'I loved *The House Share*. A great premise, compelling characters and a twisty plot kept me totally gripped'

PAUL BURSTON

Praise for

Kate Helm

'Original and pacy'
CLARE MACKINTOSH

'Fresh, wonderful and unexpected'
LISA JEWELL

'Hugely original, unexpected and completely fascinating'
JILL MANSELL

'Clever concept so brilliantly executed'
ARAMINTA HALL

'Smart, absorbing and brilliantly original'
T.M. LOGAN

'Incredible, unique and compelling'
ANGELA CLARKE

'Expertly plotted, beautifully written'
SJI HOLLIDAY

Kate Helm was born in Lancashire, and worked as a journalist covering courts and crime, before becoming a BBC reporter and producer in news and current affairs. She also wrote documentary and drama scripts, including the BBC1 programme: *Angel of Death: The Story of Beverly Allitt*. Kate Helm is a pseudonym for author Kate Harrison whose non-fiction and novels have been sold in 20 territories and sold over 800,000 copies. Kate lives in Brighton, this is her second book under the name Kate Helm.

http://kate-harrison.com
@KateWritesBooks

Also by Kate Helm

The Secrets You Hide

The
House
Share

The
House
Share

Kate Helm

ZAFFRE

First published in Great Britain in 2020 by
ZAFFRE
80–81 Wimpole St, London W1G 9RE

A CIP catalogue record for this book is
available from the British Library.

ISBN: 978-1-78576-774-6

Also available as an ebook

1 3 5 7 9 10 8 6 4 2

Typeset by IDSUK (Data Connection) Ltd
Printed and bound in Great Britain by Clays Ltd, Elcograf S.p.A.

Zaffre is an imprint of Bonnier Books UK
www.bonnierbooks.co.uk

WELCOME TO . . .
THE DYE FACTORY

TOP FLOOR: PLAY
roof terrace, mezzanine,
honesty bar, gaming

studios:
BUENOS AIRES: Bernice
LIMA: Lucas
KYOTO: Immi

SECOND FLOOR: RETREAT
yoga, fitness, emotional
support animals

studios:
BALI: Ashleigh
WARSAW: Veronica
PARIS: Camille

FIRST FLOOR: NOURISH
kitchen diner, food stores

studios:
MARRAKECH: Dex
NEW DELHI: Zoum

GROUND FLOOR: FOCUS
co-working, library,
video-conferencing

BASEMENT
laundry, housekeeper's
accommodation, sauna
(disused) historic dye pits

Every man is surrounded by a neighbourhood of voluntary spies.

Jane Austen

Prologue

Sunday 22 June 2008

Sam stands on the edge of the roof terrace, watching the mechanical sweeper clearing away last night's grime.

Is it time?

When you can't sleep, you're meant to get up and do something – anything – instead of tossing and turning in a bed steeped with early-hours fears. Sam's body craves rest, but his brain won't let it happen.

It's midsummer; already the hungover city pulses with heat. He considers walking to the Thames, chasing the hope of a breeze. But the streets will smell of piss and worse, and his stomach turns at the thought.

Sam, you don't belong here.

His penthouse has the best view in Bermondsey and he's got to know all his neighbours' routines. In ten minutes' time the owner of the café opposite will raise the shutters. He'll wash down his little patch of cobbles with bleach and set out his cast-iron tables. Maybe ninety minutes later, old friends will drift in from all corners of London to brunch like there's no work tomorrow. New couples will try to fill the awkward morning-after silence with coffee-shop bustle. Flat-sharers will come to escape their housemates before they kill each other.

You have nobody but me, Sam.

He ought to do it now. He doesn't want to ruin anyone else's morning.

If only he could avoid the violence and *will* his body to break down into motes, lighter than air. Better still, if he'd never even existed, because however he does this, it will hurt people.

He has written and destroyed a dozen messages, before settling on a cookie-cutter suicide note to his parents. An apology, reassurance that no one else is to blame, vague references to workload and insomnia and stress.

He hasn't written a note for his sister because she would see through his lies. As it is, she might still think it's her fault.

Sam, you should never have left us. Left me.

London – manic, anonymous, liberating London – was supposed to mean freedom from the inescapable burden of love.

But instead it brought the most shameful emotion of all: loneliness. A city crammed with millions of people, yet he has no one to 'brunch' with, and no one to notice his absence except the guys at work who'll curse him when he doesn't show up tomorrow.

Perhaps if he'd been made to rough it like a normal person, Sam would have made friends. The penthouse was a gift from his parents, but it feels more like a curse. He can hear his neighbours in the flats below, laughing and making love. And sometimes other sounds. Sam is a rational person, but this building was once a place of slaughter. When he's trying to sleep, he imagines he hears obscene animal noises bouncing off the brick walls, or smells an acrid stench seeping up from between the floorboards.

On Friday he bought more sleeping pills than usual from the dealer under the arches. That would be a gentler way to go. But in this weather, his body will rot, and his poor cleaner shouldn't have to see that.

So the chatty café owner will be his only witness. He's the closest thing Sam has to a friend, even though their conversations never go beyond the weather, Sam's accent, or the ridiculous hours they both work. The man is in his forties and has the look of someone who has seen it all before so Sam hopes he won't be too haunted.

Sam. Come home.

No!

The café's rusting metal shutter screeches as it rises. The owner shields his eyes against the sun as he emerges with a red plastic bucket and mop. The sodden strings look like a sea monster as they lash against the stones.

The bricks are warm underfoot as Sam steps onto the wall, slightly away from the centre so he won't hit the metal wall-crane as he falls. As he looks down, he's afraid for the first time.

Is this high enough to be sure?

So much planning, yet he didn't check how far you have to fall to be certain of death.

But he is nothing if not resourceful. At the bank's recruitment day, he scored the highest ever mark in 'Creativity and Flexibility'. He is good at thinking on his feet.

Sam positions himself like a diver – knees bent, neck tucked in – but now moves his hands to his sides, grinding his fists into his waist to fight against any survival instinct that might make him grasp at the air when it's already too late.

And he dives, head first, onto the cobbles of Tanner's Walk.

Incredible People Wanted for Dream House Share in Zone 1 Warehouse

Do you have what it takes to join us in *the* best house share in London, and quite possibly the world?

The kind of person who'll fit right in will be:

- Outgoing and interested in others, but not a complete party animal;
- Committed to joining a sharing, socially responsible community;
- Solvent, with great references.

In return, we can offer:

- A wonderful, spacious home from home in the heart of Bermondsey, just a few steps from London Bridge Station;
- Your own en-suite studio in a Victorian warehouse conversion packed with Instagrammable original features and designer furniture;
- Amazing communal spaces across four floors where you can work, eat, rest and play;
- A programme of 'City-zen' social activities and perks including yoga, organic veg boxes, games nights and even an honesty bar stocked with craft gins *and* low-alcohol options;
- A unique affordable-rent scheme which means you pay what you can manage, so we don't exclude those on a low income;
- The most fabulous housemates you'll ever meet.

To apply, please complete our online form.

NB1: As key workers are currently under-represented in our house, we guarantee all suitable applicants employed in the public sector will be offered an interview.

NB2: We operate an upper age limit of 35.

1

Tuesday 24 April 2018

Immi

I don't belong here. Anyone can see that.

Even my best dress screams 'cheap' compared to the sleek tailoring of the people I pass on Bermondsey Street. When I stop to check my hair in the window of a florist's shop, I look like the porcelain Pierrot on my mother's mantelpiece, a single tear rolling down its pale cheek.

Except I'm sweating, not crying. The make-up I applied in the staffroom has melted during the journey to London Bridge. I sidle into an alleyway and try to fix my eyeliner, though really I should scrub it all off and start again. But I don't have time for that.

Tanner's Walk is next on the right. The thought makes my mouth go dry and I struggle for breath. The panic attacks have started up again in the weeks since Al threw me out. I try to remember the meditation my old therapist taught me, her lisping voice in my head: *Imagine ripples flowing across a tranquil pond. Breathe with them. Everything is safe. Nobody can hurt you again . . .*

The panic ebbs away and my heart slows. Time to focus on being the ideal flatmate.

I know I am anything but: I'm antisocial and neurotic and fearful, and I have zero interest in getting to know the people I live with.

But I can *pretend*. I'm good at that.

Of course, no one should have to jump through hoops for a roof over their head, but it's a fact of London life. After everything I've done, there's no way I'm going home to Mum and her houseful of Pierrots and superstition.

I pat my hair to flatten the frizz and turn right. Tanner's Walk is a cobbled street, narrower than it looks on Google Maps, barely wide enough for a single car. There's a terrace of houses and a hipster café on one side, but they're dwarfed by the brick warehouse opposite.

The Dye Factory.

I laughed out loud when I read the address in the email. So pretentious and so typical of round here. But the building itself is a handsome beast, made of red bricks that glow in the early evening sun. The vast windows are framed by black metalwork, and the original wall-crane projects out like a gallows, with a timber platform that must once have lifted goods into the warehouse.

The photos on the ad seemed too good to be true, but the reality is even better.

Tanner's Walk is quiet, too, just far enough away from the braying drinkers and snarling vapers cluttering the pavements on Bermondsey Street.

I try to imagine myself coming home to *this* every night after school. I could actually walk it in fifty minutes. Even when I was living with Alastair, the commute from Highgate took an hour and a quarter – and since he threw me out, I've been sleeping on mates' sofas in the suburbs, and the journey is usually twice that.

I have to give this all I've got.

I walk towards the tall warehouse doors, which are painted oxblood red. There's a brass plaque with an engraved inscription: *The Dye Factory is named after the leather tanning and colouring business that existed here during Victorian times.*

Next to it, there's a note asking interviewees to push the entry-phone to be buzzed in, then take the lift to the top floor.

Before pressing the button, I take a moment to psych myself up.

From nowhere, I hear a sudden burst of laughter. High-pitched, almost hysterical. Children's laughter?

I scan the street, trying to work out where it's coming from. There's no playground that I can see, and the café opposite is closed.

I shake my head but the laughter continues, shrill and familiar. Like a new mother, I cannot ignore the cries of children. If Icelanders have a hundred words for snow, then I could invent just as many for the noises made by a classful of kids. Their Monday morning moans. The tap-tap-tap of feet on lino, counting down to home time on a sunny afternoon.

The chatter and hum I can hear now sounds like the build-up to a big fight that's been brewing all day.

It's coming from above me.

I look up and it all makes sense.

There's a terrace on the roof of the Dye Factory building, four storeys up, and the noise comes not from kids but from hyped-up adults. The competition, I suppose. To win, I'm going to have to join them up there, flirt better, pretend better. I close my eyes, try to picture the eddies of the River Thames only streets away, to calm myself.

I hear the fast whir of wheels. Open my eyes to see a cyclist in a black hoodie speeding towards me on the narrow strip of pavement.

Fast. *Too fast.*

He's heading straight for me.

My body freezes. Breath leaves my lungs.

Wake up, Immi. Don't be a victim! Act.

My hand goes to the pocket I've sewn into my dress and my fingers close around the wooden handle of the small hunting knife.

I twist out of the way, moments before he ploughs into me, but one of the heels on my smart shoes catches between the cobbles and I trip over, my ankle twisting under me and my two bags and the knife falling onto the stones.

'Shit!'

I reach for the knife first, as the bike stops millimetres from my body. Next I grab my handbag. He's welcome to the tote bag, it's got nothing in it except Year 6 exercise books.

'Get away from me!' I shout. 'Don't hurt me!'

I brace myself for a blow. But instead of trying to grab my stuff, he pulls the hoodie down to reveal his face. Not some thieving teenager, but a man my age. Handsome, too, like a young Idris Elba.

'I don't wanna hurt you!' He sounds almost as freaked out as I do.

I get to my feet, nerves shot, body still primed for fight or flight.

'Pavements are for bloody pedestrians.'

He shrugs. 'I didn't actually hit you, you fell.'

'You were going too fast. If there's CCTV, you could be fined for what you just did.'

He looks alarmed, as though I'm *actually* going to call the police for something so trivial. 'I said sorry.'

He turns away from me, lifting up his bike, and presses the entryphone button for the Dye Factory. When a female voice answers, he says, 'Hi, I'm Dex. Dex Shepherd, here for the interview?'

I cringe. He's here for the room, too. And he's a perfect candidate: good-looking, sporty, with a silly name.

My reaction seems ridiculous now. What if he saw the knife before I grabbed it back? At three inches, the blade is just short enough to be legal – that's why I bought it – but it's not something I want people knowing about.

The lock hums, and he pushes the Factory doors open, carrying that fancy bike over the threshold with just two fingers. Titanium, like the outrageously expensive one Al bought for himself, but never used.

I step towards the door.

Dex turns sharply, wariness in his eyes. 'Oh. You're here for the same reason as me, I guess?'

'Yes,' I say.

I am thinking: *But I need this more.*

2

Immi

The door closes behind us and I hear the electronic lock engage, trapping us inside. I can never relax somewhere new until I've worked out the escape route.

The lobby is dark till Dex finds a switch and the light blinds me momentarily. The wall lamps are made of vintage medicine bottles, labelled 'sulphuric acid' and 'calcium hydroxide'.

Ahead of us is a wide, brick staircase and a Victorian lift with concertinaed iron shutters. The floorboards would merit their own account on Instagram, they're so artfully scuffed and dented. To the side, there's a heavy timber door with the word 'Focus' chiselled into the wood.

'They didn't lie about this place, did they? It's sick.'

Sick? That's a word even my geekiest pupils have stopped using, but I guess super-cool Dex has been overcome with excitement. It makes me like him a little more.

But not enough to let him win.

'Yeah, it's right on-trend,' I say, becoming Immi the Perfect Millennial Flatmate. I press the call button for the lift. Next to the cage, there's a distressed steel cabinet with pigeonholes for post, labelled with the names of cities I could never afford to visit:

Buenos Aires

Lima

Kyoto
Bali
Warsaw
Paris
Marrakech
New Delhi.

The pigeonholes have sushi flyers in them, except Kyoto and Marrakech, which are empty.

'Those must be the two rooms they want to fill,' Dex says as he locks his bike to the bannister.

'Two? They didn't mention that to me.' The emails I've had from Hanna, the admin person, have been blunt and brief, in contrast to the original, chatty advert on Spareroom.com.

We step into the lift together. The shutters have to be pulled all the way across, like prison bars, before it'll move. There are four enamel buttons to choose from, marked 'Focus', 'Nourish', 'Retreat', 'Play'. Dex presses Play, the top one.

As we move up, I catch tantalising glimpses of the building through the bars. First, a glass ceiling underneath us shows what lay behind the Focus door: bookshelves, reading chairs, standing desks and the biggest video-conferencing screen I've ever seen.

Next comes Nourish, with the kind of pro-kitchen you see on cooking shows.

Retreat has beanbags, yoga mats and soft lighting.

'I guess the studios must be behind those doors,' Dex says, pointing towards the front of the building.

'Studios?' I repeat, wondering what might be filmed here. But then I remember that's what they call the bedrooms. The ad described them as small but well-equipped, all en suite. *We want you to love your neighbour,* the application pack said, *so it helps not to share a bathroom with them.*

The lift stops at Play. The party voices are much louder now, but there's only one person waiting for us as we slide the shutter open.

'Hi, I'm Lucas,' he says, holding his arms out like a showman. 'Welcome to the Dye Factory.'

Is he a threat? If in doubt, always assume the worst.

Lucas is my age, a little taller than me, with floppy brown hair and shrewd eyes that wrinkle at the outside corners, as though he's still laughing at a joke made before I got here. He wears suit trousers and a light-blue shirt that looks bespoke. A red rose sits in the chest pocket.

Dex steps out of the lift and reaches for Lucas's hand. 'Hey, I'm Dex.'

Lucas drops Dex's hand as though it's radioactive, and turns to face me. 'And who do we have here?'

'Immi Sutton,' I say. The handshake goes on a moment longer than I expected – it's Lucas who doesn't let go.

'A pleasure to meet you,' Lucas says with a wink. 'We had over three hundred applications for the two spaces, so you must be pretty special people to be down to the last dozen.'

Twelve people – so I have a one-in-six chance.

'Any hints on how we get selected?' Dex asks.

Lucas shrugs. 'Be yourself. Try to imagine if you'll be happy here. The Factory isn't for everyone.'

'I can't imagine anyone not digging this place; it's a hipster's dream,' Dex says.

The Play floor is stunning: a double-height vaulted ceiling above us, and a ladder to our right leading to a mezzanine suspended from the oak rafters. Over Lucas's shoulder, there's the inevitable table football game, plus an arcade-sized screen with various consoles. Vegas-style lights spell out the word 'Play' on the brick wall, while a chandelier made of more medicine bottles hangs from the central beam.

'Some parts do look dated already, the place was made-over in 2010,' Lucas says. 'But the industrial chic fits the building's history. That light fitting is made from bottles of the poisons they used to tan and dye animal skins.'

'And the bedrooms?' I ask.

'*Studios*,' he corrects me and points at a row of doors on the right: Buenos Aires, Lima, Kyoto. 'Kyoto is up for grabs. Great space, though because it's got windows onto the roof terrace there can be noise when there's a party. The other free studio is Marrakech, on the Nourish level. You'll get a tour later, but let me take you outside, introduce you to the gang.'

He leads us towards the terrace. A woman's shape appears in the doorway, so slender that at first it looks like a trick of the light. But as she steps inside, I see her face and feel a jolt of recognition, followed by fear so powerful I want to turn and run.

Where do I know her from?

'Camille, meet our guests,' Lucas calls to her. As the woman crosses the room, her loose linen dress billows behind her like a shadow. Thick black hair skims her bare shoulders.

My handmade dress with its cheery print of Russian dolls was meant to look ironic. Next to her, I look ridiculous.

'Camille, this is . . .' Lucas seems to have forgotten already.

'Dex.' My rival reaches out to shake hands but instead, Camille brushes his wrist with her long fingers and turns to leave. He follows her outside without another word.

Lucas and I are alone. 'Shall I fix you a drink here? It's heaving on the terrace.' I follow him towards the bar, which is made of railway sleepers and copper piping, with mint and borage plants growing up towards the ceiling. 'I work in the booze industry, so we have more kinds of gin than are dreamt of in your philosophy.'

I smile at the Shakespeare reference; perhaps he's testing me. 'Maybe Hamlet would have been chirpier if he'd had gin to see him through.'

Lucas laughs. It's a short, odd sound that bounces off the high ceiling. 'Take your pick. Though there's a lot to be said for good old Gordon's.'

'I'll have that, please.' I watch as he places two giant rocks of ice in balloon glasses then pours from the green bottle. He keeps looking at me, and I don't quite know what to do with my hands.

'A large one?'

I smile and he keeps pouring.

'Funny way to choose a flatmate, right?' He takes a lime from a bowl, and scythes off a long, flawless strip of zest with a knife at least as sharp as mine. 'But this isn't just a house share. It really is a community. We can't risk destabilising that by picking the wrong people.'

'How can you tell who the right ones are?'

'Well, we've made a few mistakes in the past. But we've learned from them. And Bernice – you'll meet her soon – she's been here from the start and she's very intuitive.'

He hands me the drink; the lime zest sits on the top of the ice in a perfect spiral.

'I'm only here as the charity chase,' I say. 'I'm a teacher.'

Lucas gives me a curious look, then pours his own drink, almost all gin, no more than a splash of tonic. 'It's not about your job, it's about who you are. You've got the same chance as everyone else. Cheers.'

The gin feels like ice and fire as I swallow. 'Does having a giant chip on my shoulder rule me out?'

'No, but a sense of humour helps.' He sits on the arm of a weathered leather sofa, and I cradle my drink in both hands. 'Look, in a way, this whole party is all about you guys. So own it. Everyone who lives here already is wearing a red rose, to help you see who you should flirt with to win their vote.' He taps the flower poking out of his shirt pocket.

I swallow down a wave of nausea. 'Is that what it takes?'

He grimaces. 'Sorry, that wasn't very woke of me, was it? Charm, not flirtation. It'll be easier once the gin kicks in.'

'Charm comes more easily to some people. You've got buckets of it.'

Lucas laughs that cackling laugh again. 'Fine line between charm and sleaze, which I've been known to cross. But if it helps, you've got my vote. I prefer to live with women.'

'Maybe that did cross the line into sleaze,' I say. It's a risk, but he grins.

'Ha! See, you'll fit right in. Ready?' He reaches out his hand to escort me through. A friendly gesture? Or a contract: if I help you, will you do something for me?

No. As my therapist said till she was blue in the face, not all men are like that.

Lucas's skin is warm against my palm, which has been chilled by the glass.

'Two last tips, Immi, because I like you. One, think about what talents or skills you can bring to the Factory. So, I mix a mean cocktail. One of the Dyers leads yoga, another fixes any IT problems we have.'

'Dyers?'

'It's an in-joke. We call ourselves Dyers, because we live in the Dye Factory. Better than residents, which makes us sound like we're in a mental hospital.'

'OK. I'll see if I can think of a hidden talent. And the other tip?'

'Give us a story in the interview.' He leans closer and I smell the juniper on his breath. 'Your best TED talk. Lay it on as thick as you like.'

'A *story*?'

'Tragic childhood, a brave fight against a glamorous but preferably non-contagious medical condition. To make us feel good about ourselves for picking you. The Factory loves lost souls.'

'Right. Thanks.'

As I step onto the terrace, preparing to face the opposition, I'm ready. Stories I *can* do. The truth would not help me at all.

3

Immi

The crush is intense: twenty-five, maybe thirty people packed onto the tiny terrace.

All it would take is for one candidate to elbow another out of the way to start a chain reaction that could send us toppling like dominos towards the low walls and off the side . . .

'Let me introduce you to the boss,' Lucas says, his hand still in mine as we weave through the bodies. I can smell Mediterranean herbs and tomato shoots. The thump-thump of drum and bass pulses through me.

Dex is ahead of us, talking to a tall, blonde woman with a ski-jump nose. She has a rose pinned to her fussy silver top and I can see the strain in his face as he tries to look interested.

'. . . Of course, people assume insurance is a dull sector to work in, but I can assure you, my colleagues and I party *hard* . . .'

Lucas lets go of my hand as someone pulls him away. I am alone, which usually suits me fine.

But I know Lucas is right: I have to network. As I look around for people with red roses, the ones I must impress, the figures move apart momentarily so I see the skyline for the first time . . .

The Shard catches my eye first, hundreds of panes illuminated from the inside, making a jagged mosaic against the violet evening. Closer by, warehouses like this one form a boxy circle around us, their roofs like steps up to the sky. We are the tallest.

I want to hold this panorama in my head. I know I won't be picked, but even *seeing* this secret view once is something this girl from Crewe would never have expected.

I make the mistake of looking down.

The world spins with the same falling sensation I felt that night, the surprise at still being alive, accompanied by the knowledge that he wasn't done.

'Are you OK?'

A hand rests on my shoulder, a soft grip, but one that promises more strength if I need it. The memory recedes.

I turn round. The hand belongs to a rose-wearer so I smile brightly. He's Asian, solid without being fat, and the flower pinned to his preppy white polo shirt is made of plastic.

Safe. I never feel like this about someone at first glance.

'I'm fine. It's warm up here.' I stick out my hand, aware too late that it's clammy from my vertigo. 'I'm Immi. Lovely to meet you.'

Before he takes my hand, a jet of cold water hits my cheek and I jump. Look up. The sky is still blue, no clouds.

Another jet.

This time I see where it comes from: the plastic rose.

The man giggles. 'Sorry. It is my little test, to see if candidates have a sense of humour.' He lifts a small pump out of his pocket and holds my hand up against the flower as he presses. The water tickles.

I laugh at my own shock, and at the silliness and incongruity of the practical joke in the midst of all this very serious networking. 'How many have passed so far?'

'Only you. The rest have given me the cold shoulder.' He has an accent, but I can't tell where he's from.

'You still haven't told me your name.'

'Azoum. But everyone drops the A to make it Zoum, which makes me sound like a character from a superhero movie franchise.'

'How long have you lived in the Dye Factory, Zoum?'

'From the start. I am one of only three survivors, thanks to my cunning. And my superpowers, of course. The rest have been culled.'

'You're actually *talking* like a movie character now.'

'Yeah, and I am only half kidding.' He smiles.

He's got one of those faces that becomes more handsome the longer you look at it, with long eyelashes framing unexpectedly pale green eyes. But there's none of Lucas's innuendo. 'Can I give you some advice, Immi?'

I nod. I wonder if it'll be the same as Lucas gave me.

'Run out of here as fast as your feet will carry you. Try Surbiton or Brockley or somewhere that actual human beings still live.'

It sounds like another joke. 'Is that advice for me in particular, or do you say that to all the candidates?'

'The rest are clearly sociopaths. They will fit in just fine. But you seem too nice for this place.'

I think of my knife and the reason I carry it. 'Don't be fooled. Underneath my primary school teacher disguise, I'm as warped as everyone else. And I need somewhere to live just as much.'

He shrugs. 'Don't say I didn't warn you. But if you *really* want it, you've got my vote.' And he gives me an extra squirt from the rose, as if he's sealing the deal.

The woman with the upturned nose, who was talking to Dex, crashes in between us. Even her large breasts, which are the first thing to enter the circle, seem designed to intimidate.

'Hi, I'm Veronica. Who are you?'

I answer her, but I don't think she hears me. She's pulling another person into the conversation, a tall man straight from hipster central casting, from his round specs and beard to his Allbirds trainers.

Dangerous. I sense that straight away.

'Zoum, have you met Holden yet? He's got his own fair trade, vegan ice-cream start-up.'

Ugh. He has to be a shoo-in.

Holden grins. 'I can offer unlimited supplies if you pick me!'

Zoum catches my eye and he winks. A jet of water shoots out of the plastic rose, right against Holden's glasses. He flinches. Frowns. A second jet of water follows, right into the beard.

'Oh, for fuck's sake, Zoum,' Veronica says, sussing out what he's done and pulling the trick flower off his clothes. 'Ignore him, Holden, he's got a mental age of five.'

'You'd better not have broken my rose,' Zoum says.

Holden scowls as he realises where the water came from.

'You see, this is the problem with the Factory,' Veronica says, her plummy voice rising above the rest of the chit-chat. I can imagine her shouting instructions to the slackers in her lacrosse team. 'The accommodation is fine, but the residents are mostly insufferable. And you have *zero* privacy.'

'Like in every other flat share, then, Veronica?' Zoum says.

'You only have to look at the speed of turnover to see we have a problem.' Her voice is more conspiratorial now and she moves a little closer. I can smell a strident perfume, and the hint of city sweat underneath. 'The whole set-up is toxic. Even without this grim business with poor Jamie—'

I see Zoum's hand slip behind Veronica's back and she winces. I don't know if it was a prod or a pinch, but she shuts up.

'We agreed to focus on the future, didn't we?' Zoum tells her.

Veronica huffs. 'Well, I didn't agree anything—'

Holden looks interested for the first time. 'Who is Jamie?'

'The last person to leave,' Zoum explains. 'And Veronica's not happy because she wanted his room. But no one on his floor wants her to move because she snores so badly. That's all it is.' He stares at Veronica.

She won't make eye contact with any of us. 'Don't say I didn't warn you, Izzie.'

'My name is Immi.' I wonder why she's aiming all the negativity at me, not Holden. Maybe she's one of those women who only likes to hang out with men.

She shrugs. 'But if you do end up moving here, try not to shag any of the other residents. It makes everything a thousand times messier.'

Zoum laughs. 'That I *will* agree with. And neither Veronica nor I have ever swapped bodily fluids with others. Which is probably why we're still here and in one piece.'

'Everyone here seems to love giving out advice,' I say.

Veronica does glance at me now, her expression mildly contemptuous. 'I've missed out the most important tip. Have *nothing* to do with the committee. Lucas – or Louche-as, as I call him – would screw anything with a pulse, and even the pulse is optional after he's done a few lines. Camille is vacuous and vain. But Bernice is the worst.'

'Which one is she?'

Veronica laughs. 'If she hasn't made herself known to you yet, then you're wasting your time. You're clearly not on her shortlist.'

'Take no notice, Immi,' Zoum says. 'The night is young. But you probably do want to say hi to Queen Bee. She is right over there . . .'

He points to a group of six people, all attractive and well-dressed, as though they're posing for a stock photo promoting London as a place for doing digital business.

But there's no doubting which one is Bernice.

4

Immi

The first thing I notice is that Bernice holds everyone's attention, though she's much smaller and slighter than the others. The second thing I notice is her hair: coppery curls that explode out of her scalp as though she's just suffered an electric shock.

Her clothes seem designed not to detract from that spectacular hair: white linen shirt, knee-length navy shorts, tan slip-on espadrilles. The *opposite* of a fashion statement. As I get closer – ready to introduce myself, even though it makes me cringe – her pale complexion looks flawless. No eye make-up, but she wears a solid block of pillar-box red lipstick, matte and uncompromising.

I try to ignore the suffocating crush, and push into the group, all my attention focused on Bernice.

'. . . The building was one of the first in Bermondsey to be developed into flats. But when it was refit time, the owners decided to do something more experimental, in the form of an urban community . . .'

I don't say anything, but my presence is enough to stop her talking. Bernice is older than I thought initially: early thirties perhaps. She gives me a scan up and down, the way a man would. But I don't think it's about sex. It's more predatory than that.

'Hello, Bernice, I'm—'

'Immi Sutton. I know who you are. You're the only one I haven't met yet.' She talks with crisp, confident consonants, like a radio announcer.

I notice that there are no other rose-wearers in this circle of acolytes. They introduce themselves to me grudgingly. I don't bother to remember their names; the chances of any of us meeting again are slim.

We all wait for Bernice to choose the next topic. Instead, she glances at her watch – a man's vintage Rolex, heavy on her slim wrist. 'Time to get things moving.'

She withdraws from the group, and we rivals are left staring at each other, like wild animals working out who is the most vulnerable.

Bernice, Camille and Lucas gather together at the far end of the terrace. They step up onto the low wall as though it's a small stage. There's a metal barrier behind them, but even so, I keep imagining how it'd feel to fall . . .

I wasn't always like this. I made a conscious effort to be the opposite of my mother, who is afraid of the outside world, small spaces, open spaces, doctors, other people, her own shadow. My teenage rebellion was to become fearless and rational.

That got me to London, but then London made me scared all over again.

'Good evening, and welcome to our gathering,' Bernice says. The music quietens, as though it too is in her thrall. 'We're thrilled to welcome you to the Factory. This is a unique place to live . . .'

Camille and Lucas smile in agreement. *The committee.* After Veronica's warning, I search their faces for malevolence, but they look the same as everyone else: glossy, smart, upbeat.

'We know this selection process isn't easy for you guys. But life in the Factory isn't for everyone. We interview people this way because it gives us a good sense of whether you'll fit in or not. So simply be yourself and it'll turn out fine.'

Looking at my competition, their eager body language and fixed smiles, I'd say none of us are 'being ourselves'. When the prize is a Zone 1 palace, instead of a dingy box room in the suburbs, it's no wonder there's a *Hunger Games* vibe.

'One more thing before we kick off the interviews. You might be worrying that it's too good to be true. I know we all did at the start.'

It was my uni mate Sarah who found the ad for this place. She had an ulterior motive: to get shot of me. I'm currently occupying the sofa in the tiny flat she shares with her loathsome boyfriend, Mack. But even she had her doubts about the Factory. *Just make sure they haven't got secret cameras in the bathroom that they're streaming to pervy businessmen worldwide.*

Bernice smiles. 'I promise you, the Factory isn't *Big Brother*. There's no hidden CCTV or microphones. The owners of this building are philanthropists who wanted to trial a new kind of living, with a view to rolling it out in other cities where it's needed. This community can help with so many issues that trouble our generation: loneliness and anxiety as well as the cost of accommodation. That's another reason it's so important we choose the right people.' Bernice smiles again. I want to believe her.

'While you wait for your interviews, please take a tour. Check the big screen to see who'll be showing you round. Enjoy the drinks, the music. And remember, what will be, will be.'

A female 'guest' kicks off a round of sycophantic applause, which spreads as we all compete to show the most enthusiasm. I break away before the others to check the touchscreen, which is two metres across, mounted on the weathered brick wall. I click on my name and it tells me my tour will be led by Ashleigh. I sense someone behind me.

'Hi, I'm Ashleigh. Are you in my group?'

I turn towards the excited voice. Ashleigh is the youngest of the residents I've seen so far, her fair hair pulled into tight braids that don't flatter her pretty moon face.

I introduce myself and she leans forward to give me a hug. She's dressed in flappy harem pants and a too-tight vest top, and her warm skin smells of lavender oil.

'You're the teacher, aren't you?' Ashleigh gushes, in a soft Welsh accent. 'I'd love to talk to you more about getting girls into science and technology, it sounds amazing.'

I shouldn't be surprised that everyone who lives here has read my application form – I ticked the box giving permission – but it does give me a momentary jolt. 'Definitely, it's a passion of mine and—'

But already the rest of the candidates gather round Ashleigh, who has memorised something about each person in her group. There's Holden the vegan ice-cream seller, plus an app developer and a pop-up restaurant entrepreneur. Finally Dex shuffles over.

'Hi, Dex. Documentary and fashion photographer, am I right? And don't you look the part!' Ashleigh says it without any sarcasm but Dex looks slightly shamed.

'I guess I need to work on my disguise.'

'Are you guys ready to see what the Factory has to offer? Then let's get going.'

5

Immi

Ashleigh starts by taking us up the ladder to the mezzanine, where the fancy sofas are about a hundred times more comfortable than the grim futons and blow-up mattresses I've spent the last sixty-four nights trying to sleep on.

'We call this the Nook,' Ashleigh says. 'It's got a laid-back vibe, and it's a great place to read. We get a curated selection of small press magazines each month. I *love* beautiful print.'

Next we go all the way back to the lobby, to avoid another tour group. 'Those stairs lead to the basement, where you go for your interview,' she continues. 'On the ground floor, we've also got the Focus zone: HD video conferencing, standing and sitting desks, a very full-on massage chair. Great place to swap ideas, too. The Factory encourages cross-fertilisation.'

She talks as though the place is a living thing. I glance at Dex. He is looking at the exit, as though he can't wait to get out of here.

Good. If he leaves, my odds of success improve. Nothing has gone right for me since Al made me leave. I need this. I *deserve* this.

The next floor up is Nourish, the kitchen and dining area. 'No more thefts from the shared fridge here,' Ashleigh says, pointing to a bank of shiny stainless-steel appliances. 'Your secure larder is operated by an app on your phone. But there's loads of free communal food: dairy and non-dairy milks, organic fruit-and-veg boxes for everyone to enjoy. The water is filtered centrally and we discourage single-use plastic, of course. Oh, and this is *my* baby.'

She pats an industrial-style iron shelving unit, laden with crocks and Kilner jars filled with shocking-pink and orange pickles.

'That's my fermented food zoo,' Ashleigh explains. 'I get a small salary to run our well-being and outreach programme. So I started making live foods, to reduce food waste and benefit your microbiome, which can reduce anxieties . . .'

It'd take more than pickle to get rid of my anxieties. As she talks, I try to focus. What can I say in my interview to make me stand out?

'Is that kimchi?' Holden says. 'I literally *live* for kimchi.'

Ashleigh beams. 'Right? My recipe is vegan, I leave out the fish sauce . . .' She must notice that the rest of us couldn't give a toss. 'OK, let me show you Marrakech.'

She walks towards the row of doors on the right. 'Our studios are named after cities where UN Climate Change conferences have been held.' Ashleigh holds her smartphone up against the hotel-style swipe panel mounted on the enormous oak door. I spot a delicate tattoo around her wrist, a chain of stars and planets. 'The app is encrypted.'

'No one else can get in?' Dex asks. I lean forward to hear the answer.

'It even records failed attempts, for security reasons. The only other person who can access the space is Hanna, our housekeeper.'

The door buzzes and Ashleigh pushes it open, holding back so we can file inside.

The ceiling height is the first thing I notice – well, I can't see anything else because my rivals pile in first. A giant wooden beam and a macho iron girder form a cross in the centre of the ceiling.

'Could I squeeze in, please?'

My rivals reluctantly clear a space. The room is small, but well-designed. There's a double bed, made up with white linens, a wardrobe, and ladder shelves supported by copper pipe brackets, plus more of the poison-bottle lights. It's boutique-hotel cute, but also irresistibly anonymous. I can really imagine myself here, starting over, where no one knows how badly I screwed up.

The humiliation of moving out of Al's house still hurts, even nine weeks on. He stayed away when I came to get my things. As I staggered down the stone steps alone, struggling to carry bin bags full of clothes, I sensed the yummy-mummy neighbours watching through the gaps in their frosted glass bay windows.

One of the bags split, inevitably. My underwear and a box of tampons spilled out across the reclaimed black-and-white tiles of Al's path. The cabbie didn't help but at least the sunglasses I was wearing stopped them seeing that I was crying.

'What's the water pressure like?' Holden asks Ashleigh as we take it in turns to inspect the tiny en suite. The basin is copper, the shower has a dustbin-lid-sized head, and a pristine bath sheet hangs from a meat hook: our monthly rent includes fresh towels and linen changes.

'Like being pummelled by a sumo wrestler. Kira, who used to live here before she went home to Australia, said she'd miss the shower as much as she'd miss all of us!'

'When do we get to see the other room?' Dex asks.

For the first time, Ashleigh frowns. 'It's had new flooring so you can't walk on it, sorry. But it's just as nice as Marrakech. Now, it's time for your interview, Holden. I daren't mess up Bernice's schedule.'

Holden salutes her and she smiles back. I reckon his vegan virtue-signalling has got him her support. The rest of us troop up a floor to the cocoon-like Retreat, where Ashleigh talks about yoga classes.

'. . . In summer we move the meditation sessions on to the roof. We also run a buddying scheme, where new residents are matched up with another person, so you can chat through any issues that are worrying you.'

The pop-up restaurant man frowns. 'Sounds a bit touchy-feely. Is it compulsory?'

I see irritation flash across Ashleigh's face, till she manages to restore her sweetest expression. 'It's . . . encouraged. But we also have an anonymous alert system, in case you are worried about another resident.'

Seems like overkill. Unless . . . 'Have there been mental health issues here?' I ask.

Ashleigh flushes but shakes her head. 'City living is hard for everyone, right? That's why we need to find modern ways to build better communities. Now, for the final bit of the tour I need complete silence.'

She leads us into a small, cordoned-off space behind the gym. It's dark, and I can smell straw and urine.

'These are the last two residents: Edward and Bella. One at a time, please,' she says, holding her finger to her lips. Somehow,

I'm at the front as she lifts up a cotton sheet to reveal a huge metal cage.

Two sets of round, black eyes look out at me.

'The health benefits of keeping pets are proven, so we rescued these two and took votes on what to call them. The rabbit is Edward – with those fangs, how could he *not* be? – and the guinea pig is Bella. You wouldn't think they'd get on, but they're actually soulmates.'

The rabbit is like a Facebook Easter gif, a floppy-haired creature with golden fur. Bella just looks belligerent. After a moment, they scuttle to the back of the cage.

'Who looks after them?'

'There's a rota,' she says, but then she sighs. 'To be honest, though, it's mostly me.'

'I'd help. I love animals,' I say, though that's a slight exaggeration. Mum never let me have pets, not even so much as a stick insect. But I'll keep my word if it helps me get in. Feeding and mucking out a couple of furry friends is a small price to pay for utopia.

6

Immi

My turn to face the committee.

The lift doesn't go down to the basement, and the treads of the old stairs dip treacherously, the bottom one crumbling away. The ceilings are low, and damp pushes through the whitewashed walls, making salt deposits shaped like roses. It stinks.

Straight ahead, there's a breeze-blocked wall with a plywood door and through the gap, in the shadows cast by strip lights, I see a series of channels made of stone or concrete, like farmyard troughs, five or six in a long row.

I wonder what went on down here. Lucas mentioned using poisons to dye animal skins. I'm not squeamish; I know where meat and come leather from. But still, I hate to think of animals being led to their deaths, hearing the distress of those just ahead.

Pull yourself together, Imogen. Think of Marie Curie. Rosalind Franklin, Ada Lovelace. The voice of my favourite teacher is stern in my head: *Women are the opposite of feeble.*

I step past bags of building rubble and a stack of old fridges and appliances, towards a door marked 'Office'. The wood-patterned laminate has split and when I knock, it sounds hollow.

Lucas opens the door. 'Welcome to the hot seat.'

A video camera faces a plastic chair, and he waves at me to sit down, while my three inquisitors sit opposite. The set-up reminds me of those videos terrorists send of hostage victims.

'This is how it works,' says Bernice without preamble. 'Your application was good and the online personality test showed you'd fit in well. But now we want to know the real you. We'll ask you some fun questions, which we'll record to show the other Dyers. After all the interviews are done, we'll make *our* recommendations, but it's a secret ballot. We let you know the results in the morning.'

Fun questions sound the most terrifying part of the process, but I smile in what I hope is a *fun-loving* way. 'Sure.'

Camille hasn't spoken yet. Her face is calm, but her presence unsettles me; I can't shake the feeling that I know her from somewhere.

'Ready?' Lucas says. He turns on a light mounted on top of the camera and I can't see their faces any more.

'Who, living or dead, would you like to have dinner with?' Bernice reads from a clipboard.

'Ada Lovelace. Female computer pioneer. I think she'd blow my mind.' Easy-peasy. I can thank my old teacher for that one.

'G and T or herb tea?'

'G and T after six. The one I had here was perfect. Herb tea or strong coffee in the mornings. I need something to wake me up before I face a class of ten-year-olds.'

'Special skills?'

I knew this one was coming, thanks to Lucas. 'I make my own clothes. I'd be happy to take trousers up, sew on buttons for my new neighbours. I find it relaxing.'

'What's your most annoying quality as a housemate?'

You're a fucking fraud, Immi. Alastair's parting words to me sting all the more because they are true.

'I'm too tidy,' I say, and it's not a lie. 'I grew up in a slightly chaotic household, and it's made me like everything to be in the right place.'

The 'fun' questions continue and I try to keep it light but 'authentic'.

'What would you like to leave behind, after you've gone? Your legacy?'

I don't have to think about this one. 'My work is my legacy. I know it sounds cheesy but I became a teacher to show kids that their background or family doesn't have to dictate their future. I had a teacher who did that for me so I'm paying it forward.'

'Many people come to the Factory looking for something they cannot find elsewhere.' Camille's voice is whispery, with just a hint of a European accent I can't identify. 'Does that resonate with you?'

This is my chance to tell the kind of story Lucas suggested: one to make them feel good about themselves if they pick *poor Imogen.*

'Yes. Yes, it does. It's . . . difficult to talk about but I feel safer here than I have for months. Years, maybe.'

And that, at least, *is* the truth. Security, order, minimalism are what I crave. But if I tell them the real reasons, I know they'll hate me every bit as much as my ex does.

Lucas leans forward. 'If you want to confide in us, we'll turn the camera off now, Immi. Nothing you tell us will go any further than this room.'

He doesn't wait for my answer, and when the camera light is turned off, flares of colour float in front of my eyes.

I close them and I see Alastair's rage the day he understood who I really was. It still hurts to know he loathed me, and that telling the whole truth would only have made him hate me more.

As I tell them about his anger, I hate myself too, but it's the only story I can think of that will buy me the space I need.

After it's over, Camille takes me back up to the lobby. Her hand closes around mine and she squeezes.

'Thank you for your openness,' she says. 'Sometimes, we say that you don't find the Factory, the Factory finds you. We will be in touch.'

'I appreciate that.' I'm still struck by the familiarity of her face. 'I hope you don't mind my asking, but I'm sure we've met before. Do you remember?'

Camille smiles. 'Do you watch a lot of Scandinavian dramas?'

I didn't, but Alastair was a big fan. 'A few.'

'I was in the Danish TV show, *Salt Marsh*. The body that was eaten by wolves? They used my image in all the posters and trailers, though I never got to speak a single word. The perfect woman, many men would say.'

Now I remember: an ethereal naked figure on a forest floor, her skin artfully decayed and bitten, but her exquisite face preserved by the cold or the salt, blue-grey eyes wide open. I blush, as though I've been caught looking at porn or someone's private emails. 'Oh yes. I do remember now.'

'It is an unsettling feeling, knowing everyone has seen you naked,' she says. 'But that, I know, is the fate of the actor. Goodbye, Imogen. You will hear from us soon.'

7

Dex

'What is your most annoying quality as a housemate?' Camille asks.

Their questions are so lame it's hard not to laugh.

'Hogging the shower and using up all the hot water. I work out a lot, see. But it's better than hanging around in my sweats after a run.'

'And of course you can't use up the hot water here. It's unlimited,' Bernice says, smiling at me. 'Next question: what's your signature dish?'

What bollocks this is. I'm having to fight the urge to tell them to stick their studio where the sun don't shine.

But I can't. Because the Dye Factory is the perfect place to lie low, and to be picked, I have to convince them that *I* am the perfect candidate, that I'm *outgoing and interested in others, but not a complete party animal* and all the other stuff they were looking for.

'Cheesecake. I make a vegan version too, with tofu.' That's for the sweet hippie girl. 'There's never a crumb left over.'

'And the last fun question. If we were planning a big community event, a party, what role would you take?' Bernice asks.

When I first saw her on the terrace, I couldn't stop staring at her, or rather, at her gleaming red hair, because of who she reminded me of. It felt like fate was trying to fuck with my head.

And now it feels like she's doing it again.

'Mixologist?' she suggests, sensing that I am struggling to answer.

'DJ?' says Lucas. There's a guy who is doing way too much coke. Pink eyes, raw nostrils, a jitteriness he can't hide. I know the signs well enough.

Bernice tuts at him; maybe she thinks he's being racist, assuming that my skin colour or background makes me good on the decks. But I can't blame him. I'm the one who is pretending to be street, when I am nothing of the kind.

'I can rap, sure,' I lie. 'But it can get a bit . . . angry.'

'It's obvious,' Camille says. She is easily as beautiful as most of the models I've photographed. 'Dex should take the pictures!'

They laugh but I notice Lucas write something down. They won't forget that I was stumped for an answer, but they could never guess why.

'To round off the Q&A, a more serious one,' Bernice says. 'What would you want to be your legacy? What will people remember you for?'

You do not want to know.

'I guess if I could take a brilliant photograph that would make people think – maybe in a war zone or a place where change is needed. That would be enough.'

It's not a lie: I used to think I would change the world, before I realised how little talent I really have.

'What else can you bring to the community?' Bernice asks. She's an air traffic controller. She'll like facts.

What if I gave her the real facts? That I am the last person they should pick, that no one should get close to me, that I don't deserve to be close to people; not now, not ever.

'I'm freelance, so I get spare time between jobs. I've taught photography to kids on the estate where I grew up, so maybe I could run workshops here?'

'Sounds good,' Bernice says.

Camille studies me closely. 'The Factory was partly created to help people escape the isolation that city life can bring. But it does mean we're more close-knit than conventional house shares. How do you feel about that?'

I get how this works – I need to talk the talk, to make them feel good if they choose me over all the other hard-luck cases.

'Where I'm living at the moment, it's . . . full-on. A twenty-four-hour party house. Mainly other photographers, wannabes. That's just not my tribe these days.' I hesitate. 'It's turned kinda toxic. I worry about where it could end . . . The Factory feels like a safe haven.'

All true. Just a shame this interview is two weeks too late.

Camille nods. 'I am an actor and in my world, too, partying can take a heavy toll. Are there any . . . particular issues you need help with? We are very supportive here.'

Is she hinting about what I could say to bag a space? I shift in my chair, take a deep breath and feed them another lie. 'You want honesty? I am trying to get sober. I hope that doesn't rule me out.'

Bernice's pixie face lights up. She leans in, touches my knee. 'Not at all. We don't judge here. We'd do whatever we could to make that easier.'

Lucas raises his eyebrows; he looks less convinced. 'Is there anything you'd like to ask us?'

What I want to know is what's really going on, because that philanthropist landlord story sounds as made-up as my own answers, but I daren't sour things.

'You guys are for real, aren't ya?'

Lucas scoffs, but Bernice places her hand on his arm to stop him saying more.

What's the deal with these three? There's this atmosphere between them, as though they're telepathic or have spent so much time together they can finish each other's sentences. They're probably all shagging too.

'What do you mean?' Bernice asks.

'In my world, there are a lot of fakes.'

She nods. 'This place is for real, I promise. We look after each other. You won't find anywhere else like it.'

Once I'm outside I pull up my hood again, even though the night's still hot. The chance of being recognised has got to be lower in this part of town, but I'm not going to risk it.

The cobbles make the bike shudder as I cycle back up to Bermondsey Street – I learned my lesson from my near-miss with that bossy teacher girl when I got here. If I'd hit her, or she'd called the police, it'd have been game over.

There's a postage stamp of a park ahead. Behind the swings, almost out of sight, a couple are talking. It looks like a deal: the man hands something to the woman.

I glance up a second time and realise who they are: she's that stuck-up blonde from the Factory, Veronica, the one who kept telling everyone who'd listen that the place is somewhere between a cult and a knocking shop.

And the guy is Holden, the wanker who makes vegan ice cream, which should be *illegal*.

Maybe he's bribing her to vote for him. I don't blame him. Who wouldn't lie, cheat or break the rules to improve their chances of being picked? I'm doing the same myself.

What I don't know is if it's worked.

Jesus, I hope it's worked.

I turn left, against the traffic, towards the Thames. The ride takes me twenty minutes and soon I'm dripping with sweat, stinking of my own fear. Only when I'm back at the hotel, do I risk shrugging off the hood.

In my room, I take the vodka out of the mini-fridge and pour a big slug. Despite what I told them, drinking is not my problem.

Bloody wish it was something so easy to fix.

8

Immi

Two hours and seventeen minutes to get back to Sarah's. By the time I get off the bus, tucking my knife into my palm in case anyone jumps me, all the gin and hope they served up in the Factory have completely worn off.

I'm a fraud. This city will never be my home.

As I walk the final block towards her basement flat, I hear angry voices through the open window.

'. . . I know she's your friend but we can't live like this, Sar. Especially not now.'

'Look, she drives me crazy too, but what am I supposed to do? Chuck her out? She's broke, Mack. And when she does find something new, she'll have to scrabble around for the deposit.'

'She's not our bloody responsibility. I'm going to the pub. You've got to tell her when she gets back.'

'Or what?'

'Or . . . just tell her, all right?'

'Mack, wait—'

Sarah's boyfriend comes flying out of the front door and up the flat's steps. He sees me, looks down at the open window, and has the grace to blush. 'Hi, Immi. I'm going . . .'

'To the pub. I heard.'

He slopes off. Coward. There's never been much love lost between Mack and me, but I hadn't realised Sarah was sick of me too.

Sarah and I met at uni, a third-rate place I only picked because it was close to home, and she only chose because her grades were too shit to study Law anywhere else. We've done OK, both of us. No one else from college made it to the bright lights of London.

She spins round when I come into the living room, then adopts a forced smile. 'How'd it go?'

Do I pretend I didn't hear what she said to Mack? I don't have the energy for a row. 'Went well, I think. The place is amazing.'

'Great,' she says, not looking me in the eye. 'Look, I'm a bit knackered so I'm going to have a bath and get straight to bed. Mack won't be back till late, so enjoy having the place to yourself. There's some wine in the fridge. You've earned it.'

Later, when Mack crawls in from the pub, he stumbles over the end of the sofa bed, and swears at it, at himself, and at me.

And the making-up whispers I can hear through their bedroom door soon lead to make-up sex. If the Factory doesn't work, I am going to have to come up with a plan because I've run out of places to crash.

Go back home or . . . there is always the other option.

No, I can never go back to that.

Home it is.

Work drags on Wednesday, even though the hot weather is perfect for our school-wide insect survey. I've been planning it for weeks and I'd usually be down on the ground with the kids, stoking their enthusiasm for the secret universe that exists in only a handful of soil. But today I'm too distracted checking my phone. *Nothing.*

The deadline has passed – it's no longer 'in the morning'. I've failed to get into the Factory.

Even Fatima, my head-in-the-clouds TA, has noticed that I can't muster my usual enthusiasm.

'You've a face like a bulldog chewing a wasp. Is it a boy messing with your head?' Fatima, married for fifteen years, takes vicarious pleasure in other people's more complicated love lives.

'It's not a boy. It's a house share.'

She loses interest and goes to help some of the boys inspecting the tired-out earth.

All their lives revolve around this small patch of London. I hadn't realised until I moved here that the city isn't big at all, it's just a collection of tiny towns with borders you never see on maps but which exist nonetheless. Some of my families view going to the West End as a once-a-year trip, though it's only half an hour away on the bus.

I want to widen the kids' perspectives, especially the girls.' I know what it's like to have your expectations limited by people who believe they have your best interests at heart. I also know how good it feels to break away.

'Watch the beetles under your feet!' Fatima cries out. 'They're meant to be alive when we put them back.'

Home time approaches, and the kids are mobbing me to show off their discoveries.

'Miss, Miss, you'll never guess how many insects I found in my sieve, Miss!'

I look into Agata's eager young face and snap out of my funk. 'Let me try. Five?'

'No! Try again!'

'Ten?'

'Thirty-three,' she shrieks.

As I look at her chart, my phone vibrates in my pocket. *Private number.* I never answer it at work but this time I have to.

'Immi? This is Bernice, from the Dye Factory. I've got what I hope is some very good news . . .'

Week 1: How we live

Welcome to the Dye Factory. We hope you're going to be very happy here.

We'll be sending these induction messages to your app once a week – they're designed to help you learn how the Factory works and what's going on. Because as you'll find out, Ashleigh always has something new up her sleeve.

Your buddy will meet you for the first time this week to talk through all the practicalities, from the air conditioning in your studio, to the honesty bar and the VR games you can enjoy on the Play floor (that's if Lucas ever lets go of the headset).

You'll have four get-togethers with your buddy, one for each week of your trial period. After that there'll be the vote to confirm you as a 'Dyer'. But any of us are happy to help if you have concerns or questions at any time.

We love how we live and we're sure you will too!

From all your new neighbours and – we hope – your new friends . . .

9

Sunday 29 April

Dex

I look under the bed, in all the drawers and on top of the wardrobe to make sure I'm leaving no trace of myself behind. Checking out feels weird. This shabby hotel room has been home for nearly three weeks now, and it's cost me over two thousand pounds.

One last thing to do. I turn my phone on and call Mum's mobile. She picks up straightaway.

'Hello, kiddo. We were just talking about you.'

My muscles tense, the fight-or-flight thing kicking in. 'Oh? Nothing bad, I hope?'

'We were considering a search party or reporting you to the police as a missing person.' She laughs. I think she's in the garden. I can hear the trickle of the fountain, and the dog yapping in the way he only does at birds.

'Yeah, don't do that, eh, Mum? I'm sorry. I've been really busy because of my new assignment. I've been rushing round sorting out flights and visas and currency.'

'Visas! Wow, that sounds exciting. Not dangerous though, is it, D?'

'It . . . No, we've got minders and security, and I've had all the injections. I don't want to jinx anything by telling you too much, though; it might not happen even once I get there.'

'Where? Give me a clue. I deserve to know where my son's gonna be, don't I? Especially if I'm going to pray for you to get back in one piece.'

'Um . . . Pakistan.'

There's a long pause.

'That sounds dangerous to me.'

'No, the trip's being run by the NGOs who're used to working out there. It's a brilliant opportunity, Mum. Exactly the kind of work I've been trying to land since I came to London.'

I hate lying to my mother but this is the only way till things settle. The lies are better than her ever finding out the truth about what I've done.

The barking has intensified. 'Freddie, stop that! The birds are ignoring you anyway.' She sighs. 'You promise you won't do anything stupid. You read about journalists getting kidnapped, sold to ISIS, and worse . . .'

'I promise. But it is going to be tricky to phone you at times because we'll be quite remote. So text me and I'll text you back when I can. And don't worry about me. I know how to look after myself.'

'May I tell your sisters?'

'Might be better to wait till I get back.' Though, knowing my mother, she won't be able to stop herself saying something.

I hear her sigh again. 'Love you, kiddo.'

She wouldn't if she *really* knew me. 'Love you too.'

When the call ends, I turn the phone off, take out my new one and call a cab to Bermondsey.

It's Camille who greets me when I arrive at the Factory.

She threw me the lifeline that made me play up the stuff about drinking during my interview. I'm pretty sure that's the lie that got me in.

'Welcome home,' she says. Her voice makes me think of fjords and icy skies, and her face is one I would love to photograph. 'I personally am very glad we agreed to select you.'

'I'm flattered.'

'I believe you can be trusted,' she says, and her manga-sized blue eyes lock on to mine. 'Can *I* trust you, Dexter?'

'Of course.' *Liar.*

We take the lift up to the Nourish floor. 'You've been allocated Marrakech, the room you saw on your tour,' Camille explains as she slides open the lift shutters with a loud clang. 'Bernice decided who should go where, based on how you might affect the balance of each floor.'

So Bernice is a control freak. Not a surprise.

Camille opens the door to the studio with her phone. She allows me to step inside first. It's smaller than I remembered, but still bigger than my horrible hotel room.

Don't get too cosy. This is temporary, *everything* is temporary.

Camille is waiting for me to say something.

'It's great. Really. Suits me just fine. Who is the other person you chose?'

'Her name is Imogen. She is a teacher. Had hair in a short bob, like a . . . What is the word for the girls in the 1920s?'

'Flappers. I remember her.'

'Yes. She arrives this afternoon.'

Another person with no notice to give? Maybe my own situation has made me suspicious, but surely that's a bit odd.

None of my business. I've got lucky here, very lucky. I was sure my fake references and bullshit about my bank account being hacked would make them withdraw the offer. Instead they just asked me to pay double the usual deposit. 'Great news!'

Camille smiles; it makes her face less ethereal. 'Yes. In confidence, I will tell you that you scored the most votes. Bernice was a real fan of yours. The second vote was a tie, between Imogen and another person. Hanna the housekeeper had the casting vote. She has a sixth sense for if someone is going to fit in.'

It seems odd to tell me all this. 'I'm guessing Imogen doesn't know she almost didn't get in?'

She frowns again. 'No, and please do not share this with her. I am only telling you because . . . I am not sure she will survive the trial period, so maybe you prefer not to become too close to her.'

'Thanks for the warning. But it might be me you want to get rid of.'

'Either party can leave without comeback before the end of the four-week trial. Though I hope you will stay,' she says, and there is a hint of a blush on her pale skin. 'Oh. We have removed all accessible alcohol from the kitchen area, though the honesty bar upstairs remains. Would you like us to ask your neighbours to help by keeping an eye on you?'

Invite them to spy on me? I suppose I have to say yes. 'That's very thoughtful. But I do have another bad habit I haven't kicked: vaping. Is that allowed?'

Camille wrinkles her nose as though she can already smell the sickly vapour. 'Not in your studio or communal areas. But we have created a vaping pod on the roof terrace.'

'A vape with a view. I like that.'

'I will leave you to unpack. Tonight, we're planning drinks for you and Imogen. But for now, settle in. And, again, welcome home.'

Unpacking takes sixty seconds: I leave most of my gear in the suitcase. I need to be ready to run.

Once I'm done, I go out into the kitchen area and make a coffee. The espresso machine takes a few minutes to figure out, but I'm pleased when the thick liquid pours into my cup, alongside that wake-up smell.

I sense someone nearby.

When I turn, it's Veronica – the big-nosed woman I saw with one of the other candidates in the park across the road.

'Hi. I'm Dex,' I say, smiling.

'Yes, you are.' She doesn't smile back.

'Fancy a coffee, now I've sussed out how this works?'

'Don't bother. We're not going to be friends, you and me. Friendship doesn't exist here.' Her voice is so loud I imagine it must travel through the whole building. 'People pretend, but they'll stab you in the back when you're not expecting it.'

Before I can reply – and how the hell am I meant to? – she turns and walks up the stairs to the next floor.

What the hell brought that on?

I wait till she's gone and then take my coffee up the two flights of stairs to the terrace. When I reach the rooftop, I feel less hemmed in. In the hotel, the double-glazed windows were sealed shut, trapping me inside with my thoughts. I couldn't even run, in case someone recognised me. At least here there's a gym and open space to go out for a run. I can breathe city air and watch the world, while I work out if I can ever rejoin it.

I find the vaping pod at the far left – it's not as fun as it sounds: a small shed with two office chairs, and just about enough space for one, or maybe two people who know each other *really* well.

As I squeeze in, I brush against the mint and herb pots by the entrance. The smell brings memories flooding back and makes me nauseous. It takes a good few gasps of nicotine before I feel OK again.

'Another sinner! Hooray!'

Bernice is manoeuvring herself into the space; her red hair shocks me, as it did the first time I saw her. She sits opposite and our knees almost touch. She looks exactly the same as she did at the interview: bright lipstick and white blouse.

I think of what Camille told me earlier, about how Bernice supported me at the vote. *Why?*

'Hello again, Bernice. I'm so happy you guys chose me. Thank you.'

She reaches out and pats me on the knee, almost playful. 'It's great you could move in so quickly. We were keen to be back to full capacity; it really helps to make things more fun around here.'

She's less uptight than I remember, perhaps organising the recruitment evening made her seem more stern.

'This place is an oasis compared to my old digs.'

'You're going to love it. You don't have a choice actually, because I'm your buddy, and I never fail at anything.'

'Great.' I hesitate. 'Can I ask why you chose me?'

Bernice looks at me thoughtfully. 'Fishing for compliments already? We just thought you'd fit in. I know the interview was a bit of an ordeal but it's critical we get the right people. On the rare occasions we have made a mistake, it upsets the whole ethos.'

'Veronica doesn't seem convinced I'm the right person.' I regret it as soon as I've said it – I'm the last person to rat on someone.

'Ah. Strictly between us, she's a mistake we're still having to live with. We chose her before we'd fine-tuned the selection process, or introduced the buddy system. There's no way she'd pass now.'

'Am I allowed to ask why?'

Bernice smiles. 'Let's just say her rudeness is nothing personal. She harbours a list of grudges as long as your arm. But we have plans. If she doesn't cheer up, we'll find someone who is less of an energy vampire.'

I nod, though the contract said once you were in, there was no way you could be evicted. 'Right.'

Bernice breathes out a long puff of vapour. 'I don't want to waste any more time on her,' she says. 'But I do want to hear *much* more about Dexter Shepherd.'

10

Immi

Sarah and Mack drive me to Bermondsey – they clearly don't want me to change my mind about moving out.

'This is swanky,' Mack says as we pull up on the cobbles outside.

It really is. I keep wondering if the committee mixed my name up with someone else's, and they're going to turn me away when they realise it's me.

But then I remember the look on Bernice's face when I told my sob story. I deserve this. Maybe I'll be damned for eternity for lying about some of it – Mum is pretty hot on hellfire – but if it means I get my corner of heaven while I'm alive, it might be worth it.

Sarah helps me unload my stuff from the boot. 'Like when your parents drop you off at your halls of residence,' she jokes.

Except she's remembering her own past, not mine. I lived at home the whole time I was at uni. I wasn't strong enough then to make the break.

Mack's getting increasingly mardy. 'You've landed on your bloody feet. Why did we never find anything like this, Sar?'

'If it's any consolation, I don't think they allow couples,' I say, pushing the entryphone button.

Mack looks at his watch. 'I don't suppose you feel like con-
tributing to the petrol, Immi, because—'

The door to the Factory opens. Lucas is there, smiling broadly.
He embraces me, his lips brushing my neck. Every muscle in my
body tightens up: the familiar rictus.

Calm down. He doesn't mean anything by it.

Sarah raises her eyebrows at me over his shoulder, and
mouths, *Hello!*

'Welcome, Immi!' Lucas says, ignoring the others.

'I hope you're not inducting my friend into some kind of
cult,' Sarah says to Lucas, before she heads back to the car.

'If it is a cult, then she's coming willingly,' he replies, laughing that strange cackle I'd forgotten. He turns his back on her to
help move my things into the building. Despite his slim build, he's
strong: sinews stand out like cords in his neck as he hauls my case
into the lift with one hand, and my sewing machine with the other.

The door slams before I can wave goodbye to Sarah.

'Self-closing,' Lucas explains. 'And that camera up there
records a snapshot of everyone who enters or leaves. I thought
you might find that reassuring . . .'

I hate myself for lying to them about something so shitty. 'It
does feel very secure.'

'I told them it was what you needed. At the vote.'

He *really* wants my approval. Before I can reply, the lift gates
slot into place and the cage moves up slowly. As we pass the
Nourish space, the aggressive woman with the blonde hair sits at
the long dining table, alone. When she sees me, she freezes, her
coffee cup halfway to her mouth.

'Is she OK?' I ask.

'She's just jealous you've got a studio up on the terrace,' Lucas says. 'There are people here who'd kill for Kyoto.'

'You got the refurbishment finished in time, then?'

'Refurbishment?' He frowns.

'Ashleigh said they were relaying the floor and that's why we couldn't see the room last week.'

'Oh that. Touch and go, but yeah.'

When we reach the Play floor, I'm dazzled again by the scale of the room, the height of the rafters.

'Pretty special, isn't it?' Lucas gazes up too. 'The leather tanning trade was an ugly business, but the architects still made the building beautiful.'

Is this the real Lucas speaking, or part of his charm offensive? Veronica warned me at the selection evening that – what were her exact words? – *Lucas would screw anything with a pulse.*

'Would it be all right for me to see the room now?' I ask.

'Sorry, got carried away. Can I have your phone?'

'Why?'

'So I can set up the app for you.'

I watch closely as he installs the program. Even now, I worry the Factory could be one giant scam. *If something seems too good to be true, it normally is,* as my mother never tires of saying.

'Just pick a PIN, confirm with your fingerprint, and you're good to go.' Lucas passes it back to me.

I turn away to punch in a number. When I hold my phone against the sensor, the light glows soft green and I push open the door.

This room is lighter and bigger than the one we were shown downstairs. There's a full-sized oak desk, and the iron bed must be a king-size. Instead of the beams downstairs, I have *actual rafters*. The window looks out on to the far edge of the roof terrace, and the city beyond it.

'At night, you can just glimpse the Shard,' Lucas says, his breath on my neck. 'There's a blackout blind and double glazing if people are partying out there when you need to sleep.'

Sleep. I haven't slept properly for thirteen months. Even with my knife under my pillow, part of me always stays alert.

I step towards the window, relieved to have a reason to move away from Lucas. Does he expect some kind of thanks for persuading the others to let me move in? The thought passes through me, shadowy and cold. But I don't owe him – or any man – a thing.

'I absolutely love it.'

Except one thing about the room is niggling me.

When I turn round, Lucas is bundling in my case and boxes. 'I'll leave you to get unpacked.'

'Lucas, which part has been redone? Ashleigh said it was the floor but it looks . . .' I look down. The oak boards are beautiful, but they're worn, not new. 'I'm not complaining. Just curious if anything's still drying because there's no smell of varnish or . . .'

He doesn't answer for a few moments. Eventually he says, 'I wasn't involved. Bernice would know. Maybe Ashleigh got it wrong. She's very in tune with her chakras, but not so much with real life.'

I shrug. 'No worries.'

He gives me a quick smile. 'Oh, we're having welcome drinks for you and Dex, the other new Dyer, starting at seven. At least you don't have far to go.'

Dex is the photographer who nearly ran me down with his bike. Weird. I was sure it'd be that hipster ice-cream maker. I wonder what Dex did to win *his* place.

The door closes softly behind Lucas.

I sit on the bed, and exhale. *Home.*

A smile spreads across my face. Life has dealt me some shitty luck since I moved to London – and I've made some terrible decisions.

But maybe this, finally, is my second chance.

I fold and stack and stow like a Japanese decluttering guru. The drawers and wardrobe doors seem stiff but that's probably because the furniture seems as old as the building itself.

When I've finished, the space looks as minimalist and calm as it did when I first opened the door. If it wasn't for my iPad on the bedroom shelf and my sewing machine on that lovely old desk, it would almost look like no one lives here. A couple of years ago, I read that hoarding can be inherited. I won't let my genes get the upper hand.

There's only one thing left to put away, out of sight. Maybe it can go in one of the desk drawers. I sit down and wonder about the person who sat here before. Did they feel this excited on the day they moved in? I cannot imagine giving this up without a really good reason.

Their loss is my gain.

One drawer I've already filled with pens and pencils and the double-ended *Great Work/Watch Your Sums* stamp I use when marking. But the other one kept sticking and this time I pull with a bit more force, finally wrenching so hard that it shoots out. Something drops from inside the framework, and I crawl underneath to pick it up. At first, I think it's a petty cash bag from a bank and I wonder if I've stumbled on a stash of money hidden decades ago.

But, no, there's nothing inside it. I stand up straight, and am about to throw it in the bin when I notice there's a bar-coded sticker on one side. And when I turn it over, there are two words printed on the plastic: *Evidence bag.*

11

Immi

I turn the bag over twice and unseal the top. There's definitely nothing inside, but it looks like the real thing.

Why is it here? Maybe the desk came from a house clearance after a crime. Or perhaps the bag is some kind of ironic gift. Whoever lived here before me might have been addicted to *CSI*, and someone bought the evidence bag as a joke.

But I *do* have a use for it.

I take my box of pills and put it inside; it fits perfectly. Then I run my finger along the raised edge to seal it, and place it underneath my pencils, which I always arrange in the same order. There's no reason for anyone to go snooping – and with all this security, no one can get in – but this way, I'll know for sure.

I change out of my 'moving house' clothes and look for something to wear tonight. Most of my dresses are handmade: sewing is the one useful thing Mum taught me. It doesn't fit people's stereotype of a feminist science nerd, but dressmaking is all about measuring, logic, 3D visualisation.

I choose a simple blue chambray shift with a hem I topstitched with gold thread. I pull it over my head, and transfer my knife from my old jeans into the secret pocket under the hem. As I straighten the dress, I see myself in the mirror. Alastair liked me in this frock, because it makes me look old-fashioned, almost demure . . .

Enough. I need to do something to take my mind off the past. At the bottom of the wardrobe there's a big bag of washing I felt too awkward to do at Mack and Sarah's. Laundry is the perfect distraction.

I take the lift to the ground floor, then walk down the steps to the basement, following the tickly scent of washing powder towards a windowless room.

Someone's sports gear is revolving round the drum of one machine, but a second is empty so I load my stuff inside. I don't have any detergent but there's a row of bottles, each labelled with a Dyer's name. So much for *sharing*.

I siphon some out of Veronica's bottle, mainly because hers also has DO NOT USE written bossily on the side.

And now I jump, because I realise someone else is in the room. I turn slowly to see a pale, dowdy woman about my mother's age, dressed in a beige smock.

'Hello, Imogen.'

I suppose it's quite obvious who I am, but even so, I hate it when someone else has the upper hand.

'Hi. Do you work here or . . .?' I wish I hadn't said that. Is it wrong to judge someone because they look older than the people I've met so far? Though I remember the tenancy agreement did stipulate an upper age limit for residents; I think it was thirty-five. I bloody hope I've got my shit together by then and can afford a place of my own.

'I am Hanna. I run housekeeping.' Her clipped accent sounds Eastern European.

'Oh yes, we've been emailing each other.' I hold out my hand. 'Good to meet you. You must know everything about what goes on in the Factory.'

She doesn't offer her hand, or a smile. 'No. I live down here. Mostly stay out of the way when I am not working.'

On second glance, she's not dowdy at all: her grey-blonde hair is cut into a long bob, much more precise than mine, and the smock is fitted, made from a high-quality linen. If I look like her – rather than my mother – by my mid-fifties, I'll be delighted.

Yet however good she looks, working and living underground to service the needs of a bunch of twenty-somethings is no one's dream job. She must have had limited options.

I know how that feels.

'I think I'll come back when this is done,' I say, hoping she didn't see me steal Veronica's detergent.

She says nothing in reply, and I wonder if she doesn't speak much English. She simply stands there, and I have to back out, awkwardly.

I want to run back upstairs, into the light.

I'm reapplying my lipstick just before seven when there's a knock at my door. Is this what it's like here? People 'calling' for each other, asking if I'm coming out to play.

As I open the door, I expect Lucas, and brace myself for an overly intimate embrace.

'All right?'

Dex. When we first met he scared me, then irritated me with his lazy slang. But now he counts as a familiar face. A pretty handsome one, as it goes.

'Do you want to come in?'

He nods and when he's taken a look around, he grins. 'You got the best room.'

'I didn't get a choice.'

'Hey, don't get defensive. I still can't work out why they let me in at all.'

'Me neither.' It's a relief to say it out loud.

'Weird, isn't it? Which is why I thought maybe we could stick together, in case it all goes a bit *Big Brother* during the welcome drinks.'

He's dressed more smartly now than at the interview, the sweatpants and hoodie swapped for shorts and a crimson T-shirt.

He raises his arm and I link mine through it with a grin. My door buzzes closed behind me, though the other two studios have their doors propped open. I can't ever imagine being that trusting.

Dex lets me step outside first: half the terrace is bathed in late-afternoon sunshine, but the faux grass stops it being too dazzling. At the other end, in the shade, Bernice and Camille are filling vintage drinks dispensers.

'Sample these for us, you guys!' Bernice calls over, and we cross the terrace, still arm in arm.

She embraces me first, then Dex. 'Look at you two, like the Prom King and Queen! We're so delighted to have you here.'

Camille tips ice into the dispensers before holding out a limp hand. The cold has turned her skin yellow and it's freezing against mine. 'Yes, you are both very welcome.'

'Now,' Bernice says, 'Immi, this drink is an extra-potent Pimm's, with fresh mint from our herb garden. And we made this one specially for you, Dex. Cranberry, with lots of lovely fresh lime.'

I raise my eyebrows at Dex.

'I'm cool if Immi knows,' he says. 'Alcohol is . . . problematic for me. So I'm not drinking right now.'

'Oh. Right, well . . .'

'That's why the Factory is going to be such a great fresh start.' Dex smiles virtuously and raises his glass. 'Here's to us and our new, squeaky-clean lives at the Factory.'

'To clean living,' I echo.

As we toast, I notice Bernice and Camille smiling at each other. So they're going to get their kicks out of Dex by detoxing him.

What are they planning for me?

12

Immi

Bernice wasn't kidding about the Pimm's being potent. The sweetness disguises the alcohol, but even before my first glass is finished, a horrible wooziness kicks in.

I move away from the edge of the terrace to try to reduce the dizziness. There are no chairs laid out, so I perch on the wooden edge of a plant box full of herbs: spiky stalks of rosemary and lush bunches of basil and mint.

Zoum, the joker with the plastic flower and the dire warnings, comes over.

'You ignored my advice to stay away, then.' He's holding a bottle of low-alcohol beer. I need to find one of those before Bernice or Camille foists another knockout Pimm's on me.

'Well, Surbiton and Brockley were full.'

He grins. 'I voted for you, like I promised.'

'The best of a bad bunch?'

'No. But I did think it'd do us good to have some people with normal jobs in the Factory.'

'What do you do, Zoum?'

'Freelance IT. As boring as it gets.'

Didn't Lucas tell me someone fixed the Dyers' IT problems for free? Zoum must be the tech Good Samaritan. 'How about everyone else? I know Camille is an actor, but that's all.'

As the others show up, he gives me potted biographies: Bernice is an air traffic controller – suddenly her clear, forceful voice makes sense. Lucas works in PR for the alcohol business, and Veronica, who arrives wearing the same furious expression as last time, is something senior in insurance.

'What about Dex?' I ask.

'A photographer, I think. And Ashleigh' – he nods as she shuffles onto the terrace in badly fitting Moroccan beaded slippers – 'is saving the world one random act of kindness at a time.'

I give him a stern look. 'She seems to mean well.'

'So well that you have to wonder what she is atoning for.'

Is he joking? I don't know him well enough to ask. 'Are there a lot of community activities like this?'

'Ashleigh leads wake-up yoga most mornings, and every Tuesday she reveals her latest City-zen plans to improve our lives at a community meeting. Oh, and there's earth hour once a month, where we get together by candlelight. Virtue-signalling on a massive scale, but it is nice. Chilled.'

'What if you don't fancy taking part in stuff?'

'It's a good idea to show willing till the vote on whether you're allowed to stay permanently, but after that, you can ease off. So long as you do not steal anyone's washing powder, and refrain from storing dead bodies under your bed, you'll be left alone.'

I try not to blush, wondering if he's somehow worked out what I did in the laundry earlier. But the mention of bodies reminds me of the evidence bag. 'The person in Kyoto before me. Why did they leave?'

Zoum takes a swig from his bottle. 'Ah. We . . . agreed, before you and Dex moved in, that it was best to put what happened with Jamie behind us.'

Jamie. Veronica mentioned him at the selection evening, when she was trying to put me off the Factory. 'Was it bad?'

He shakes his head. 'No, but it created a few divisions that have not been repaired quite yet. You understand.'

I don't, but I decide not to push it. Flatmate feuds can erupt over nothing at all; I know that from the shared houses I endured before I met Alastair. 'Onwards and upwards, eh?'

He nods, then leans in to whisper, 'Between you and me, I am not convinced it's fair to keep you and Dex in the dark. So if things do rear their ugly head again, I promise to tell you what you need to know.'

Before I can say anything else, I see Bernice marching in our direction, almost as though she knows what he just said to me.

'Now, now, Zoum. We can't have you hogging Immi all night long. She is the guest of honour, you know!'

After sunset, the languidness of the spring evening morphs into a more intense, wild-eyed mood. The music changes too and people take turns to choose tracks from the virtual assistant's infinite library. Conversations start and don't quite end before another one takes over. I become the centre of attention, which is unfamiliar but flattering.

Everyone is fantastic. *I* am fantastic.

No. I am drunk.

'So do you think the human sacrifice comes tonight, or later?' I say to Dex when we're getting another drink.

'Too soon. Probably at the midsummer solstice. Fatten us up first.'

'So long as there's no orgy this evening, I haven't shaved my legs . . .' I stop talking, embarrassed at how flirty I sound.

But he's grinning. 'Haven't shaved mine either.'

I giggle, feeling less stupid. 'You know what . . . I didn't think I liked you when I first met you, but . . .' Again I say the words before engaging my brain.

'But?' He still looks amused, his eyes wide. I notice how long his lashes are, too, like little brushes sweeping under his eyes.

'But I was wrong, Dex. You're nice.'

He smiles. 'I think you're nice too, Immi.'

'Are you a proper alcoholic?'

'Wow. That's direct.'

'*Shit,* sorry. It's none of my business.'

'I don't know what a *proper* alcoholic is. But I regret things I've done when I was drunk. So I want to try living life sober.'

I nod, and it makes the room spin. 'I wish I was sober right now.'

'Let me get you some water.' Dex heads towards the drinks' table, but the mention of water makes me realise I'm bursting for the loo. I buzz myself back into my room and catch myself grinning stupidly in the bathroom mirror.

All I needed was somewhere safe, a place to lick my wounds. What if I have stumbled on something much, much better? Still smiling, I head back outside, planning to drink only water from now on, when I hear raised voices from the mezzanine 'Nook' above me.

'. . . And which one of you is planning to screw Immi? Or are you just planning to screw her over, like you did Jamie?'

I recognise the voice: it's Veronica, her tone venomous. I shrink back underneath the beams. I'm stuck here because I can't go through the door to the terrace without being seen.

'Veronica, stop being such a child.' Bernice, sounding bored. 'I know you're pissed off we caught you out, but you should be grateful we're giving you another chance.'

'*Grateful?* You're forgetting how royally I could fuck you all over.'

'You wouldn't dare.' Lucas's voice. 'They'd ruin you if you break the agreement.'

'I promised not to volunteer any information about Jamie, but what if Dex or Immi asks me outright? They deserve to know what they've got themselves into before it hits the newspapers.'

'It won't.' Camille, her voice low. I hadn't even realised there was a fourth person there.

'Oh, Hanna can silence the media too, can she? You forget that her power counts for nothing in the real world. You can't keep this secret forever.'

The floorboards creak above me, and I duck behind the bar area as Veronica climbs down the wooden ladder, and stomps to the main stairs, presumably going back to her room.

'We can't trust her anymore,' Lucas says. 'She's too volatile.'

'She's bluffing,' Bernice says. 'But I'll talk to Hanna, see if she can make Veronica an offer she can't refuse.'

Lucas laughs. 'Just don't make me leave a horse's head on her pillow. Are you OK, Cam?'

I hear a muffled 'yes'.

They start to come down the ladder and I stay crouched, despite the cramp in my thighs, fighting a drunken compulsion to pop out of my hiding place and ask them what that was all about. One thing is clear from what they said, and Zoum too: they don't think this is any of my business.

Except Jamie lived in my room, slept in my bed. That evidence bag I found could be connected to him, but how?

I wait till they've all gone back out to the terrace, then pour myself a tonic from the honesty bar.

Should I ask Veronica? No, I'm too drunk. Anyway, things will probably make more sense in the morning.

After I finish the drink, I go to bed without saying goodnight to my new neighbours, though I can hear them on the terrace until about one, when everyone finally drifts away.

But I still can't sleep. I get up and wedge the chair underneath the door handle. Electronic locks are all very well but I want advance warning if someone uses brute force.

13

Monday 30 April

Immi

I never sleep well in a new bed, so I'm tired and groggy when I get up. But my power shower wakes me up and I drink my coffee on the roof terrace, which is miraculously clean despite last night's party. The city looks glorious from up here – but the best thing about being so central is that I can *walk to work*.

Before I lived in London, I didn't realise what a big deal that is. It takes me fifty brisk minutes, which sobers me up. Just as well, because the only thing tougher than Monday morning with Year 6, is Monday morning with Year 6 *and* a hangover.

'OK, everyone, settle down. The weekend is over and it's time to get down to work.'

All day, I'm there in body but not in spirit, desperate to go home. I half-expect to find my stuff dumped on the pavement of Tanner's Walk, with a note attached saying: *Sorry, we made a mistake, you don't belong.*

I force myself to stop thinking the worst and concentrate on what I might pick for dinner from all the goodies in the communal kitchen. While I was staying at Sarah's, I used to eat sandwiches on the bus home, to avoid crowding her and Mack out.

When I get back, I find Dex on the Nourish floor, making a salad.

'I feel like I should be going full *MasterChef* in this kitchen,' he says.

I rummage around the communal veg box and take out a mysterious gnarled, brown tuber. 'Yeah. I'm the same. But what do you think we're meant to do with this?'

He grins. 'Just don't ask Lucas that question. I bet he'd have a few suggestions.'

I smile. Knowing Dex has sussed out what Lucas is like – and finds it funny – makes me feel less vulnerable. Dare I ask Dex what he thinks of Veronica too?

No. After what I heard yesterday, I'm staying out of Factory politics. I get some yogurt from the communal fridge, add a banana, nuts and some organic raw honey. 'Have you had your first buddying session yet? Who did you get?'

He cringes slightly. 'Bernice.'

I nod. 'She scares me a bit. I've got Ashleigh. Maybe she'll make me stroke the bunny rabbit to help me relax.'

'Or slit its throat. You let me know if they start talking about satanic rituals, yeah?'

We both laugh, but I sense he's edgy about this place too. 'It's gonna be OK, right?'

Dex hesitates just for a second, then puts the knife down, reaches over and pats my hand. 'Sure. And if we hate it, it's not Hotel California. We can check out any time we like.'

I sleep better on Monday night, though the chair stays pushed against the door. On Tuesday evening, after work, the others drift onto the roof terrace and I join them. Ashleigh arrives last, hair released from its braids and now a halo of golden frizz.

'Guys, especially Immi and Dex, gather round, it's time for terrific Tuesday! Once a week, I round up any community news, and introduce cool stuff I've found to improve our lives as part of my City-zen programme.'

People pull up deckchairs and beanbags – I think it's a full house, till I notice Veronica isn't here. Maybe that's why everyone looks so relaxed.

'So, we always kick off with a kind of show-and-tell, so we know what's happening in each other's lives.'

Camille begins, telling us about an audition she's got this week. 'It has been quiet for me recently, so I am hoping it might work out. There's so much competition.'

Dex nods. 'Creative industries are really hard like that, aren't they? I'm waiting on commissions too, so if anyone wants help around the Factory, let me know.'

'Cheers for that, Dex,' Ashleigh says. 'So, in Nourish news, my latest batch of ferments are coming on. Thanks to the warm weather they should be ready tomorrow. The milk kefir is going to be amazing.'

'But don't accept any from Zoum,' Lucas warns us. 'Last time, he swapped the real stuff for sour milk.'

Zoum grins. 'It was just an experiment to see if anyone could taste the difference.'

Ashleigh pretends to laugh but I get the impression that she struggled to see the funny side. 'Now, I'm always looking to use tech or other innovations to make life even better.' She picks up a remote control and within seconds a strange, wild noise surrounds us – a combination of high pitches and low hums.

It's whale music. I've played videos of it to the kids at school when we've studied the oceans.

'Are they shagging or do they always make that noise?' Lucas asks.

Ashleigh gives him a dirty look. 'It's *relaxing*. Basically, this uses the fire alarm system to play music wirelessly into the studios and other floors. Instead of shocking us out of our beds, it could chill us out. I want to experiment with different tracks to increase wellness levels.'

Wellness is one of my least favourite words, but I'll try not to hold it against her. She's handing out cards and asking us all to keep track of emotion and mood, so she can work out the most effective sounds.

When the meeting ends, Zoum comes over to me and Dex. 'So, what did you think of your first "terrific Tuesday"?'

'Great,' I say.

'You're not worried Ashleigh's going to brainwash us into going vegan by playing subliminal messages in our sleep?'

'I know you're joking, Zoum, but I'm already worried I've joined a cult and you're not helping.'

He laughs. 'It's not a cult, it's a *community*.'

'What's the difference?'

'We don't have a leader, at least, not an official one.' He glances meaningfully at Bernice, who is whispering something to Hanna. I hadn't even realised she was at the meeting, and it surprises me. Though perhaps it shouldn't: she's responsible for the day-to-day running of the Factory.

Even so, there's something about the way the two women are standing that makes me look again.

Despite Bernice's status as Queen Bee, it's Hanna who looks like the one in charge.

Much as I like the terrace and the kitchen, it's always a relief when I can close the door behind me and stop pretending. I'm trying to model myself on the person spec from the advert, but I'm not sure I can keep this up for another three weeks and five days.

Except . . . I have to. I just need to pace myself, withdraw occasionally. So on Wednesday, I grab a slice of pizza on the way home and eat it on the banks of the Thames, taking in the view. Tonight I'll stay inside my studio, get lesson-planning done. And if Ashleigh decides to pump whale music around the speakers, at least I have the *very* expensive noise-cancelling headphones Alastair bought me for Christmas, only a month after we moved in together – and two months before he dumped me.

The pizza sticks in my throat and I struggle to swallow it, along with the hurt. If I don't let myself feel it, it's not real.

It's my only way of coping. If I start to let it out, I fear it'll turn into some unstoppable tsunami that will force me to face the other shit too. I think it would drag me under.

Suddenly the Thames, with her murky depths and her strong tides, seems less calming, so I walk briskly back to the Factory. I ignore the voices on the roof terrace and let myself into my room, ready to crash out.

Something is different.

I know immediately. What's changed? My bed looks the same, roughly made, and the biography of Ada Lovelace I was reading is still on the bedside table, a half-drunk glass of water sitting on top.

But I *know* someone has been here. The air is too clear and fresh, as though the window has been opened during the day. There's none of the soupy warmth that's been there the previous two nights when I've come home from school.

Who has been here?

The keycode is meant to be completely personal, my room only accessible by me.

Pressure builds in my chest, as though boulders have been dropped onto it. My breathing is fast but I'm not getting enough air, and my brain pulses, as though it's too big for my skull.

My space has been invaded. *It's intolerable.*

The bathroom door is ajar.

Is that how I know? Because I close it every morning, to make sure the fan works at maximum efficiency after I've finished my shower. I have a thing about mould.

Or maybe it's because the left-hand desk drawer is not quite shut . . .

My sleeping pills.

I wrench the drawer open, the blood rushing in my head – and exhale with relief when I see the clear plastic evidence bag is still there, and the box inside it. Untouched. Am I imagining this?

My breathing is beginning to return to normal.

But now I see the way the pillow has been placed against the headboard. I never do it like that.

And I can smell even more proof: a soapy scent of detergent that makes me certain who has been in my room.

No. This is *not* what I signed up for. I tear out of the room, slamming the door behind me.

My anger is too vast to hold in.

14

Wednesday 2 May

Dex

Bernice and I are starting my first 'buddying' session in the vaping pod when Immi bursts in.

'I need to speak to you, please, Bernice. Privately?' she says, ignoring me completely. Her eyes are crazy.

It makes her look hot.

Stop that. You're not here to get laid, not after where it led last time.

Bernice raises her eyebrows at me, but goes out onto the terrace and tries to calm Immi down. The smell of herbs wafts in from outside – overpowering, *nauseating.*

I can't hear every word of the row, but it seems to be about Hanna the housekeeper accessing Immi's room without permission.

'. . . It's standard for her to go in and change the bedding and towels, Immi. She only gets access via the app twice a week.' Bernice's voice is soothing. I guess she uses the same tone with irritated pilots stuck in the stack above Heathrow Airport.

'I've only slept in that bed three times, I don't need my sheets changed!'

'But as I was about to explain, if you want to opt out, just select that on the app, and she'll leave the linens outside. Or you could cut down to one change a week. It's really no big deal.'

Immi is facing me, her cheeks red with anger. But her eyes aren't furious. There's something else there: she looks vulnerable.

'I can't believe she's allowed in to snoop on us, that's all.'

Snoop? A nerve above my eye twitches.

Bernice reaches out to touch Immi's hand. 'Imogen. Seriously? You shouldn't be angry with Hanna, you should feel sympathetic. A woman her age, stuck doing our dirty washing in that basement?'

'I'm not comfortable about the invasion of privacy.'

What is she worried Hanna might find? Immi doesn't seem like the kind to have secrets.

I check myself. I've got to stop projecting all my own feelings onto other people. I'm the only one in this place with *real* skeletons in my reclaimed wood closet. 'Fine. That's what the opt-out is for. Though it's not exactly in keeping with the community spirit. Perhaps the Factory isn't right for you.'

I hear the warning in Bernice's voice. Immi flinches. 'I'm not complaining, it just takes some adjustment . . .' Her voice sounds meeker now.

'OK. Understood. But please don't say anything to her. Hanna's not the brightest, but she does care about us all. She'd hate to know she's made you angry.'

Immi sighs. 'I won't.'

Bernice raises her eyebrows as she shimmies back into the vaping pod but there's a slight smile on her crimson lips, too. 'Who rattled *her* cage? Anyway, where were we?'

'Buddying.'

'Oh *yes*,' she says and there's a gleeful look in her eye as she inhales deeply from her slimline black vaper. 'What happened there is a classic example of someone who hasn't got a handle on the ethos of our community yet.'

It seems harsh, considering we've only been here a few days. 'In what way?'

'Privacy is important to everyone. But the practical advantages of having your room cleaned for you, your laundry done? I mean, they're worth compromising for, surely?'

'I guess.'

'What you have to understand here is that we're about lowering the defences, Dex. About embracing a different kind of living.'

'I thought it was a house share,' I say as mildly as I can.

She blinks. 'It's a community. Maybe we could unpick that together. As part of the buddying? What community means to you.'

I laugh. 'Woah. Does the therapy get thrown in free?'

Bernice says nothing. The silence grows. A small bird lands on the cut-down tin drum someone – Ashleigh, I bet – has filled with water. It bathes, flicking its wings rapidly, always watchful, before flying off.

'I hope you're not going to disappoint me, Dex,' Bernice says eventually. 'My judgement is usually pretty good.'

It's the same tone she used with Immi, and I realise I have to be careful too. 'No, man. Community is what I'm missing. It was part of my childhood, before I fell in with the wrong people.' All true, but Bernice will probably be imagining tower-block life on the breadline, with a little police brutality thrown in. The truth is very different: barn dances in the village hall, Scouts, our neighbours patting themselves on the back for graciously allowing the *coloured family* to assimilate so well.

'Do you think that is why you struggled ... Why you ended up ... in your current situation?'

She means my imaginary drinking problem. But she's right, by accident. My current shitstorm all started when I left home.

I nod and she smiles, satisfied. 'So, let's move on to life here. I notice you're spending a lot of time in the Factory, which is cool. The real world is a bit of a disappointment in comparison, right ...'

When the session is over, I go back to Marrakech, knackered from lying. It was pretty full on. I take out the bottle of vodka I've hidden in my wardrobe, pour a double and down it in one. Rinse away the smell, brush my teeth.

I should be making a plan but I guess there's no hurry. The last few weeks have taken everything from me.

Enough with the pathetic self-pity. I don't deserve any peace after what I did.

The sound is enough to wake the dead.

An electronic alarm, two tones that make my ears hurt and my head throb. A police siren? Are they coming for me?

'*The fire alarm has been triggered. Please evacuate the building, using the stairs only.*'

A recorded woman's voice issues instructions, calm but uncompromising, in between the shrill notes. She sounds like Bernice.

I reach for my phone and leave my studio. There's no smell of smoke. Veronica is heading down the stairs too, wiping her eyes with the back of her hand. Red lights in the wall flash to show the way.

Hanna stands at the main entrance doors, checking people off as we leave the building. She must have run up from her room in the basement to organise the evacuation.

'Hurry, hurry,' she says, copying the tone of the recorded announcement. She looks like a nurse in her pale nightshirt and white slip-on shoes.

I do a count myself: Immi, Camille, Lucas, Veronica. Bernice emerges looking dishevelled, the first time I've seen her with a hair out of place. Another siren approaches.

'The fire service have to come out when the alarm goes off because of the number of residents, and the number of floors,' Lucas is telling Immi.

Zoum and Ashleigh are the last out.

'Satisfied, are you?' Veronica shouts at Zoum.

'Come on, Veronica,' Lucas says. 'It might be the real thing.'

'Yeah, right. I have a seriously important compliance meeting in' – Veronica checks her smartwatch – 'ugh, three hours. And thanks to Mr Joker here, I am going to be as much use as a chocolate teapot.'

'Why me?' Zoum says. 'I like my sleep as much as the next person.'

'Rubbish, we all know it was you. And Ashleigh, next time you come up with some genius idea for improving our quality of life, keep it to yourself, will you? Because this moron will always find a way to use it against us.'

Bernice steps forward. '*Did* you set the alarm off, Zoum? Honestly? Because if you did, we can let the firefighters go and deal with a genuine emergency.'

Zoum shakes his head. 'I swear.'

I wonder why they are all so desperate to blame him for what could simply be a fault in the system?

Though it is a pretty major coincidence, I guess. One day Ashleigh is saying how brilliant it is that she can use the fire alarm system to pipe shitty spa music into our rooms, and the next night, the alarm itself is triggered, as though someone is mocking her.

As the fire engine turns into Tanner's Walk, there's only just enough space in the narrow street. Hanna shows the crew inside but already I'm certain this *is* a false alarm.

What kind of freak *does* that? The last time it happened, I was in primary school and even then, we thought the kid who did it was juvenile.

I look at the people I live with and wonder who is up to no good.

Bernice might pretend we have a community here. But not everyone is on the same page.

15

Friday 4 May

Immi

By the time the bell goes on Friday, I'm almost on my knees, thanks to whoever set off that stupid false alarm.

The fire service had no idea what caused it and the Factory's supposedly high-end security system didn't show how it was triggered either. Though Veronica insists it was Zoum, as he's notorious for his so-called sense of humour.

But as we all trooped back to bed, he stepped into line with me on the stairs, touched my arm to slow me down. 'Do not believe them, Immi. I play a few jokes, but I never mess with life and death.'

When I didn't reply, he leaned in closer. 'Think about it. Who knows inside out how the system works? Ashleigh, that's who. Some people are only ever happy when they have maximum attention.'

At the time, I half believed him. Yet as I take the bus back towards London Bridge – I'm too tired to walk this afternoon – I try to think of other explanations.

It was Zoum who joked about playing subliminal messages in our sleep. And don't cults use sleep deprivation to break people down?

Ugh, tiredness also makes you paranoid. It was a fault, that's all.

I focus on the bank holiday weekend ahead. I plan to do nothing except lie on that roof terrace and drink home-brewed kombucha. I need to be on my best behaviour. Bernice made it clear that my outburst about Hanna changing my sheets was a black mark against me.

I need her support. Because even with fire alarms, nosy cleaners and cultish tendencies, the Dye Factory beats any other house share hands down.

'How *are* you?' Ashleigh asks as I sit down on a gym ball in Retreat. It's Saturday and I am wide awake, hangover-free and ready for buddying.

'I'm great. Had a fantastic night's sleep and I'm sure your kombucha is raising my mood!'

She smiles but there's a steeliness in her eyes. 'It's a shame you haven't had time for buddying until now. Any reflections on the last six days?'

'I love it. Everything just *works*. The design is gorgeous, and all the little extras, too. Especially the things you've put in place.'

It's the truth. I was sceptical about the fermenting areas and the emotional support animals, but at lunchtime, people happily pile their plates with 'living' salads from the crock pots Ashleigh tends. Plus I've gone to Retreat to read a few times, and Bella and Edward seem to get quite a few visits. Bernice stayed longest and I'm sure I heard her cooing.

'Good. But you're not such big fan of our housekeeping arrangements, right?' Her lilting Welsh accent doesn't soften the implied accusation.

'Oh, that.' *Are they in some WhatsApp group, commenting on our behaviour?* 'It'd been a long day and I was freaked out. I don't want to go into detail but . . . something happened to me a while back that's made me quite jumpy.'

She leans in, bouncing gently on top of her gym ball. I'm pretty sure she doesn't know the story I gave to the committee at the interview, but who knows? 'Imogen, you're among friends here. Anything you tell me will go no further.'

Friends is pushing it. I hardly know her. 'Thank you,' I say, closing it down.

A flash of irritation crosses her round, pretty face. 'You'd be surprised how good it can feel to share. When I first came here, I was pretty shut down. Yes, even me, with my crystals and my meditations. Spending time here at the Factory helped me fully embrace what community is.'

I don't really know what she means. 'How?'

'You're never alone here. We all have . . . experiences that have shaped us in the wrong way. My brother had very big problems.' Her mouth curls as she says this. 'It affected the entire family but especially me. I became very defensive, very closed off.'

'I'm sorry to hear that.' Though I can't ever imagine her that way.

She blinks. 'It took a lot of work for me to get through it, become the woman I am now. Pain can unite us. Are you certain you don't want to share?'

All I really want is to get off this bloody gym ball as sitting on it is making my thighs burn. 'Not right now. I hope that's OK.'

A pause, before she says, 'Sure. It can take some time to get used to the kind of openness we embrace here. And you do have three more weeks before we decide your fate.' She giggles. 'So, have you thought about the community contribution side of things? Paying it forward?'

I nod, pleased to be on safer ground. 'I thought I'd bring my machine out, and help anyone who is interested in upcycling or mending clothes that are looking a bit tired . . .'

Afternoon. I'm lying on a sunlounger on the terrace, wishing I had a real drink in my hand.

'That looks suspiciously like one of Ashleigh's gut-gurgling potions,' Lucas says, emerging from inside with a bottle of white wine so cold that beads of condensation are already appearing on the glass.

'It's elderflower and dandelion,' I say primly.

'Ah well. If you prefer gooseberry with an overtone of kiwi, I've got the answer.' He unscrews the top of the wine. 'New Zealand Sauvignon Blanc. Unlike that stuff, it won't make you fart.'

'I'm fine, thanks.'

He shrugs and joins Queen Bee and Camille on the fake grass speckled with daisies that they've laid out. To my right, Dex is chatting to Ashleigh. He's dressed only in shorts, the cross-hatched pattern of his abs on display. Not that he looks like he's showing off on purpose but Ashleigh seems hypno-tised. She laughs at everything he says, and keeps tucking the same strand of hair behind her ear, as though she's a love-struck eleven-year-old.

Why am I being such a bitch?

I'd better not be developing a soft spot for Mr Shepherd myself. A rebound crush is the last thing I need.

I get up and go back to my room, trying to focus on lesson plans for next week, but the words swim in front of my eyes. Even the wonder of science can't compete with a day as beautiful as today.

Plus, my mother will be phoning soon, and I don't want the Dyers to overhear me.

I drag myself out of the Factory and walk through Bermondsey, towards the river. When I lived with Al, we'd spend weekends in Primrose Hill, or shopping in Hampstead, but I think I prefer this part of London. The banks of the Thames buzz as I walk to the Tate Modern and the Globe, then cross over the Thames and make my way back towards Tower Bridge.

I live here. When the tourists clamour for selfies, I almost pity them. These are *my* buildings, my views. I am a Londoner!

Mum always calls me between four and six on a Saturday; she doesn't like me phoning her, in case she's 'napping', which is code for *sleeping off the booze.*

There's an element of control, too. She wants to hold on to a part of me, to believe I might surrender and come home. It's easier for both of us. Till I found the Factory, I thought she might get her wish.

I'm staring up at the forbidding walls of the Tower of London when my mobile rings.

I pick up immediately. 'Hi, Mum. How's the weather where you are?' I always try to start upbeat, but she usually drags us down.

'Dreadful. So muggy that I can't get comfortable, or sleep at night. I bet it's even worse in London.'

The sun is bright, there's a light, refreshing wind, and the newspapers say we're warmer than the Costa del Sol. 'It is pretty oppressive, yes. The crowds don't help.'

I imagine her bunched up on the sofa, shuddering at the idea of crowds. Whatever I say, she takes as a slight. If I tell her I hate my life down here, she asks why I won't come home. If I tell her everything is going well, I am apparently rubbing it in.

I want her to be happy. But not enough to sacrifice my own life.

'Is Alastair with you?'

Alastair is the only thing I've ever got right in Mum's eyes so I've pretended we're still together. Telling her it's over would destroy her.

'No. He's working – last-minute crisis in the office.' My accent has started to mirror hers again, without having to think about it.

'Again?' But there's admiration in her voice. He visited her a couple of times after we met, and though she's too agoraphobic to visit me in London, she's seen pictures of his house. She thought we were teasing when we told her how much a terrace in Highgate had set him back. *You could buy my house and the neighbours' both sides for that,* she'd said, and we'd laughed along with her, though actually he could probably have bought the whole street.

'You know how ambitious he is,' I tell her, and she almost purrs back.

'And school?'

Back and forth we go. The reality of my life is so different to the one she imagines. Soon the conversation switches to health and the various conditions afflicting her and everyone she knows. In her world, illness is currency. I hope if I ever get to that stage, they'll have legalised euthanasia.

Eventually, she runs out of news.

I suppose I need to get it over with.

'Do you . . . need anything from me at the moment?'

'I'm fine, thank you, Imogen.'

I tell her I love her, which I do. When the call disconnects, the view of the river looks duller and the people seem to be smiling to spite me, so I decide to head home to the Factory.

Home.

That word makes the world bright again.

16

Immi

Play is empty when I get back, and the roof terrace too. I go to the honesty bar, planning to pour one of Ashleigh's kombuchas, but my resistance is low after talking to Mum, so I settle for a very small gin.

I climb the ladder to the mezzanine, but when I'm halfway up, I realise Lucas is up there, reading a newspaper.

'Oh, sorry, I'll go somewhere else—'

'Not on my account, Immi. Come and join me.'

He pats the circular velvet sofa. It's big enough for ten people, but it'd be stand-offish to sit at the other end, so I get close enough to see what he's reading.

'Not a surprise, is it?' Lucas says, pointing at a photo of the latest actor facing #metoo allegations. 'He always looked like a sleazeball. It's getting so it'd be a news story to find a star who *isn't* a sex pest.'

This is the last conversation I want to have, but I try to keep it light. 'The casting couch isn't too much of a worry in primary school teaching as we're ninety per cent female.'

'Well, it's rampant in the booze industry and it's not only women who are targeted. When I was younger, I was a bit of a pretty boy and I seemed to bring out the worst in women of a certain age. Not that I objected too strongly!'

It's hard to imagine him as *pretty*. He looks exhausted. I can smell wine on his breath but I suspect alcohol is not the only substance he's abusing.

I smile tightly. 'It's not the same. Men are usually stronger, physically. Plus they're often the ones in charge. Did you ever feel your career would suffer if you said no?'

Lucas gives me a long look and shakes his head. 'Sorry, Imogen. I'm out of order. I know I shouldn't be flippant about this stuff.' He closes the newspaper and puts it on the floor. 'Tell me how you're settling in.'

'Even better than I expected. It's so nice not to be sofa-surfing. To have a place to call home.'

He nods. 'That's great to hear. And the other Dyers?'

'Everyone is so friendly!'

Another curious look. '*Everyone?* Really?' His eyes are bright, inviting me to slag off one of our neighbours.

I'm playing it safe. 'Well, obviously it'll take time to get to know everybody properly.'

'Yeah, some of them you don't want to get to know.'

I *could* ask about Veronica now. 'Who do you mean?'

Lucas leans towards me. 'As you might have gathered from the fire alarm on Wednesday night, Zoum can be a pain in the arse. But Veronica is the main problem here.'

'She seems . . . unhappy.'

'That's one way of putting it. She gets off on causing trouble.'

I think of the argument I overheard on my first night. 'Has the community not helped her at all?'

He frowns. 'You can only help people who *want* to be helped. People who're . . . open to the ideals of the Factory.'

I nod. 'Well, I *love* it.'

'I *knew* you'd fit in. It's a crazy kinda place but if you're willing to go with that, it takes over your life. In a good way, obviously.'

'Right.'

He points at my glass. 'Top-up? Let me see if I can guess which gin you're drinking. It's my specialist subject.' He shifts closer towards me, and takes the drink out of my hand. 'Can I taste it?'

'Sure.' I feel as though he's asking permission for something else but I don't know how to refuse without looking pathetic. The atmosphere has changed.

He tastes, licks his lips. 'I'd say . . . Hendrick's.'

'No. Try again.' I sound flirtatious though I definitely don't mean to.

'I think I need another' – he leans in – 'taste . . .'

His lips are moving towards mine, and for a moment I wonder if this is what is expected. Whether kissing him is the real price of living somewhere so good.

Can I do this? It's just a kiss.

But now his hand is on my leg and his breathing is speeding up and that crushing sensation begins again . . .

My body says no, rearing back. When I look down, my left hand is bunched into a fist and my right is poised to rip the knife out of my pocket.

'*Get off me!* No!' My voice is shockingly loud.

Lucas freezes. He looks stunned, then momentarily pissed off, before he manages to rearrange his face into an expression of contrition. He moves back, so there is space between us. 'Oh Immi, I'm so sorry, I thought—'

Thought I wanted it?

Or simply didn't care either way?

He revolts me. But I cannot lose his support. 'I . . . Sorry, it's not you, you're attractive, but . . .'

'Shh. It was completely my fault. Fuck, you'd think I was actually Harvey Weinstein or something.'

'No, I don't think that.'

'I really shouldn't drink during the day. Forget it, please. And if you *could* bring yourself not to tell any of the others, I'd be really grateful. I promise I don't make a habit of this.'

The more he protests, the more the anger rises inside. I've had enough of men who think they can do what they want without caring if *I* want it too. But I am on probation. I can't say any of that. 'All right.'

Lucas stands up. 'I'll leave you in peace. And sorry again.'

'It's forgotten.'

Except, it's not. Was that *really* a misunderstanding, or was it some kind of test? Perhaps I was meant to go along with this to get Lucas to vote for me to stay permanently.

I close my eyes and think of cooling ripples of water, inhaling to the count of seven, exhaling to the count of eleven. In, out. *You're safe.*

As my pulse slows and the heaviness on my chest starts to lift, I convince myself it was an overreaction to a clumsy come-on. This has nothing to do with Lucas, and everything to do with what happened to me.

Week 2: What we want from you

Your friendly app here to wish you a happy Sunday!

The first week can be a whirlwind – but now it's the start of your second week here, we hope you're starting to feel like one of the gang!

When you applied, we asked what you thought you could bring to the Dye Factory, and this week, we'd really love to get a glimpse of that in action. Don't panic, you don't have to redecorate an entire floor or do the washing for Hanna! We have found that small gestures of kindness are what makes this a happy place, so anything *you* can do to pay it forward this week will help us see what the community will be like with you here for good.

It's also a great reminder to all of us old-time Dyers that we have to put in as much as we take out . . .

And, same as last week, your buddies are around to guide you. Have a great seven days,

Your neighbours

17

Sunday 6 May

Immi

I wake up wanting to hide from Lucas and the others. But eventually hunger – and the subtle pressure of the message on the Factory app to socialise – forces me to leave my studio. As I emerge, Camille is sitting on the sofa facing my door.

I smile but she stares back at me. It's the same look she had on the posters for that TV crime series, dead-eyed and tragically beautiful.

'Morning, Camille.'

'It's afternoon now,' she replies, still frowning. 'I wondered . . . Would you like to talk to me about anything, Immi?'

'Um . . . what about in particular?'

'I had a visit from Lucas last night. He was concerned about what happened between you, but was worried that coming to see you himself would make things worse. I thought it would be better perhaps if you and I discussed it, woman to woman. We could go to my studio?'

The *last* thing I want to do is talk about it with anyone. But I don't trust him to have told Camille the truth so I have to find out what he said.

'OK.'

Her studio is Paris, on the Retreat floor, along from Ashleigh and Veronica. When she lets me in, I can smell peaches. The scent is so strong I assume it's air freshener, until I see a bowl of the cut fruit on her desk, the brilliant orange flesh the only colour in the room. Everything else is white, even the furniture.

'Wow, I can't believe how different your studio feels from mine.'

Camille smiles. 'I like tranquillity. I think the studios do take on something of the essence of the people who live here, though the history of the building persists.'

'Yes, those poison bottle lampshades are brilliant.'

She shakes her head. 'I am talking on a much deeper level. We are always surrounded by spirits. In a way, it's comforting. To know that whatever we are dealing with, the people who worked in these rooms are still with us.'

I don't find it comforting, or likely, but I don't say so. 'You wanted to talk to me about Lucas.'

She sits on the bed and pulls out her chair for me. The perfume of the peaches gets stronger. 'I am close to Lucas but I can also see his faults. He has many insecurities that lead him to seek . . . reassurance. When he's drunk too much, or taken something, he crosses the line.'

So he *did* tell her the truth about what happened, even though he made me promise to say nothing. At least he has a conscience, I suppose.

Camille is waiting for me to say something. 'It was unexpected.' Though, was it? I'd been getting sleazy vibes from him since the first time we met.

'He feels very bad about it. Especially given what happened to you with your abusive ex.'

I close my eyes, apologising to Al again in my head for the lies I told about him to get my place here. He is not to blame for the damaged person I have become.

'I too have been hurt badly by someone I trusted, Immi. I know how it shakes the foundations of who we are, how we see the world.'

When I open my eyes, she's staring out of the window. Her view is more built-up than mine – the red bricks and roofs of the buildings opposite. She looks on the edge of tears.

'Camille, I appreciate it, but I don't want you to cause yourself any distress, so please don't feel you have to share.'

'I want to help, that's all. I sensed it from the first time I saw you that we have ... damage in common. I think it's natural to recognise this in someone else. Neither of us have siblings, right?'

I nod, though I don't know how she knows.

'It makes for a lonely time growing up. And not the easiest of childhoods, either? Forgive me if I am being presumptuous or projecting my own experience onto yours.'

She's not wrong about my childhood. It makes me wonder what exactly happened to her.

'I'm not a counsellor, but as an actor, I am fascinated by how we become who we become. My own early life was extremely chaotic. I learned not to trust, to build a shell, which I know can make me seem aloof. But now the Factory has come into my life, I am trying to open myself up more, despite my early experiences. And more recent disappointments ...'

I wait, as it feels as though she wants to say more. I don't look at her, but try to give her space, gazing at the peaches instead. The kernels look as though they've been hand-carved, and around them, the orange flesh has grown red threads that look like tiny veins.

'I'm sorry,' Camille says suddenly, her voice different now. 'This was meant to be about you, not a therapy session for me. Lucas just wanted you to know he's very sorry and he won't do anything like that again. And *I* want you to know I am here, if you need to talk . . .'

Could I ever confide in someone I know? I had to stop the counselling after a few sessions because I couldn't afford it, even though I knew I still needed help.

And Camille is almost a stranger, and willing to listen.

No. My priority has to be keeping a roof over my head, instead of straightening it out.

'That's very kind of you,' I say, standing up. 'But I think for now I want to focus on looking forward, not back.'

I walk towards the door but she calls me back.

'These are for you, Immi.' She holds out the bowl of cut peaches and I carry them out with me.

When I get back to my studio, my mouth dry, I bite into the flesh. But after what we talked about, I seem to have lost my sense of taste and smell. It's like chewing cotton wool.

18

Immi

I need something to take my mind off the crap Camille's chat has dredged up.

So when I get back to my studio, I start work on a new sewing project. It's a bias-cut summer dress in midnight-blue silk that slithers as I try to cut out the pieces on the bed. I bought the fabric months ago, but sofa-surfing doesn't really allow for hobbies.

Soon the challenge of making sense of the pattern absorbs me. I barely notice the afternoon passing by as the dress takes shape. It's going to be beautiful.

There's a soft knock at my door.

'Who is it?'

'Ashleigh. We're about to kick off with earth hour, which means the power gets turned off in about ten minutes' time.'

'Oh.' No more sewing for me, then.

'Are you joining us?'

After all those weeks with no privacy, the last thing I want is company. 'Will I be very unpopular if I don't?'

She pauses for long enough for me to get the message. 'It's not compulsory, but it would be . . . noticed. And I don't like to boast, but my twilight meditation is awesome. Everyone takes part, even the cynics.'

Twilight? It's even later than I thought.

'OK. Let me change, I'll be out soon.'

'Great. Oh, and it's best to light the candle in your lantern before you leave your studio. There's no moon so later it'll get pretty dark.'

When I step out onto the terrace a few minutes later, I'm self-conscious, aware that Lucas will be there too. But the way everything's been set out for the meditation takes my mind off it. There are indigo-dyed woven mats laid in a patchwork, with soft cotton pillows around the edges. The terrace wall has been lit with dozens of tealights in glass mosaic holders that cast a kaleidoscope of colours against the brick. The sky is just begin-ning to turn pink and after a day of sun, the smell that drifts from the herb garden is hypnotic.

'Beautiful.'

It's Dex. His breath on my neck makes the goosebumps spring up, but not from fear. It's more an awareness of how close we are, of his presence.

'All Ashleigh's handiwork, at a guess,' I say.

He takes his place on the mat. Camille is already sitting down, self-contained and graceful in a lotus position, with a small drum resting on her knees. Gradually the others drift in too.

I flinch when I see Lucas but he sits down on my other side and grins as though nothing happened last night.

'Are you two ready for fun and games? Turning off all the power is a licence to commit mischief.'

So much for being contrite.

Dex smiles but it doesn't reach his eyes; he *really* doesn't like Lucas. 'I thought it was about saving the planet,' he says.

Lucas raises his eyebrows. 'Killjoy.'

Ashleigh stands at the front. Is everyone here? I quickly check behind me: no Veronica again.

'As always, let's begin with gentle stretches from this lotus position. Follow me, or do what your body tells you to. And as you feel the strength and flexibility of your muscles, thank them for holding you up, and taking you through this day . . . and every day . . . without you even having to notice they are there . . .'

As I mirror her movement and breaths, I try to forget about everything else. Camille begins to tap softly on her drum and I let my breath follow the rhythm.

'And now let that kindness travel beyond yourself, to those who surround you right now, on this rooftop. Your neighbours and friends, sharing this magical space. Think about the month since we last met. The everyday kindnesses that have been done to you. The way you have responded and repaid those kindnesses.

'When you're ready, lie down on your mat. Feel the warmth of the fabric against your skin. The sun did that. Rising and setting each day. Giving life . . .'

Ashleigh's voice rises above the pattering of the drum. Her words seem to melt into me, and I *do* feel that benevolence towards the people around me, and the sun, and the planet.

Except I cannot, will not, feel benevolence towards the man who changed me.

And I can't forgive myself, either, for allowing it to happen.

I try to breathe away the fear. But it keeps coming: the tightness in my throat, the blackness studded with stars, the stale smell of a hotel room and the certainty that everything was shutting down for the final time.

'We are here for the blink of an eye. Enjoy the gift of being here on this planet without bearing grudges or dwelling on what cannot be changed.'

Ashleigh is right. I *must* let go of what happened to me. I let her words wash over me . . . healing me.

But now I can hear something else: underneath her voice, underneath the drumming, a noise that isn't quite human.

I open my eyes to see if anyone else is hearing this. Ashleigh is at the front, still seated, but her head swaying gently as she speaks, lost in her own world. Everyone else seems to be absorbed too.

It's getting louder, clearer. What is it? More whale music? There's definitely an animal quality to it.

But isn't the sound system meant to be turned off?

The noises are getting louder. Clearer.

Cries. *Howls.*

Lucas opens his eyes and sits up. He stares at me, questioning.

Ashleigh's voice falters. She opens her eyes too. Camille stops drumming. The only sound is layers and layers of animals in distress.

It's horrific: the soundtrack of the slaughterhouse.

'What is this?' Ashleigh cries out. 'Where the hell is that coming from? All the power's been turned off.' She covers her ears and runs across the terrace, towards the AV controls by the door.

I get up and join her as she jabs her fingers against the touchscreen, trying to override whatever glitch has made the speakers turn on again, producing these terrible noises. The volume keeps rising, the animal cries reverberating at the highest pitches. People in the neighbouring buildings must be hearing it too, the waves of sound travelling across Bermondsey.

'I can't turn it off,' she's screaming, clutching her hand against one ear as she swipes wildly.

'Let me!' She backs away as I try. But the touchscreen seems to be locked, and nothing I do makes a difference. The others are crowding around now, making suggestions, asking where the speakers are.

And all the time, those nauseating sounds . . .

It's Zoum that reaches over me in the end, and presses some combination of buttons that instantly turns the screen black and stops the noise so abruptly that the silence is almost as shocking as the wails were.

No one says anything. What *was* that? Not a glitch, surely. A deliberate act. But who would be sick enough to want to do something that upsetting?

I hear crying again, but this time it's human. I turn towards Ashleigh, who is raging. 'Which one of you bastards did this? How *could* you? After everything I've done for you all . . .'

Bernice touches her arm. 'Ashleigh, it's over now. We'll find out what happened.'

But Ashleigh shakes her head. 'Don't fucking patronise me. You're all a bunch of ungrateful bastards.'

She turns and runs back into the Factory.

'Shouldn't someone follow her?' Dex asks. But we all look at the floor.

Bernice sighs. 'Don't all volunteer at once, eh? Looks like it's down to me, as usual.' She follows Ashleigh into the building.

Leaving me wondering who would do this to Ashleigh, and why.

19

Monday 7 May

Dex

They bring the weekly community meeting forward to Monday night, after the headfuck of that horror soundtrack.

'This was *not* a glitch,' Bernice says. She's chairing the meeting instead of Ashleigh, who still looks traumatised. 'This was deliberate, though I can't actually believe any of us would do such a thing.'

'You must be able to find out who it was from the computer?' Immi says.

'Unfortunately, the hard reset that Zoum did to shut the sound system down also cleared the cache of historical data.'

All eyes turn towards Zoum, who shrugs. 'Which does not mean it was me, OK? I like jokes but I would never do anything intentionally to hurt people.'

'That's not strictly true, is it?' Veronica says. 'When you messed about with Ashleigh's kefir, you could have poisoned all of us.'

He scoffs. 'Nonsense. Anyway there is only one person who could have turned the power back on. Where were *you* during earth hour, Veronica? Because you were not on the roof with the rest of us.'

I watch them as they bicker. So much for community.

'Hanna has suggested we disable the sound-streaming enhancement to the alarm system until further notice,' Bernice breaks in. 'I'm afraid Immi and Dex are not entitled to vote, but can I have a show of hands from the rest of you?'

The vote is unanimous.

'Can a rollback of the software be organised, Hanna?'

The housekeeper nods. 'Tomorrow. I will have to call engineer.'

Maybe *she's* behind it. In horror movies, it's always the quiet one.

'I have to remind you all,' Bernice continues, 'that Ashleigh gives a lot of herself to make the Factory a good place to be. So after this mess, please can we make a special effort to support her new project?'

Ashleigh stands up, not making eye contact with anyone. 'Thanks, B. Onwards and upwards, right? So, I made a discovery in the basement. You know the boarded-up part behind the partition wall, by the dyeing troughs? Turns out there's a sauna there, behind all the rubbish. A relic from the first conversion in the 1990s. It's been unused for over ten years but I've had the structure checked out and it's sound. I think we should refurbish it.'

Veronica laughs. 'Not wishing to piss on your bonfire, but it's pretty hot at the moment outside. Isn't a sauna more of a winter thing?'

Bernice shakes her head. 'Supportive, remember, Veronica?'

'It's OK, I'm happy to answer that,' Ashleigh says. 'There is a tonne of evidence that suggests taking a sauna every day reduces heart problems and stress.'

Bernice nods. 'Less stress has got to be a good thing, doesn't it? So, Ashleigh is looking for volunteers to get the sauna back in business. And I expect *everyone* to do their bit, especially our probationary Dyers. Perfect chance to pay it forward. No bloody excuses.'

I'm the first to sign up. It'll make a change from pounding the treadmill or doing endless weights to pass the time while I'm hiding inside the Factory.

I have my routine now. I wake early but wait till the worker bees – Lucas, Immi, Bernice if she's doing days – have left. Then I take a coffee onto the terrace. It never gets old, the bird's-eye view. I can see everything, and nobody can see me. Perfect.

Ashleigh appears, all springy from her early-morning yoga. She seems to have bounced back, and is even more full of good-will towards the rest of the human race.

'When do you want to get started on the sauna?' I ask her.

She comes and sits alongside me with a steaming mug of herbal tea that looks and smells like pee. 'After this, if you're free? We need to move all the old electricals out of the way, wash everything down, measure for what we need to buy new . . . I say new, it'll be recycled timber, obviously, and . . .'

I zone out when she starts talking. Her voice is as relaxing as wind chimes. When we've finished our drinks, we go down to the basement. Camille is already there. She's wearing old clothes, but still manages to look like she's stepped out of a Hygge-themed photoshoot.

'How are you feeling about your audition yesterday?' Ashleigh asks.

Camille shrugs. 'Bad. I would have expected a call-back by now. My face did not really fit, *again*.'

'Oh, how could *your* beautiful face not fit?' Ashleigh coos. 'I could watch you in anything.'

'I have had four auditions in the last fortnight,' Camille explains to me. 'And four rejections. But it's a numbers game, so I keep going.'

Ashleigh fills two buckets with water and hands out rubber gloves.

She has a key for the plywood door that blocks off most of the basement. When she steps through, I see nothing until she flicks a switch.

No one says anything for a moment. It's so . . . freaky.

The space is vast. There's room to park forty or fifty cars, and in this area, that would make *serious* money. But it's unusable, because of these weird pits. Most of the floor area is criss-crossed with low stone walls, like the foundations of tiny buildings.

'Down here makes me think of Pompeii,' Camille says.

That's exactly what it looks like – the remains of a miniature civilisation that was wiped out by some terrible disaster.

'So what are they?'

'They used the pits for dyeing and tanning animal hides,' Ashleigh says. 'Though the dyes weren't the kind we have now. They used dog shit, human urine, sulphuric acid. Imagine the stink.'

'Sometimes I don't need to imagine,' Camille says. Even in the odd colour cast by the strip lights, she is stunning, the shadows around her blue eyes like voids. The urge to go upstairs and grab my camera is really powerful.

But I won't. The results would only remind me how untalented I am.

'What are you talking about, Cam?' Ashleigh asks.

'Now and then, I think I can smell the past. The chemicals and the putrefaction.'

Ashleigh frowns. 'Camille has a very vivid imagination. It goes with being creative. Or Danish. Or both.'

Camille shakes her head. 'I tell you, I *do* smell bad things. Maybe what happened here was so toxic it seeped into the bricks and sometimes finds its way out. The smell of suffering. Human and animal.'

Ashleigh's gone silent. It's only now I make the connection between the awful animal sounds that were played during earth hour and the history of this place. It makes the 'trick' played on us all even more cruel.

When I first heard those horrible screeches, I wondered if it was my own mind playing tricks, my guilt driving me nuts. It was almost a relief when the others started hearing it too.

Despite her cute new-age schtick, Ashleigh is the boss from hell. First I get lumbered with the back-breaking work of moving a bunch of rusty old fridges and heaters out of the way. Then I join the two of them inside the sauna: it's a tight squeeze.

'We're using a bleach solution to remove the black mould from the benches and cladding,' Ashleigh explains.

The sauna was built on top of two of the dyeing pits, with a space underneath for ventilation, and the stove and sauna rocks on top. Apparently it was designed for six, but it feels very cramped, even with only three of us in here.

A couple of times, Camille touches me, apparently by accident, except her hand stays on my arm or knee for longer than feels comfortable. I try to ignore it, but even Ashleigh keeps giving me lingering looks.

Believe me, ladies, you do *not* want anything to do with me.

Eventually, Ashleigh sees how knackered we are and calls it a day.

'Thanks for your help, guys. Won't be long before sauna time!'

She says this as though we should be looking forward to cramming ourselves into a sweatbox with our neighbours.

'Can't wait!' I say.

Climbing the stairs back into the light of the main Factory building is like emerging from a prison. Back in Marrakech, I shower away my sweat.

My old phone is on charge and I hold my breath as I turn it on. It's the only way my family can get in touch so I check it daily, but the guilt always makes me dread this moment.

The sound of a new SMS echoes around the studio. I force myself to look at the screen. If the police have been in touch, then I think I'll have to leave the Factory. But fuck knows where else I can go. Sleeping rough has never been my style.

I open the message: it's from my sister, Selma.

Hey little bruv, hope it's going well in Pakistan. Stay safe, all right, and don't do anything too stupid. We want you home in one piece.

Mum did tell my sisters after all. I knew she would and now they're also worrying about me having my head chopped off by some ISIS thug wanting his fifteen minutes of fame on YouTube.

Another reason to feel like an utter shit.

20

Saturday 12 May

Immi

It's been a crazy week at school, catching up after the bank holiday, so it's Saturday teatime before I have time to 'volunteer' down in the sauna. There was no way Ashleigh was going to let me off the hook.

But when I get down to the basement, I find Dex is in charge today. I suddenly feel self-conscious in my baggy old clothes. I try not to look at him. The last thing I need is to be attracted to another Dyer.

'We're putting the flooring in,' he says when I go down to the basement. 'The old wood was too rotten, so we're making new duckboards.'

'Cool,' I say, suddenly unable to string a sentence together.

When Zoum arrives to help out, I don't know what to say to him either. He's still got to be the number one suspect for the fire alarm and that earth-hour nastiness, even though he's never felt threatening to me.

'I am not what you would call a handyman,' says Zoum, eyeing up the power tools laid out on the concrete floor outside the sauna. 'My skills are more cerebral than practical.'

Dex and I exchange a glance. 'Then you'll just have to hold things in place and hope we don't miss with the hammer,' Dex tells him.

We get to work measuring the floor area of the sauna and sawing the long pieces of cedar to fit. Dex is methodical and a good craftsman. I just wish he was wearing more clothes, because I can't stop staring at his body.

Yup, it's official, I have a full-blown crush. Just what I *didn't* need.

Zoum is on vacuuming duty, getting rid of all the sawdust. The woody aroma doesn't cover up an awful stink that must come from the walls or the floor.

'Did someone die down here?' I ask.

'I can't smell a thing,' Zoum says. 'Maybe I've got used to it.'

'How long have you been here?' Dex asks.

'Since the beginning, along with Bernice and Camille. The original gang.'

I'm surprised. 'You don't seem very close to either of them.'

Zoum laughs. 'I chose not to get involved. They did try to lure me in, but it wasn't really my scene.'

Is he talking about friendship, or more? 'They tried to get you into bed?'

He looks away. 'I . . . They would be wasting their time with me. I am gay, though I do not make a big thing of it.'

'Oh, right . . .' It makes total sense, now he's told me. The fact that when I met him at the selection evening, he was friendly but not flirtatious. And the way I never felt the immediate threat I did around Lucas.

'Enough gossip,' Dex cuts in. 'We have *work* to do here, you guys. If you're short of things to do, these last planks are rough.

Grab those sanding blocks and the sandpaper to smooth out the splinters, please.'

It's strange – I wouldn't have expected Dex from the 'hood to be a DIY expert. But seeing how he works with his hands makes him even more attractive.

'Sorry, Commandant Shepherd,' Zoum says. 'Your wish is our command.' And he gives me a sly wink.

Dex does a quick survey of our progress. 'We need to fix the boards so we don't fall through into the dyeing pit underneath. I'll go and get the glue from Ashleigh, but keep sanding till I get back.'

'Slave driver,' Zoum whispers.

'Is it pretty normal for people to sleep together here, then?' I ask, when Dex has disappeared up the stairs. 'I thought there was a ban on relationships.'

'*Exclusive* relationships are a no-no. Meant to reduce cliques, although you may have noticed it has not worked. But casual sex? I am as certain as I can be that Lucas and Bernice and Camille all know each other *intimately.*'

'So is Bernice with Lucas, or Camille?'

'Maybe both? Everything else about this place is almost *designed* to encourage sex, wouldn't you agree? Beautiful people, free alcohol, all those king-size beds.'

I remember Sarah's caution when she first found the advert, advising me to check for hidden cameras. 'What are you saying, Zoum? You think there's another agenda here?'

Zoum nods. 'Ha! You are a scientist like me, Immi. You refuse to take things at face value.'

'Well, my mother says, if something seems too good to be true, it usually is. I mean, who funds this place?' I sand the corner of my plank of wood a bit, so Dex will be pleased with me.

'You should ask *Hanna* that question.'

I lower my voice, aware she might be in her office, on the other side of the partition wall. 'She barely speaks English.'

'Ah, you Brits are always so keen to judge immigrants, which is something we can use to our advantage.' He shakes his head. 'She understands everything but has so far resisted my attempts to get her to talk. In the meantime, the best resource I have found to explain the Factory would be the Wikipedia page on cults.'

It's one thing for me and Dex to joke about it, but it's another to hear it from Zoum. 'You think that's what the Factory is?'

Zoum sees the look on my face. 'No, but there are some commonalities. The world outside is made to seem like a poor imitation. The yoga and mind manipulation, control of diet. We even have our own made-up words. The Dyers. The City-zen programme.'

I think it through. 'But doesn't a cult need a leader?'

'Bernice fits the bill, no? Charismatic, clever.'

I force myself to laugh. 'All right, Zoum, tell me how I avoid brainwashing?'

'Do what I do. Stay out of the power games. Keep it light.'

'That isn't what you do at all. You're always playing tricks.'

He holds up his palms in protest. 'Not me. I swear. Someone is playing dirty. There is another necessity for a cult to work: a scapegoat. Until recently, someone else played that role, but now it seems to be a split between myself and Veronica.'

'She doesn't seem to go out of her way to make friends and influence people.'

Zoum sighs and makes a token effort to blow away the tiny bit of sawdust he's generated. 'When she first came, she was desperate to belong. *They* rejected *her* but I have no idea why.'

I suspect there's something he's not telling me, but I have to play this carefully. 'Why would they scapegoat *you*, Zoum?'

'Who knows? I am used to being ostracised, Immi. As a refugee, with my family. At school. In those settings, I used humour to defuse difficult situations but maybe it has backfired on me here in the Factory . . .'

There's sadness and confusion in his voice. 'Things blow over. Maybe if Dex and I get voted in for good, we might balance things out again.'

Zoum grins. 'He *is* very cute.'

'Who is?'

'Dex. Come on, Immi. The chemistry between you two is obvious. But remember, if you do get close, everything has a knock-on effect. Collateral damage can be dangerous. And I say that as a guy who grew up in Kabul.'

'Is that what happened with Jamie? He slept with the wrong person?'

He frowns, and opens his mouth to say something but we both hear Dex thundering down the stairs again.

'No slacking, you guys. I have glue now and we're gonna finish this floor even if it takes us till midnight.'

Week 3: Never break the Factory code . . .

So, we don't want to get heavy on a Sunday morning, but communal living does mean accepting a few ground rules. When the Factory first came into being in 2016, there were none. Peace and love were meant to be all we needed.

It didn't quite turn out that way, which is why we worked out a code. Nothing tricky. Just some stuff about keeping the shared areas tidy, respecting each other and avoiding gossip.

The code is designed to keep everyone on an equal footing and avoid cliques or nastiness. We also discourage intimate relationships between Dyers – you could say that's none of our business *but* in such a tight-knit community, exclusive relationships can't help but pose a risk to the equilibrium. If you *do* think you've met your soulmate, though, please inform the committee, to keep things transparent.

Bottom line? We're more into the carrot to encourage good behaviour here. But if necessary, we can resort to the stick. You have been warned . . . As always, ask your buddy if you want anything clarified,

Your Factory friends

21

Sunday 13 May

Immi

After finishing in the sauna, I go to bed, but it takes a long time to fall asleep; I keep thinking about the people I'm living with, seeing them through Zoum's cynical eyes. The Wiki page about cults makes for interesting – no, chilling – reading. So many things resonate. But one thing jumps out that Zoum didn't mention: *cults seek out vulnerable people.*

The more I get to know my housemates, the more I believe this could be true of every one of us. Me, Camille, Ashleigh and Zoum all seem to have something in our past that makes us lost or insecure. What's to say the same isn't true for Dex and Lucas and even Bernice, once you scratch the surface? And as for Veronica . . . being ostracised must be the most painful thing of all.

I think back to my interview, too, and the way they encouraged me to tell a sob story. Was that because they picked us on the basis of who would be easiest to control?

The Factory app wakes me with the new message on Sunday morning. As I read, it almost feels like they've read my mind about my crush on Dex.

Except what if it's mutual? Zoum said he thought there was chemistry, which suggests Dex might like me too.

I stay in my studio most of the day, not wanting to see the others. By the time I head onto the terrace, it's dusk. The sky is darkening but the mood lighting is on, so there's no threat of any of the 'mischief' Lucas threatened before earth hour this time last Sunday.

Dex is waving me over to the loungers at the far end of the terrace, the ones with the best view of the city.

'You went to bed early last night,' he says. He still seems to smell of cedarwood from the work we did on the sauna.

'Keeping tabs, are you?'

He puts down his magazine. 'We gotta look out for each other. As the newest recruits.'

'All for one and one for all.' I hold my glass up to his. 'What are you drinking?'

'Coke. Bernice has even banned me from kombucha as Ashleigh says it can contain a massive half per cent alcohol. She's worried I might relapse.'

I make the mistake of looking at his face, and his eyes draw me in and he doesn't break the gaze.

I take a big gulp of wine. 'Is it weird, being sober when everyone else here is getting drunk?'

'I miss the taste more than the buzz. Which I guess means I wasn't as hooked as I'd thought. Plus, I'm not the only one who stays sober.'

'No?'

Dex nods towards Bernice, who is resting her head on Lucas's shoulder. Her body is floppy, as though she's been drinking for hours.

'She pretends but she never touches a drop. You notice these things when you don't drink.'

'Why would she act drunk, then?'

Dex shakes his head. 'I gave up trying to figure out *why* people behave as they do a long time ago.'

There's a weariness about his voice. What's his Achilles heel? His only quirk is that he never seems to leave the Factory.

'How's work?'

He frowns. 'It's tough out there. Instagram makes it look so easy to take good photos, so there's less work for the pros. Or maybe I'm making excuses for the fact I am not half as good as I think I am.'

'I'd love to see your work.' It comes out before I have a chance to think about it. I sound too keen.

'Would you?' He's grinning again now. 'It's mainly fashion plates. Anorexic girls in terrible clothes.'

'Isn't that every man's dream, though? Getting to boss models about?'

He looks at me so intently that my face burns, and the heat begins to travel down. 'They're so not my type.'

I try to look away, but I can't. Desire is building inside me, the feelings I thought had been obliterated by bitter experience. 'And what *is* your type?'

He waits and waits before answering. 'I have a feeling you already know the answer to that, Immi Sutton.'

I don't know exactly when I make the decision. Everything is hazy, in a good way.

I do know the other Dyers have been looking at us. I know, too, that we have spent too much time together. It's late. The minutes have turned into hours, blurred by wine that keeps appearing in my glass. It's not Dex topping it up. Maybe it's Lucas, or Bernice.

Is this part of their plan, a kind of voyeurism? Right now, I don't care either way.

A fresh bottle of wine appears next to my sunlounger. I should mingle with the others, pretend that what's happening between Dex and me is not real. I look at his face and I don't want to talk to anyone else.

With every sip, my willpower lessens.

Without warning, the terrace empties, except for the two of us. I feel the almost-touch of his hand on my arm as he brushes away a lazy bee, and the current that passes between us is powerful. I got an electric shock, once, from a dodgy socket in Mum's living room. I remember the wobbliness and the feeling that I would never be able to let go.

Dex is like the pleasurable version of that.

I giggle.

'What?'

'You're like an electric shock.' My words sound clear to me, but he looks puzzled. 'Forget it,' I say.

'Is this the kind of shock you mean?' he asks, touching my hand. He leans forward and his lips touch mine. 'Or is this more like it?'

A long time afterwards, I answer him. 'That was shocking. In a good way.'

There is fear there too, maybe there always will be for me now, but I want him so much I *will* overcome it.

We kiss again, but something jars. A sense we're being watched. My studio windows aren't the only ones that face the terrace. Either Lucas or Bernice could be watching from their rooms. They might be observing us together.

I break away.

'Is this not OK?' Dex asks.

It's more than OK, and that frightens me. The way I feel now is so different to how it was when I first kissed Al. Then I was still numb. Now I'm on fire. But I'm scared too.

Before the bad memories can come back, I kiss Dex again, then I whisper, 'Come to my studio. But not right away, we don't want it to be obvious. Pretend you're going to bed, make lots of noise, and then come back up.'

'Seriously?'

I think of Zoum's warning about collateral damage. I could stop this, now, with no harm done.

No. I don't want to play by the rules. Look where that's got me.

I kiss him again. He nods.

Decision made.

Dex and I are *good* together.

Even though I think we're both holding back. As I come, I try not to make too much noise, aware of how close our neighbours are. We've closed the window so the room is hot and airless.

My chest tightens suddenly, as though my breath is being stolen from me. But I try to tell that this is safe. Dex is safe. Maybe, just maybe, I can trust my instincts again.

'Happy?' he asks, moving to lie next to me, his arm around my shoulders, the heat of his skin and mine almost too much to bear.

'You can't stay. You saw the app message, they don't like things to get complicated.'

'They?'

'The Factory people. The committee.'

His eyes widen. 'Right.'

'This . . . us, it doesn't have to be complicated,' I say, pulling away completely and not looking at his face. 'It was just a spur of the moment thing. We're drunk.'

'I'm not.'

'Still. These things happen, right?'

'I'd quite like them to happen again,' he says and his hand on my shoulder generates that current again. We could probably power the entire Factory for a week; Ashleigh would approve of our renewable energy.

'You really should go, Dex.'

'And I will go.'

And he does. But not for another two hours.

I wake up early on Monday: alone, mildly hungover, aching. Smiling.

I shower away our sweat. I brush my teeth, though the sourness of the wine remains.

At my door, I hesitate. We agreed when Dex left that we would act exactly the same as before. The other Dyers might suspect, but they can't know for sure. I rein my smile in, make out it's an ordinary Monday morning.

And ordinary Mondays begin with coffee.

I open my studio door, ready to act normal. My foot touches something soft on the floor.

A fresh set of bed linen, neatly folded into a perfect square.

My arms rise up on instinct, as though I am naked and need to cover myself up.

Hanna isn't due to provide new linen till Wednesday.

How did she know?

22

Monday 14 May

Immi

At work, I keep getting distracted by flashes of memory of Dex and me together.

And when I'm not thinking of that, I move on to wondering why Hanna put new bedding outside my studio. Is Zoum right when he says she's the one who knows everything that goes on in the Factory?

I go straight to my studio when I get home, worried I won't be able to act normal if I bump into Dex. After a bit of lesson prep, I go back to working on my dress. As I touch the silky fabric, I imagine how it'll feel to wear it, the soft coolness against my skin, and it makes me think of last night again . . .

A knock on the door brings me out of my daydream.

'Ready for mentoring?' Ashleigh calls out.

My heart sinks. Last time, she was so relentless in trying to get me to reveal my innermost thoughts. And now I have an even bigger secret to keep.

'Yeah, great!'

She suggests we go down to Nourish, which is the last thing I want, knowing Dex will be so close by.

'I want to get some Instagram shots,' she says. 'I'm trying to really grow my followers, and right now it's all about pulses.'

I help her to arrange a rainbow of different beans on slate platters and olive-wood boards. She asks me to take her picture next to the pulses. 'From a high angle, please, to minimise my chins!'

'You don't have chins,' I lie.

'Ugh, I really do. I have a very slow metabolism. It's so unfair, I hardly eat *anything*.'

As she puts on her Instagram face, I think of Dex only metres away, on the other side of the door to Marrakech. He's bound to be there. He's like a vampire – only goes out when it's dark.

Can I get away with sneaking into *his* studio tonight? I'd forgotten sex could be that good. When Al and I made love, it was never that intense and I assumed it was because my body would never again respond as it had before I was attacked . . .

Last night showed me I was wrong.

'So, today we're meant to be chatting about our rules and stuff,' Ashleigh says as she stirs the pan of black beans she's cooking for her #pulsepower story. 'I personally think you've already got a handle on it, but I guess the committee want to make sure we don't get a repeat of last time.'

I look up, surprised. 'And what was that?'

For a moment, she looks panicked. 'Um. Oh sorry, thinking aloud. I mean, nothing bad. We just don't want to get into a situation where we have two studios to fill again, it's really disruptive.'

'Sure. The girl in Dex's room went back to Australia, is that right?'

'Kira, yes, she was brilliant. I really miss her.'

'What about Jamie?'

Ashleigh stirs the pot vigorously and the steam obscures her face. 'I can't talk about that. Sorry.'

'So the openness we're meant to embrace only goes one way, right?' Irritation makes me sound more aggressive than I mean to.

'I'm afraid satisfying your curiosity is not a good enough reason to tell you, Immi.' She matches my tone. 'What happened hurt people and it won't help to rake over it. If you're going to live here long-term, you have to accept that sometimes decisions will be taken that are about the City-zen community rather than the individual.'

It sounds unconvincing, as though she's repeating someone else's words. The Wikipedia page mentioned cults can use 'groupthink' to ensure compliance and it reminds me of that.

But I don't want to turn it into a big deal, so I nod at Ashleigh. 'I suppose it's like school. Not all the kids are going to agree with the rules, but we need some or it'd be anarchy.'

Ashleigh looks relieved. 'Exactly!'

Except, of course, in the Factory, we're all adults.

The desire to knock on Dex's door wanes gradually. By Wednesday, I can even focus on work again.

On my way home from school I go shopping in Bermondsey. The over-privileged people who live here used to irritate me, but I'm beginning to act more like them, glancing at the immaculately styled displays in the windows of the delis and boutiques. Even the newsagent's racks look 'curated'.

It's muggy but the subsidised rent I'm paying means I can actually afford two scoops of exorbitant gelato from the organic place on the corner. I ignore my mother's voice in my head – *I don't spend that on food in an entire week* – and give into the richness of the chocolate and the sharpness of the lime . . .

I shiver. Once, twice. It's not because of the ice cream.

Something has changed.

Someone is watching me. I'm certain of it.

I look up and down the street, trying to work out where my observer might be.

A figure in my peripheral vision moves suddenly, and I jerk towards it.

Towards *her*.

'Veronica?'

She's standing on the opposite corner, staring at me. Her mouth is open as though she's about to call out, but now she's turning away and starting to run.

'*Veronica*, stop! Let me talk to you.'

Her long legs are faster than mine and she seems to know where she's going. Not towards the Factory, or into the crowds of drinkers where I might lose her, but to the tower blocks.

As I try to keep up, the rational part of my brain is telling me to stop. She lives in the same building as me. We could chat any time.

Yet I keep following. My ice cream falls to the pavement – almost five pounds' worth.

When she does slip out of sight, I am half relieved. But there she is again, in her bright-red T-shirt, her blonde hair bouncing in a bunch between the bumps of her shoulder blades before she disappears.

Fine. Whatever. I'm too tired for games.

I pivot past the end of the high-rise, knowing I've lost her.

'You should work on your stamina, Imogen.'

I look left. She's standing there, arms crossed, unruffled.

I can't speak for thirty seconds. As I recover, I try to make sense of what this is. Why we're both here.

'Why . . . did you . . . run?'

'To get away from the Factory so we could have a chat in private. You can't have a poo there without the committee knowing about it.' Her accent stays cut-glass, and I imagine she learned at school that *proper* swearing is bad manners.

'What do you . . . want to talk about?'

Veronica glances around, checking no one is nearby. 'You're starting to see it, aren't you, Immi? You're realising I was right.'

'Is this about Jamie?'

'What do you know about him?'

'Only that he lived in my studio before me. But I think he did something bad and that even though no one will talk about, it's still affecting people.'

Veronica's eyes dart left and right. 'Jamie didn't do *anything*. I used to work with him. I was the one who got him in so I blame myself.'

'For what?'

'For them ruining his life.'

'What did they do?'

Veronica wrings her hands. I've never seen anyone do it so obviously before. 'Look, they made me sign a confidentiality agreement, and it's watertight; Hanna made sure of that.'

'Well, Hanna isn't here now, Veronica. And you must have wanted to tell me something, or you wouldn't have got me here.'

'Google him, OK? James Henderson. It should come up. If not now, then definitely within the next fortnight. And if it all comes out and they ask where you got the name, say . . . I don't know, you could have found an old envelope addressed to him or something. Though they turned his room upside down.'

I think of what I *did* find: the evidence bag. 'Were the police involved?'

Veronica's eyes narrow. 'How do you know that?'

'Just what you said about the room being turned upside down.'

She sighs. 'Look, you can't do anything about Jamie. But you can decide to protect yourself. And your boyfriend Dex.'

I stare at her.

'Oh, Immi, don't be naïve. Nothing stays a secret at the Factory. You think you can stay out of it, but the whole thing is a power game. Even the interviews – they never did that when I joined.'

Joined. Even though she's warning me against the place, it's as though she wishes she still belonged. Has being ostracised made her so bitter, or was she like this already? 'They told me they'd made mistakes with other residents,' I say.

'Like me and Jamie. Yeah, they would say that. But does that give them the right to root out all your secrets?'

Is she talking about the interview or something else? 'I understood what they were doing. I played the game.'

'You think you did but that was only the beginning. They're already grooming you to think like they do. Sometimes I even wonder if all the practical jokes aren't Zoum after all. Maybe it's *them*.'

'Or you?'

She scoffs. 'I see I'm too late, you're already on their side. At least I tried.' She turns away.

'So what would you do, Veronica? I need somewhere to live. We don't all have rich parents and a trust fund.'

It's a guess, but it makes her look slightly shamefaced. 'All right. Suck up to them, till the vote. But hold a part of yourself back.'

If she knew what I'm holding back, she wouldn't care what happens to me.

I try one last time. 'What makes no sense, Veronica, is if the Factory is so bloody awful, why are *you* still living there?'

Music and voices drift out of the flat windows above us, and the cries of lads playing football in the car park bring me back to reality. Suddenly all this drama seems ridiculous, the attention-seeking behaviour of a woman who is sulking because she's not number one, and she can't get her way.

'Because I want to be there to see their faces when Jamie gets justice.'

And before I can ask any more, she starts to run again, faster than before. This time, she doesn't want me to catch her up.

When I'm back in my studio, I do google Jamie Henderson. I get over 132 million results, but nothing that mentions the Factory.

I have two choices: believe Veronica, or believe the others. Maybe Veronica is just bitter about being excluded from the 'in' group. It would make a kind of sense. She and Bernice are both head-girl types, yet there can only be one Queen Bee.

23

Friday 18 May

Immi

On Friday night, people gather on the terrace for impromptu drinks, but I only have half a glass of wine before retreating back to Kyoto. I don't trust myself to be in the presence of drink *and* Dex at the same time.

Through my window, I hear small talk that lasts an hour at most, then my neighbours drift away. I lie on the bed, trying to focus on work stuff. But my mind cycles between thinking about Dex, and wondering what happened to Jamie, the man who *used* to lie exactly where I am lying now.

Eventually, I must fall asleep because the next thing I know, something wakes me with a start.

A sound, in my room.

A quiet scrabbling.

Not human.

I open my eyes but the rest of me stays frozen. The noise is persistent, a scratching that seems to travel around the room, fast and nervy.

Mice? The thought makes me nauseous and I sit up. When I was five, we had an infestation in the house. Our neighbour came to get rid of them. Not because he wanted to help – Mum always made it clear she didn't welcome interference – but because they were breeding and threatening to infest the whole street via the shared attic spaces. Each morning I'd go into the kitchen to get my cereal and see them running along the lino and the counter, scuttling back into their hiding places.

That was bad. But the traps that snapped the rodent bodies in two were even worse.

My head pounds. The scrabbling continues. Too loud to be mice. They do say in a city you're never more than a few feet from a rat.

I stand up, look under the bed, check the en suite. Not that I know what I'd do if I found myself face to snout with a rat. The scientist in me knows the animal would be far more frightened than me. But the little girl I used to be remembers how even a dead mouse, its body broken and pinioned by a metal spring, made me wet myself with terror.

The noises fade away, until they're gone completely. Did I imagine them?

It's coming up to five a.m. and I lie down again, unsettled and craving more sleep.

The knocking comes just before eight on Saturday morning, tentative but rapid.

'Immi, are you there? I need help.'

It's Ashleigh.

When I open my door, her eyes are red and she is hyperventilating. 'It's Edward and Bella.'

For a few moments, I try to work out how I could have completely forgotten two housemates, before realising she's talking about the emotional support animals. 'Are they sick?'

'No. Worse. They've gone. Either they worked out how to unlock their cage, or someone deliberately let them out.'

The scrabbling. Was that the rabbit and the guinea pig, lost in the pipes like lab rats in a maze? I've not exactly bonded with them, but I certainly don't wish them any harm.

I tell Ashleigh what I heard.

She nods. 'Yeah. I knocked on Dex's door before, and he's downstairs in the basement, trying to work out if they might have got into the service ducts. Will you go and tell him what you heard?'

After avoiding him for days, I'm not sure how I'll react to seeing Dex, but Ashleigh is distraught.

I turn to head down there, and she whispers after me, 'If you see Bernice, don't mention it yet. She loves those animals even more than I do.'

I go downstairs and find Dex in a utility area behind the office and the laundry. Hanna is there too, and they're both studying plans, with the baffled look of people trying to decipher hieroglyphics.

'I heard them moving about. I think they might have been in the walls or under the floor somehow,' I say, trying not to look at Dex. 'Can I see?'

The sketches were made when the building was remodelled for communal living, and show that the plumbing and heating system is interconnected, with the pipework running in the walls and floors. My brain is good at seeing how things fit together in three dimensions. I tap a section.

'I think that's where they might be.'

Dex and Hanna study the drawing too. 'So, can we open up the pipes and grab them?' he asks.

'No. Even if we did, the length is too long for us to reach and the diameter is way too small to allow any of us to climb inside. And they must be terrified, so they're going to run away from us, and further into the system.'

'Unless we use food,' Hanna says.

She's right. I head upstairs to ask Ashleigh what a rabbit and a guinea pig might find irresistible, and realise Dex is following me. I pick up my pace, but while we're between Nourish and Retreat, he reaches out and touches my wrist to stop me going any further. My skin burns.

'I've missed you, Immi.'

'Yes. But . . . we agreed to keep our distance. At least till the vote.'

Except I don't shrug him off and he doesn't pull away. I want to kiss him, to forget about lost animals and Factory politics. We lean in, our lips millimetres apart and . . .

Veronica is above us, dressed in her running gear. Dex and I jump apart and he lets go of my arm. She narrows her eyes and I wait for her reaction.

'Excuse me,' is all she says. She jogs past and a few seconds later, I hear the front door slam.

'Shit, that was close,' Dex says.

I don't tell him she already knows. That maybe *everyone* knows. 'We both need to keep our eyes on the prize. The animal stuff is bad enough without us fuelling the mind games.'

'You think Edward and Bella were released on purpose?'

I'm surprised at how naïve he seems. 'There's no other explanation. But it's nasty. Who uses animals for pathetic point-scoring?'

Dex looks up the stairwell, as though he's working his way through each room and each resident.

'Could it be Zoum?'

I remember the way he spoke to me during the sauna refurb session; I believed him when he said he only used humour to defuse tension. 'I don't know. He's a bit of a joker but I don't think he's *cruel*. What about Veronica?'

He shrugs. 'Maybe. God, this is a screwed-up place sometimes. Still, at least we know it can't be either of us. This is all about ancient history and grudges, right?'

I nod. Except I don't agree about it being ancient history. Whoever did this seems determined to keep fear and resentment very much in the present.

24

Saturday 19 May

Dex

When I turn up for my third mentoring session in the vape pod, Bernice isn't wearing her killer lipstick, and her eyes are as pink as poor missing Edward's.

'What kind of person does this?' she says, her voice cracking, before she inhales a giant lungful of grapefruit-scented vapour.

The more I've thought about it, the more I realise I wouldn't put it past any of my neighbours, except Immi and maybe Ashleigh. But instead I say, 'We're doing everything we can to tempt them back.'

'If you ask me, maybe they're better off out of here. Sometimes I wonder what's happening here. It feels out of control . . .'

I can't think of an answer. I turn on my vaper, to drown out the smell of the fresh herbs outside. I have to brush against the pots every time to get into the pod, and that fresh aroma always triggers the one memory I fight to keep buried.

She looks up at me and shakes her head. 'Ha. I'm meant to be telling you how lucky you are to be here, and making sure you want to stay. Doing a shit job, right?'

'It's normal to be upset.'

'Normal.' She scoffs. 'So, do you?'

'What?'

'Want to stay here? We need to know by this time next week. If you hate the place, we won't bother to do the final vote.'

'Are you kidding me? Only a complete screw-up would walk away from something this good. They'll have to carry me out in a coffin.'

Bernice flinches. 'Or they'll throw you out once you hit thirty-five. Whichever comes sooner.'

'I'd forgotten about the age limit. Is that even legal?'

'It's all in the contract, which no one forces us to sign,' she says. 'Just be careful what you're signing up for, eh, Dex?'

I'm about to make some flippant remark about thirty-five being a lifetime away, but I look at her now, tired and make-up free, and I notice faint lines between her brows, and a few white hairs in the line of her parting.

I force myself to look away so I don't see her vulnerability. I *want* her to be Bad Bernice, our Machiavellian Queen Bee, because somehow, if she's weak, it means this whole set-up is built on nothing.

'Cheers for the warning. Though it's all irrelevant if you guys don't vote for me.'

Bernice laughs. 'Ditch the false modesty; everyone loves you. Especially Ashleigh. You're her right-hand man – all that volunteering you're doing for her.'

'Keeps me occupied.'

She exhales. 'Do you think it's helping your problem, being here?'

'Definitely.'

'Because that is the point of this place. It's meant to help, otherwise it's all for nothing.'

I should probably go overboard now, tell her I feel like a different man, that she's a lifesaver. But I don't want to deceive her any more than I have to. 'Has it helped you with anything, Bernice?'

It's hard to imagine how she'd need fixing. She's beautiful, confident, successful . . .

'I thought it had.' She looks at the ring finger of her left hand and begins to pick at the glossy red varnish, pulling away fragments to reveal the bare nail underneath. 'I was married, before I came here.'

Married? I can't picture Bernice in a couple, because she appears so complete in herself. 'What happened? You don't have to tell me but . . .' *But* I have the feeling she wants to.

'He had . . . mental health issues. I should have kept him as a friend and tried to fix him that way but instead I convinced myself marriage was the best way to save him. None of it was his fault but the divorce settlement wiped me out. The Factory came along at exactly the right time.'

'Yes. I saw the ad for the Factory when I really needed it too.'

Bernice has moved on to her middle finger now, systematically removing the varnish, scattering scarlet confetti all over her shorts. 'Incredible, right? Hanna appears like the fairy godmother and sprinkles Factory fairy dust over all of us.' She looks up at me, almost challenging me to push her further.

'Everyone who lives here is fucked up, is that what you're saying?'

She smiles. I like Bernice, but I wish she didn't gossip about everyone. I know all about Ashleigh's binge eating, and Zoum keeping his sexuality from his parents, and even about Camille pretending she comes from Denmark rather than Finland, because Denmark is better for her image.

I wonder what Bernice would do if she knew the truth about me.

'I suppose we *are* all fucked up, Dex. And no amount of twilight yoga or fermented cabbage is going to sort that out. Still, there are worse places to live out our existential angst, right?'

'I'll say.'

Her green eyes look enormous. 'The Factory has given me so much. It's like a family. Protecting that isn't work for me. I know it sounds mad, but it's almost . . . a calling.'

We both peer through the door of the pod, out towards the haze that makes London look like something out of a watercolour painting. 'So what happens when you leave?'

She stops smiling. 'I am sure there'd be people happy to fill my shoes. I've been saving for a deposit on a place near the airport, but my heart's not in it. Imagine swapping this for a poky flat under the flight path?'

I smile. 'When you put it like that, Bernice, I don't think I'll ever want to leave either.'

Week 4: Do you belong?

Hey, hey, hey, it's Sunday! How does it feel, to belong? As you enter your fourth week here, you will have a sense of whether you want to stay or not. So we thought we'd ask the Dyers when it was that they realised the Factory was the place for them.

I got it the first time I saw the sun set from the roof terrace and I looked round and saw the others' faces in that amazing light and I knew they'd always be my friends.

Bernice, Croydon

I came to London prepared for the rejection every actor accepts as part of their life. I found acceptance at the Factory.

Camille, Copenhagen

For once, it's not about the gin. It's about knowing people have got your back!

Lucas, Cambridge

No one else would have me.

Zoum, Kabul

25

Sunday 20 May

Immi

Edward the rabbit can't resist the lure of bok choy from the organic veg box and he emerges from a duct a little dishevelled but floppy ears intact. But by Sunday night, we're beginning to give up on Bella.

There was a big row about it earlier. I heard raised voices through my studio window and went to look. Zoum was sitting on the terrace, trying to read, while Lucas stood over him, accusing him of messing with people's heads for fun.

Zoum ignored him for a while, but I saw Lucas poking him, and then Camille and Bernice started shouting too.

I was on the point of getting up and going to defend him – I hate bullying – when he finally picked up his book and left. Lucas had the last word.

'That's right, sod off. If you don't want to contribute to this community, you shouldn't enjoy the benefits either.'

Should I have stepped in? I like Zoum, but I also know I'm going to need the committee on my side to get voted in as a permanent Dyer. After that, I never have to talk to bloody Lucas again.

Despite him, I like more of my neighbours than I expected. Dex, of course, but Ashleigh, too. And even Bernice can be kind. Twice a day she renews the veg to try to encourage Bella to come out of the ductwork.

One evening, I find her standing stock-still with her ear against the wall. 'Everything OK, Bernice?'

'I thought I heard something in the pipes. I hate to think of that animal trapped inside there, and all because of our petty arguments.'

I thought Bernice would rather die than admit to any flaws in the Factory, or take personal responsibility for them.

My desire to make people feel better kicks in. 'It's probably found a way out into the Thames by now, and is developing its own colony of guinea pigs.' I don't actually believe that for a second, but it's the kind of thing they say to kids when a pet disappears.

Bernice gives me a dismissive look. '*She* clearly wouldn't survive for thirty seconds out there, but thanks anyway.'

It was a stupid thing to say – even my Year 6s wouldn't have bought it. 'Who do you think opened their cage, Bernice? Everyone seems to be blaming Zoum but I'm not sure.'

She looks at me searchingly. 'The trouble is, it could have been any one of us.'

This surprises me even more. She can't mean she even suspects her friends? 'I was wondering about Veronica. She seems unhappy.'

'Has she been talking to you?'

I shake my head. 'Not at all. She mostly ignores me, to be honest.'

Bernice's eyes don't leave my face. Can she tell I'm lying?

She sighs. 'What we need most of all here is some stability. We only have to get through the next fortnight, and it'll get better, it has to.'

Fortnight? 'But the vote's this time next week, isn't it?' The idea of having to keep up my 'happy Immi' act for a further week makes me feel exhausted.

'Yes, but then—' She stops. 'You're right. Sorry. My shift patterns mess with my memory. It won't be long till you guys are permanent and we can get everything back on an even keel.'

It's only when she walks away that I realise she's assuming Dex and I *will* be allowed to stay.

I should be relieved. I *am* relieved, but I wish there wasn't this undercurrent of uncertainty, too.

Because they're still lying to us about what happened before we came here. I'm guessing we won't be told the truth until we've signed on the dotted line.

I'm out with Sarah after work tonight. I'm buying her dinner in exchange for her looking at my rental contract.

We meet in a bar on the South Bank. She wanted to nose around the Factory but I didn't feel comfortable inviting her there. There's nothing in the rules to say we can't have visitors, but I haven't seen any outsiders in the building since the night of my interview. It seems safer not to challenge the status quo until after I've been voted in.

Sarah looks knackered, and I remember how the commute used to turn my skin that same pasty shade. It's only when she asks me to get her an elderflower cordial, instead of sharing a bottle of wine, that I realise.

'Holy shit, Sarah, you're pregnant!'

She pulls a face, but it doesn't disguise the delight in her eyes. 'Looks that way.'

After we've done all the hugging – I know she'll make a great mother, though I'm not so sure about Mack as a dad – she tells me it was unplanned. 'Total own goal when it comes to work. I was aiming for partnership before we had kids. I wanted to apologise to you as well. I was really grumpy in that last fortnight you were at ours. Now I can blame my hormones.'

'Yes, but what's Mack's excuse?'

I come back with the drinks and after a bit more chat about swollen boobs and nausea, she interrogates me about the Factory. I tell her the good bits first: the walk to work, the facilities, the rooftop yoga. 'And then there's Dex.'

'Tell me more!' At uni, Sarah was the wild child and I started out as the innocent – Mum never let me out long enough to be anything else and I didn't want to get pregnant and be stuck in Crewe forever. But in my first term, I met a guy I liked enough to sleep with and discovered, to my surprise, that I enjoyed sex every bit as all the 'normal' girls.

'But there is a catch.' I explain about the Factory's no-relationships rule, and a few of the other strange things that have happened: the yoga with slaughterhouse sounds, the missing animals, Veronica's melodramatic warnings. 'And I feel they're all hiding something about the guy who was there before me.'

'Maybe they're just embarrassed about Veronica. She sounds like a nightmare who'd whinge about anything.'

I sip my wine, wishing I could believe that's all there is to it. 'Except . . . it sounded serious. She backed down from telling me more because of some confidentiality agreement. She told me his name – James, Jamie, Henderson – but it's a *shit* name on Google. There are millions of them and none seem to have a connection.'

'As long as I've known you, you've worried that things are about to go wrong, Immi. It *is* possible that this time you've just lucked out.'

Sarah comes from one of those families where nice things are expected. I hope she never understands why I see life differently.

'Yeah. Glass half empty, as always,' I say, holding up my glass. 'Actually, completely empty now. So while I get a top-up, this is the contract I have to sign if they vote for me to stay on Sunday.'

'Hand it over to your Auntie Sarah.'

When I get back from the bar, she's frowning. 'Woah. This isn't quite the standard tenancy agreement, is it? The three-month notice period is pretty extreme but maybe that's the price you pay for luxury. Can I hang on to it to check it all the way through?'

'If you're sure you don't mind.'

'Sure, it'll give me something to read on the nightmare bus home.'

'Will you stay in your flat? It's a bit small for you two plus a baby.'

Sarah groans. 'Tell me about it. Mack thinks we're gonna have to move near his parents in High Wycombe. Ugh. Still, London is for bankers and Russians. We're like homing pigeons. You'll leave one day too.'

The thought makes me nauseous. 'Over my dead body.'

As I walk home, sunlight dances on the Thames and the sounds of people flirting in a dozen different languages surround me. In Crewe, Mum will be washing her dirty dinner plate in cold water, turning her fingers ghostly white. Not using the hot tap saves money, according to my mother. *Look after the pennies and the pounds look after themselves*, she says, as though it's the heating bills, rather than the credit cards, that have got her into, well, hot water.

The Factory might have its quirks, but nothing would be as intolerable as going home.

26

Tuesday 22 May

Immi

I oversleep on Tuesday morning. When I'm rushing down the stairs to try to make up time, I crash into Veronica as she's coming out of her studio.

She jumps even higher than I do, but immediately turns away from me.

'Veronica, wait.' I lower my voice. 'Could we meet later? Same place we met before? I need to ask you something.'

'You've already done enough.'

'What are you talking about?'

She narrows her eyes at me. Behind her, the door to her room is ajar. Woah. It's a serious mess in there: clothes and other stuff thrown everywhere, as though she's interrupted burglars. I know *way* too much about people who live that way thanks to my mother. The disorder inside their heads is even more dramatic.

'Veronica, do you need help?'

She scoffs. 'As though I'd take it from you. I got it wrong. You do belong here, with the rest of the vipers.'

She slams the door behind her and the bang reverberates around the space. As I walk down towards the lobby,

I expect people to come out of their studios to see what's going on.

No one does.

After a school day full of misbehaviour, followed by an exhausting parents' evening, I'm relieved to be home. But as I let myself into the Factory, I hear raised voices coming from the Focus space on the ground floor.

I try to listen in, but the soundproofing is too good for me to make out the words. I can only hear the tone: angry. This is becoming the norm in this bloody place.

I go upstairs. The rest of the building feels deserted. I pour myself a glass of water and sit alone on the terrace, enjoying the peace and trying not to speculate on what the latest arguments are about.

Something has changed. I am no longer by myself.

I turn to see Dex standing behind me.

Knowing we're alone makes the hairs stand up on the back of my neck.

'Do you know what's going on downstairs?' I ask, not moving any closer.

'Well, it's not your usual terrific Tuesday, is it? No one mentioned it to me, but they all kinda drifted inside just before nine.'

I look at my watch: it's past eleven o'clock. 'They've been in there all this time?'

He nods. 'It means trouble.'

I cannot take my eyes off him. 'It also means . . . they're distracted. That they don't know where we are.'

Does he want what I want?

His eyes blink a yes. 'Your place or mine?'

I lead the way back into the building, past the door to my studio and towards the stairs. I hold my breath as I walk down, aware of Dex behind me, and hoping this isn't the moment they choose to break up the meeting.

Dex holds his phone against the lock and opens the door to Marrakech. He beckons me in.

I've been in here before, of course, when we toured the Factory on the selection day. But it looks different at night.

It *smells* different too. Not of Dex, but of *alcohol*.

He reaches his arms around me to kiss me, but I pull away. 'Have you been drinking?'

Dex shakes his head.

'I can smell booze. Are you sure you haven't been drinking in secret?'

Even in the darkness, I can see something in his face that makes me suspicious.

'This is going to sound weird, Immi, but sometimes it *does* smell really strongly of alcohol in here. For no reason. Like someone has spilled it on the floor or in the basin. But no one comes in here. I asked for Hanna not to clean because I don't like the idea of her going through my things.'

His stupid lie brings me to my senses. I turn to go. I'm not going to have sex with someone who invents a story like that to cover their arse. 'Whatever.'

He reaches out to stop me. 'OK. OK, I do have some vodka in here. But it's not like it seems.'

'For fuck's sake, Dex. You're meant to be teetotal. That's the whole point of you being here, isn't it?'

'I might have . . . exaggerated how much alcohol is a problem for me,' he says, not meeting my eye. 'You remember what it was like at the interview. They *wanted* people they could fix, to make them feel good about themselves. I played up to that.'

If I hadn't done the same, maybe I'd be more shocked. 'So . . . you're not an alcoholic?'

He sighs. 'Not *exactly*, no. I never wanted to lie, especially not to you. But I *needed* this room, Immi. Just like you needed yours. Do you believe me?'

Should I?

He takes my hesitation as a yes and leans in to kiss me again. And that makes up my fickle mind for me.

The darkness intensifies everything. We fall asleep at about four a.m., just as the dawn arrives. I should return to my own studio but I can't quite bear to leave Dex yet.

But something jolts me fully awake. Sounds coming from the floor above. Footsteps and thumps.

Retreat is the next level up. Maybe one of the Dyers has got insomnia and is trying to tire themselves out in the gym. I'll have to wait till they've finished before I can risk going back to my own studio.

Except as I listen, I realise it's not one person: it's several. I can make out a woman's voice, and two men.

'I can do that myself, thank you!'

Veronica. Irritated rather than afraid. The men grunt in agreement. I hear clattering, the rumble of wheels against wood. The lift ascending, the shutters opening and closing again.

Dex is still deep asleep. I consider waking him up, but instead I creep out of bed and go to the window. His studio looks down onto Tanner's Walk itself. There's a white van parked on the cobbles, its rear doors open.

Veronica leads the procession, dragging an enormous suitcase over the stones, not caring how much noise it makes. Behind her are two huge men carrying boxes, bin bags and a leather armchair. They load the van and then get in the front.

She follows them, but before she climbs into the passenger side, she stares up at the Factory. I dart back quickly, not wanting her to see me gawping. I remember the humiliation I felt when I left Al's place. If I could have moved out at midnight, without anyone else seeing, I would have.

She's still staring up at the building. For a moment, I think she's crying, until she thrusts her hand towards the building, her middle finger pointed up.

'*Fuck you all!*' she calls out. I don't actually hear it but I see the words leave her lips.

27

Wednesday 23 May

Dex

Maybe it's not weird that Veronica left. But what *is* weird is the way no one is talking about it.

Correction. They're not talking about it to me.

Conversations stop dead when I come into the room, or walk onto the terrace. The whole day, nothing has been said in front of me.

I try to check out Veronica's room when people go to work, but someone has put paper over the glass to stop anyone seeing through the spyhole. When I step back, no light gets through.

Someone is behind me . . .

I turn slowly, as though it's no big deal. And then breathe out when I realise it's Immi. I've been wanting to talk to her all day but we agreed we wouldn't hang out together for another few days.

'See?' she says. 'She's definitely gone.'

I nod. 'I guess last night's secret meeting went wrong.'

'Or right? The committee have been trying to get rid of her, I think.'

Immi walks downstairs to Nourish and I follow. She takes a ripe mango out of the communal bowl and begins to slice into it. She's wearing a vest, and the muscles in her arm tense as she runs the knife under its skin and cuts into the flesh.

It's making me horny again. Everything is: the texture of the fruit, the methodical way she works, the exotic perfume. But I have to stop this. Not just till after the vote, but for good. I am not safe to be around and though I don't know what happened to Immi before she came here, I have a strong sense that safety is what she needs most.

'Has Bernice spoken to you about Veronica?' she asks.

I overfill the kettle, so it'll bubble noisily when it boils, masking our voices. 'No. Weird, right? But they're all talking to each other.'

'You seem pretty close to Bernice. You could ask her outright?'

Is Immi jealous? 'I wouldn't say close. She's my mentor, that's all.'

Immi looks unconvinced. *Definitely* jealous. I look around the floor. There's nobody else around. I step towards her, slide my arm around her waist, my hand under her vest, up towards her breasts.

So much for stopping this.

She inhales sharply but gently moves my hand away. 'Not now.'

'But maybe later?'

Her answer is to jump away.

I look around and realise Camille is coming down the steps. Did she see us?

'I am glad I found you together,' Camille says. 'You may have noticed . . . changes.'

All of us look up, towards the Retreat floor.

'It's no secret that Veronica had been unhappy in our community for some time and now she has chosen to leave. It is nothing to be concerned about.'

She sounds like a spokesperson on a dictator-run TV channel. A load of questions form in my head but I don't ask any of them.

Immi frowns. 'I thought there was a notice period?'

'She's rich. You knew that, didn't you?' Camille says. 'People with money can afford to walk away from difficult situations, even if they are partly responsible for creating them.'

'What happens now?' Immi asks.

'The Dyers need to meet to decide whether to advertise her room immediately. We will let you know later this evening, if at all possible.'

Camille turns and climbs the stairs again. I no longer feel horny. Probably best, for all our sakes.

They come for me much later in the evening. Bernice, Camille, Lucas. No Zoum, or Ashleigh. Just the big guns.

We go to the Retreat area where Immi is already waiting. I can hear the rabbit scuttling in its cage. There's still been no sign of Bella; Edward must be lonely without his cellmate.

'Thanks for your patience,' Bernice says. 'There's nothing to be concerned about.'

When two people tell me that on the same day, I *am* concerned.

'It's not usually like this here,' Lucas says. 'But Veronica was the bad apple and now she's gone—'

Bernice interrupts him. 'We're getting ahead of ourselves.'

Lucas raises his eyebrows at me as if to say, *Women, eh?*

Bernice continues: 'Veronica found it hard to adapt to communal living. Or rather, a non-hierarchical style of communal living. She went to boarding school and I think she imagined it would be the same here, just without the cold baths.'

Lucas laughs his creepy, psycho laugh.

Bernice holds up her hand to stop him. 'I accept responsibility for picking the wrong person. Her behaviour could be . . . erratic. I think she told you both how terrible the Factory is, even before you were accepted.'

'As you guys know' – Lucas takes up the story – 'we don't have many rules here, but we do ask for complete honesty and trust.'

There's a pause as they let the words settle.

Bernice says, 'We discovered recently that Veronica had attempted to undermine that. She recommended a candidate for one of *your* rooms, who pretended to be an ice-cream maker. He was actually a tabloid journalist and he paid her for the opportunity.'

Holden the vegan was a reporter? I remember seeing him handing Veronica money, but I never guessed that would be the reason.

For a moment, I imagine what might have happened if he'd been picked, instead of Immi. Would he have ended up snooping around my background too? That would have been a bigger story than anything else he might have uncovered in the Factory.

'Why would a journalist want to live here?' Immi asks.

'We can only assume he thought we were some kind of cult,' Bernice says. 'Obviously, he would have found nothing newsworthy, but we had to take action over Veronica's breach of trust and continued negativity. Ashleigh made numerous attempts to improve her attitude, but she threw it back in our faces.

'So last night, after taking advice from the landlord, I informed her that the management were giving her four weeks' notice – this is an exception to the usual three months. She . . . didn't respond well. It seems that she decided to move out more quickly than that. Under the circumstances, it's probably for the best.'

Camille sighs. 'Even though we're all very sad we didn't get to say goodbye.' I can't work out if she's being sarcastic.

'So what happens now?' I ask. 'Does her room go to the next person on the list from the interviews?'

'As a committee, we've decided it would be too disruptive to bring someone else in right now,' Bernice says. 'Instead, we'd like to wait until after the weekend, when your probationary period ends and we know what's what.' She gives me a quick wink. 'Though I am sure we've chosen well this time.'

I look away. They couldn't be more wrong, in my case. I am going to betray their trust too before long.

'Any questions?' Lucas asks.

'Is there a copy anywhere?' Immi asks.

Bernice leans forward. 'Of what?'

'The exact rules we're not to break.' Her voice is sharper than I expected. 'You've sent us something vague on the app, but it sounds like there's a whole other set of traps you're willing us to fall into.'

'Hey, it's not about *dos* and *don'ts*,' Lucas says. 'We're more laid-back than that.'

'Clearly not that laid-back if you've evicted Veronica.'

I want to kick Immi under the table but she's too far away. If she really wants to stay here, she might want to dial back the spikiness.

Bernice stares at Immi. 'It's just a case of being considerate. But if you need clarification on anything specific, you only have to ask.' She closes her folder, pushes her chair back so violently it almost topples over and leaves the room. The others follow and finally I am alone with Immi.

I look at her. 'Maybe that wasn't the best moment to pick a fight. Bernice isn't used to being challenged.'

'Damned if I do, damned if I don't . . .' Immi looks so vulnerable right now. I want to put my arms around her, but she seems to read my mind and shakes her head. 'Better if we don't see each other tonight. Not that it won't be a hard habit to break . . .'

As I watch her go, I sense it's not just about tonight. That it's over between us, whatever 'it' was. I know it's for the best. Especially for Immi. She doesn't need someone like me in her life.

The last few weeks almost convinced me that I'd got away with what I did. But I'm kidding myself. It could take years, but sooner or later I will slip up and be found out.

I deserve punishment. If it weren't for my family, and what it will do to them, I would hand myself in right now.

28

Saturday 26 May

Immi

The vote is tomorrow.

I'm trying not to behave any differently around the people who'll decide, but of course, that makes me even more self-conscious.

By Saturday evening, I can barely walk across the terrace because I've forgotten how to put one foot in front of the other 'normally'. Dex seems to be having the same problem.

He's alone in the vaping pod, staring at us through the door. The repetitive action of bringing the vaper up to his lips, inhaling, exhaling, reminds me of those zoo animals on YouTube who've been driven mad by captivity. I want to go to him, ask what's wrong, but I daren't risk it. Plus, I'm already drained by my usual lie-packed Saturday chat with my mother.

The Factory is quiet tonight. Bernice is working a night shift, Zoum is at his parents' house and Ashleigh's gone to a yoga retreat, coming back first thing for the vote. I'm guessing both of them will support us.

But the committee could still outvote them and after my outburst about the rules, I worry they might hold it against me.

Camille comes out from the Play area with a tray full of drinks. 'I have made an extra gin and tonic,' she says. 'Would you like it?'

It seems like a peace offering so I take it and follow her to the sunloungers where she and Lucas have been hanging out most of the afternoon. They both seem drunk already and when I taste my drink, it's more gin than tonic. After talking to Mum, maybe I've earned it.

I'll stop at this one, though, then I'm going to bed.

'Big day tomorrow,' Lucas says. *Creep.*

'I'm nervous.'

'Don't be, you're among friends and you fit in perfectly. You're nice to look at, you tidy up after yourself . . . and you have that slightly tortured quality that all Factory residents need, just to give things an edge.'

I pretend to laugh, but it's all too close to the truth.

Before I can reply, a shadow passes over us. Dex has emerged from the vape pod, smelling of artificial berries.

'It's Dexter the beefcake!' Lucas calls out. 'Come and have a gin! Ah, silly me, you *don't.* Another tortured soul.'

Dex gives me a *what-the-fuck?* glance. 'I'll get myself a tonic.'

By the time he comes back, I've steered the conversation into safer waters: holidays and plans for the summer. Lucas is going to Australia on an extended work trip. Camille has relatives who decamp every year to their lake house in Denmark, and she might join them. Dex says something non-committal about exploring more of Europe. As he hardly ever leaves the Factory, I don't think any of us believe him but we let it go.

The discussion is forced, but there's never a break long enough for me to leave the terrace without feeling I'm snubbing them.

'I'm bored,' Lucas pronounces. 'And I'm feeling *naughty* without Bernice to keep an eye on us. While the cat's away . . .'

'You could show me the virtual reality stuff,' I suggest. It's one of Lucas's things, surprisingly. He spends hours with a mask over his face, arms and body swaying and dancing. Zoum told me he reckons Lucas has found the 3D lap-dancing channel. *'Or maybe he's developed a hologram of himself to get off with, the ultimate in masturbation.'*

Lucas shakes his head. 'VR is more of a solo experience. What else . . . ?' He smiles. 'Ah. I have an idea. Why don't we christen the sauna?'

Dex gives me a helpless look. 'No. We shouldn't spoil Ashleigh's grand opening next week. Assuming Immi and I are still here.'

Lucas laughs. 'Like I said, chill. We're voting for you. Unless you're too *boring* to be part of our fun-loving community.'

Camille laughs too. 'A sauna *would* be perfect right now.'

'I don't want to hurt Ashleigh's feelings,' Dex says, though his protest is half-hearted. The threat if we *don't* do this couldn't be clearer.

'She never has to find out,' Lucas says, taking Camille's hand. 'What happens in the sauna, stays in the sauna!'

They move swiftly and Dex and I follow. *This time tomorrow, it'll be over. Then I can be as antisocial as I like.*

Sarah has checked the tenancy agreement for me and, though strict, it's all kosher. Once I'm in, I'm in, and they need to give three months' notice to kick me out, unless I do something shitty.

Hanna isn't around and the basement is in darkness so I walk right into the pile of junk next to the door before Lucas turns on the strip lights. The dyeing pits look like catacombs, and I can smell hot cedar.

'Did someone leave the sauna running?'

Camille steps inside and the smell gets stronger. 'No, I helped Ashleigh test it this morning. Now it has been made completely airtight, the sauna retains all the heat.' She pronounces it the Danish way of course, as *sow-na*, and I have a vision of naked middle-aged men thrashing each other with twigs.

Naked . . .

I glance at Dex, but he looks through me, as though he's sleep-walking. As he steps into the sauna, I catch a whiff of something unexpected on his breath.

Alcohol.

Is he mad? He told me he'd exaggerated his 'problem' to get in but why risk them discovering the lie so close to the vote? Bernice and Ashleigh would never forgive him if they found out.

I hold back at the sauna entrance, but Lucas grabs my hand and pulls me in. 'Immi, come on, we're losing the heat.' His palm is cold and when I look at his other hand, he's holding a chilled bottle of Prosecco.

I sit on the lowest bench and feel the heat through my cotton shorts. I think they *planned* this.

But why?

Dex sits next to Camille on the upper level of the L-shaped platform.

Almost in slow motion, Camille peels off her vest top. Underneath, her bra is sheer and flesh-coloured, her nipples porn-star hard. She might as well be wearing nothing at all.

What the fuck is she doing?

Lucas looks at me. 'Not feeling the urge to cool down yet, Immi? This'll help.'

He shakes the bottle of fizz and when he pops the cork, Prosecco spurts out. Most of it seems to go over me and Camille, who just smiles. Is she under Lucas's spell? The night after he kissed me, she told me he sometimes crosses the line. Perhaps he's manipulated her into this.

Dex tries to wipe the Prosecco off the sauna bench with the sleeve of his T-shirt. 'Now Ashleigh will definitely know we've been here.' He tuts. 'The smell will be a dead giveaway . . .'

'Loosen up, Dexter, you're *boring* me,' Lucas says and takes a swig from the bottle, before passing it to Camille. She drinks too and then holds it out to Dex.

'Lucas, stop tempting him,' I say, before turning to Dex. 'Don't drink anything. Bernice is bound to find out.'

But he holds the bottle up to his lips anyway. Bloody idiot.

Lucas cheers like a football yob as Dex gulps.

He takes the bottle from Dex and hands it to me. 'Your turn.'

They're all watching me, so I drink, just to make them stop. It's shockingly cold as I swallow, compared to the sauna temperature. Dex is sweating and Camille's bra has turned more translucent, from Prosecco and heat.

Lucas claps his hands. 'Party time.'

Camille turns towards Dex and reaches her pale hand up to his face; her fingers turn his head towards her and she begins to kiss him. Her eyes seem blank.

Lucas is sliding his hand up my leg, his face near mine, his breath smelling of stale wine. I look at Camille. She was the one who apologised on his behalf, she was the one who said he was flawed.

Why is she letting this happen?

'Relax, Immi. No one knows we're here.' His breaths are short. 'I've wanted to do this ever since I saw your photo when you applied to live here.'

His lips graze mine but I pull away. 'No. I . . . This . . .'

I look to Dex for support, but to my horror he hasn't pushed Camille away. He even seems to be responding.

The hot air burns my throat and lungs and I don't feel I'm getting enough oxygen.

Lucas's cackling laugh bounces off the walls. 'Ah, don't worry, Immi, you'll get your turn with Camille, she loves *everyone*. We're all one happy Factory family . . .'

His hand is still on my leg, making my skin hot and itchy. I squirm out of the way, trying to stand up.

'This is against the rules. We're not meant to get involved.'

Camille and Dex are no longer kissing but watching us.

'Fuck that,' Lucas says, sharper now. 'We know the two of you are screwing. What the rules say is, no *serious* relationships. This is your chance to prove you're happy to get involved in community activities.'

Is that what the Factory is really about? Or is this just about Lucas amusing himself with some sick game?

'No. I'm *not* doing this.'

Lucas shrugs. 'Shame. I really thought you might be more open-minded.' He turns to Dex. 'But you're happy, right? We can all keep a secret. Bernice would be so disappointed to know you've had a little relapse, Dexter.'

'Dex, don't listen to them.'

But Dex is still not shrugging Camille off; his glazed eyes seem unfocused.

Is this who he really is? I am disgusted with him, and with my own stupidity in trusting him.

Wrong again, Imogen. You cannot trust your judgement.

I push hard against the sauna door but it doesn't budge. I realise it opens inwards and when I wrench it open, the wooden handle burns against my palm.

'Close the door behind you,' Lucas mocks me.

I hear them all laughing as I run, out of the basement, up the stairs, my feet clanging against the metal steps, my breath ragged. When I get into my room, I realise I'm crying.

I jump onto my bed. What a fucking idiot I am for thinking I could play the system. There's no chance I'll be able to stay now.

And if I can't live here, I'll have to leave London for good.

My phone is buzzing. When I look, I've had a couple of missed calls from Sarah. My heart hammers. Is it the baby?

A text says: *Check your email, found something odd. Sar x*

When I open her message, I expect to find some minor suggested change to the rental contract. But instead, she's written: *Could this be your Jamie Henderson?*

I click on the link below.

Week 5: Should you stay or should you go?

It is decision day! We hope you've enjoyed the last four weeks as much as we've enjoyed getting to know *you.*

But now the end is near and so we face . . . Ah, wrong song! The voting process will be as stressful for us as it is for you but we have to ensure the stability of the Factory. And you won't be happy long-term if this is the wrong place for you.

The vote is a secret ballot of all full community members. We will inform you of our decision asap. If, unfortunately, things do not go your way, you may take up to fourteen days to find other accommodation and your deposit will be refunded in full on the day you vacate. No hard feelings.

If you are accepted, we ask for the contract to be signed and a further month's deposit will be taken. The notice period for full community members is ninety days, to allow us time to find the right successor. After recent experiences, no exceptions can be made so we do recommend you take independent legal advice before signing.

And as soon as you do – let's party!

Love from all the party animals at the Factory

29

Sunday 27 May

Dex

I wake early. My head throbs *so* badly from the drink. No one else has stirred.

I walk up to the terrace, look out at the panorama of London. By the end of today, I could effectively be homeless. Why didn't I just go through with that miserable threesome last night? This place could have been my haven for months, till I figured out how to get away from everything that's happened.

Last night showed me what the Factory is really about: people using each other to get a fix of whatever floats their boat. Maybe I am the same.

But is Immi different?

Maybe. She left the sauna first.

As soon as she'd gone, I was jolted into reality. Camille's lips on mine felt suffocating, and her hand rising up my thigh made me think of a butcher manhandling a side of beef.

As I tried to stand up, Lucas was smirking. 'Your girlfriend's gone now so you can stop pretending you don't like it. We can have some fun.'

'I don't want this to happen.'

'Come *on*, Dexter. You looked like you were well up for it a minute ago. *Up* being the operative word . . .'

I reared back and hit my head, a sharp crack that made the world go wavy for a few seconds.

'Think carefully before you go,' he said. 'Who are your real allies here in the Factory? Bernice talks a good game, but she bores easily. Whereas Camille and I are *very* loyal to the people we care about.'

'So if I fuck you, I get to stay, is that what you're saying?'

I expected outrage.

But he just shrugged. 'I don't want you to fuck *me*, mate. I'm more of a spectator.' Like he was talking about *Wimbledon*.

'Lucas, let him leave.' Camille's voice sounded flat but Lucas laughed again. 'You're already too far into the game, Dexter Shepherd. If that's your name.'

Even remembering that moment this morning, I feel the loosening in my gut and a twitch of the muscle under my eye. Lucas saw it too, knew he'd rattled me.

'I'm done here.'

'Not quite. Thing is, Dex, a web search can tell you so much about a person. But it's weirder when a search can't even find the basics. Especially for a photographer. Not even a proper portfolio. No wonder you're not getting much work.'

It was true. Dex only has the most cursory online presence. I set it up at the hotel: a couple of social media accounts, a monochrome website featuring other people's images, and a contact email that doesn't exist. 'I find work through word of mouth.'

Lucas held up his hands. 'Whatever you say, *mate*. It doesn't matter anyway. Poor Bernice put so much effort into helping you stay off the booze. She's going to be very disappointed in you when she finds out you've let her down.'

I ran out of the sauna, knowing he was right. But I was more worried about Immi. I arrived on her floor gasping for breath. Knocked and knocked again on her door, picturing the look of disgust on her face when she saw me kissing Camille.

'Immi, it's me. Open up please. I'm sorry. Nothing happened.'

But there was no answer.

Should I try again now? Before I can talk myself out of it, I walk to Kyoto. Knock once, twice.

No reply.

Ashleigh bounces up the stairs, bright-eyed after her day-long silent retreat. I think about the sauna and shame makes my skin burn. I hope they cleared out the fizzy wine, so she won't guess what we did.

She smiles at me. 'You won't get an answer. I saw Immi go out half an hour or so ago.'

'Did she have any stuff with her?'

Ashleigh looks puzzled. 'Just a handbag. I'm sure she'll be back in time for the vote. Are you nervous?'

'A little.'

'Everyone loves you, Dex, and with all the work you've been doing for the community, I can't even imagine why someone wouldn't want you to stay here forever.'

I try to smile. Poor Ashleigh is even more naïve than I thought.

My 'neighbours' meet at four o'clock.

I wait in my studio. What next? If they throw me out, I get two weeks to find something else. What then? I could buy a tent, go off-grid . . .

Except I am a wimp. My sisters call me that with affection, but there's nothing cute about my lack of survival skills.

At half past four, I head down to the Focus space, as instructed. They've pulled across sliding partitions to create a soundproofed meeting room plus a narrow waiting area.

No Immi, still.

After a few minutes, Bernice comes out of the meeting room. Her face is unreadable. 'Have you seen Imogen?'

I shake my head. 'Ashleigh said she went out earlier.'

Bernice tuts. 'Does she actually *want* to live here or not?'

I shrug. 'I'm sure she'll be back soon. When will we have the decision?'

'Soon.' She doesn't look at me before she turns to go back to the other Dyers.

Finally, the front entrance rattles and Immi comes into the Focus space, her face pink and hair unbrushed.

'Where have you been, Immi? Bernice has already been out looking for you once. She looked mad. You'd better come up with a good reason.'

She looks through me. 'What do you care?'

'Immi, last night – I swear I didn't do anything more than you saw. I was drunk and when I realised—'

'Forget it. I was wrong about you but I'm glad I found out before—' She stops.

I sense Bernice standing behind me.

'Dex first,' she says. 'At least *he* didn't keep us waiting.'

I walk into the meeting room, scanning the faces for clues to whether I'm in or out. Lucas stares at me. Camille looks away.

The transparent Ghost chairs are arranged in a circle – two of them are empty. Does that mean both Immi and I have been approved?

'Sit down, Dex,' Bernice says, showing me which chair to take, before sitting next to me. There are no spare seats now.

One of us is out.

'So, we have made a decision, Dex.'

They're getting rid of me.

I catch Ashleigh's eye but she doesn't smile.

'But first, would you mind telling us what happened last night?'

I look at Lucas again. *Really? You want to go there?*

Bernice leans forward, her eyes narrowed. 'There's no obligation. But to move on, we would need you to admit you have a more serious problem than you have suggested.'

Is she offering me a way to stay? 'A problem.' I search her face for clues as to what I have to do to buy myself time.

'You were drunk, weren't you?'

I nod. 'I . . . The stress of not knowing if I could stay. I needed something.'

'Have we not supported you enough?'

'No. You all have, and especially you, Bernice. I'm sorry.' And I am, because I know how much effort she's put into trying to fix me.

'Why do you think it happened last night in particular?'

I look at my 'neighbours'. Is this part of their game – wanting to humiliate me, break me down? That's how a cult works.

'I was lonely.'

'You should never feel alone here,' Bernice says. 'We are a family.'

Ashleigh frowns at me. 'Bernice feels very let down, Dex.'

I nod. 'I really am sorry. Is there anything I can do?'

Bernice sighs. 'We've decided that we *could* extend your probation for a further month on two conditions. The first is you agree to attend an organised rehab programme, with our support.'

The thought of lying to even more people who want to heal me is unbearable. 'But I—'

Lucas says, 'Listen, *mate*. We can't help if you won't even listen.'

I want to smash his face in. But instead I take a breath, remembering what happened last time I lost control.

'And the second condition is that you change mentors,' Bernice says. 'I've obviously failed you.'

'No, you haven't.'

She doesn't reply.

'Do I get to choose who I have instead?'

Lucas smirks. *Shit*. Is it him?

Camille stands up, walking across the circle to embrace me. As she gets closer, I smell scorched cedarwood.

'It's going to be all right,' she says, laying her cold hand on my cheek. 'We'll get together very soon, and help you find a way forward.'

Over her shoulder, Lucas is grinning at me.

30

Immi

Bernice emerges from the meeting room. But instead of escorting me back inside, she sits down in the chair opposite. She looks smaller than usual.

'I need to talk to you.'

'You're evicting me, aren't you?'

Twenty-four hours ago, I would have feared this news more than any other. But now I have a way of fighting back, thanks to Sarah.

'It's not that simple, Imogen.'

'What was the decision?'

She brushes a thick strand of red wiry hair out of her eyes. 'There was no absolute veto but a couple of people abstained. This hasn't happened before and . . . there's no real protocol.'

Lucas and Camille.

'If no one objected strongly enough to vote against me, surely I can stay?'

Bernice sighs. 'Under normal circumstances, yes, but after what happened with Veronica, I'm extremely worried about the future of our community. Letting someone stay who doesn't enjoy everyone's support could be a disaster. Not just for us but for you. Are you *sure* you still want to be here, Immi?'

Her face is open, as though she really does care, but I dismiss the thought. She only cares about staying Queen Bee. 'You don't fool me.'

'What's that supposed to mean?'

'The trouble here goes back a long way before Veronica, Bernice.'

She stares at me, trying to work out what I mean.

'I know about Jamie.'

Bernice blinks. 'Jamie used to live in your room, yes. So what?'

'Veronica tried to give me clues without breaking her confidentiality agreement. Gave me his name, told me to google him. The weird thing is, when I looked him up on the Wi-Fi here, nothing relevant came up. But my friend found stuff straight away, including a report about him being charged with harassment and distributing revenge porn.'

She stares at me.

'That's why Jamie went, am I right? He was charged the same month that he left the Factory.'

Bernice exhales. 'Immi, we did plan to tell you both the truth.'

'When exactly? You've known everything about *me* from day one. You lapped it up at my interview.' I'm so furious about their deceit that I forget my own – the fact that the story that secured my place was just that: a story. 'Didn't you owe it to me to tell me I was replacing a *sex* offender?'

I'm shouting, now, and I don't care. Let them all hear.

'There seemed no point in worrying anyone unnecessarily.'

'That's so considerate. And of course, it had nothing to do with the fact no one in their right mind would choose to walk into such a toxic situation.'

She stares at the floor. Maybe she's ashamed of this now she's been called out on it.

Tough luck. I keep going. 'At least there's one good thing to come from this, Bernice. Because Veronica might have been bound by a confidentiality agreement, but I'm not, until I sign a permanent tenancy. What's to stop me going to that Holden guy, telling him what I know. A fat cheque from him would help me with a new deposit.'

Bernice's expression changes. 'What's your price, Immi? An apology? Compensation?'

I see weakness. I feel power.

'I want to stay.'

Lucas scowls when he sees me following Bernice into the meeting room. *Good.*

No more Nice Immi.

'Ashleigh, get Immi a chair, would you, we seem to have one too few seats by accident.'

Ashleigh blushes and I'm pretty sure she was told the exact number of chairs to put out. This was no mistake. When she puts the chair next to me, she's smiling. 'You're in?' she whispers.

When I nod, she beams back. 'Great news.'

Bernice waits till I'm settled. 'As a result of today's vote, I am delighted to welcome Immi as a permanent member of the Factory community. Dex will be staying for another month with a view to being confirmed at the end of that period, if he takes further steps to address his alcohol problem.'

I wasn't expecting that. When he denied anything happened after I left the sauna, I didn't believe him. But why else would Camille or Lucas land him in it?

'After the disruption of the last few months,' Bernice continues, 'it's good to have two people who we can now call friends.'

Silence, until Ashleigh starts off a muted round of applause. I don't join in. None of these people – except perhaps Ashleigh and Zoum – are my friends. I want to stay because the Factory is central and convenient and cheap. The rest is bullshit. That's what the last four weeks have taught me.

'Drinks upstairs are called for,' Bernice says. 'But first, there's another issue we must address. Because we have a tough week ahead. It is *imperative* we stay strong.'

Dex looks up, confused. 'Tough, how?'

Bernice sends me a warning glance. 'One of our former residents is going on trial on Tuesday accused of . . . harassment-related offences. It should be over by Thursday but there *may* be some media interest.'

I hadn't realised the trial was so soon.

'Harassment?' Dex repeats. 'What did he do?'

The report had mentioned Henderson's job in insurance, so I imagine it's some kind of City-boy sexual harassment suit gone wrong.

Bernice narrows her eyes. 'As a committee, we've decided to protect the privacy of the victim, which means I can't say any more. In addition, we ask that no one here attends, unless you're a witness.'

A witness? A cold feeling spreads down my spine. The Factory must be more involved in the crime than I realised. Maybe it even happened here . . .

'Journalists might try to contact individuals.' Bernice speaks slowly and clearly, in full air traffic controller mode. 'We don't believe they will be legally allowed to name the Factory. However, they may still be looking for a scoop. Please, think of the victim.'

Bernice nods, as though that is that.

Zoum is on his feet. 'Hold on. So we get no discussion, no chance to disagree with what you've decreed from on high?'

'Zoum, this is difficult for everyone and—'

'Pretty difficult for Jamie, too, right?'

Lucas stands and squares up to Zoum. 'What the fuck is your problem, mate?'

Bernice jumps up too, pushing herself between them. 'We have to have faith in the legal system.'

'Even though you are trying to ban us from going to court and hearing it so we can make our own minds up?' Zoum says.

'It's going to be hard enough for those of us directly involved, without people we know gawping at us in the witness box.'

Zoum scoffs. 'Justice is meant to be seen to be done.'

Ashleigh and Camille watch open-mouthed. As do I. It's a stand-off: Lucas and Zoum staring at each other with thinly disguised loathing.

'What do you know?' Lucas spits the words. 'You're not even British.'

'That's enough, Lucas!' Bernice says.

Zoum shakes his head. 'This isn't over,' he says, before marching out of the room. His footsteps clang against the metal stairwell, before he slams his studio door. Dex catches my eye but I look away. We're not lovers, or even friends. Not now.

Bernice turns her back on Lucas. 'Maintaining a dignified silence is the right way to handle this situation. Unless anyone wants to make this even more painful than it already is?'

I consider speaking out. But do I have the right? Maybe the victim of whatever happened is sitting in this room and deserves privacy.

'Good. Let's try to look ahead to our community open day on Saturday, when the case should be over. In the meantime, I think we could all use a drink.'

My neighbours file out of the meeting room silently. Dex holds back, wanting to talk to me.

I brush past and take the lift up to the roof terrace, where Ashleigh is laying out a table of drinks. I reach for a bottle of Prosecco and a single glass, and take them back to my studio without a backwards glance.

I'm in.

It's a hollow victory but for now I don't have to go home. I am going to celebrate that, at least. Alone. Because there's no one else I can trust.

31

Monday 28 May

Immi

Monday is another bank holiday and I stay holed up in my studio, working on my dress, which is almost finished. Now I'm about to sign on the dotted line, I don't have to pretend to be someone I'm not.

On Tuesday, I have a lie-in, because it's half-term. I wait till I've heard Bernice and Lucas leave before I venture out myself.

The Factory is silent. The only other person I can find is Ashleigh, who is decanting sour-smelling pickles in the kitchen.

'Is it usually this quiet during the week?' I ask her.

'Kind of. But it's also because the court case starts today.'

'I thought no one was going.'

'Well, the victim . . . They'll be giving evidence.'

So the victim *does* live here. And she's *not* Ashleigh. I check myself: it's not a given that the victim is a woman.

'And you won't tell me who?'

'It's not won't, it's *can't*, Immi. The person wants to stay anonymous for very understandable reasons. But by the end of the week, things will be more normal, hopefully.'

'Will they, though?' I shake my head. 'First the poor animals going missing, then Veronica going, and now this.'

'Of course, they're all connected,' Ashleigh says.

'How?'

'By Veronica. She was the one who suggested Jamie in the first place. Back when we recruited by word of mouth.'

Recruited. Such a weird word to use. 'You can't blame her for something someone else did.'

'No, but . . . she was always troubled. A lot of the pranks Zoum has been blamed for, I wonder if she was really behind them.'

Veronica could have left the bedding outside my room the night Dex stayed, rather than Hanna. A tiny act, but it unsettled me at the time. 'Why would she do that?'

Ashleigh shrugs. 'Divide and conquer? It's another reason we need to pull together, Immi. This place *matters*.' She finishes decanting one bowl of ferments and puts an even larger one onto the worktop. The smell of chilli and garlic makes my nose itch.

'That's a lot of kimchi,' I say.

'Prepping for the community open day on Saturday. The timing could be better, but it's important to go through with it. Maybe it'll mark the start of something more positive.'

'Will the trial be over by then?'

'Should be, Bernice says. It's one person's word against another's.'

When I was attacked, I never went to the police for that very reason. My chest feels horribly tight, suddenly. I breathe it out. 'Can I help?'

She smiles at me. 'That'd be great. How do you feel about massaging salt into sliced cabbage for the kimchi? It can be a very positive way of releasing any tensions.'

We work alongside each other, the squelch and squeak of the cabbage the only sound. But it doesn't make me feel less stressed. I'm sick of being in the dark. If none of them will tell me what's going on, there's one way to find out for sure. Tomorrow I am going to court.

This building is nothing like the courts I've seen on TV; instead, it's a scrappy building with all the dignity of a multi-storey car park.

The security guards X-ray me and my bag, and point at the list of dos and don'ts on the wall before I can go in. No talking, no music, no use of electronic devices. Regina vs. Henderson is in Court 2 and the trial is already in session by the time I arrive.

A set of concrete stairs leads up to the public gallery. Will another Dyer be there? There's a glazed window at the top of the steps with a 'Quiet in Court' sign next to the handle. I peer through, holding my breath. Two rows of seats, and only three people seated: a middle-aged couple and a young woman with hair tied demurely back.

Should I be doing this? Never mind what was agreed by the committee, it's possible the evidence might trigger bad memories of my own.

But that's in the past. I'm here because knowledge is power, and I need to understand the Factory if I am to stay.

I push open the door, take a seat and look down at the court below. A couple of officials down there give me a cursory glance, then return to what they were doing. The surroundings are as shabby as outside, but the gowns and uniforms make it intimidating. I ignore the judge and the lawyers and the young guy who is giving evidence in the witness box, and try to get a glimpse of the dock instead. It's tricky, because the dock is directly underneath the gallery but I lean over.

It's empty.

And that's when I realise: it's Jamie Henderson in the witness box.

He looks so *young*. In reality he's probably only a couple of years younger than I am, but fresh-faced with plump cheeks and soft-looking hair, like a baby's. He doesn't belong in court, flanked by guards.

When I look to my left in the public gallery, I see the family resemblance – the couple are his parents, the girl is clearly his sister. But the older man looks furious, as though he might jump down to tell someone – everyone – how badly they're getting it wrong.

Henderson has a quiet voice, and the acoustics are terrible, so it takes me a few moments to tune into what he's saying.

'. . . And my colleague put in a word for me and so I moved into the Factory.'

Veronica was the colleague, of course.

'Communal living is rather different to a normal house share. Can you tell us about the arrangements?' The lawyer sounds friendly – I am guessing this is his defence barrister.

Jamie smiles – he is a pretty boy. That and his soft Scottish accent make an attractive package. I wonder if the Factory's residents hit on him as they did me and Dex.

'It was great at first. I could walk to work and the building was amazing. My room wasn't huge, but all the shared parts are enormous and *really* cool. I even got to do some gardening, which is something I love. To top it all, it was pretty cheap. They did an affordability test to determine your rent, and I only earned a trainee's wage.'

'And how did you find your new housemates?'

'They seemed . . . friendly, at first. There was maybe more drinking than I was used to. And I did become aware of . . . how can I put it . . . clickiness.'

'You mean there were cliques?'

Henderson blushes, aware he got the word wrong. 'I tried to stay out of it. I went to boarding school as a kid, see. I'd had enough of bullies. I aimed to be nice to everyone.'

'And what about women? Were you used to living around them?'

He blushes even deeper. 'Well, my sister and my mother, of course, when I wasn't at school, which was all boys. At uni, I mostly shared with other guys. I am a wee bit shy, but I get along with everyone.'

'Still, was there anyone who caught your eye?'

Henderson shakes his head. 'At the beginning, I thought they were all out of my league. But, um, then there was one who began to be more than friendly. I didn't believe it at first.'

'And who was that?'

I wait, sensing I am about to learn the name of his alleged victim.

Henderson hesitates, looks up at his family in the gallery, gulps.

'It was . . . Cam. Camille Jarvis.'

Hearing her name should be shocking, yet somehow I already knew. She told me she'd been hurt by someone she trusted. Her cool blankness makes sense, instantly. Detachment is a way of protecting yourself. I cut myself off from real life too, after what happened to me.

The barrister leans forward. 'The woman who says you harassed her. Coerced her. Humiliated her to get revenge. What do you say to those allegations?'

'*No!* I never would. I never *could*. I loved her.' He looks up to the gallery, at his parents. I see his mother nod back: *I believe you*. His sister – younger, I think, but not by much, looks away.

My instinct is always to believe the victim. But what about the Camille I saw on Saturday, the one who stripped off in the sauna and tried to seduce Dex?

Unless Lucas was pulling her strings.

Henderson's evidence continues. The picture he paints of the Factory is one I recognise: a feverish yet fragile community, where friendships and more are made or fractured over late nights and long, strong drinks.

But the stuff about Camille and their relationship is not so clear-cut.

'At what point did you begin to think Miss Jarvis might be interested in more than friendship?'

'At midsummer, a few weeks after I'd moved in. There are always parties at the Factory and they had one for the longest day. Someone had brought a firepit onto the roof terrace, and we were drinking hot toddies and burning logs as the night got cold. It was . . . cosy.

'I went to the vape pod. And Cam . . . Miss Jarvis came to join me. She began to kiss me. It was a surprise, but . . . well, it was nice, too.'

'And you're sure it was her who kissed you first?'

Henderson shrugs. 'Yeah. I'm not someone who reads signals all that well. I wouldn't have made a move . . . Even though I was drunk, I didn't want to embarrass myself.'

I believe him.

'How far did it go that night, Jamie?'

Now he's really blushing. He won't look up at the gallery, at his mum.

'We . . . went to her studio room. And we kissed and touched and . . . she wanted to go further. To have sex. But I thought if she *liked* me, maybe we'd have a relationship, so I wanted to wait.' He clasps his hands together. 'It sounds stupid now. With everything that happened.'

'Were you undressed?'

He closes his eyes. 'Yes. We were both naked. She touched me . . . I had an orgasm, too quickly. I was ashamed. Got dressed, went back to my own bed.'

'And what happened after that?'

'It was like it had never happened. For her, anyway.'

And this is when it gets muddy. Because according to Jamie Henderson's own account, he was confused, hurt. Angry. He became determined to persuade Camille there might be a future for them. The more distant she became, the more he sought to change her mind. Perhaps she thought he'd lose interest, but as the weeks and then months passed, he became even more convinced they should be together.

'This was a long time to hold a candle for someone. Did she ever complain about you? Object to your being persistent?'

'She didn't. Sometimes she was nice to me, sometimes she ignored me. Lucas warned me, though. Another one of the residents in the Factory. He told me I was coming on a bit strong.

I mean, they were just gifts. Flowers. This is how men have always won girls over, isn't it?'

'Now we move on to the events of the night of November tenth. Your honour, I wonder if now might be an appropriate time to break for lunch?'

I find a café round the corner. I'm not really hungry but I eat a sandwich while I think it through. Jamie is clearly awkward, inexperienced, a virgin even. Maybe he misread what happened between him and Camille. The things he did to 'win her back' could be seen as sweet or sinister, depending on the mindset of the person being pursued.

It'll all come down to the evidence this afternoon. Did he force his way into Camille's room? Or did she play with his emotions? There's no assault charge, as far as I know. It's harassment, and circulating a sex tape, via colleagues at work.

So the result will probably depend on who the jury like the most.

I did my research, after I became a victim. The chances of a conviction – or even of a case going to trial – are low for sex offences. Where there's been a previous relationship, it's muddier. And where there was something even more shameful involved, as there was with me, bringing a case becomes a waste of everybody's time.

But this is not about me, it's about Camille. I try to imagine how hard it must have been for her, still living in the place where she was harassed and filmed, 800 miles from her home and family.

When someone abuses their power, it changes you. On the outside, you seem harder, but inside, the knowledge that you're a victim makes everything about the world seem foreign, suddenly.

Not about me? Everything I've done since it happened is about me.

I leave half the sandwich, force myself to drink a coffee and then head back to court, walking briskly past Jamie Henderson's family. They have an aura of well-groomed privilege – boarding school doesn't come cheap. The lawyer defending him looked older and more expensive than the one for the prosecution.

I don't look through the window when I reach the door to the public gallery. I push it open and realise someone has got there before me.

32

Immi

Hanna.

I turn and run.

Down the steps, out of the court and as far away as I can get. Hanna can't know I've been here. I don't think she saw me.

But what the hell was *she* doing in court?

I go into a café to get my breath back. Fragments of the morning's evidence come back to me but I needed to hear the testimony this afternoon to make sense of what really happened.

When I finally go back to the Factory, they all see me as I arrive on the Play floor: Bernice, Lucas and Camille watch from the terrace. Do they know where I've been? I ignore them, let myself into my studio.

Hanna is sitting on my bed.

'You're not supposed to be able to get in here anymore.'

She shrugs. 'I can ask to override the app in an emergency.' Her voice is low and calm but I notice she's closed my window so no one on the terrace will hear us. She is a few inches smaller than me, yet her presence is intimidating.

'How is this an emergency?'

'You need to know about the evidence you missed.' Her accent sounds less stilted than before, and her English is much more fluent, just as Zoum had said.

'You mean the evidence the committee told me I had no right to hear? I was instructed not to go to court, if you remember.'

Hanna runs her palm across the top of the bright white duvet, as though she can't bear to see a crease unsmoothed. 'I did not approve of that decision. I understand the desire to protect a vulnerable person. But to me, it reinforces what many believe about sexually motivated crime. That it is something the *victim* should feel shame about. Should keep a secret.'

I hadn't expected to agree with her. 'You're right about the shame. But why are you so convinced he's guilty?'

'Because I was living here, Imogen. Jamie appeared to be a shy, likeable person in the beginning. But he developed an obsession. He would not let her be. I witnessed this. And the more people tried to warn him off, the more he persisted. He couldn't hear *no*.'

No. No. No. I'd said it too, but no one heard me either.

I lower my voice, aware Camille is only a few metres away on the terrace. 'What actually happened, Hanna? The charges are quite vague.'

'I believe there were two significant encounters between them. The first time, she ended it before full sex. She said later it was a mistake, that he was more like a brother than a lover. But he could not accept this. When the gifts and flattery failed, he pretended he was low. Suicidal. She let him into her studio to try to help him feel better and he gave her alcohol. A little after that, they did have sex.'

I close my eyes. I don't want to hear this. Yet I can't stop myself picturing it: Jamie turning up, being let into the studio, the door closing, the situation escalating . . . 'Consensual sex?'

Hanna shrugs. 'Camille has never remembered it fully – she was semi-conscious. I believe she was drugged. After he left, she lay there for several hours before sending an SMS to Bernice, who discovered her. But Camille refused to let the police be called. She felt it was not clear-cut.'

Her word against his.

'What changed?'

Hanna blinks. 'Two things. One, Jamie wanted it to happen again and his attentions became even more . . . frightening. And the second was, Camille discovered he had filmed their intercourse and shared it with workmates, who then shared it more widely. Remember, her face was well-known as a result of the billboards advertising the TV drama. The sex tape can still be found in certain places on the internet, despite attempts to take it down.'

It comes back to me now, what Camille said when I asked her why I might recognise her: *It is an unsettling feeling, knowing everyone has seen you naked.*

I imagine how it would have been if images of what happened to me had been available for anyone to see, to *masturbate* over. My view of Jamie changes in an instant. I want him to get what he deserves.

'Did he try to explain what went so wrong when he gave evidence?'

Hanna frowns, the lines again failing to reach her forehead. 'He stressed that she was the experienced one. That this was some . . . kink of hers, to seduce younger men. I hope the jury will see through him.'

'The case is meant to end tomorrow, right?'

'Yes. A guilty verdict will be closure for Camille. I hope perhaps after that, emotions here will be less . . . unpredictable.'

And if the verdict is not guilty? I don't ask that question.

I nod. 'Thanks for telling me, Hanna. I . . . um have some work to do now, so if there's nothing else . . .'

She doesn't move. 'Will you return to the court?'

'I don't know.'

'In my opinion, Imogen, it may be better for the community if you do not. I will not mention to anyone that I saw you there today.'

Her voice is as steady as before but her expression is steely.

I shrug. 'All right.'

Hanna stands up and smiles. 'Good. Now you can focus on letting yourself enjoy your time as a full member of the community. I know how hard you worked to be accepted.'

33

Wednesday 30 May

Dex

My first mentoring session with Camille is this afternoon, and I am dreading it. I stand on the terrace wondering what the hell I'm going to say if she tries it on again, or if Lucas is in the room too.

Music is drifting through from inside and I follow the sound: it's coming from Bernice's studio.

She knows how to handle Camille. I hurt Bernice by drinking after all my lies, I know that, but maybe asking her advice could help us get close again. I head for Buenos Aires before I have the chance to change my mind.

She doesn't answer immediately so I have to knock again. She's in her work clothes and looks startled to see me there. 'Sorry, was I disturbing you with the music?'

'No. I like it.'

The sound is soulful, like the tracks Mum plays sometimes when she's had one drink too many, trying to cajole my father into dancing.

'Sure you're not lying to get back in my good books, Dex?'

I shake my head. 'Wouldn't dare.'

'I was born twenty years too late,' Bernice says, waving me in and pointing at the old-fashioned turntable. 'This is Northern Soul – bit perkier than Motown. They played it in the clubs around Wigan as an escape from factory life.' She laughs. 'And as we know, Factory life can be grim, right?'

The state of her studio freaks me out. It's cluttered, even dirty. 'Just back from work?'

'Yup. All life-threatening incidents avoided, as per usual.' She moves her flight bag off the chair for me to sit down and opens her wardrobe. I thought she'd have ranks of dry-cleaned shirts and shorts, but instead stuff is spilling out. She begins to change and though there's nothing sexual about her undressing, I look away. The scent of grapefruit fills the air: she's vaping in her studio.

'Isn't vaping in here against Factory rules?'

She steps in front of me, dressed again now, and though it's her usual casual 'uniform', the shorts are creased and stained. 'Sometimes I want privacy. Is that a crime?'

She's jumpy, but then we all are, while this court case happens. No one has told me precisely what it's about, but it makes me wonder how they'll react if I'm ever caught.

How would it feel to confess for what i did? I imagine saying the words to Bernice right now. I wonder whether it would be a relief.

I'd happily take *my* punishment, but I can't bear knowing my family would get a life sentence too.

'It can be a goldfish bowl out there,' I say.

She sighs. 'Why are you here, Dex?' The old Bernice, cutting to the chase.

'It's my first mentoring session with Camille later. I'm anxious not to cause any more upset so I wanted to ask your advice.'

'Are you a gambler, Dex?'

'No. It's the one addiction that's never appealed. You?'

'Not in the conventional way.' She takes a deep drag of the e-cig and a cloud of vapour blurs her face as she exhales. 'Look. The mentoring relationship isn't all one way. Camille needs help to take her mind off a few things right now and she likes to play cards.'

I look into Bernice's eyes. Is she hinting that Camille was Jamie's victim? She looks away first.

'Thanks,' I say. 'I'll suggest it, if you really think it'll help.'

She laughs. 'What do I know? The longer I live here, the less I understand what makes any of us tick.'

The music throbs, some guy singing about heartbreak. It stops suddenly, and the grinding of the needle is all that's left. Bernice stares at the player but doesn't do anything.

There's something so vulnerable about her right now. Should I try to reach out? She's so proud and I don't want to offend her. 'Bernice, you seem different. Can I help *you* for a change?'

She looks as though she's considering it, before she shakes her head. 'Just tired. And with Camille, don't force it. The gambling thing was just an idea. She's good, but she plays for cash, so never stake more than you can afford to lose.'

I take a pocketful of small change with me when I meet Camille in Focus, in case she does want to teach me poker.

She's at one of the standing desks, working at a laptop. The teleconferencing screen next to her plays an animated screensaver of a roller coaster. It dips and soars so violently it makes me feel sick.

She turns. 'Hello, Dex.' Her smile doesn't reach those blue-grey eyes. The deadness there reminds me of how she was in the sauna. 'I was beginning to think you weren't coming.'

'I wouldn't dare.'

'It's for your own good.'

'Right.' Sarcasm creeps into my voice, even though I'd decided to play nicely while I was still on probation. 'Look, I don't know what you and Lucas are trying to do to me, but I'm not going to be blackmailed into sleeping with either of you.'

Camille looks down. 'That stuff was not my idea.'

'Whatever. But you mentoring me? That's rubbing my nose in it.'

She shakes her head. 'No, Dex. Actually, I need *your* help, if you are willing.'

She clicks the laptop and an image of herself appears on the screen. It's the one that made her famous. I never saw the drama on TV, but the Underground ad was impossible to ignore. A woman lying in a forest, black hair spread out as though she's floating in dark water, leaves and soil scattered across her naked body.

It's the wounds . . . Prosthetics, obviously, but horribly realistic work: flesh that had been bitten by wolves, and the early stages of decay.

Before I can say anything, the image begins to move. As Camille lies motionless, wolves crowd around her in a kind of dance. Music blasts out of the speakers, a disturbing dirge with a heavy bass beat. The size of the screen makes it even more difficult to watch – she is five times life-size, a waif and a giant at the same time.

And then her eyes snap open.

It makes me jump.

'This is my showreel,' Camille says, pausing the video. 'For acting. It's not getting me work and I hoped as you're in a similar business you could give me a second opinion? There is a . . . controversial change I am considering.'

It's the last thing I expected but at least it doesn't involve *me* getting naked. 'OK. If I can help, I will.'

'I'll play from the beginning.'

I watch as it spools back to the titles, with Camille's name and agent details, mixing through to the wolves sequence. It's what she's best known for, but even so, a clip of an actor playing a corpse doesn't seem a great way to demonstrate her skills.

The video continues with three more clips of Camille acting in another language. I guess these must be Danish soap operas. *She's not that good.* If anything, the language barrier makes it clearer. Her facial expressions and movements seem stilted.

I'm wondering what positive feedback I can give when the shot changes again, to a big close-up of her face, shot to look as though it's been recorded on a phone, low-res, as her features fill the entire screen. Her eyes are half-closed again.

As it plays, I'm relieved because I finally have a suggestion. She should cut this because it's too similar to the wolf trailer.

Yet when the Camille on-screen opens her eyes properly, there is *real* terror in them, an intensity that makes me re-examine my judgement of her acting skills. Her mouth is slack, like she's drunk, and there's no dialogue, so it's all about that raw fear in her eyes.

She stops the video, her back to me still. 'Well?'

'That last clip is very powerful. You manage to convey so much without speaking. Is there any more from that production?'

'There is plenty. Tell me, how much would *you* use?' Camille selects another file on the laptop.

Another shot of her face appears on the screen, from the same angle, but this time there's a soundtrack: a man's voice, panting and whispering. It's a sex scene, though I can still only see her face.

'Oh, Camille,' the man is calling out. 'You are so beautiful.'

Camille? Why is he using her real name?

The shot widens to show more of her body: a T-shirt has been pushed up to her neck to expose her breasts. The man filming this is having sex with her, the one telling her in a strange, high-pitched Scottish accent that he loves her *more than anything.*

Yet on-screen Camille stays silent.

I want to leave but I can't move. 'What the fuck is this, Camille? Is this *real*?'

She turns back towards me and I realise tears are running down her cheeks.

'You must be the only person who has never seen this,' she says between sobs. 'I thought the whole world had.'

And now I realise what I'm watching, and who Jamie's victim was.

34

Friday 1 June

Immi

It's the end of what feels like the longest week in the Factory.

Yesterday, the jury was sent out to consider its verdict, but after a couple of hours, the judge sent the jurors home until this morning.

Now, the heaviness of the wait engulfs the building. We know the verdict is coming. Camille hasn't left her studio and everyone creeps around, not wanting to disturb her.

I need a change of scenery so I go to the café at the Tate Modern, and try to work surrounded by mothers and kids squabbling during 'educational' half-term day trips. I never did this kind of stuff with *my* mum – her fear of the outside, of crowds, of life itself, saw to that.

Eventually I finish my paperwork. I google the court case, in case there's anything online about a verdict. But there's no trace. I remember the row I overheard on my first night at the Factory, when Veronica told the others *something* was going to hit the media. It must have been the case, but I guess it wasn't a big enough story after all.

To pass the time – and delay going back – I google the Factory instead. If it really is a pioneering experiment, surely there must have been some coverage before things started to go wrong?

First, I find a property site which collates three decades' worth of prices and estate agent particulars of properties across London. It's searchable by postcode and the Factory appears, though not under that name. The first pictures are scanned copies and show boxy 'yuppie' apartments, with interiors decorated in 1990s style, all dark wood and chrome furniture and astonishingly low prices. The sauna gets a mention too.

There's a reinvention around the millennium, uncovering the false ceilings and partition walls to create huge luxury flats, one per floor, with rental prices that still seem low compared to today.

By the time of the building's reincarnation as the Factory, the ads stop. But I *do* find a PDF of a piece from an architectural magazine about the redesign. It majors on brief, which '. . . focused on the idea of fostering community and connection, in contrast to the often alienating urban environment of one of the world's most iconic cities'.

There's nothing about the owners of the building, though the designers remark on the generosity of the budget.

We had a lot of financial and design freedom. Each floor is themed around Maslow's hierarchy of needs, reimagined for the millennial generation. Places to eat, drink, rest, recharge and simply be – all designed to foster collaboration and fight loneliness. The final requirement was, of course, very big beds. Young people like sleep – and sex.

I shudder, remembering the sauna. But why would property owners or developers spend so much to improve the lives of random young city-dwellers? Despite what Ashleigh said about the owners being philanthropists, the rich are not known for their generosity to strangers.

Whatever the initial aims, there's an even bigger question mark for me now. Has the community worked, or made things worse?

In my five weeks at the Factory, I've seen sexual tension, rivalry, anger, manipulation, guilt and pain. Hardly 'fostering community and connection'.

I close my laptop and walk back to the Factory. It's early afternoon and Ashleigh's preparations for the open day tomorrow are everywhere – signs and posters and the smell of gluten-free lemon cake baking in the oven.

As I climb the stairs to the top, I decide to spend the afternoon helping her. Ashleigh does seem to enjoy a little martyrdom but mucking in will take my mind off what's gone before.

I'm just about to let myself into Kyoto when I hear a shriek that sounds more animal than human.

It's coming from Camille's studio.

35

Immi

Not guilty.

By a majority of ten to two, which means two of the jurors believed Camille's version of events. But that can't be any consolation.

After the shriek, Bernice goes to Camille in her studio. She sends me a message asking me to tell the other Dyers when they arrive home.

Out of unspoken respect, no one uses the terrace tonight, and people congregate in the Nourish area instead. When Bernice arrives, we ask how Camille is and she just shakes her head.

'We should cancel the open day,' Ashleigh says, even as she pours agave syrup over the tops of her tray bakes. 'The last thing Camille needs is strangers traipsing through her home.'

Bernice sighs. 'No. She'd hate to spoil it. She just needs time to heal, on her own.'

'The problem is, there's something going on in all the areas,' Ashleigh says. 'Sauerkraut-making down here, yoga in Retreat, plus Zoum is doing the international co-living video conference in Focus . . .'

He smiles shyly. It's good that he's doing something at the open day, maybe it'll help heal the rift with the others.

'Have you organised any activities in the basement?' Lucas asks.

'No.' Ashleigh looks put out. 'If you remember, I was planning to unveil the sauna but some of you jumped the gun and have used it already.'

Lucas ignores the whinge. 'Then I'll take Camille down to Hanna's office for the day. I'm sure she won't mind, and I have absolutely no desire to meet the great unwashed. We'll get drunk and hide till they've all gone.'

So on Saturday, we welcome almost a hundred people into the Factory, preaching that communal living is the future. But all the while, we know that a broken person is cowering out of sight, trying to come to terms with something awful that happened within these walls. I can't be alone in wondering if the Factory can survive this.

Ashleigh is a star, leading her mindfulness class and her ferments workshop and her tours with a manic cheeriness. The guests are suitably wowed and giddy on 0.5 ABV kombucha. If I didn't already live in the Factory, I'd be joining a waiting list for the next available room. I wear my new dress, talking to people about how I made it and where they could learn sewing themselves.

'And they're all gone,' Ashleigh announces at just before five, after everyone has handed back their visitor badges and left the building. 'Time to add the gin to the kombucha, don't you think?'

I go to get fresh lemon for the gins from the kitchen and find Dex there. He's been helping out behind the scenes, washing up and wiping down in the storeroom on the Nourish floor, rather than interacting.

'Shouldn't you have been photographing the event for posterity?'

He shrugs. 'Not in the mood for small talk with strangers.'

There's an odd quality to his voice. I walk towards him and he recoils.

'Shit, Dex, you stink of booze.'

'What's it to you?'

It's a fair question. My brain has been so full of the court case that I haven't spent any time with him. But he's not sought me out either. Already, our two nights together are beginning to seem like an aberration, maybe even the result of the clever design that forces Dyers together.

'It might not have worked out between us, Dex, but I do care about you. Is there anything you want to talk about?'

He shakes his head. 'Stay away from me, Immi. For your own sake.'

The knock-back hurts; that's the last time I'll try with him. 'Suit yourself.'

I head up to the terrace. Ashleigh is there with Zoum and Lucas. At least those two are no longer at each other's throats. Bernice is here but looks knackered.

'Is Camille OK?' I ask Lucas.

He shrugs his shoulders. 'She's . . . getting there. Thanks for asking.'

I pop slices of lemon in everyone's glasses while Ashleigh talks about the energy that the open house has brought into the Factory.

'You saw how envious people were when they came round today. We should remind ourselves how lucky we are to have this space and each other.'

We raise our glasses. Nowhere is perfect. But perhaps there is still hope for the Factory, if we can pull together.

The week's stresses catch up with me and I go to bed early. Only Bernice and Lucas are left together on the terrace.

A moaning sound wakes me. Not sexual, and very different to the shriek Camille made when she heard the verdict. I can't ignore it: it's coming from somewhere here on the Play floor. I stumble out of bed, pocket my knife, and follow the noise.

Bernice is standing at the entrance to her studio, her chest heaving, as though she's just run a mile without stopping.

'What is it?' I ask, realising the moans are coming from her. The door to Lima, Lucas's studio, is open too.

'I . . .' Bernice is trying to say something. She points into Buenos Aires.

I follow her outstretched hand. It's messy in here. Magazines and books are stacked on the shelves and the floor. A vintage poster celebrating air travel hangs over the bed.

At first I don't realise what it is I'm meant to be looking at.

But then I see it, and I gasp.

It's Bella the guinea pig, lying on the rumpled bedsheets. How weird that she should reappear after all this time and immediately go to sleep . . .

But she's not sleeping.

She is dead.

Feeling nauseated, I step towards the bed to touch the creature. Perhaps the noise of the visitors brought her out of her hiding place and she died here of a heart attack?

My fingers touch stiff fur. And there's something even stranger: the animal is icy-cold, her face in a rictus expression, suggesting that Bella has been dead for some time.

Which means somebody put her on Bernice's bed on purpose.

Bernice and I sit on the terrace with two large brandies, while Lucas deals with the animal. His unexpected compassion is too much for me to process right now.

'Have a bit more,' I urge Bernice. When I took her hand to lead her away from the studio, her skin was clammy and I thought she might faint. Now she cradles the glass as though it's an object she doesn't recognise, still less comprehend what it's used for. 'It's good for shock.'

'Who c-could do such a thing, Immi?' Her voice sounds so different to the clear, confident one I am used to. 'Bella did nothing to harm anyone. But someone let her and Edward out of their cage and then . . . Well, they must have killed her.'

'Though there wasn't a mark on her. Perhaps they found her already dead and then . . .' I tail off. It's hardly comforting to imagine someone discovered the rodent's corpse, kept it somewhere – even froze it in their personal larder – before placing it on Bernice's bed late at night to scare her witless.

'The person who did this *knows* I care about the animals. Knows I'd be more horrified by this than . . . well, if they'd killed one of *us*.'

I doubt that, but as I lift the glass up towards her lips again, I am wondering about the culprit too. Zoum gets the blame for most mishaps, but he's never been mean to me, and I can't believe he'd do this. But with Veronica gone, the list of people who might want to lash out at Bernice or the committee has shrunk.

Over Bernice's shoulder, I see Lucas carrying a pathetically small bundle wrapped in a bath towel. He places it in a box and then moves it into his own room, presumably so she never has to see it again.

He comes out with a third brandy glass and pours himself a generous measure. 'Fuck, B, what kind of people are we living with?'

She doesn't look up.

'I don't think we should tell anyone what's happened,' Lucas says. 'It'll just churn stuff up, and give him the satisfaction of knowing he's achieved exactly what he wanted.'

I look at Lucas. 'Him?'

'Come on, Immi, who else would it be except Zoum? Let's not give him the attention he's craving.'

I don't want to argue. 'I suppose it's best not to upset Ashleigh, it'd really hurt her.'

'Bernice? Are you happy with that?'

She looks up, her eyes dazed. 'I . . .'

Lucas raises his eyebrows at me, as though he's at a loss. 'Is it OK if I leave you to get her to bed?' he says quietly. 'I had a fairly intense time with Camille all day.'

'Of course.'

He puts his arm on Bernice's shoulder and squeezes it. I see her flinch. 'Try not to let it get you down, B.'

She says nothing till his studio door has shut behind him.

'Immi, can I trust you?' she asks finally, her voice quiet yet oddly high-pitched.

I nod. 'You know you can.'

'I think I'm done. With the Factory. It's too fucking cruel.'

'What's been done to you *is* cruel, Bernice. But you're the lynchpin of this place. It wouldn't be the same without you.' I can say that without it being an untruth. Whether I like her or not doesn't matter.

'But what if I got it all wrong, Immi? What if it's *my* fault this place has become so . . . toxic.'

Part of me wants to push her further, ask her what she means. But she's in shock. If I take advantage of that, I'm as bad as the rest of them.

'Listen, things will look better in the morning. They always do.' That's another lie, but a well-intentioned one. 'Let's get you to bed.'

Lucas must have tidied up her room while removing Bella's little body, and at least there is now space on the duvet for Bernice to sleep. She lies down but doesn't seem to want to let go of my hand.

'There are things you need to know, Immi. About this place. It's only fair . . .' But already her speech is slurring as tiredness takes over.

'Not now. Tomorrow. We can talk about whatever it is tomorrow.'

Back in my own studio, I try to convince myself that the new week might bring some respite from the extreme pressure we've all been under.

But I wouldn't want to put money on it.

Week 6: Let's stick together

Good morning, everybody. In the light of recent events, we've decided to keep the Sunday messages coming for the foreseeable future, to help us pull together.

We've all been through the mill, but let's look ahead. There is still so much to look forward to. Our midsummer celebration is now less than three weeks away and it is always a very special one, cementing the closeness we do our best to nurture.

Whether you're a new Dyer or an original, let's do all we can to come together as never before. Bad times are behind us: let's unite for the next stage.

36

Sunday 3 June

Immi

Camille emerges from her studio pretending she's getting her head around the *not guilty* verdict. But little tics and tells give her away. Her left eye twitches. She starts sentences that she never finishes.

I, too, pretend this is a normal Sunday. That a dead animal wasn't dumped on someone's bed. That the Factory isn't harbouring hatred.

There's no formal yoga class today, but I need to clear my head so I grab a mat and stand facing Ashleigh as she goes through her daily practice. Her movements are now so familiar it's easy to mirror them.

She's tried so hard to keep the community together. She can *never* know about Bella's fate.

Slowly, the poses begin to do their work, and my limbs relax, though my spine and neck are still rigid.

After a few minutes, someone slaps down another mat behind me. I turn slowly.

Bernice.

She's a yoga sceptic, insisting that vaping is better for relaxation than stretching. *So why is she here?*

I try to relax but she's ruined it for me. I watch from the corner of my eye: Bernice is clumsy and self-conscious, even though Ashleigh keeps shooting her encouraging smiles.

When the session ends, Bernice refuses Ashleigh's offer of herb tea down on the Retreat floor, and follows me to my studio door.

'Can we talk now? Please?'

I don't want to get involved.

It's a visceral reaction but it's based on experience. Going to the court was a mistake. So was trying to help Dex, and even talking to Veronica.

And for the first time, I worry that the pranks are a sign of something even more toxic. People who hurt animals can graduate to hurting humans . . .

'Bernice, is there anything to be gained from going over what happened?' I lower my voice. 'Lucas was right, we have to act normal, to try to catch out the person who did that to Bella.'

'They want me out,' she whispers.

'Who do?'

'Whoever did this. I've put everything into this place, Immi.'

She's wearing a T-shirt and grey tracksuit bottoms that make her seem so much smaller. I want the old Bernice back, the sassy Queen Bee in her off-duty uniform of starchy shirt and pressed shorts.

'No one doubts that, Bernice. We're all upset by the court case, but it'll blow over, won't it?'

She shakes her head. 'No. It won't. They know that I lied and they're going to use that—'

'What did you lie about?'

But she's not looking at me anymore. She's focused on the stairs. I can hear footsteps from Retreat below.

'I lied about my age,' she says quietly. 'I said I was younger than I am. I'm thirty-six now and they can use that to get rid of me.'

'The age limit thing? I'm sure that's not an issue now you're settled here.'

But she doesn't seem to be hearing me. 'Lies can be used against us,' she says, her fake smile at odds with the words. 'Nothing here stays a secret . . .' She begins to laugh. 'And I think yoga is definitely not my forte.'

I stare at her, confused at the sudden change of direction.

Lucas and Camille are walking up the stairs towards us.

'Yeah, you're definitely not a naturally bendy person, are you, Bernice?' Lucas says. 'Still, I admire you. Good to get those old bones moving, right? We're not as young as we used to be.'

I've really had enough of their constant bitching and infighting. I go to Nourish to get food so I can hole myself up in my studio for the rest of the day, sewing and reading and working. Anything is better than getting embroiled in other people's arguments.

Zoum is in the kitchen, mixing dough, his fingers scrabbling in the flour to bring it together.

It *can't* have been him, can it? My skin crawls as I think of Bella's frozen body.

'All right, Immi?'

'What are you making?'

'Flatbreads. I thought I would test out my mother's recipe and then finish them off on the firepit later, for everyone to share afterwards.'

I go to my fridge and take out a yogurt. 'After what?'

'Earth hour, of course!'

Shit. 'I'd forgotten all about it.' I tip the yogurt in a bowl, add gluten-free granola from the communal hopper.

Zoum smiles. 'I think it is excellent timing. A chance for the community to come together again. I know I have not always helped but I am committed to helping us start. Beginning with breaking bread.'

'Really?'

Zoum has shaped his breads now and places them under tea towels. 'They need time to rise.'

'And you haven't laced them with laxative?'

He shakes his head. 'I promise they are unadulterated. My practical jokes are behind me now.'

'Why the change of heart?'

He takes butter out of the fridge and places it on the tray, along with a small dish of onion seeds. 'I think ... whatever happened between Jamie and Camille caused a lot of damage to both of them, and the rest of us. But it is time to put that behind us. To try again.'

Should I tell him about what Bernice said, how rattled she seems? No, because then I'd have to tell him about Bella and ...

'That's good,' I say instead. 'I'll see you later on.'

Back in my studio, I try to weigh it all up. Zoum was ostracised for disagreeing with them all about Jamie, but he's trying to be the bigger man now, for the sake of this place. If he can put all the bitterness behind him, then surely I can too?

There's a knock at my door: Ashleigh.

'You're joining us for earth hour, aren't you?'

I follow her out onto the terrace. The firepit has already been lit, and Ashleigh has laid yoga mats in a circle. One less than last time, when Veronica still lived here. Perhaps she and Jamie poisoned the place, but now they're gone, we can start over.

It seems that we're all hoping for the same thing. Even Dex appears, ready for the yoga session.

'I want you all to close your eyes,' Ashleigh says softly. 'And I want you to breathe in through your nose to the count of three . . . two . . . one . . . and then out through your mouth . . . five . . . four . . . three . . .'

My breath slows. Every time she repeats the numbers, the pause between them lengthens.

'We are a community,' Ashleigh continues. 'We are connected by hidden threads, and sad moments and joyous ones. We need to come together again. To heal.'

Something makes me half-open my eyes during the meditation. Bernice is sitting opposite me. Her eyes are closed but I see the glint of candlelight reflected in water on her cheeks.

She's crying.

No one else has noticed. Even Ashleigh has her eyes closed.

I shut mine too. Proud Queen Bee will be glad no one else has seen her this way.

After earth hour ends, I feel tired but cleansed. Outside it's quiet, as my fellow residents have gone to bed early too. Finally I begin to feel the pull of sleep and . . .

What was that?

It sounded like a crash, something shattering. Maybe it was the imagined thud of my own body as I came out of a nightmare and fell back onto the bed.

Or someone staggering from Bermondsey Street to have a piss against our walls?

I pull myself up in bed, listening. It's past midnight. Is one of the Dyers getting some night air on the terrace?

But the noise is coming from street level. A scream. Words I can't make out.

My feet touch warm floorboards as I climb out of bed and leave my studio. Nobody is around. I walk out onto the terrace. Nothing moves.

But the words from Tanner's Walk are getting louder and shriller. I peer over the terrace, the drop making me dizzy. There seems to be a potted lavender missing but I can't see anyone.

'Who is it?' I call down. 'We're trying to sleep here!'

'You have to come,' someone shouts back up.

I don't have to do anything, sunshine.

Instead I force myself to take another step towards the edge of the wall. I stoop, holding on to the low rail.

And when I look down this time, I see something: two figures leaning over a shape that could be a bag of rubbish or a discarded coat.

Except for the pool of purple that is spreading around it, like the halo around the street lamp that lights the scene.

37

Monday 4 June

Immi

I'm running.

I can't feel the soles of my feet on the steps, and my body seems a long way away, but my brain is sharp.

Who is it lying down there?

It could be a tramp in a stupor. A girl who's had too much to drink. A cyclist hitting the kerb.

But I heard a thump. If someone had stumbled at street level, there'd have been no noise at all.

As I run, I'm aware of doors opening behind me, Dyers coming out to see why someone is clattering down the metal steps.

I speed up. Who fell?

Or jumped . . .

The faces of my neighbours flash through my mind as I near the ground floor. Which of them might be desperate enough?

Zoum, haunted by past mistakes?

Dex, drunk and burdened by whatever keeps him awake?

But one face keeps appearing. *Camille.*

I know how it feels to loathe your body so much you want to leave it. To see yourself as some man did, as an object not a person; to want that feeling to stop. Even if it means obliteration.

I wrench open the entry door. A couple are standing over the figure on the ground. The man is talking breathlessly down the phone: 'No. She's not breathing . . . she . . . I am pretty sure she's dead.'

She.

The young woman rushes towards me. 'We were at the other end of the street when we saw something fall. We thought it was washing or bin bags caught by the wind. Except for the sound . . .'

I have to force myself to look at the motionless shape between them. Petite. Red hair.

Bernice.

No. it can't be her.

'Bernice. Wake up.'

But already I know she can't hear me. The side of her head has been flattened and blood pours out. It's obvious that the person inhabiting that damaged body has gone.

Yet still, I fall to my knees and in a gesture that must be more to comfort myself, I cradle Bernice. Soon the blood covers my legs and hands, seeps into the T-shirt I'm wearing. Pieces of terracotta pot are scattered around the pavement, along with black soil. Broken green spikes of the lavender are caught in her beautiful hair and I can smell its perfume.

Oh, Bernice.

Too fucking late to hold her now, my conscience is screeching. *If you had given her any comfort at all yesterday, when she was begging you for help, maybe she'd still be alive.*

I try to position myself over her body, to give her a little privacy. 'Please, stop anyone else getting closer, at least till the emergency services arrive,' I ask the witnesses. 'No one needs to see this.'

I don't know how long it is before the lights of the ambulance are so close that they illuminate her face and all the blood. I hadn't even heard it approach.

And behind it, a police car draws up, and officers leap out and it occurs to me that it must only be months since the last time they were called to the Factory.

I don't want to let her go, but the paramedic persuades me gently, and as I stagger to my feet, someone wraps a blanket round my shoulders. I don't feel cold, but the blood all over me must be shocking to other people because when Lucas sees me, he looks horrified.

'Fuck, Immi, what have you done to yourself? I heard the ambulance and—'

That's the moment when he realises I am not the casualty.

I can't let him see Bernice. Not like this. I push him away but in the process, I spread some of her blood across his arms. 'There's been a-an . . .' I'm about to say accident but it's not, is it? 'Something bad has happened, Lucas. The medics are dealing with it. Don't crowd them.'

He's staring over my shoulder and I turn too. They're doing CPR. Perhaps it makes family and friends feel better, to think that everything was tried. Bernice's body is not visible as the crew crowd round, but her bare feet move slightly in time with them pounding on her chest.

I see the nail varnish on her toes. Pillar-box red. The same colour as the lipstick she always wears.

Always *wore*.

'It's Bernice?' he asks, his voice plaintive as a child's.

'Don't watch, Lucas.'

He's crying out as I try to usher him away again. 'What's wrong with her?'

'I think she . . . fell. Off the terrace.'

He stops sobbing for a moment and looks up at the roof.

I remember standing here on the day of my interview, the sounds of the party coming from above, the voices reminding me of kids in a playground.

'*Fell?*' Lucas repeats.

'I didn't see anything. I just heard . . . something.' I don't want to describe that thud, so I add, 'The people who called the ambulance . . . I heard their voices.'

'Did she . . . speak to you?'

'No, she was unconscious.'

Behind us, more residents are watching: Dex, Ashleigh, Camille, Zoum.

They were all closer to Bernice than I was. *Yet it was me she tried to talk to.* Was that because I was the only person she could trust?

I step towards them, using the bossy hand movements I employ on school trips when I'm trying to marshal the kids away from something they shouldn't see.

And then a policeman is coming towards us, with even bossier movements than mine, and of course it's me he is looking at, because I am half-naked, covered in blood.

Someone else is in control.

The instant I realise that, the strength leaves my legs, black stars glitter before my eyes and I am falling too.

'Imogen? Open your eyes for me, will you, love?'

I do as I'm told, though the light is blinding and the realisation of where I am makes me want to black out again.

I am in the ambulance. It seems odd to me at first. Surely Bernice should be in here in my place. She is the one who has been injured.

But of course, she's not injured. She's dead.

'My friend?'

The ambulance man has eyes that have seen everything. He doesn't need to speak for me to know my first instinct was correct.

'Where does it hurt, Imogen?' he asks me. 'You took a tumble and there's a graze on your knee, but aside from that?'

I mentally check myself, top to toe. 'I think I'm in one piece.'

'You weren't attacked, or wounded by anyone, were you? Or . . . anything you'd rather talk to my female colleague or the police about?'

I've wondered hundreds of times what it would have been like if I'd reported what happened to me before. I suppose it would have been a lot like this.

I shake my head. 'This is *her* blood: Bernice's.'

'I wish I could clean you up but I think the police will want to take your clothes.'

I nod. My body has started to shake. When I close my eyes, I see the shape of her head and now I can't even picture Bernice as she was before.

'Take your time. The police can wait a few minutes. Better for them if you're calm and able to tell them exactly what happened.'

They let me change in the office in the basement. Hanna is there as they bag my T-shirt and knickers, and she brings me fresh clothes from my studio – with my permission, for once – to change into.

Two police officers – one male, one female – talk to me, their body cams recording what I say. Not that there's much to tell. I sense them relaxing when I tell them there was no fight or altercation, that my only involvement was hearing the sounds from outside and coming down to find Bernice.

'I think ... I think she must have jumped,' I say, wanting them to contradict me.

The woman stays poker-faced. 'Obviously, there will be a full investigation, as there always is with an unexplained death like this.'

Hanna flinches at the word *death*.

When they let me go, I find the other residents have gathered around the table in the Nourish area. They watch me walk up the stairs. A strange sound comes from the end of the table. Camille. I'd never known what the word *keening* meant till now. It's a shrill wail, almost too high-pitched to be heard by humans.

Ashleigh sits next to her; her skin has lost its country-girl colour. But no one is trying to stop Camille making that awful, unforgettable noise. It's almost as if we know there's no point.

'What did they say?' Dex asks me. His voice is thick. A glass by his hand is half-full of ochre spirit – Scotch or brandy.

'They didn't say anything. There will be a full investigation, though.'

Zoum shakes his head. 'It's obvious what happened. She killed herself.'

'We don't *know* that,' Ashleigh insists.

No one corrects her, even though there's no way Bernice could have fallen by accident.

'You were all meant to be her friends,' Zoum says. 'Where were you when she needed you?' he continues. 'The buddying and the yoga and all the other bullshit made things worse not—'

'Zoum, stop it.' Lucas's voice is surprisingly strong. He's stopped crying but his eyes are red raw.

'No. I won't,' Zoum says, but quieter. 'We all pretend we live in a community. That we *care*. But the fact is, Bernice was desperate. So desperate she wanted to die. And none of us did a single bloody thing to stop her.'

I wait for someone to argue, but the silence tells me we're all thinking the same thing.

38

Dex

I don't plan it. One minute I'm hearing all this shit coming out of Zoum's mouth, and the next I'm feeling the crunch of my knuckles against his cheekbone.

Then I feel the sting and the shame.

'Hey. Dex, what the fuck?' Lucas steps between us, though the fight has already gone out of me. The reproach in Zoum's eyes is like plunging into an ice-cold lake.

'I-I'm sorry. Zoum, believe me.' My words feel clumsy and my teeth loose, as though I'm the one who had my skull rattled. Zoum touches his cheek, which is going red, but I doubt he'll have a black eye. I'm not much of a fighter.

'Dex, go to bed,' Immi says, as though she's telling off a pupil.

Zoum shakes his head. 'I'm going anyway. You lot keep drinking till you've convinced yourselves none of it is your fault. So much easier than facing the truth, right?'

I sit back down.

Camille's wailing has turned into a weird noise, like an animal makes when it's so hurt that the kindest thing would be to finish it off. I think of the video she showed me and I wonder how much more she can take.

Yet no one who was close to Bernice wants to be the first to go to bed.

'Did she talk to any of you?' Ashleigh asks. 'About . . . I don't know, feeling . . . low?'

Low.

A dead person isn't *low*, and suicide isn't *a bout of the blues*. And once you've looked at the milky eyes of a corpse, you can never see your own in the mirror without knowing there is no *gentle passing away*, no afterlife.

Lucas grabs the brandy. Pours himself some more, then it goes around the table: Immi, Ashleigh – who pours for herself and for Camille – and finally it comes to me.

Everyone has forgotten I am supposed to be teetotal. The bottle's almost empty anyway, only an inch or so in my tumbler. As we sit around the table, it reminds me of a séance.

Are you there, Bernice? Tap once for yes, twice for fucking no.

'You know, she made a choice,' Lucas says carefully. 'She chose not to tell us how bad things were. We were her friends, especially Camille and me. She would have known she could come to us about anything.'

It's too soon to absolve ourselves.

Ashleigh nods. 'Camille knows that, don't you, darling?' She's still stroking her hand, but there's no change to the noise the girl's making.

But Lucas is lying to himself.

I get it. You start reframing what's happened, excusing yourself, inventing convoluted reasons to explain the actions you took, creating some brand-new, improved version of events.

But it doesn't help, because deep down, you still know. You can't undo what you did.

Light footsteps on the metal treads sound exactly like Bernice's. But it's Hanna, her face grey and angular under the kitchen lights.

'You must all try to get some sleep.'

Chairs scrape against the concrete floor. It's as though she's given us permission to go to bed, and thank God for that, because the alternative was sitting here until dawn breaks. Some of these people have jobs to go to.

Has anyone told Bernice's colleagues? I wonder if her work was a contributory factor in whatever drove her to this. Air traffic controllers live with pressure day in, day out.

But they're screened. They are trained to cope.

I blink. Of all the people living in this excuse for a community, she's the last person I'd have expected to do this. Bernice was in control, always. The idea of her dying *that* way, crushed on a pavement, in public, with no certainty that she wouldn't end up paralysed instead, seems totally out of character.

I think of the evening when she let her guard down, told me about her difficult marriage. Should I have seen this coming?

But I was too absorbed in my own world to listen properly. I did nothing. No, maybe it's worse than that: I caused her additional pain with my own lies, then threw her compassion back in her face. Was it the final straw?

'Come on, Camille, take this,' Hanna is saying. She has a brown pill in one hand, and a glass of water in the other. When she catches me looking, she narrows her eyes. 'A herbal sedative. Would you like one too?'

I shake my head. *The drugs don't work.* But tonight I really, really wish they did.

39

Immi

I toss and turn all night and it's only the momentum of familiar routines that gets me up and out to school for the first time in a week.

The kids are hyper, full of half-term gossip, and my colleagues aren't much better. I work on autopilot, and even Fatima the TA leaves me alone.

I sneak away from school as soon as I can after the last bell, planning to walk home, see if it clears my head. But instead, I stare at passers-by. This time yesterday, Bernice was alive, like them. What the hell happened? Bernice wasn't my favourite person in the Factory, but she had an admirable *take me or leave me* confidence.

What happened to her to change that? None of this makes sense.

The only thing I do know is I don't feel safe there. So instead of walking towards the Thames, I get the Tube towards the suburbs I used to loathe so much. I know Mack and Sarah thought they'd got shot of me, but it's still better to be an unwelcome guest on their sofa than return to the Factory tonight.

'Mate!' Sarah doesn't look pissed off when she opens her door, which is something. 'You're just the person.'

'Am I?'

'Yeah, Mack's away with work and I've got this massive craving for a Hawaiian pizza, but I couldn't justify a delivery if I'm home alone.'

I try to smile, but pretending in front of Sarah is much harder work than it was in front of colleagues or the kids. 'I need to talk to you.'

She ushers me in. There's no sign of a bump as I embrace her, but her boobs are squashier against my chest.

Already she's dialling a number on her mobile, ordering a ham and pineapple with chillies. 'And is it a quattro formaggi for you, still, or have you gone vegan now you live in that commune?'

I shrug. By the time she's finished the order, I'm crying, though breaking down in front of other people – even my closest friend – is *not* what I do.

She looks up and sees my face.

'Oh shit, Immi, hold on while I get some of Mack's cider.'

She fills my glass, and then refills it over and over, as I tell her about finding Bernice's body, and the fact the poor woman had tried to talk to me before she jumped, and that shitty business with Bella the guinea pig. Sarah pats my back but doesn't crowd me.

'You're not to blame for this,' she tells me when I've finished my story. 'The place was already fucked up, and you barely knew her.'

'Which must be why she wanted to talk to me, not the rest of them, her so-called friends. They were part of the problem.'

'Yes, but you had no reason to expect she'd do this.'

'No, but—'

'But nothing. It's sad, but not your fault. Let's focus on what happens next. Do you want to move out?'

'I . . . My head says I'll never find anywhere half as good and central and reasonably priced and . . .'

'And your gut?'

'The Factory doesn't feel . . .' I hesitate, knowing how daft I'm going to sound, but I decide to say it anyway. 'Safe. It doesn't feel like a safe place to be.'

'Well then, that's settled. You can stay here tonight and tomorrow. Mack's not back till Wednesday. And in the meantime, I'll look at the small print and find a way to get you out of your contract. If that's definitely what you want?'

The doorbell rings: pizza man. Her eyes light up, though she tries to stay focused on me, waiting for my answer.

'Let me sleep on it.'

Despite the hard mattress on the sofa bed, I sleep better than I have in days. When I wake, I know what I must do: start again, somewhere new. A building can't be blamed for a suicide, but as long as I live in the Factory, I won't be able to forget how I failed Bernice.

Maybe walking away from the others is cowardly. But as soon as Sarah can get my money back, I'll find myself a new drab room with a soul-sapping commute. Anything will be better than the sophisticated cruelties of the Factory.

At break, I do a quick search on Spareroom.com to see if there's anything I could afford if I don't get my deposit straightaway, but the only cheap places are so far out that I'd have to spend all I save on travel. I leave school at lunchtime to look at the small ads in the local shop, but there's nothing there either. When I get back from the newsagent, there's a buzz about the staffroom and a cluster of women are gathered around someone in the kitchenette.

'Here she is!' Fatima announces and steps aside to reveal a guest.

Lucas.

He looks wrong here, like a peacock in a coal mine. I've only ever seen him after work, when he's sloughed off some of the extra finesse his work must demand: the shiny, stitched shoes and the expensive watch. I'll tell him to hide the watch when he leaves the school grounds, as it might prove irresistible to one of the local gangs.

'Immi!' Lucas says, striding towards me and air-kissing both cheeks. His aftershave makes me think of the first time we met, and then the awfulness of that moment in the sauna. Yet when we separate, I notice his eyes are red-rimmed.

'Just passing, were you?'

'Clearly not. But I was worried when you didn't come home last night. We all were.'

'Let's go somewhere more private.' I don't want to provide today's dose of drama to my bored colleagues. He follows me outside to the blind spot just beyond the school gates, where the smokers go.

'I've decided to leave the Factory,' I tell him, after I've made sure no one can see us from school.

'We all feel the place won't be the same. I was one of her closest friends and I can't believe—' He stops, looks away. 'I know what she'd say, though. Decisions like this shouldn't be made when you're feeling emotional.'

'Thanks for the handy tip.' I regret it as soon as I've said it. Too harsh. He came to see me, after all. 'Why are you really here?'

'To make sure you're OK, number one. It can be contagious. Suicide? People get infected by this awful idea that the world would be better off without them.'

I stare at him, but his statement seems to come from a genuine place. I wonder what *his* story is, the wound that's led to the coke and the cockiness. 'I'm sad and I feel guilty. But I'm not going to harm myself. Are *you*, Lucas?'

'Too fucking selfish.' He looks up at the pale-blue sky, scans the surroundings. 'I admire what you do. Those kids. This place. That's the opposite of selfish.'

'Really, it's not. I get loads back from them.'

'Apples for the teacher?'

'Something like that. Look, I have to get ready for class.' It's a lie.

'Bernice was on antidepressants, you know. She shouldn't have been drinking with them.'

'I didn't know that. Do the police?'

He shrugs. 'I suppose they'll talk to her doctor. She used to avoid alcohol because she knew it could really affect her mood. But in the last couple of weeks, she started drinking again and when I tried to talk to her about it, she told me to mind my own business.'

I think about what Dex said once, about noticing that she seemed to stick to soft drinks. 'You and Bernice . . . Were you ever *together*?'

Lucas looks away. 'We . . . In the early days, we were lovers, briefly, yes. But we decided we'd be better off as friends. Best friends, really.'

That's not how it looked at the weekend, when Bernice stopped talking as soon as she saw him and Camille. She looked afraid. 'Had you fallen out about anything?'

'No!'

'I'm not blaming you, Lucas. There's mental illness in my family so I know sometimes there is nothing you can say to make things better.'

He sighs. 'Please come back tonight, Immi. We're better off together. Other people are really struggling because of what Bernice did and it's easier if we can all talk about it.'

'By people, you mean Camille?'

'Yes. Dex too. Bernice was his champion, went out of her way for him. I worry what he might do, but maybe you could get through to him, as you've been . . . close.'

'Like you and Camille?'

He actually blushes. 'All of those games seem so trivial now, don't they, Immi? We need to pull together. You can still give notice, but I think it would make a big difference if you could come back for a few days. *Please.*'

I don't say anything but I give him a small nod. He leans forward to embrace me, and I almost back away. But when I let him touch me, briefly, Lucas feels insubstantial, not threatening.

After he's gone, I replay the conversation, wondering if I've just been manipulated. Maybe. I do try to do the right thing, when I can.

I text Sarah. *Won't be staying with you tonight. Things to sort in Bermondsey. Thanks for everything.* x

40

Tuesday 5 June

Immi

From the outside, the Factory looks exactly the same. The street has been cleaned, the police tape removed, and when I look up, the pots of lavender along the roof terrace are perfectly aligned again, though one is missing.

But inside, the silence gives it away. Usually there's music drifting from one of the studios, or a conversation on the stairs, or the sizzle of food from the Nourish floor.

Nothing.

Yet I know people are in. Dex's bike is here, next to Zoum's folding Brompton. Post has been taken from all the pigeonholes except two: the ones that belonged to Veronica and Bernice.

My footsteps on the metal treads sound obscenely noisy, like drums at a funeral.

I get all the way to the terrace before I see another soul, and then three of them are there: Ashleigh, Camille, Dex. The warm afternoon is turning into a sultry evening, and when I glance over at the vaping pod, it's impossible to comprehend that Bernice will never sit in there again, our own Queen Bee, surveying her hive.

Camille gives me a wan smile and Ashleigh stands up, comes to hug me. Her eyes look pink and sore, and I smell sweat and lavender oil. I remember Bernice's split skull and the scattered lavender spikes caught in her hair.

'We were worried about you,' she says, and there's a hint of reproach. 'We're meant to be a unit. We need each other.'

'I stayed with a friend. How's everyone doing?'

Ashleigh glances at the other two. 'See for yourself. Camille is calmer now, but I think Hanna's shoving something a lot stronger than valerian into her. And Dex . . .'

Dex stares into space. His eyes are blank but his mouth hangs half-open and I know straightaway it's because he's drunk. I have to get really close before he notices I'm there and summons up a lopsided grin.

'My pal, Imogen,' he drawls, 'back in the bosom of the Factory family again. Weren't we the *lucky* ones to be chosen?'

I glance over at Ashleigh who raises her eyebrows. 'Let's talk somewhere private,' I say to Dex, and try to take his arm. He shrugs me off.

'Why bother? We're all one community, right? *Sharing, caring . . .*'

'Come on,' I whisper. 'Camille is upset enough without you playing up, so think of her.' This time he cooperates, though he lists like a freighter on choppy waters.

I sit him on the chair in my studio and fill a large glass with tap water, urging him to finish it as we talk.

'Have you actually had a break from drinking at all since . . .'

'Since Bernice threw herself off the fucking roof?'

Last time I tried to help him, his coldness made me walk away. But things are different now Bernice is dead. I have to try harder. 'Dex, I know you were closer to her than I was. I understand why you're drinking. But talking might help.'

'Not you too. Ashleigh keeps trying to get us to *talk* as well.'

'I'm sure she means well,' I say.

Though I don't know if I *am* sure. She seems almost to get a kick out of an outpouring of grief. Or maybe I'm being unfair to her.

Dex finishes his water and I refill it, then sit down on the bed. With him here too, this space feels claustrophobic.

'You're going to leave the sinking ship, am I right?' he says.

I don't want to lie to him. 'I'm . . . thinking that may be for the best. Last night I stayed with a friend, to get my head straight.'

'I thought you'd gone for good.' His voice is sad, the cynicism gone.

'Lucas came to my school today. He said it might help for us to process it all together, so here I am. But medium-term, I don't think this place is right for me. How about you?'

He laughs, but it's bitter and humourless. 'I'm staying. I don't have much choice.'

'Come on, Dex. You could buy yourself out easily if you wanted to. That bike of yours would pay most of the deposit on a new place.'

'I can't buy myself out of the mess I'm in.'

'What mess? Tell me, I might be able to think of a way out.'

'Believe me, it's all dead ends. And anyway, I'm probably better off up here, with these other freaks and away from normal people. I'm dangerous, Immi.'

The air is still.

Another version of what happened two nights ago runs through my head. Bernice and Dex, on the roof together. Tussling. Pushing. *Falling.*

'What do you mean?' My voice is a whisper.

He shakes his head. 'I didn't hurt *Bernice*.'

'But you hurt someone else?'

'Yes. I did.' He stands up, still unsteady, too big for the space. 'Listen, Immi. Some people are past helping, all right? I'm not the person you think I am.'

'Dex.' I reach for his hand but he pulls away. 'Stay and talk.'

'Gotta save up my trauma for tonight.'

'What's tonight?'

'Lucas didn't tell you? Hanna has hired someone we can all talk to. A counsellor. *So* thoughtful. Even our grief is taken care of by the kind people behind the Factory.'

Hanna's set aside an area of the Retreat floor for the counsellor to use. Thankfully she's moved chairs in from Focus, so we don't have to spill our guts while sitting on beanbags.

'The counselling is not compulsory,' she explains when I ask her about it. 'But this is a terrible event for the whole community. It feels irresponsible not to offer the option.'

To my surprise, everyone – even Lucas and Zoum – have already signed up for a session. Their scribbled names put me under pressure to do the same.

When I go down at my allotted time, the guy, Julian – bearded, younger than my stereotyped idea of a therapist – invites me to sit down and take a moment before telling him how I'm feeling tonight.

Trapped. Scared.

'Sad,' is what I actually say. 'And confused about why Bernice did this. Guilty, too.'

He nods, leaving pauses for me to expand. That beard makes it hard for me to read his expression. When I stay silent, he says, 'Tell me about Bernice.'

I think aloud, describing her composure, her magnetism, that sense that the place revolved around her.

It does help to talk to a person who doesn't know me, and never knew Bernice. I find myself recounting that noise I heard, the fear as I ran and then those minutes holding Bernice, the lifeblood leaving her as I tried to speak comforting words . . .

'Not that it mattered what I said. She was already gone.'

'You don't know for certain,' Julian tells me. 'Hearing is one of the last senses to go. She may have heard you.'

'She wanted me to listen to her the day before. If I had, maybe she'd still be alive.'

'What makes you say that?'

'Before she . . . Before it happened, she was trying to talk to me about something important. I wasn't interested. This place, it can be *political*. Cliquey. I didn't want to get involved, so I turned my back on her.'

'You never had any sense of what she wanted to talk about?'

The age thing still seems too trivial to mention. But there were other things. 'There had been some incidents. Pranks.' As I describe them – the lights, the fire alarms, and the laying of the dead animal on her bed – they seem even more sinister than they did at the time.

'This sounds like a pattern of intimidation. How did Bernice respond?'

'She was very upset about the guinea pig. If only I'd listened . . .'

'No one could have known what she was about to do, Imogen. It's not about you, or about the Factory. She made her own choice to take her life, didn't she?'

Perhaps it's his body language, or the directness of the question, but I wonder, suddenly, whether this counselling has really been laid on for our sakes. What if it's more about protecting the interests of whoever owns this place?

'You're the expert. What do *you* think?'

He folds his hands in his lap. 'That's not why I'm here.'

'So why are you here? To convince us it was all her fault. Or head off any legal action?'

Julian frowns. 'I'm not a lawyer. But Bernice made a choice that no one could have predicted.'

'Well, that's all OK then, isn't it? No harm done. Uh, except that a girl is dead. Oh, and another resident was tried for harassment, almost lost everything. How lucky we are to live in this amazing community!'

'Imogen . . .' His voice is soothing.

But I'm already on my feet. There is no calming me. 'Don't worry. Tell Hanna to tell her bosses I won't make a fuss or go to the press. But they have to let me leave this toxic mess.'

I pass Hanna on the stairs. 'Immi. You are upset—'

'No shit. I'm also done. No more fake counselling. No more clean sheets or interference. Just stay away from me.'

41

Immi

One by one, they knock on my door.

Ashleigh, Dex, Zoum. Even Camille.

I lie in the half-dark, the breeze making the blind rattle against the window. Wait for the only person I've decided I *will* allow inside. The only one who might have the answers I need.

'Immi, it's me. Can we talk?'

Lucas looks surprised when I open the door to him.

'Talk away.' I know what *I* want to talk about, but first, I'll let him take the lead.

'Immi, the counsellor's gone. I told Hanna it's way too soon.'

I step aside so he can come in and I take the chair, so he's no choice but to perch awkwardly on the bed.

'What's it got to do with Hanna?'

'She's the house—'

'The housekeeper? More like the puppetmaster. Or have you been here too long to see she's pulling your strings?'

Lucas shakes his head. 'I didn't come here to talk about her.'

'No, because none of you question *anything*. You've been seduced by the luxury so you can't see that nothing about this place makes sense.'

'You didn't ask too many questions when you wanted to join us, did you?'

'No, but that was before someone *died*.'

I see a flicker of fear in his eyes. 'You know something isn't right here, don't you, Lucas?'

He lowers his head. 'I didn't come here to argue. I wanted you to know we've found something else out. About Bernice.'

'What?'

'She kept a notebook, sort of a diary. It gives an insight into what was in her mind. Because before this, it made no sense for her to die. She was loved, with this great career.'

'What had she written?'

'I haven't read it – the police have it now – but she was having terrible nightmares, brought about by guilt. She felt responsible for pushing Camille into the court case against Jamie. Plus Bernice had lied about her age, she was worried it'd get her thrown out.'

Was that really all it was about? 'So who found this notebook, Lucas?'

'It was—' He stops. 'Hanna. OK, yeah, it was Hanna, but that doesn't mean anything, does it?'

I say nothing.

He shakes his head. 'This isn't Hanna's fault. It was mine. I was Bernice's friend. Her *best* friend . . .' He gulps. I can tell he's trying not to cry. 'If she'd told me how she was feeling, I could have reassured her. Why didn't she tell me?'

He is sobbing now. Despite all the shitty things he's said and done, I can't bear it. I put my arms around him, and his weeping is so intense that my T-shirt is soon soaked. It's the kind of crying that burns itself out eventually – I know that much from my pupils, and my mother. When he does stop, I pour him a glass of water.

'Better?'

He sniffs. 'Sorry. I've been trying to keep it together out there for Camille's sake. She had such a shit childhood. Bernice was like a mother to her, as well as a friend.'

'It's bound to have hit the two of you the hardest.'

'Yeah. Though the way Ashleigh is behaving, you'd think *she* was Bernice's closest friend. Such a fucking attention-seeker.'

This is more like the Lucas I know and loathe. It makes me feel less guilty about pushing him. 'Did Hanna find anything else? A suicide note?'

'Not as far as I know.'

'So . . . that might mean Bernice didn't plan it. Things just got too much for her in that moment, which means none of us could have seen it coming. Or prevented it.'

Lucas's eyes are a bright, brilliant blue now. 'You can't know that.' But his voice is pleading for reassurance.

'The only thing I did wonder,' I say carefully, 'is could she have found out about that night in the sauna? The thing with you and Camille and Dex?'

'The thing that *wasn't* a thing because it never actually went anywhere?' He shakes his head. 'No. And anyway, she was never jealous like that. She knew what I'm like. A bit, well—'

'Slutty?'

I regret my harshness, but he starts to laugh. 'Harsh but absolutely bang on. A weak-willed, charming slut. That's exactly how she'd have described me.'

His strange cackle of laughter stops abruptly. I've run out of comforting words but Lucas doesn't move. 'Could I sit with you here for a while, Immi? I don't feel I can go and pretend again yet.'

Vulnerability is my kryptonite: I can't say no. I still don't like him, or trust him, but right now, I see a grieving person who feels alone.

'I guess so.'

I unscrew the top of my bottle of vodka and pour a good glug into both our empty water glasses. Eventually it's dark outside and we lie down together, side by side – not friends, definitely not lovers, but not quite as lonely as we would be sleeping alone.

42

Wednesday 6 June

Immi

I hardly sleep at all, but Lucas does: so deeply that it's hard to wake him when we need to get up.

'Lucas, it's almost seven o'clock.'

He blinks, as though he has no idea where he is, or who I am. When he realises, he frowns. 'We didn't . . .?'

'Definitely not. But you need to go back to Lima, so the others don't see you spent the night here and get the wrong idea.'

For a moment he looks rueful. 'Sure. You're right – nobody needs to know. And I'm sorry for taking advantage.'

At work, Fatima is obsessed with Lucas after his visit – if he's single, if I fancy him, if he's as loaded as he looks.

If she knew what's really going on, she'd stop. But it feels too private to share the suicide beyond the Factory. *Keep it in the family.*

I begin to count the minutes till I'll be back in Bermondsey, because at least there I don't have to pretend. My night with Lucas – his vulnerability and the news of Bernice's notebook –

has made me realise this roller coaster of emotions is part of the process of grieving.

Of course we feel guilty. But it doesn't mean we *could* have changed anything . . .

School finishes early this afternoon: our INSET session has been cancelled because the trainer has flu, so the head gives us the nod to 'do some *independent* learning – whether that involves going to the cinema or a walk in the park, you've all earned it'.

I go home to get my swimming costume – I haven't been swimming for months and it might clear my head.

When I let myself into the Factory, it's deathly silent at first. But as I climb the stairs, I hear low voices. And then something else that makes me catch my breath.

Laughter.

There's no law that says we can never smile or laugh again because Bernice died. Even so, it feels too soon.

Part of me wants to catch whoever it is, to shame them a little, so I creep up the stairs as quietly as I can. The laughter's coming from Retreat so I stop out of sight.

'. . . Told you I'd get there in the end.' *Lucas.* That laugh is unique.

Someone else laughs, a woman.

'You are a very bad man, Lucas.'

Camille? She sounds completely calm.

My instinct is to run up the last few steps and ask them what the fuck they're playing at.

But I make myself wait.

'You mustn't say a bloody word to her, though, Cam. Not even a hint.'

'What is that thing people always say when someone dies? It's what Bernice would have wanted. But now that's out of the way, will you fuck her again?'

'I doubt it.'

'That's not like you.'

There's a pause before Lucas speaks again. 'Immi's sweet and she tried very hard, but I'm a one-woman man at heart. You *know* that.'

It takes me a few seconds to process what he's saying. Suddenly it falls into place, like the clunk of a coin in a vending machine.

Lucas has told her he's slept with me.

Not just spent the night with me, him falling asleep lying on my bed, me allowing it because I thought it was a comfort to both of us.

Camille thinks we had sex.

Why would he tell her that? And why the hell would they think Bernice would approve?

I hear their footsteps above me. And little gasps. They're kissing. Do I go up, let them know I am here? My own breathing sounds so loud to me, and I am astonished they don't realise I'm only a few metres away.

'You seem tired,' Camille says.

'Heavy night,' he says and laughs again.

One last kiss and they separate: Camille's delicate steps heading towards Paris, and Lucas's movements more assertive as he heads upstairs to the Play floor.

I duck out of the way and wait for their two studio doors to slam shut. The strength has left my legs and I slump down onto the metal treads of the staircase.

Everything about the Factory is rotten. If I stay any longer, can I be sure I won't be just as bad as them?

Eventually I haul myself up and leave the building. I go to the Thames and walk for miles, thinking through what to do next.

I don't want to stay at the Factory a second longer than I have to, but I need my deposit back to start again. I text Sarah, asking her to take another look at the contract. She tries to call me, but when I listen back to the message, her concern is tainted by irritation because I keep changing my mind.

'I *will* try, Immi, but I can't promise. It would have been so much easier if you'd decided to leave before you signed on the dotted line.'

She's right. But Hanna and the Dyers kept their worst qualities hidden for four weeks. Or at least, I chose not to see them.

Now, all the toxicity has been exposed. I think of myself as a resilient person, but so was Bernice. How can I be sure I won't be driven to the edge by this place?

Maybe it's even time to admit that going home to Mum could be my only option. It feels like defeat after the fighting I've done to stay in London, but it might not be as bad as I fear. Mum *has* been more stable lately, and I haven't had to send a top-up for weeks . When I am in a positive frame of mind, I let myself believe that maybe, one day, she'll take the first step outside the front door. Perhaps, after a week, dare to go beyond the garden gate.

And eventually, find her way back into the world.

I want to call her, to try sharing how I'm feeling. But I don't want to stress her out because she'll worry if I phone her.

Shit.

I haven't spoken to her at all this week. I postponed the call on Saturday because of the open day. And then Bernice died and I forgot about everything except that.

What if Mum has hurt herself, collapsed or worse? I am a shit daughter. I don't deserve her . . .

I dial her number. It rings twice, four times, six times. Shit, *shit*. Is she lying on the floor, her hip broken or—

'I don't want to talk to you, Imogen.'

I take a breath, force a smile into my voice. 'Oh Mum, I'm so sorry. I did mean to call you but it's been a manic week at work and—'

'Didn't you hear me? I don't want to talk to you. Because it's all lies!'

'Mum?'

'I've never been so betrayed in my life.'

On autopilot, I stand up and walk away from the South Bank towards a quieter spot, in the shadow of two glass office buildings. I don't even know what betrayal she's talking about yet – I have told her so many lies.

'Mum, tell me what I'm supposed to have done.'

'When you didn't call me on Saturday, I tried you but I couldn't get through on your mobile phone. So I called Alastair instead.'

My strength ebbs away. I suppose I'm lucky I've been able to keep it from her for nearly four months, but I always knew I was putting off the inevitable.

'Mum, I can explain—' Though even as I start the sentence, I don't know how.

'Don't waste your breath. Why should I ever listen to you again? After everything I've done . . .'

And she rants and rails about how terrible all of this is for her, how humiliated she felt when Al quietly explained that I no longer live with him and haven't since February, how ashamed she is.

It won't ever cross her mind to wonder why I felt I had to lie to her for so long.

Week 7: *In memoriam*

This has been the Factory's toughest week.

Only a week ago, our beloved friend Bernice was still with us. You may have guessed that she took the lead in creating these messages, to spread the philosophy of community that meant so much to her.

We may never know what led her to take her own life but we will always miss her.

We can't put a time limit on grief. But what we must do is support each other, and also begin to consider what Bernice's legacy might be. There must be a reason she came to the Factory when she did, establishing so many of the positive things that make it – still – an inspiring place to be.

So when things seem hopeless, talk to your neighbours, and when you feel sad, ask yourself: is this what Bernice would have wanted? How can we carry on what she began?

43

Sunday 10 June

Immi

The app wakes me, and as I read the new message, I wonder who wrote it, now Bernice is gone.

Ashleigh, maybe, trying to pour oil on troubled waters. Or could it be Hanna, trying to hold the Factory together for her employers?

It doesn't change anything for me. As soon as Sarah finds a way for me to break my contract without losing my money, I will be gone. But right now, it's hard to forget that this time last Sunday, Bernice and I were doing yoga on the terrace. I climb out of bed to look through my window at the skyline, rose pink in the morning sun. Crewe never looks like this.

How could she have wanted to leave the world behind?

Down on Tanner's Walk, the café shutters are rising with a screech of metal and it makes me crave a coffee to wake me up. I'm just turning away when something makes me freeze.

Movement.

In Bernice's old room.

Her window blind is half raised, so perhaps it's just a breeze . . .

No. That's a *person*.

Or a *ghost*?

I don't believe in ghosts. Is it Hanna moving around in there?

I creep out of my studio, ready for when the person emerges. They'll have to come past me to go back downstairs.

As I tiptoe across the floor, the *thump, thump, thump* of blood in my ears is the loudest thing by far. I realise I don't have my knife on me – I left it under my pillow. But there's a small paring knife on the worktop, the one we use to slice the lemons and limes for gin and tonic. I pick it up.

Adrenalin makes us see danger where it doesn't even exist. But I've made that mistake before, convincing myself I was safe when I was anything *but.*

Is it possible Bernice *didn't* kill herself? An image of the evidence bag I found in my empty studio pops into my head. It's not the first time the police have had to investigate a crime here.

But that was Jamie and he doesn't have anything to do with this.

Unless . . . *Could the person in Bernice's room be Jamie?*

I slow my breathing. I have an uninterrupted view of Bernice's door from here and I can see it opening, slowly.

My right hand closes around the little knife and I can feel the indentations in the handle. It's one of those Japanese designer knives and it cuts through lemons as though they're nothing but air.

I stare at the door frame.

Whoever this is has some explaining to do.

A man steps out.

Zoum.

I can't believe it.

He pulls the door shut behind him. As he turns, he sees me, and freezes. *Fight or flight?*

Except flight is not an option because there is nowhere for him to go.

He's carrying a sports holdall, and it's so incongruous – I've never seen Zoum do any kind of exercise – I almost want to giggle.

Fear again. Does strange things to us.

He doesn't move for ten, maybe fifteen seconds, before starting to walk towards me.

'Stop. Don't get any closer to me.'

'Immi, it's not what you think,' he whispers.

What does he imagine I am thinking right now? That he's a thief? A peeping Tom? A *killer*? Of all the people here, I trust him the most. Or at least, I did.

'What the hell were you doing in there?' My voice is low, so as not to wake Lucas in Lima only a few metres away.

He opens his mouth, then closes it again. Perhaps he can't think of a credible explanation. 'Not here,' he says. 'My studio.'

Is it safe to go with him? I stay at a distance as I follow him down the stairs. As Zoum buzzes his way into New Delhi with his phone, I wonder how the hell he got into Bernice's studio? And why he needed to?

He holds the door open for me. As I step halfway inside, my brain tells me *not* to do this. I stay close to the door so I can run.

Zoum's studio is full of tech devices and paperwork: less of a bedroom, more of a hacker's lair. He drops the sports bag and kicks it halfway under the bed. 'What were you doing in Bernice's room?'

Zoum sighs. 'It is not what you think,' he repeats. His green eyes are wide, the long lashes making him look more like Bambi than a burglar.

'And what is it I'm meant to think? Because it looked fucking suspicious.'

'I was cleaning. Look, here is the proof.' He reaches down under the bed, pulls out the holdall and unzips it. When I look inside, it's full of sprays and wipes.

'But why? And how did you get into her studio?'

He says nothing.

'Let me make this simple,' I say. 'You tell me, or I tell Hanna.'

Zoum's eyes widen. 'All right. But you have to promise not to tell the others. You are the only person here I actually trust.'

I weigh it up: I could agree now but still tell Hanna if I need to. No one else around here seems to keep their promises.

'If I believe you, I'll keep quiet.'

He nods and sits down on the bed. 'You will not like it, but I promise you it is not as creepy as it sounds.'

Great start, Zoum.

'I *was* cleaning. I have been waiting for a time when the whole Factory was empty. But Camille and Dex have hardly left the building since Bernice died so I decided to do it when everyone was asleep.'

'Hanna has already cleaned the place. She even found some kind of notebook.'

'Says who?'

Lucas. Unless it was another lie. 'Just something I heard. But why would you bother to clean her room?'

'Because . . . my problem is, I *have* been in Bernice's room before. And I did not want there to be any trace of me left, in case there are further investigations.'

'Why would there be? She killed herself, case closed.'

Zoum says nothing.

'OK, so why would there be traces of you in her studio, Zoum? I never saw you visit her. And you and Bernice weren't friends.'

'At first we were, when we first moved in, but the more she took control, the more the cliques developed, the more I tried to disrupt it.'

'How?'

'Just by unsettling them a little. I would move a book, or a pair of shoes. Leave a light on when they had turned it off.'

I stare at him. 'You've been breaking in? How?'

'The security system Hanna bangs on about? It is easily hack-able. Took me a day, and a few bitcoin, but I worked out how to get into any studio, with zero trace of me being there.'

'Have you been in my room too?'

'No. I only ever wanted to freak out our self-appointed royal family. And only then to do pranks.'

Pranks. 'Oh God. It *was* you that let Edward and Bella go. It was you that . . .' The image of the dead animal splayed out on Bernice's bed makes me want to vomit. 'You drove her to this.'

He shakes his head. 'No. I never touched the animals. By the time you guys came, I had pulled back from playing tricks. Things were already nasty enough.'

'Because of what Jamie did?'

Zoum nods.

'You took his side, didn't you?'

'Not entirely. None of us will ever know what happened that night, except him and Camille. But I cannot honestly say I think either of them were entirely blameless.'

I stare at him. 'If this is the bit where you dare to say a woman was asking for it, then I'm going.'

'No. It's not that.' He sighs more deeply than before. 'If you really want to know why the committee needed someone to stop them, I *will* tell you. But there is no going back, once you hear it.'

'I want to leave the Factory anyway. Tell me or I'll tell Hanna what you've been doing.'

He takes two steps towards his desk – the same one I have in my studio. I notice that the paintwork has been distressed in exactly the same spots. I believed mine was old but it was obviously churned out in some faraway factory. Another fake.

Zoum leafs through paperwork that's been stuffed into the left-hand drawer. For a moment, I wonder if he's about to pull out a weapon. I tighten my grip on the knife in my pocket.

Instead he hands me an A4 sheet.

'Read it. But it is going to change everything.'

44

Immi

The sheet is a photocopy of a betting slip: I wouldn't know that except for the fact it actually says 'Betting Slip' at the top, with space underneath for the details.

The handwriting that fills the space is looped and unusual, but before I can work out whose it is, I am gasping at the words.

I bet my stake that Dex will screw Immi within four weeks.

I read it twice, trying to understand what it means. At the bottom, in the space for the stake, someone has written, *£1.00.* Finally, there's a date, in the same handwriting.

24 April 2018.

'That's the date of my interview for my place here . . .' I shake my head. 'Zoum, what the hell *is* this? Where did you get it?'

'In Bernice's room. I had gone in to move a few things around, to spook her, she was being insufferable that week. I found her stash in her bedside cabinet.'

'Stash? There's more than one of these notes?'

'Yes. If it makes you feel any better, you're not being singled out. I photographed them on my phone, so she'd never know.'

'Show me the others.'

He takes a bundle out of the drawer and hands it to me: there are maybe ten pages in all.

The next sheet I look at has different writing. I recognise it as Lucas's: loose and sprawling like a lascivious uncle's.

I bet my stake that Ashleigh puts on weight AND gets ugly, UGLY drunk within her first 7 days.

It's dated January 2017. I look at the next page.

I bet my stake that I can work out what Kira's worst fear is, and have fun with it, within three months.

Bernice's handwriting. The perfect o's and right-angled T-bars seem poignant now she's dead. But the words are sinister. I think Kira was the nurse who lived in Dex's studio before she went home to Australia. Maybe *this* is why she left.

I look back up at Zoum. 'What do they mean?'

'I believe they mean that Bernice, Lucas and Camille have been betting in a game the rest of us did not even know was taking place.'

'That's ridiculous . . .' I say, yet at the same time, there's something about it that rings true.

'Read them all. See if you can find any other explanation.'

I do what he suggests. They date back over eighteen months and each new arrival at the Factory seems to have three slips devoted to them, one from each member of the interviewing committee.

All the bets seem to focus on exploiting people's vulnerabilities: sex, booze, drugs, shyness.

There are two left. The first is in Lucas's writing, dated June last year.

I bet Cam can drive poor Jamie mad with unrequited love!

My mouth goes dry. 'Seriously?'

Zoum nods. 'That one is from the day Jamie moved in. I found it in December, a couple of weeks after he'd been charged with harassment.'

'Have you confronted them?'

'I thought about it very carefully. But what if they plotted against me instead? This way, I could keep an eye on them.'

'You're *scared* of them.'

'After what happened to Jamie, wouldn't you be?'

I look down at the last sheet. Bernice's writing again. In deliberate copperplate, she's written:

I bet Lucas can get Immi into bed before midsummer's night.

Today is 10 June. He did 'get me into bed', with almost a fortnight to spare . . .

I drop the papers. I'm going to wake Lucas up right now and tell him what a wanker he is.

But Zoum has pushed in front of me to block my way. 'You can't talk to them, Immi.'

'Yes I bloody can. You're fine, aren't you? I don't see *you* named on any of these bets.'

'Because I joined at the same time as Bernice and Camille. They must have invented the game afterwards. But think it through. This might be the missing link in explaining what Bernice did. If you tell them we know, they'll try to cover it up.'

I hesitate. 'You think the games might have driven her to end her life?'

'None of us can be sure. But the police might be able to find out.'

Part of me knows he's right. Yet the game is still being played, even with Bernice dead. That's why Lucas told Camille he slept with me – for the sake of a fucking bet!

Last time someone took what they wanted from me, it damaged me forever. There's no way I'll be used all over again.

I shove Zoum out of the way, surprised at my own strength as he falls to the floor, wrench the door open and run up the stairs to Lucas's room.

I hammer on his door. It occurs to me as I do that the knife's still in the pocket of my shorts. Maybe I'll bloody well use it. Show him how it feels to be powerless.

There's a moaning sound from the other side of the door, a protest against being woken. Then: 'All right, I'm coming.'

I say nothing. I want it to be a *surprise*.

When Lucas opens the door, he still looks half asleep. Good.

'You're a lying bastard, aren't you, Lucas?'

He frowns. 'Huh?'

'All that, *Oh, I'm so sad about my poor dead friend, I need you to comfort me* stuff was an act. You didn't give a shit about Bernice.'

'Hang on, Immi, you can't say that—'

'I can say what I like. You *used* me.' In my head, I am not seeing Lucas, but another man who did the same.

I am remembering a hotel bed, a year ago. A man is on top of me, one hand holding a pillow over my face, the other clutching my throat. My lungs burn and my head boils and I am paralysed with terror till the world goes black . . . and I come round and black out, over and over again, with no power to stop the cycle. Half a dozen little deaths.

I blink away the flashbacks, take a deep breath. Behind Lucas, Camille is getting out of his bed, completely naked, rubbing her eyes as she emerges from groggy sleep and comes to the doorway.

And someone is at my side, too. Zoum has followed me, and his eyes plead with me: *Don't tell.*

A tiny doubt grows. Knowledge is power. Can I overcome my rage and use this information to get what I want?

'I heard you both talking yesterday. Camille, I don't know why Lucas lied to you, but we didn't have sex. He spent the night in my room because he pretended to be upset about Bernice and I took pity on him . . .'

Camille frowns. Somehow it makes her look even prettier. 'Is this true?'

'I . . .' Lucas looks at me, then her, then back to me. 'I *was* upset.'

'We all are. So why lie to Camille about us? I heard what you said, something about how Bernice would have been pleased we'd had sex.'

Lucas glances at Camille. 'It was . . . stupid.' His eyes dart up to the left. Kids do the same when they're trying to invent excuses for some minor transgression. 'After the sauna stuff went wrong, I was trying to prove I was attractive . . .'

Before he can finish, Camille sighs and goes back into the room. Behind Lucas, I can see her pulling on a T-shirt.

'But why the hell would you think Bernice would be *pleased*?'

'I can't explain it. All I can do is apologise, Immi. I took advantage of your kindness. If there's anything I can do to put it right . . .'

Stop lying, I think. But I know too well that once you start lying, it's almost impossible to stop.

Camille pushes past me without a word to any of us. Lucas stares at the floor.

'Just keep away from me, Lucas, OK?' I say as I turn away and his door closes behind him.

Zoum walks with me to Kyoto. 'Thanks for not saying anything,' he says, as I buzz my way in.

I'm exhausted suddenly, even though the whole day still lies ahead. 'I didn't bloody do it for you, Zoum. I haven't forgotten that you only found all this out because you're some kind of peeping Tom.'

I run the shower at maximum force and undress. As the water pounds against my head, I try to make sense of it all. Can I find a way to use their sick game to help me escape from the Factory? Or, more accurately, escape from the people inside it.

45

Wednesday 13 June

Dex

No one bothers to monitor my drinking now.

Suits me just fine. I start my day with a hair of the dog, and continue self-medicating till it sends me to sleep. The days merge into one. I think it's Tuesday but it could be Wednesday. Not like I have anywhere to go.

'Dex?'

Ashleigh, on the other side of my door, is the only one who hasn't given up on me. Even there, there's an element of performance to her kindness, as though she's trying to pass her Duke of Edinburgh's Award.

'Forcing someone to do yoga is bad karma, Ashleigh.'

'It's not that. Bernice's parents are coming to visit, they haven't been able to face it before now. We thought we'd give them a card with some messages about what she meant to us.'

That's really going to help. A picture of flowers, and a bunch of sentimental bullshit from people who let their daughter down.

But I drag myself off the bed, cupping my palms over my mouth to check halitosis levels. Average. I can live with that.

When I open the door, Ashleigh smiles with relief, but the smile doesn't reach the dark shadows under her eyes. 'You look knackered,' I tell her.

'Cheers, Dex. I don't look anywhere near as shit as you though.'

I take the open card, holding it up against the wall to sign. There are a few scrawled messages already. Camille has written: *Bernice was my friend, my supporter and my most adored of neighbours.*

Typical of an actor to think about a dead woman only in relation to herself. But perhaps what happened to Camille has made her that way. It's hard to picture her as anything but a victim now I've seen that horrible video Jamie made.

The rest of the messages are platitudes.

I close my eyes.

Remember *her.* The halo of red hair, the fear in her eyes, the moment of realisation.

I am not a friend, I am a killer.

'If you're struggling, just write that you're sorry. That still helps,' Ashleigh is saying, and I wonder what *she* knows about grief. I remember Bernice hinting she had some kind of mad brother.

I write: *I'm so sorry for your loss, Bernice was a force of nature.* But even that's open to interpretation. Too late to cross it out. I hand the card back. On the front, there are birds swooping across a blue sky. Not flowers, but still a terribly composed stock shot photo.

Like that matters.

'What time are they coming?'

Ashleigh shakes her head. 'Sometime this afternoon. Before most people get home from work. Do you want to know so you can come out and talk to them?'

'No thanks. I wouldn't even know where to begin.'

I'm making myself a sandwich when I hear the grind of the lift moving up. Hanna's voice drifts through the bars followed by a man's muted replies. I don't want to see Bernice's parents, but short of hiding under the kitchen counters, I can't avoid it now.

As they step out of the lift, Hanna's eyes lock on to mine, as though she knows what a coward I am.

'This is where Bernice would cook with her friends. Dexter here is one of the newer residents. I'm sure he'd be very happy to talk to you about their friendship.'

Her mother and father are small. Bernice was too, physically, but the power of her personality meant I saw her as a giant.

I wipe my hands on the towel and move out from behind the counter, reaching out to shake her father's hand. He recoils slightly, but goes through with it, out of politeness. Maybe he's racist.

Or maybe he sees me for what I am. A killer.

His wife keeps her hands firmly in the pockets of her beige jacket. It's been raining outside and her shoulders are wet; she smells of dog.

'Mr and Mrs Booth. I'm so sorry about what happened to Bernice.'

They look down, as though this is the most embarrassing thing that's ever happened to them.

I have this urge to fill the silence. 'I hadn't known her long. But she was . . .' I am about to repeat that force of nature bullshit I wrote in the card. What else can I say? 'It was a terrible shock, to all of us. She didn't seem the kind of person . . .'

Her mother's head snaps up towards me. Her face isn't embarrassed. It's furious. 'The kind of person to kill herself? That's because she wasn't. At least, not before she moved in here.'

'Helen . . .' Mr Booth puts his hand on her arm, but he sounds too weary to stop her. Now I look more closely, they're younger than I thought: mid-fifties. Younger than my own parents. But shock and grief have turned their skin ashen and made their bodies slump.

'What happened to her?' Helen Booth asks me, her amber eyes exactly like her daughter's. 'Why did she die?'

'I don't know.' That much *is* true.

'From the first founding of the Factory, there has been a mental health support system,' Hanna says. 'Co-listening. Mindfulness sessions, a range of—'

'A fat lot of good they turned out to be.' Helen spins round to face her. 'This is a glorified house share. Why in God's name would you go to that trouble unless you knew the whole set-up was dodgy?'

'It . . .' Hanna hesitates. 'The founders . . . The building owners have an interest in the welfare of young people. The model of communal living was imagined as a kind of urban . . . small village.'

'Reckon it's more like bloody *Big Brother*.'

Hanna shakes her head. 'No. The owners have known loss themselves. This whole idea was to give young people a safe space.'

Mrs Booth scoffs. 'Safe? This isn't the end of this, you know. We're not just coming here, picking up her things and being sent away to mourn. You tell those owners that, will you?'

Hanna nods. 'I will pass that on.'

'Come on, Hel.' Mr Booth tries again to take his wife's hand and this time she lets him and I realise she's started to cry. 'Hanna,

I don't think we want to meet any more of her friends – no offence, Dexter – we just want to see her studio room and then we'll be out of here.'

'Of course. Please follow me.'

And as Hanna leads them up towards the Play floor, she glances back at me over their shoulders. I can't read her expression, but I think it's fear.

After seeing how devastated the Booths are, I can't stop thinking about my own parents. The lie I told them about going on assignment somewhere dangerous was the only thing I could think of to explain being out of touch. But now it strikes me how selfish I've been, again. My mum will be checking the news from Pakistan constantly, imagining me kidnapped or held hostage or worse . . .

I turn my old phone back on. When was the last time I did this? I don't think I've checked since Bernice died. I'm such a fucking loser as a son.

Dare I risk calling home rather than texting? I want to hear my mother's voice. Perhaps I could tell her I am somewhere safe now – India or Thailand – but am going to do some independent travel. Keep it vague so no one would be able to track me down. It's more lies, of course, but at least they might be kinder ones?

The buzz of multiple messages is a bad sign. What if something has happened to them, or one of my sisters? Fuck. I can't keep living this way.

I start scrolling through, my fingers fumbling against the touchscreen. I know all the messages must be from Mum or my sisters, because I blocked everyone else.

Hi D, good to hear you're making progress with the assignment. Stay safe, whatever you do. We love you and want you home in one piece, Mum.

That was sent on Sunday, just after I sent my last text to her. There's another similar message from her on Monday but it's on Tuesday when the texts suddenly change tone.

Someone claiming to be your old flatmate has turned up at the house wanting to talk to you. If you get this, can you call asap?

And then, an hour or so later:

She's gone now but she said she needs to get in touch urgently. She mentioned the police, and someone dying? What's going on? Please tell me. If you're in trouble, we can sort it out. Mum xxx

Today she's sent one more:

We're going out of our mind. Please get in touch. Your dad thinks we should call the police ourselves.

And the last message comes from Selma, my eldest sister, who always puts herself in charge of any crisis.

Little bruv, I don't know where you are but I am pretty sure it's not Pakistan. We can only help you if you get in touch. If you won't do it for your own sake, do it for Mum.

Immediately, I text Selma back.

> I am OK. Promise. Things tricky but I will explain soon. Tell Mum and Dad not to worry and not to waste the police's time. Love D

I turn the phone off again the second the message is sent, but already I am panicking. Could the police triangulate my location from that single text?

And what the fuck do I do now?

I wonder who it was from my old life who came looking for me. And why *now*? Unless it was a detective pretending to be someone I lived with.

I have made this happen by burying my head in the sand, thinking everything would calm down.

Now there is nothing to do but escape all over again. Unless I actually *want* to be caught and ruin the lives of the people I love.

46

Dex

On my new phone, I call to book a night in a B&B out east, pleading with them to let me pay in cash. But even that puts me on edge. What if the police have been monitoring my ATM withdrawals?

No. They'd have found me by now if that was the case. I suppose they have dozens of murders to investigate at any one time.

I leave my studio in the middle of packing to grab food from the communal stores – some for now, some for later. Everything I do has to minimise the risk of being caught on CCTV, and that includes takeaways.

'You! It was you, wasn't it?'

Something is falling towards me, down the stairwell. It hits me on the cheek, then bounces down the metal steps, clanging as it goes.

I look up. 'What the fuck . . . ?'

A weird, cackling laugh travels down the stairs. Lucas is standing on the flight between the Retreat and Play floors. In one hand, he has a bottle of gin, and in the other, two lemons. He throws one at me, as though he's hurling a grenade. I duck out of the way just in time.

'You nicked the paring knife.' He's raving. Is it drink or drugs or both?

'I don't have time for this shit,' I tell him, and I'm about to walk past when I see him totter on the edge of one of the steps. Instinctively, I run up the stairs to try to steer him to a safer spot on Play. 'Hey, Lucas, watch out.'

There's a glassiness in his eyes that's caused by something more than booze. He's been on the coke again. Loads of it. I'm a little afraid of the guy. Or what the drug has done to him.

He moves back up the steps, to the safer territory of the Play floor. 'Fuck off!'

I back away, arms raised. 'OK.'

'We were all right till you came. You and fucking Immi. And now you've nicked the knife too and I can't even make myself a drink.'

'I haven't taken anything, but I could get you another knife from the kitchen?' Though maybe that's a stupid offer: he does not look safe to have a blade right now.

'I don't want a knife. I want Bernice back. I want everything to be the same . . .'

Lucas might be a tosser, but he's also lost. I understand how that feels. 'I know it's terrible, but there's nothing you could have done to stop her.'

'Don't lie. I'm not an idiot. And what if it *wasn't* suicide?'

'Hold on, Lucas. You think someone else could have been involved?'

He stares at me. 'I don't know anymore. There's meant to be this notebook full of stuff about her feeling suicidal, but Hanna reckons the police have got it now. And she was never a weak person. She was strong.'

'She was . . .' Except I remember the conversation we had in the vaping pod, where she talked about her life before the

Factory: marrying a man with mental health issues. Could that have affected her too? 'The thing is, none of us can ever know what's going on in someone else's head.'

Lucas shakes his head. 'I *knew* her. Something went wrong. Maybe someone played her suggestions in her sleep, telling her to kill herself. Or even pushed her off the roof.'

'Lucas, mate, try to calm down—'

'I'm not your fucking mate. It could have been *you* who did that to her!'

There's nothing I can do while he's in this state. And I have enough to think about. Lucas is not *my* problem. The Factory screwed him over – they can fix him.

As I walk back down to Nourish, Lucas keeps muttering to himself. A glass that was teetering on the edge of the honesty bar falls off and smashes and he rages again, cursing me and life and himself.

Surely if they are in the Factory, Ashleigh or Zoum must have heard him? Maybe they're feeling the same as me: it's every man for himself.

Except, I can't let it go. Halfway down, on Retreat, I decide to knock on Camille's door; she's the only person here who has his back now Bernice is gone. He might be a dipshit, but he's in mourning. That gives him a little more leeway, as far as I'm concerned.

And it's gonna play on my mind if I leave him like that.

'Camille, are you there?'

I wait for her to respond.

'Yes.'

'It's about Lucas. He's upstairs and he seems kinda upset and there's a glass smashed and I think he'll only listen to you.'

Silence.

'Camille, did you get that?'

'Lucas is an adult. Tomorrow he'll be OK again, until the next time he does coke. There is nothing any of us can do.'

'But—' I stop. Maybe she's right. Cokeheads like Lucas don't listen, especially not when they're in that state. And Camille has her own grief to deal with.

Lucas is just another taker. He doesn't deserve anyone's sympathy. People like that deserve what they get.

I walk away. Inside my studio, I zip up my suitcase: it's hardly been opened since I arrived more than six weeks ago. How could I have wasted all that precious time?

Maybe because this place gets under your skin without you realising. Makes you drop your guard so you don't see the danger till it's so close you can touch it.

47

Thursday 14 June

Immi

At first, the sound is part of my dream.

I lie in a meadow, the sunshine on my face, taking the deepest breaths. But the feeling of calm is jarred by a sense that there's something important I've forgotten.

The fire alarm starts, sounding all wrong in this empty field. The sun disappears and . . . I am back at the Factory, lying in my bed in the dark. The alarm is so loud it feels like it's coming from inside my body.

'*The fire alarm has been triggered. Please evacuate the building, using the stairs only.*'

The disembodied voice reminds me of Bernice again. As she's now dead, it sounds even more sinister than the first time.

I check my phone: 03:19.

Another false alarm?

I can't take the chance. I jump out of bed, pull on shorts and fleece, push my feet into trainers, take my phone, my purse, my laptop, and cast around for anything else that I don't want to lose.

Finally I slip my knife into my pocket.

When I emerge from my studio, the alarm hurts my ears even more. I get to the stairwell and I can see my neighbours below, moving down with purposeful speed.

Hanna appears from the terrace. Why is she up here, not downstairs? She's in a cotton nightshirt, her sturdy legs bare and her small feet in moccasins. 'Out. Go immediately down to the street.'

'Can't I go onto the roof terrace?'

She shakes her head. 'There's no safe way off to escape from the terrace. Go now, please.'

I flinch as I remember how Bernice's body was broken by the fall. 'Hanna, is this a drill? Because I can't smell any smoke.'

'It is not a drill. You need to leave.'

I can see Lucas's door is open. 'Has Lucas already gone?'

Hanna says nothing.

Typical of Lucas to get out without trying to save anyone else.

'You must go now, the emergency services are coming. Walk, do *not* run, and wait with the others.'

Something in her tone makes me do as I'm told. As I go down the stairs, the sound of the sirens gets louder but there's no sign of any fire. By the time I'm on the street, blue lights dapple the cobbles as a fire engine stops outside.

Goosebumps spread across my skin from the cold and the delayed shock of being woken this way. I head towards the others: Ashleigh in a onesie, Zoum in boxers, Camille in a wine-red kimono that hugs her tiny frame. There don't seem to be enough of us. I do a mental headcount, and the chill deepens.

'Have you seen Dex?' I ask.

Ashleigh shakes her head. 'No. I can't see Lucas either.'

We rush towards the entrance of the Factory. Hanna has come down now and when she sees us she blocks the doorway. 'You can't come back in.'

'We don't want to, but two people are missing,' Ashleigh says, her voice shrill.

'Two?' Hanna repeats, frowning.

'Dex and Lucas,' I say.

'Out of the way, please.'

I turn to see two firefighters behind me.

'What do we have?' the woman firefighter asks. 'Anyone inside?'

Hanna glances at us and moves further into the entrance lobby and the two firefighters follow. 'Yes,' she says, her voice low but still audible. 'But they are not affected by fire. Are the police on their way?'

I don't hear the rest, but soon we're being moved back along Tanner's Walk and more members of the fire crew are going into the building.

As they head up, I dial Dex's number.

It rings out and out before the briefest voicemail message is triggered: *It's me, I'm busy, I'll call you later.*

'Dex, are you upstairs? If you're out running or something, call me back, please.' I hesitate before adding, 'I'm worried about you.'

Ashleigh frowns. 'No answer?'

'Nothing.'

She approaches Camille, who is shivering, her arms folded across her chest. 'You should phone Lucas.'

'I left my mobile in my studio.'

'Borrow mine.' I hand it over.

She hesitates for a moment. But then she enters his number and lifts the phone to her ear.

Everyone falls silent. I hear the ringing at the other end.

Then realise I can hear it in stereo. The faintest echo is coming from somewhere close by.

From inside the building.

'Hello?' Camille says and I realise that however much I loathe Lucas and what he's done, I still want him to be OK.

Instantly I feel silly; of course he's OK. He's one of those people who can charm his way out of anything.

Camille is staring at the phone. Her face looks eerie in the light from the screen.

'What's the matter?' Ashleigh asks.

Camille hands the phone to me.

'Hello?' I say, expecting Lucas's mocking laughter at the other end.

'Is that Imogen?' A female voice. Hanna? Except she sounds different. Hesitant. 'Ring off now. We will be down again soon.'

I see another firefighter heading towards the Factory, carrying a red rucksack and a large green bag marked 'Defibrillator'.

He disappears into the building without another word.

I turn away from Camille and the others and whisper down the phone. 'Is it Lucas? Is he hurt?'

I hear Hanna inhale. 'He is not currently breathing.'

As I try to work out what to say, the phone buzzes against my face as a message comes in. When I look at the screen, it's Dex.

I left last night for a new place. I couldn't stay. It's bad for me. Maybe one day I'll be able to explain. I'm sorry I didn't say goodbye.

48

Immi

It's different this time, when the police arrive.

The team is bigger, the work more focused, the attitude to those of us who are left less sympathetic.

As dawn breaks, we're escorted from the street into the basement office, with a policeman to keep an eye on us all. *Standing guard* sounds dramatic but I think that's exactly what he's here to do.

'Are we allowed to talk to each other?' Ashleigh asks.

The officer looks uncertain. 'Maybe not about what's just happened,' he suggests, even though it's the only thing we want to talk about.

The others know that an ambulance crew entered the building ahead of us an hour ago. Because I spoke to Hanna on my mobile, I am the only one to know Lucas was still inside and had stopped breathing. Surely if they'd managed to resuscitate him, he'd have been taken to hospital?

Instead, the sounds of frantic activity we heard through the window have been replaced by more muted noises. From the police dramas I've watched, I think they may be *preserving the scene*.

'Lucas is dead, isn't he?' Ashleigh says.

Nobody replies.

The policeman points at the kettle and boxes of tea on top of the fridge: Hanna's stash. 'I'm dying for a cuppa. Anyone fancy making a brew?'

Ashleigh volunteers. As she bustles about, my thoughts speed up. Hanna must have set off the fire alarm herself, but why? Did she find Lucas injured or unconscious? Perhaps he tried to kill himself, like Bernice did.

If she killed herself at all.

Everything has changed. However hard I try not to jump to conclusions, if two people from the Factory are dead, the police *must* be considering the possibility of murder.

I look up at Camille. Her fingers are clenched in her lap, knuckles white. Has it occurred to her that she might be the only member of the committee still alive?

The other unknown is Dex's disappearance. I tried calling again after his text, but the police have taken our phones now, so I don't know if he's responded.

A woman knocks and enters without waiting.

'We're going to work in order of rooms, starting at the top, so I'm looking for' – she looks down at a list – 'Imogen Sutton?'

I'm almost relieved to get away from the others. We take the lift to the Retreat floor. They've pushed the beanbags to one side and set up three chairs instead – one for this detective and her colleague, and one for the 'witness', which I suppose is what I am.

Though I didn't witness anything, so maybe I'm more of a suspect.

As I sit down, I realise the male detective was here before, when Bernice died.

They introduce themselves – I forget their names straightaway but the woman is in charge – and ask me to talk through what happened this morning. There's no space for me to ask *them* anything about what's gone on.

I tell them my version: the alarm waking me up, seeing Hanna, noticing that Lucas's door was open, evacuating the building.

'And when did you notice that two of your housemates were missing?'

They know about Dex. Well, they've got my phone, of course they do.

'Pretty much straightaway. The numbers just ... looked wrong.'

'I gather you called' – she checks a note – 'Dexter Shepherd first. Tell me your version of what happened.'

Version. They don't trust us anymore.

I explain about it going to voicemail and lending my phone to Camille so she could try Lucas. About it ringing out until Hanna answered ...

My mouth is dry. 'Can you tell me what's happened to Lucas?'

She exchanges a glance with her colleague. 'I can confirm that, unfortunately, Lucas Callaghan was found unresponsive by a member of the fire service, and that despite their efforts, and those of the ambulance service, he couldn't be resuscitated. I'm sorry. At the moment, though, I can't go any further.'

'But ... had he been attacked? Please. We *live* here. I was here when Bernice died ... I found her body, do you remember?' I appeal to the male officer. 'If his death was violent, we might all be in danger.'

Saying the words out loud makes them solidify, as though they might suffocate me.

'That's precisely why we're taking this very seriously. We cannot ignore the possibility that both Ms Booth's and Mr

Callaghan's deaths were deliberate acts, or at least in some way connected.' Her face softens a little. 'But I can tell you that there were no obvious signs of an assault.'

'Did you have a response from Mr Shepherd?'

I reach into my pocket automatically but of course they have my phone already. Instead my hand closes around the handle of my knife. How will *that* look if they search me? I need this to end quickly. 'You've got my phone, you must have seen what he said.'

The woman says, 'The timing here seems very . . . convenient. Did you have any idea he was going to move out? I understand the two of you have been close.'

What has Hanna told them? 'We both moved into the building at the same time. We had a . . . very brief relationship.' As predicted by those bloody betting slips. Should I mention them? Except I have no evidence. Zoum is the one with the copies.

He *has* to hand them over now that two of the people who wrote them are dead. And Camille is the only survivor of the committee that used to rule the Factory. Does that put her at more risk?

Maybe I am seeing connections where there are none.

'Why did your relationship with Mr Shepherd end?'

I shrug. 'It was like a freshers' week thing, when you bond with people who are in the same boat before you realise you don't have much in common. Look, I don't think it's Dex, but you need to talk to Jamie – the guy who lived here before. He has a very good reason to want to hurt people here.'

'We know our jobs, thank you, Ms Sutton. And what about Lucas? How did you get on with him?'

It's the *did* that makes it hit home. Despite all the good reasons I have for loathing Lucas, I can't bear the idea that he's dead.

By the time they finish interviewing everybody, I need to leave for school. While we were all corralled downstairs, the forensics people removed Lucas's body. I walk back to my studio to get dressed and see his door is taped shut. When I go onto the terrace, his window is papered over from the inside.

Hanna summons us to the kitchen area.

'I'll keep this brief as I know you all have work to do but I have made contact with the building owners and they have agreed to a significant upgrade in external security.'

As I listen, it strikes me yet again how wrong I was about Hanna when I first met her. I realise that she was playing up to the 'untrained migrant' stereotype, but even so, I wonder who else I've misjudged.

'This is a just precaution. There is no evidence that Lucas's death was suspicious but I know you will want to be reassured.'

Zoum sighs. 'Not suspicious? Two otherwise healthy young people die and it is just *one of those things . . .*'

'I didn't say that.'

'Plus, increasing security will only keep *intruders* out. If Lucas died . . .' – Zoum pauses, considering what to say – 'at someone else's hand, surely it is more likely one of *us* was involved? Murder victims are almost always known to the perpetrators.'

No one has said the word *murder* until now.

'I am doing this only to reassure you,' Hanna says. 'I . . . I know what I saw and I do not believe he was murdered.'

'No disrespect but I would rather wait for a pathologist than take *your* word for it,' Zoum says bitterly. 'Meanwhile, we have one member of the community who decided to move out on the exact same night as all this happens. And if we do not feel like blaming Dex, what about Jamie? We could accuse him, just for old times' sake.'

'Zoum.' I put my hand on his. 'Not now, please? We all want answers but right now, this is too soon. We're in shock.'

Hanna gives me the briefest nod of thanks. 'I understand the police are making inquiries about Dex. In addition they have informed poor Lucas's immediate family but they have requested we do not talk about it outside the Factory for now.'

'How convenient for you and the owners.' Zoum's sarcasm is wasted on Hanna. I grip his hand tighter. Maybe he feels that if he'd gone to the police about the betting slips before this, Lucas might still be alive.

Hanna stares at him. 'Let me remind everyone there is a privacy clause in your contract, forbidding you from discussing other residents with the press.'

'And what happens if we do? Eviction? Well, bring it on,' Zoum says. 'Any sane person will be leaving as soon as they can anyway.'

Hanna shoots him a poisonous look. 'This is a time for the community to come together, not tear ourselves apart. Any more questions?'

No one speaks.

She nods. 'I will advise when the security upgrade is done. In the meantime, we have temporary swipe cards for each of you to allow access to your studios while the police have your phones.'

She hands them out and when she leaves, the others disperse too. I want to talk to Zoum, but Ashleigh holds me back. Her eyes are swollen and red.

'Immi, I know we're not meant to discuss it, but what did the police ask you?'

'A bit about how everyone got on. But then they honed in on drugs. Whether I knew what Lucas used, how much.'

She nods. 'They asked me the same. I mean, he used to cane it but . . . he was young. Healthy. He wasn't addicted or anything.'

'Except I'd noticed he seemed more . . . needy,' I say gently, 'since Bernice died. He even said to me that suicide could be contagious. It's awful, Ashleigh, but if it *was* drugs, then at least we know there was no one else involved. That we're safe . . .'

But as I say it, I don't know if I believe that.

'I've failed,' she says, her voice plaintive. 'My job was to keep people happy. That was the whole point of the bloody yoga and the community events and the rest. I was meant to make a difference, to make up for what I did before.'

I am about to ask her what she means when I realise she's crying. 'Oh, Immi, what if I made things worse . . .' she says between sobs.

I take her in my arms. 'Ashleigh, no one who knows you could doubt that everything you've done was with the best intentions.'

At least, that's what I thought till now. But though it's obvious she's upset, it's strange the way she's turned Lucas's death round to making it all about *her*.

49

Immi

I get through the school day thanks to caffeine. Every break, I heap four spoons of instant into my cup, and borrow Fatima's phone to call Dex until I get sick of hearing his voicemail message.

And all the time, my sleepless brain turns over last night's events without making any sense of them. As the end of the day approaches, I begin to dread going back to the Factory. I *know* I can't stay there much longer. It's time to admit defeat and go home.

The head teacher, Diane, appears in my peripheral vision. 'Can I have a word?'

That's all I need to end my day: a bollocking for my lack of attention. Of course, she'll have noticed. She understands everything that goes on in her school, from the tiniest child's acting out, to full-on staffroom politics.

As I take a seat in her office, I wonder if now's the time to warn her I am going to have to leave my job. It makes me feel sick; Diane's put so much trust in me over the last two years, grooming me for big things.

'How are you doing, honey? You look really knackered.'

'I'm sorry. I've had a few bad nights' sleep but it's only temporary—'

'I haven't called you in to tell you off, Imogen. It's the opposite. How do you fancy trying your hand at deputy head?'

I gawp at her. 'Seriously?'

'You're ready. And Mo has just told me she's pregnant again. Pretty far gone, too. I'll have to clear it with the governors, but I'd love you to step up to cover her from September till next summer. After that, who knows?'

My eyes smart. After all the things I've done to survive in this city, the news is overwhelming.

'Thank you,' I manage to say. 'For believing in me.'

'I should be thanking you. I can't wait to be able to put my feet up.'

But as she goes through the details, reality bites. I've always wanted a leadership position, and Diane is my dream mentor. But none of this changes the shitty truth: without the Factory or a wealthy boyfriend, I can't afford to stay in London.

'Any questions?'

I shake my head.

She stands up. 'Oh. I nearly forgot. We should be able to organise a temporary salary rise. Not untold riches but it should make a difference to what you take home.'

I walk back to Bermondsey, trying not to get my hopes up. I need to look at pay scales, but it's *possible* that the temporary promotion might just be a lifesaver.

Because if I say yes, the acting-up pay might allow me to leave the Factory without getting my full deposit back. I'd have to juggle my credit cards like a circus clown to pay a deposit for a new place but it *might* work, especially if I could negotiate a shorter notice period with Hanna.

So when I see her rearranging the beanbags in the Retreat space, I approach her.

'How are you doing?' I ask.

Hanna looks unruffled, her linen tunic fresh on, her bob neatly styled, the grey hairs giving an aura of seriousness.

'It is almost impossible to believe that Lucas is dead too,' she says. 'But we must carry on as usual. Without routine, we fall apart.'

She's trying to shut down the conversation, but the promotion news makes me reckless. 'We're already falling apart, can't you see that?'

'The Factory will find its own equilibrium again.' She picks up another beanbag and shakes it to redistribute the filling.

I reach out to catch her arm. 'No, Hanna. It's like Zoum said: any sane person will be looking to move on as soon as they can.'

She freezes. The sense that I've invaded her space is strong enough to make me pull away.

'The security upgrade is complete now. You are safe. Now we must support one another. The alternative is anarchy.'

I stare at her. 'No. The alternative is to accept that the Factory experiment hasn't worked. I want to leave.'

'Are you *sure*, Imogen? Perhaps you have a rose-tinted view of what you came from and what you did to get here.'

For a moment, I feel as though she's hinting at what really happened to me, rather than the story I told at my interview. But no one here knows about my old life. 'Staying on friends' sofas wasn't ideal, but it beats dying.'

'Tsk. Such exaggeration! If you are hoping for an early release from your tenancy agreement, I will not support it.'

Her attitude riles me. 'With respect, Hanna, it's none of your business. I'll write a letter for you to pass on to your bosses. Or just give me their email address. If that's not too much trouble.'

I hear a scrabbling from Edward's cage in response to my raised voice. Poor creature is even more trapped than the rest of us.

'Do you really think I have no other options but to work *here*, Imogen? People make assumptions about who I am, where I come from. I could have my pick of opportunities in my home country, or even here.'

'I didn't think—' But of course, I did underestimate her. We all did.

'The Factory is a project I committed to. I want to support young people as they set out in life. But part of that requires tough love, making sure you don't give up the moment things get a little difficult.' She stacks the chairs the detectives used and puts them by the door.

'*A little difficult?* Is that what you call two people dying?'

'Imogen, these deaths were tragic. Avoidable, almost certainly. Bernice was so lonely. Lucas was an addict, though he concealed it. I *do* feel partially responsible as I am sure you do, but now we must focus on those of us who remain. Especially Camille.'

It's the first thing she's said I agree with. 'How is she?'

'In shock. And afraid. I've tried to explain the random nature of her friends' deaths but she doesn't see it that way. She's been having nightmares about Jamie and, of course, she is the only member of the committee left. It's our duty to stand by her.'

She turns away, and works her way through the candles, trimming the wicks, so her thumb and forefinger end up coated with black soot. The world might be falling apart, but Hanna clearly can't bear the idea that the candles might smoke at the next yoga session.

I think about the betting slips and my sympathy for Camille wanes. 'Doesn't she have any other friends or family?'

'Not really. Has she ever shared anything about her childhood?'

'She said it wasn't the easiest.'

Hanna nods. 'That is an understatement. Going home is not an option for her. She wants to be where her friends died, to find closure. In the meantime, she needs continuity, which you and Ashleigh and Zoum could offer.'

'Don't try to use emotional blackmail.'

Hanna shakes her head. 'It's not blackmail, it's about your values, Imogen. But we can't force you to stay. If you wish to leave, we will keep the two months' deposit you've already paid, plus we require an additional month's rent from you if you breach the full notice period.'

'*What?* I don't have that kind of money.'

'The contract is clear. Full community members are liable for the full three months. Debt collectors will be engaged if you do not pay up. But . . . there might be room for negotiation.'

'Like what?'

'If you show a little commitment to the community, I *could* ask the landlords about reducing the notice period. Say, to coincide with the end of term? We could even store your belongings, rent-free. You might go travelling over the summer. Come back to London in time for a brand-new term, a fresh start elsewhere.'

It surprises me that even in the midst of this drama, she is aware of my term dates. And that she understands me well enough to know this actually appeals. Especially now, with my promotion and pay rise.

I don't want to be at the Factory a single day longer than I have to be, but perhaps it's easier to pretend I'm considering the offer, while Sarah tries to find me a legal escape route. 'Would you ask them, on my behalf? In the meantime, please consider this the first day of my three-month notice period. I'll confirm it in writing.'

'As you wish.' She smiles. 'Imogen, these are the times that can make or break an individual. Helping a person in need is never something you will regret.'

I play-act the caring person Hanna wants me to be all evening, trying the role on for size.

I try to empathise with Camille and what she's endured. There's a difficult early childhood, followed by Jamie's trial, and now the loss of her two closest friends. I think about the timing; from what Zoum said, those awful betting games only started after Lucas joined the Factory, so perhaps he was the one who turned everything toxic.

Ashleigh and I smother her with kindness, offering drinks, chatting to her about everything and nothing. Even Zoum cuts her some slack.

We're rewarded with occasional smiles, which give me the same satisfaction as the purr of a timid cat you've encouraged to sit on your knee.

'You're a lot softer than you look, Immi,' Ashleigh says to me when we're in the kitchen, making herb tea.

'Do I come across like a bitch normally then?'

She blushes. 'No. But when you first got here, you didn't get involved unless we held a knife to your throat.'

The words make me flinch, but she can't *know*, it's just a turn of phrase. 'I was unsettled by how close you all were. I felt I was an outsider.'

'Not anymore. Maybe something good could even come out of this tragedy.' Ashleigh smiles but I know she's forcing it, this Pollyanna view. It's so different to what she said this morning, when we'd learned the news about Lucas. *I was meant to make a difference, to make up for what I did before.*

What the hell does *Ashleigh* have to atone for?

I pat her hand. 'I hope you're right.'

Before bed I try Dex again – the police returned our phones tonight but I wonder if they're monitoring us.

Even if they are, it's no crime to be worried about a friend. It doesn't even ring before his voicemail kicks in.

I sleep deeply, not waking until almost seven o'clock.

Only twenty-eight hours since poor Lucas was found, but I feel calmer. And when I remember the promotion Di offered me, a warm tingle spreads from head to toe.

Does that make me a bad person? Maybe. But as a scientist, I know the self-preservation instinct is one of the strongest.

I *can* do this. Pretend to be committing to the community for a few days, then get Hanna to talk to her bosses. I'd rather leave immediately, but now I'm less knackered, I see that what happened to Lucas and Bernice has nothing to do with me.

The sun is out as I step onto the street. But despite that, I shiver.

I glance over my shoulder.

Someone has followed me out of Tanner's Walk and on to Bermondsey Street. A man. My age, roughly. Round glasses, a beard. Oddly familiar, but probably because he looks like most of the men round here.

The pavement is busy enough with potential witnesses, so I make a judgement call.

Turn, stop.

He almost runs into me. And now I do know who he is.

'Holden?' The guy from our original interviews, who pretended to be an ice-cream seller but was actually a journalist.

'Immi, right?'

Has he remembered my name, or has Veronica put him up to this?

'Whatever it is you want, I am not talking to you.' It surprises me to hear the tremble in my voice.

'Come on, Immi. I don't bite. I only want to talk to you about what's happened in the Factory.'

I keep walking. 'I'm running late. I'm not interested.'

We hit one of those walls of people you get at this time of day. He's next to me now. I can even smell his aftershave.

'Are you sure? Because there could be money in it for you. A *lot* of money, if what the police are saying is true.'

'Oh, and what's that then?' I can't resist.

'That your man there was murdered.'

'Bullshit. Lucas was on drugs, so—' I stop, realising what I've said.

Holden smiles. 'It must be a terrible time for you all.'

'Piss off or I'll start to scream.' I step up the pace.

'It's going to get worse, Immi. There'll be journalists outside every day when this comes out. But if you talk to me, give the inside story, that'll kill it for the other journalists.'

I keep walking, though I feel unsteady. *Murdered?* It crossed my mind immediately after I realised Lucas was dead but since then, the police seem to have been focusing on drug overdose as the cause.

It's probably Holden lying to get me to talk.

'Think about what I've said, Immi. Because if you don't do it, you can bet your life one of your neighbours will. And I promise, we pay way more than anyone else so you just have to name a price and . . .'

I step out of earshot, trying not to think that the money could allow me to leave the Factory straightaway.

No. I won't stoop that low. That would make me as bad as the rest of them.

50

Saturday 16 June

Immi

On Saturday morning, Ashleigh walks onto the terrace holding a copy of *The Sun*.

I almost laugh. 'Not your usual reading material, Ashleigh—'

And then I see the headline: THE HOUSE SHARE TO DIE FOR

'It says . . . It says Lucas was murdered.' Her voice is a whisper.

'But how . . .?' I take the paper and read the story, *Exclusive by Holden Wright*. It's packed with lurid inaccuracies. Lucas is an 'international booze guru' and the Factory is a 'cultish commune for the rich elite'. I try to cut through the bullshit for the facts.

> The body of Lucas Callaghan, 29, was discovered after an apparent hoax fire alarm led to the trendy warehouse building being evacuated in the early hours of Thursday morning. When one person didn't come out, fire crews went into the building and found the city slicker's body.
>
> 'At first it looked like a drugs overdose,' a source said. 'Like so many wealthy city workers, Callaghan was hooked

on cocaine. But the recent death of another resident — who apparently took her own life — led the police to order urgent toxicology tests.'

The story introduces Bernice and her 'mysterious early-hours fall from the luxury roof terrace after a decadent party. The Factory has free booze on tap and a reputation for bed-hopping'.

I suppose they got those bits right.

When the results came back, they confirmed the worst. Callaghan didn't die from too much cocaine. Instead, it's thought he'd been injected with a massive dose of insulin.

Callaghan was drunk, which meant his liver couldn't react and process the insulin safely. He died of a heart attack.

Police confirmed last night: 'This is now a murder inquiry.'

Someone really did kill Lucas.

And that someone must be one of us. As Zoum said, extra security won't protect us if the threat comes from inside.

I sense my chest tightening, my throat closing down, and that all too familiar paralysis that makes me feel I'm dying all over again.

There's a final section inside the newspaper.

Detectives will be interviewing the wealthy residents again this weekend. But an insider also said they're looking into a link with a recent harassment case. A former Factory resident was acquitted of revenge porn charges, but police are likely to revisit the case.

The alleged victim cannot be named but it's understood to be Bernice Booth, who plunged from the roof terrace only a fortnight ago.

Other disturbing incidents are also troubling detectives, including the disappearance of a guinea pig kept in the building as a 'companion animal' to the spoiled residents. 'It's well known that psychopaths often rehearse on animals before graduating to murder.'

I look up, unsure what to say to Ashleigh.

'Whatever happens, Camille can't know about this,' she says.

I hand the paper back and there are little greasy marks where my fingers were. 'True. But they got it wrong about Bernice being the victim in the court case, so the rest could all be bullshit too.'

'They got the insulin right, though.' Ashleigh's eyes are glassy.

'But where would that have come from?'

Tears start to fall but she doesn't seem to notice. 'From me,' she whispers.

'Sorry?'

'I'm a diabetic. It's one of the reasons I'm' – she motions down at her body – 'plump. I find it hard to control my sugars. I have to use insulin, have done since I was little.'

Why has she kept this a secret? 'OK . . .'

'A friend texted me about the story this morning and I went to buy the paper. When I saw what they say killed Lucas, I checked the box where I keep my supplies. Most of my vials are missing.'

'How much?'

She makes a choking sound. 'A month's supply.'

'Fuck, Ashleigh.'

She begins to sob properly now. I get up to give her a hug, just as the entrance buzzer sounds. Someone is at the front door.

The police? The press?

It buzzes again.

Neither of us moves. We stay locked in the hug, waiting for Hanna to answer the door.

The last courtesies have gone. The police summon us to the basement office. I go with Ashleigh; Camille and Hanna are already there, and Zoum is the last to arrive.

He gives me a resigned smile but I can't reciprocate. Because I realised as I walked down the stairs that Zoum is the only person except Hanna who can access every room in this building without leaving a trace.

An overweight male detective enters the room. He's much more senior than the others, you can tell from the way his colleagues defer to him.

'The leak to the newspaper is unfortunate, and packed with inaccuracies, but it is true that we are treating Mr Callaghan's death as suspicious. We will also be looking more closely into Miss Booth's. This whole building is now a crime scene which means you are going to have to bear with us, as it's such an extensive property.

'We need to interview all of you again. We are also planning to talk to former residents. We need answers.'

Ashleigh stands next to me. I sense energy coming off her, like when a clever kid has their hand up, desperate to answer a difficult question.

'But do you think it *was* a double murder?' Zoum asks.

The detective huffs. 'I am hardly going to share my theories with witnesses *or* suspects. But I should stress that while Mr Callaghan did *not* die of natural causes, we will be keeping an open mind about whether another party is involved. Are there any questions?'

Now Ashleigh gets her chance.

'I need to speak to someone now,' she says, 'about the insulin and—'

I reach over and pinch her arm. We discussed this before we left the terrace. She shouldn't say anything about this in front of the others.

She stops.

'OK,' the detective says. 'Let's talk to you first. No one is to leave the immediate Bermondsey area, so you are all nearby when we need to interview you. Sadly, you'll have to pay for your own ruddy cappuccinos while our forensics teams are here, because the kitchen and other communal areas are temporarily out of bounds.'

I hang back with Ashleigh, pretending to be the supportive friend.

The woman officer from Thursday night turns to me and says firmly, 'You can't stay with her during the interview, you know that?'

I nod. 'Of course not. But . . . I have something else that you need to know.'

51

Immi

After they've taken my statement and Ashleigh's, we both go to the café over the road. The humidity makes it unbearably stuffy inside so we sit at a wrought-iron table on the cobbles.

'What did you tell them?' she asks me.

I can't bear to say. I feel shitty enough about it as it is. 'I . . . We're not meant to talk about it, are we?'

'No. But surely we can tell each other how we feel. I need to tell someone. I'm certain they think *I* did it, because it was my insulin.'

'Shh. I'm sure that's not true. Did anyone else in the Factory know about you using it?'

'No one except Hanna because I had to put it on my application form,' she replies. 'But what if someone else had access to that? Because, well, there was this *thing* that kept happening . . .'

I wait but she puts her finger to her lip, like a kid who has shared a secret they shouldn't have. 'What thing?'

'Sometimes there were these smells. In my studio. Of cake and bread, chocolate. All the things I shouldn't eat.'

I smile patiently. 'Your room is right above Nourish, Ashleigh.'

'Yeah, but who the hell in the Factory eats cake? Most of the Dyers are gluten-free.' Ashleigh frowns. 'Plus the smell was *only* in my studio, not in the communal areas, like it was being pumped in on purpose.'

'Oh, Ashleigh, come on. Why would someone do that?'

Her cheeks colour. 'Please don't tell anyone, but sometimes I . . . binge. It goes back to when I was a kid, not being allowed what I wanted by my parents, because of the diabetes.'

Is bingeing her vice? It seems inconsequential compared to the other secrets Dyers seem to hide from each other. 'We all like comfort food sometimes, Ashleigh.'

'The smells made my cravings so much worse, like someone was manipulating me.'

'Maybe.' I try to brush it off. Except I remember something else: the way Dex's studio always stank of booze, even when he insisted he was barely drinking.

Was that Zoum playing tricks? They seem particularly mean-spirited ones for the guy I thought I trusted.

But not out of character if he really is a killer . . .

'You're right, Immi. I'm being paranoid.'

We sit in silence until the barista delivers our drinks. I look up at the Factory. In the dull daylight, it looks like two-dimensional movie scenery: the set for a chilling blockbuster.

For fuck's sake. I'm becoming as much of a drama queen as Ashleigh. I hated telling the police about Zoum, and even now I can't believe he's a killer.

But someone is.

Jamie? But surely he'd have attacked Camille, not Lucas, if revenge was his motive. And it doesn't explain how he'd know about the insulin, or how he got into the Factory.

Which leaves Dex. He loathed Lucas. He hasn't responded to any of my messages. And there was that time when he told me to keep away from him because he was dangerous . . .

What about Camille herself? I know she's suffering, but perhaps a part of that is guilt. And then there's Ashleigh, who seems almost to enjoy the bonding that's come from grief. Even though she's given so much to the community, Zoum and Dex both hinted to me that she's on some ego trip. Could that lead to murder?

This is madness. I am trying so hard to come up with crazy theories when surely the most obvious suspect is the one I've been closest to. Dex.

'Immi, look.'

Ashleigh is pointing at the Factory. The entrance doors have opened and a uniformed officer emerges.

Behind him is Zoum. He's not handcuffed but there's something proprietorial about the way the policeman and the female detective stay close as he steps onto the cobbles.

I look away, but he's already spotted me. We're close enough that I can see the beads of sweat on his brow.

'I'll be back soon,' he calls out as they escort him towards a police car. The two officers open the rear door but he resists being manoeuvred inside. 'I had nothing to do with this. But someone killed Lucas and you won't be safe till they find out who did it.'

His head disappears as they lose patience and move him into the car with a little more force than they might show to someone they think is innocent.

Ashleigh and I stare after the car as it drives along the cobbles, back towards Bermondsey Street and wherever they're taking him to be questioned.

Once it's gone, I realise Ashleigh is staring at me. 'It was *you* who told the police to go after Zoum, wasn't it? It must have been, because they've only spoken to the two of us so far and I said nothing about Zoum.'

'Ashleigh, I—'

'What the fuck did you tell them, Immi? What just got Zoum arrested for murder?'

It's as if all the rage Ashleigh might have been hiding behind the yoga-bunny exterior comes out in an unstoppable tsunami.

'They're all being taken away from me.' Her blue eyes darken almost to black. 'This was my safe space till you got here. I *mattered* to everyone but it's all *meaningless* now. You've broken us. Broken *me*.'

The idea that Zoum might be a killer seems to disturb her less than *my* betrayal. But I let her rant because I think I know what's behind it: her own sense of guilt. It was *her* insulin that killed Lucas.

When she finally runs out of energy, I speak. 'You know, none of it is my fault, or yours. And now we have to leave it to the police.'

But she pushes her chair back so hard it nearly topples, and walks away.

'Ashleigh, remember the detectives said we're not to go too far from the building!' I call after her.

'Why would that matter, now you've apparently solved the bloody case for them?'

I consider going after her, but it's probably better I let her calm down. I go into the café to pay for us both. The man behind the vintage coffee machine looks like a 1950s relic himself, with dyed black hair as shiny as the polished chrome counter. He gives me an odd look – he must have heard some of what Ashleigh said.

'Sorry about that,' I say. 'Flatmate trouble.'

'You're from over the road, aren't you?'

I nod.

'You want to be careful talking about it in public. This place has been crawling with journalists.'

Must be good for business. 'Thank you for the warning.'

'Bad enough for your friends to die, without people making money out of it.' He waves away my debit card. 'On me. I know how crap it feels to be caught up in something so awful.'

The unexpected act of kindness floors me momentarily. I nod a thank you and turn back to go into the Factory. As I do, I'm aware of a movement from the corner of my eye.

A car sits on the double yellows. In the passenger seat, I make out a man's silhouette, but what dominates is a giant camera lens. The driver's door opens and a woman gets out, calling out to me, 'What do you know about the people who've died?'

Bloody journalist.

I fumble with the outside door, clumsy in my haste to try to get in before she reaches me.

'Was he a junkie?' she's shouting. 'Were you one of his lovers?'

Finally I manage to open it and get into the lobby, slamming the door behind me.

'Aren't you worried you might be next?'

Inside, a team of three forensics officers are working their way through the many possible scenes of crime. Ashleigh's and Zoum's studios have been turned upside down, and parts of the communal areas are sealed off with tape. They've got their work cut out: two people are dead, one missing, one under arrest.

I don't want to get in anyone's way, so I retreat to my studio. I haven't eaten today but I'm not hungry. Fear, maybe.

Though shouldn't I feel safer now the police have got Zoum in custody?

I try calling Dex but it goes straight to voicemail again. I text my mum, saying I'm around for a phone call if she wants, but she just sends back a short message: *No thank you. I will be in touch when I have forgiven you.*

I can't focus on my book or on sewing, so I lie on my bed, listening to the low voices of the officers.

I must have been dozing because it's almost dark when I hear a knock on my door: tentative, unthreatening. Even so, I clutch my knife in my palm as I get out of bed and peer through the spyhole.

'It's me,' Ashleigh says, her face distorted by the fisheye lens. 'I'm sorry for what I said before. I didn't really mean it.'

'It's fine. We're all strung out.'

'Could I possibly come in, Immi?'

My chest tightens. 'What for?' I don't really believe that Ashleigh is a murderer, but I've misjudged people many times before.

'The police have gone for now. I can't sleep on my own. I wondered if I could stay in your room tonight. Sort of . . . safety in numbers.'

I remember when I let Lucas stay the night. Eight days later he was dead. Would anything have been different if I'd turned him away?

But tonight, I don't want to be alone either. I slot the knife into the pocket of my shorts and open the door.

She blinks, surprised. 'I didn't think you were going to let me in.'

I'm not exactly the most tactile person, but I can tell a hug is what she needs. 'Come here.'

We embrace and her lavender oil scent reminds me of the first time I met her, at the selection evening, when I would have said anything to get accepted into the Factory.

But it also reminds me of the smashed pot of lavender I found next to poor Bernice's body.

Eventually, Ashleigh falls asleep, her arms and legs splayed out like a child's, her tie-dye top riding up at the back. I go to pull my duvet over her when I see a dark bruise on her shoulder.

I look closer.

It's not a bruise, it's a tattoo, and it's very different to the delicate star-and-planet design around her wrist. This is a spider's web as big as a fist, the navy lines thick and uneven, like it was done by a teenager. But she couldn't have done this herself.

In the centre, an ugly rendering of a spider waits for a fly.

Week 8: A message from management

This is Hanna here. As no one has sent me a message to distribute via the app this week, I have decided to send one myself.

The effect of what has happened will stay with us all for life. But for now, we must take one day at a time. I can promise that I and the Factory's owners will do everything necessary to ensure your continued safety.

The investigations will involve some disruption but we are all anxious to get justice for our friends, Lucas and Bernice. Once we have the all-clear from the police, I am happy to consider any further changes that make you feel more secure. Please find me, I am always available.

One thing has not changed: the aim of the community is to support and nurture those who live within it. This is more important today than it has ever been.

Hanna

52

Sunday 17 June

Immi

Ashleigh creeps out at first light, to my relief. Even after I covered her spider tattoo with the duvet, I couldn't unsee it. Why does she have it? What does it mean?

Instinct told me not to ask her.

The forensics people come back so I leave the Factory and walk aimlessly around Bermondsey, among the Sunday crowds. I sit on a bench in the park and google: 'What does a spider's web tattoo mean?'

It is most associated with doing time in prison, involvement in gang violence, or being trapped in the system.

I thought I was past being shocked by my neighbours, but I was wrong. I remember her rage when she found out I'd got Zoum arrested. Perhaps that was closer to the real Ashleigh than the chilled-out version she presents to people.

Whatever it means, I need to protect myself. I call Sarah, after planning what I will say, to avoid freaking her out too much.

'Hey Immi.' She answers immediately and I can hear she's in the car. 'I hope your day is looking brighter than mine. We're on the way to beg the in-laws for a loan to help us buy our suburban dream home.'

'Did you see yesterday's paper?'

'No, why?'

So I tell her about Lucas, and the toxicology, and the fact that the police seem no nearer working out what's gone on.

'Shit. I'll revise what I just said about my day being bad because yours is worse. I take it you've given notice.'

'Of course. But I don't think I'll last the full three months and they're not massively into negotiating a shorter period. Was there *anything* you found that might help me escape?'

'There is a bit of case law that might allow you to break the agreement due to "extraordinary circumstances". It might not stand up in court, but would the people behind that place really want to take it that far? I could write to them, suggest it's counter productive to keep you against your wishes. It's the nuclear option, though.'

I try to picture Hanna's response to that kind of letter. 'I can't see the management taking it very well. But she sent a more conciliatory message to all of us this morning. I could try talking to her one last time, before going legal.'

'Do you feel safe, Immi?'

No.

But then, I haven't felt safe for over a year. Sarah has no idea what happened to me, I couldn't tell her because it would have meant telling her *everything*.

So even now I can't stop lying. 'You know me, Sarah. I have cockroach-level abilities to survive Armageddon.'

'Still. I hate to think of you in that place, alone. You let me know as soon as you want me to press the button.'

Another bloody journalist ambushes me as I buzz into the Factory.

'Do you know the refugee?'

I stop. 'What the hell are you talking about?'

'The one they've arrested,' she says. 'He's a refugee from Afghanistan. Is he a Muslim?'

I should have guessed the newspapers might take that angle – *crazed immigrant goes on the rampage.*

'You know *nothing* about him.'

But then, neither do I.

The forensics people must have finished because there's no one around. As I go downstairs to look for Hanna, I consider the journalist's question about Zoum. Maybe I was so desperate to find a friend here that I ignored the warning signs.

Religion has never seemed important to him, but perhaps what he witnessed before leaving Afghanistan might have affected him at a deep level.

No. I don't believe that. The only reason I spoke to the police about Zoum was because he could hack into the security system. Hopefully he's already explained it to the police and they're looking at the other Dyers – Dex, Camille, and now Ashleigh and her horrible tattoo. Not forgetting Jamie . . .

I shiver, and not only because it's cold down here. I step into the office; there's no sign of Hanna, but it reminds me of what a peculiar existence she has. There's no natural light and the smell of laundry detergent doesn't quite mask the dampness. It's not much of a life.

I turn to go.

'You were looking for me?'

She's behind me, so close I could count her eyelashes.

'I've thought about what we said, but I can't stay at the Factory, Hanna.'

'We discussed this. Are you reneging on your agreement to support Camille and Ashleigh?'

'It was never a definite agreement. And things have changed now we know Lucas was actually murdered. My lawyer thinks so too.'

Hanna's eyes widen. 'Your *lawyer*?'

'I have to protect myself, Hanna. She wants to write a formal letter to the owners, but I came to see if we could come to an agreement without going down that route.'

She smiles at me, then sits down in the old office chair next to the computer. 'And your . . . *lawyer* is aware of your own full circumstances, is she? So that she can be certain to pursue your best interests?'

'Thanks for your concern, but yes. My best interests are served by getting out of here and getting my deposit back so I can move somewhere safe.'

Hanna sits down at the computer. She has her back to me as she logs on. Maybe she's bringing up my contract, to show me a hidden clause that means I can't leave without sacrificing my right kidney.

'Imogen, when you accepted a place here, you committed to something greater than yourself. As part of the screening process, we needed to ensure we were bringing the right people into our community.'

Fuck that. I'm heading for the door. 'You should change your interviewing process then because it's not working.'

'On the contrary, when it came to your screening, some alarm bells *did* ring. But I decided to give you the benefit of the doubt.'

'I really, really wish you hadn't bothered.' I get to the doorway and glance back. On the computer screen, I see a face.

My face.

And I realise what this is all about.

53

Immi

'What the hell are you doing with that?'

I am too shocked to play dumb.

Hanna swivels the chair around so she's facing me. 'I feel genuinely sorry for young people these days. In my youth, indiscretions could be forgotten, but now there will always be a trace, however hard you try to wipe it out.'

'Spare me the sympathy, Hanna. Where did you get that?'

She turns back to the screen and brings up another picture: a screenshot of me in a shimmery gold evening dress – an outfit that breaks the rules about showing either cleavage or legs but never both.

'You know exactly where it's from, Imogen. Or should I call you Isabella? A sophisticated name for a whore.'

Shock overwhelms me, followed by shame.

'Close it down. *Please.*'

'You look beautiful, in a slutty way. And it seems you were a natural. Did you get a bonus from the agency for all these five-star ratings?'

'They told me they'd taken the profile down. I double-checked.'

'Nothing ever really disappears, as I said.'

My head fills with fragments of what I did, and what was done to me. I can't think, never mind speak.

'Imogen, I am not judging you. Though many would, sadly. Your mother might struggle to understand. And it's hard to see your colleagues sympathising with what you did to stay afloat. Never mind the parents of the children whose minds you are helping to form.'

'I . . . need to sit down.'

Hanna stands up and I take her place in the chair, too close to the screen and to images I hoped I'd never see again.

It took a few goes to get them right, using a selfie stick because I could hardly ask my flatmates for help. The agency advised me on what I should wear, how I should pose, what to write on my page. It was a parody of a dating profile: my make-up too vivid, my answers loaded with innuendo. The men who browsed these pages weren't looking for a life partner.

'Who else knows about . . . Isabella?'

'Only myself and the person who does our background checks. None of the residents. We take privacy very seriously.'

I stare at her.

'But that may need to change. If you left now, Ashleigh and Camille might blame themselves. Showing them these would at least reassure them that you were already untrustworthy.'

Why does she think I'd care about them knowing? Judging from Ashleigh's tattoo, she can take care of herself.

Hanna continues: 'I'd also be concerned that your instability might affect your work with minors. It would be my duty to share what I know.'

Shit. At school, it'd be game over. And if my mother found out, it would break her. I'd never be able to start again, not even back home.

'You'd ruin my life over a few weeks' notice?'

Hanna shakes her head. 'It's a matter of principle and loyalty, Immi. Surely you can see that?'

No, I fucking can't.

Shame has faded, anger taking its place. 'Why are you so desperate to save this place? They're not your kids. And it's not like this can be your dream job? You live in a basement, you do our dirty washing—'

'I explained before. I am here to protect all of you.'

Like a cornered animal, I want to lash out, but it won't help. I breathe, breathe, breathe . . .

'What do you want me to do?'

'Only what you promised the other day. Hold on till this passes.'

'It won't pass. Two people are dead!'

'Immi, all things pass. But I must focus on the greater good. Think it through. I can rearrange the studios so you're all close together and feel more supported. Then, at the end of term – only just over a month from now – you move out, with your full deposit returned, and do what you please.'

'But what about the photos of me?'

'Our background checker is also the best when it comes to . . . cleaning up a reputation online. That would be your little bonus if you help us now.'

I pretend to think it through, though of course I have no choice. 'Do you have information like this on everyone who lives here?'

'As I explained, Immi, I take privacy very seriously so I would never share anything about them with you.' But the self-satisfaction in her eyes leaves me in no doubt that she knows *all* our secrets.

Except, presumably, who killed Lucas, and whether Bernice jumped or was pushed.

I stand up, desperate to get away from her. 'Do you get off on the power, Hanna? Because at the end of the day, you're only a glorified fucking cleaner.'

She shakes her head. 'And you're a glorified *fucking* prostitute. Let me know your decision tonight, please. The last thing we need is further uncertainty.'

I only just make it up to my studio before I throw up. Afterwards, I brush my teeth to take away the taste, but the smell lingers.

I stare at myself in the mirror afterwards, at the plainness of my features and the grey shadows under my eyes. Not exactly escort material.

But it's amazing what make-up and vodka can do: the former sends out the signal of availability, the latter blurs the lines. When I came to London in August 2016, I didn't *plan* to end up sleeping with men for money. Does anyone? My salary went up, but my student loan repayments did too. All manageable, until Mum confided in me that she was struggling, now I wasn't there to help her manage her spending.

I started off sending small amounts, to cover the odd bill, but the more I sent, the more she seemed to need. Introducing her to the internet was supposed to help her feel less isolated. Instead, it sent her shopping habits into overdrive, as she was able to fill the house with even more junk from the comfort of the sofa.

I ended up paying *her* rent, along with my own. Every time I got on top of things, she'd have some new crisis. Once she called me five times during assembly and I sneaked out, thinking she must have been taken ill or had an accident. Instead she'd handed the phone to the bailiffs, who were threatening to take all her furniture and the telly unless I did a bank transfer before morning break. Guilt stopped me ever saying no, and within six months, I was in so much debt myself, I couldn't see a way out.

It was a magazine article about students selling sex that gave me the idea. The girl they featured looked so ordinary, but she lived in Zone 2, owned nice things, and was even saving up to buy a flat.

My first time was horrible, though the client was no more or less loathsome than the ones that followed. I did it one night a week, earning more than I took home for a week's work in the classroom. My life became easier in every way. I was a better teacher, a better flatmate. I tried to lock away what I had to do to make that happen.

The plan was to stop once I'd earned enough to get a deposit on my own rental. I knew this was corrosive, potentially risky, even though most clients were just lonely or even 'time poor'. The majority of my hours involved being paid to flirt and eat and drink, no worse than a date. The only difference was that they paid to ensure our evening would end in sex. It was simple.

Until I met a client who thought that because he paid, I couldn't say no to anything.

I got home at four the following morning, a different Imogen. Before I left for school, I logged on to the agency website with shaking hands and suspended my account. It wasn't the only thing I stopped doing. I no longer wore make-up (except for the thick concealer to cover the bruises on my throat), bothered to style my hair, or wanted to spend time with anyone except the kids I taught.

A few months later, on a night out Sarah *forced* me to go on, I met Al. I'd become invisible to most men, but still he bought me a drink, took it gently on the first few dates until he realised I needed security and quickly offered that and much more. It was a whirlwind.

But it was also a lie. The woman he fell in love with was a reserved primary school teacher. He never suspected there was a different, feisty, funny, sexy Imogen. She had almost ceased to exist.

Perhaps I would have been able to bury her for good, if I hadn't gone to his office party on Valentine's night. I recognised his boss immediately as we air-kissed, but he narrowed his eyes, trying to work out where he knew me from. I hoped he would never remember.

He'd been one of the first people to hire me, not for himself, but for three international clients at a 'soirée' arranged in their honour. He had ordered all the expected commodities – gourmet food, fine wines, compliant women. It wasn't a terrible experience, as these things go.

But he *did* remember, and he did tell Al on the Monday morning.

When Al confronted me that night, I stayed silent, even though there were so many things I *could* have told him: that no one sells sex out of choice, and *Pretty Woman* is a fairy tale. That I had always known I would be punished again.

Fuck this. I go to my drawer and take out the evidence bag, with my sleeping pills in it. I begged my doctor for these after the attack, and though I hated the fogginess and the metallic taste, they were the only thing that broke the crippling cycle of insomnia.

I take one. To be sure of oblivion, I should wash it down with gin. I sneak out to the landing and steal a whole bottle of gin from the bar, without writing it down in their bloody honesty book. Let's add theft to my misdemeanours.

54

Immi

Evening and the police have gone. I am lying dazed on the bed, when I hear voices. *Male* voices.

Despite the pills and gin, I am instantly awake. With Zoum under arrest, it's only women left living at the Factory.

So who the hell is out there now?

It takes a few seconds for me to get my balance when I stand up. I put my phone in one pocket, next to the knife. Walk down the stairs, past the silent Retreat floor, towards the voices that seem to be coming from Nourish. A uniformed policeman is holding open the door to New Delhi. I get closer to see that inside, Zoum is packing a bag.

He looks up and when he sees it's me, he shakes his head.

'What's going on?'

'They let me go, Immi, *that's* what is going on.'

'Mr Akhtar has been released on police bail pending further inquiries,' the policeman says.

'You're coming back here?'

'Oh, do not worry,' Zoum says, not looking at me as he folds up T-shirts and underwear. Behind him, his room has been stripped of all the equipment and personal belongings. I guess the forensics team did that. 'I am just dropping in for a change of clothes, and my officer friend here is making sure I do not . . . interfere with anything. Not that there is much left to interfere with.'

'Are they taking you to prison?'

Now he looks at me. 'Worse. I am bailed to stay at my parents' house. It is fair to say they are more thrilled about this than I am.'

His eyes lock on to mine. Despite everything, there's amusement in them and it hits me: I don't believe he killed anyone. 'Zoum . . . You know I had to tell them.'

He zips up the holdall and pulls it off the bed.

'All done?' the officer asks. 'I have to see you out of here but I can drop you off at the Tube, if you want? Might as well.'

Zoum shakes his head. 'Thank you but I could do with the fresh air.'

I step aside as he leaves the room. 'You said we weren't safe. Outside the café. What did you mean?'

'It is not rocket science, Immi. The police still have me in the frame but lack the evidence to keep me in custody. As soon as I get my computers back, I intend to prove my innocence, but until then, whoever killed Lucas is free to do whatever they please.'

'If it's not you, who do you think it is?'

I almost add: Dex or Jamie? *Hanna?*

Zoum sighs. 'Conveniently, all the latest records of who was coming or going in and out of the Factory have been wiped, and the back-ups too. The police assume I am the only one with the skills to do that, but obviously someone else has hidden talents.'

'You must have some idea?'

He walks out of the studio, down towards the lift, the police-man following him. 'Why would I share it with you if I did, Immi?'

I say nothing.

Just before he steps into the lift, he turns. 'Look, maybe it is over now. Maybe Lucas and Bernice did actually kill themselves after all.'

'Tell me this, please. Would you stay here, if you were allowed to?' I ask.

Zoum half smiles. 'Probably not. But then, it all began to go wrong long before you got here. Maybe as a relative newcomer, you are safe.'

The policeman pulls the lift bars shut and they descend, the sound of the hydraulics fading till there's nothing to be heard but the buzz of the coffee machine.

I'm getting sleepy again when Hanna comes to my door.

'You have made your decision?'

I nod. 'It wasn't really a choice.'

'In which case, you are moving into Warsaw,' she says.

Veronica's old room has multiple advantages, she tells me. It's already been deep-cleaned. There's no apparent connection between her and the deaths so the police are happy. Plus, it's on Retreat, next to Ashleigh and Camille.

'You can all look after each other,' Hanna explains.

I don't protest. 'All right. I'll pack up tomorrow.'

'No, tonight.'

'It's nearly ten o'clock.'

'Better this way,' she says, in a way that makes it clear the decision is made.

Ashleigh helps me carry my sewing machine down and stays with me while I unpack. I can't stop picturing that tattoo. I won't say anything – it's not in my interests to antagonise her – but there'll be no more cosy sleepovers. Veronica's room feels more claustrophobic because the window looks out onto the modern flats on the other side of Tanner's Walk.

'There's a good vibe on this level,' Ashleigh says, back to her perky self, 'so it'll be a fresh start for you. I know it's late, and you've got school tomorrow, but what about a welcoming meditation? Ten minutes?'

Like the good girl Hanna wants me to be, I agree. I change into sweatpants and a vest, and cross the floor to the studio. Soft acoustic guitar plays from invisible speakers and Ashleigh has lit the candles so the light flickers along the walls. The scent of the forest fills the room and three yoga mats are arranged in the shape of a triangle.

Ashleigh brings Camille into the space. I don't think she leaves the building anymore, so maybe it doesn't matter to her whether it's eleven a.m. or p.m. She barely acknowledges me as Ashleigh helps her sit down on one of the mats.

'Let's hold hands,' Ashleigh says, once we're all seated and facing each other.

Her hand is warm and reassuring, but when I reach out for Camille she won't look at me, and I have to force apart her clammy fingers to take hold. Even that feels like an assault.

Ashleigh leads us through an exercise to bring down our heart rate. Slowly, Camille's skin begins to warm up against mine and the claw-like grip softens.

'We're in this together,' Ashleigh says. 'Yes, we're grieving for the people we've lost but also supporting each other.'

Ashleigh's grip on my hand tightens a little in a reassuring gesture and I find myself doing the same to Camille. When she grips back, it feels like there's a real connection between us all.

'There's no obligation, but if we want, we can share how we're doing. Let me begin.' Ashleigh's voice is a conspiratorial whisper. 'I feel our collective sorrow but I also feel our strength.'

Camille makes a choking sound. I open my eyes to see she's crying. She tries to pull her hand away to wipe her face but Ashleigh says, 'Let the tears come, Camille. Let it all go, we're here to listen.'

'They're gone . . .' Camille says.

I can't take my eyes off her face as the tears fall and fall. Her heart is breaking but she's still beautiful.

She gulps. 'And I'm still here and I am so scared that Jamie will come for me too. That this was all about punishing me. Sharing the video of me wasn't enough punishment for rejecting him. He had to kill my friends, because they looked after me. I won't ever be safe again . . .'

Ashleigh gives me a look that says: *I'll handle this.*

'You're wrong, Camille,' Ashleigh says softly. 'The police are on it. And Hanna has improved the security systems so there's no way now that he can access the building. You're completely safe.'

What Ashleigh doesn't know, but I do, is when someone has robbed you of your sense of security, you never feel one hundred per cent safe again.

'Have you considered seeing a therapist about what happened with Jamie, Camille?' I ask. 'It can make a difference.'

Her eyes meet mine. 'What use is a therapist if Jamie won't let me forget?'

As she speaks, I picture Jamie in the dock. He has the strongest reason to want revenge. But the police must have spoken to him, checked his alibi. Zoum says the records of who came and went have been wiped, but Jamie couldn't possibly have had the access or knowledge to do that.

Who could, except Zoum? Dex? No. He never showed any interest in computers.

But there is one more person who has access to everything that makes the Factory work. Hanna.

'. . . Or maybe it would help to go home, spend time with family?' Ashleigh is saying to Camille.

She shakes her head. 'I won't run away because of him. And anyway, *you* are the closest I have to a family now.'

When Ashleigh smiles, it looks a little smug to me. 'See, Camille, that's better. Immi, would *you* like to share how you feel, now?'

Trapped and deceitful and . . .

'Grateful . . .' I say, and I try to make myself feel that way. 'Grateful that I have you two close.'

The music soars and I breathe out. Camille has shut her eyes again and her hand in mine is warm and open.

Could I still find something good in this situation? If I can just bide my time, then come September, I could make a new start as deputy head with no skeletons in my closet.

I nod, making the decision. 'Camille?' I say, 'You think you'll never feel OK again but there is hope. I had something . . . similar happen to me and though I'll never be exactly the same, I have been able to carry on with my life.'

Ashleigh grips my hand a little tighter. 'Have you ever told anyone about this before?'

'No.' A half-sob sticks in my throat.

'You know, if you want to, you could tell us. Nothing goes outside this circle.'

I close my eyes. Maybe it's the sleeping pill lowering my inhibitions. Or it might be the buried feelings that resurfaced after seeing those pictures of me as Isabella. But I think I finally want to talk.

'Just over a year ago, a man did something to me without my consent and . . .'

'Go on.'

'I thought I would die and . . .'

'Close your eyes and tell us, in your own time,' Ashleigh says.

And I do. I don't explain how I came to be in bed with that man, but I tell them everything else: the hand around my throat closing down my windpipe, the other hand holding the softest of pillows against my face. The pressure in my head, burning in my lungs and that blackness. *That terror.*

And waking up to his cries of pleasure at bringing me to the point of death.

I open my eyes and Ashleigh is nodding at me, approving. 'Thank you for sharing. We are definitely stronger together.'

Camille is looking at me intently. 'I always knew that what we had in common went deeper than what you told the committee at your interview. I'm sorry this happened to you.'

'Hopefully it's helped,' Ashleigh says.

I *do* feel lighter, for being heard and believed.

It's only when I am lying in bed afterwards that I realise both Camille and I shared something of ourselves: our deepest fears.

All Ashleigh did was reflect them back at us, without revealing a single thing about herself.

55

Monday 18 June

Immi

Teaching provides a little respite from Factory stress, but when I check my phone at break, there are three missed calls from one unfamiliar number. As I walk out of the playground to the street, it rings again.

'Immi? I'm sorry.'

It's Dex. *Alive.* That's something. But I have so many questions, I don't know where to begin. 'Where are you? Why did you leave?'

His breathing is laboured, as though he's been running. 'What happened to Lucas had nothing to do with me. I swear. On my sisters' lives.'

Sisters? He's never mentioned them before. I know *nothing* about him, including whether he has it in him to kill. 'You *ran* away, Dexter. On the night someone died. Makes it hard to believe it was just coincidence.'

There's a silence. 'I know. It's . . . complicated.'

'You've got to come forward, for the police to rule you out, because right now, you look guilty as hell.'

'You think I don't know that?' He sounds desperate.

I am on the cusp of offering my help. I've been rescuing lost souls since I was a kid and propped up my mother. But no one

ever props *me* up. I make a decision. 'Look, you have to go to
the nearest police station, talk to them. If you had nothing to do
with it, you'll be OK.'

'I can't do that.'

I scoff. 'Don't be stupid. You have to help yourself, Dex, and—'

'I'm not Dex.'

'*What?*'

'You want something to prove you can trust me? Something
nobody else knows? My name is Davy.'

'Why would you even tell me that? It just sounds like
another lie.'

In the background, I hear birds crying out, the hum of cars
and lorries driving fast.

'I'll explain if you come to see me, Immi. But you must promise you won't tell anyone else where I am.'

I'm so sick of people telling me what I *must* do. 'Forget it.
I don't need this cloak-and-dagger shit. Especially not when two
people I lived with are dead!'

I hang up and head back into school. I have to protect myself,
not Dex, or Davy – or whoever the fuck he is.

All I have to do is keep my door locked, my knife to hand,
and count off the days. Twenty-nine to go before I can forget
about Dex, the Factory, Alastair, the scumbags who hired me
as Isabella, and everything else that's stopped me living the life
I want.

It's about survival.

Except, of course, old habits die hard.

By lunchtime, my resolve has weakened. Dex and I were never
in love, but we *were* close, and now he's hit rock bottom. I know

how that feels, yet since I confided in Camille and Ashleigh last night, my spirit does feel a tiny bit lighter.

Perhaps that's what Dex needs: absolution.

Plus, I still need to know if he killed Lucas. I type out a text: *Against my better judgement, I will meet you. But somewhere public. After school.*

He sends back a postcode and a *thank you.*

Google Maps takes me to Green Park, a place I've never visited before. I wonder if Dex has either, because arranging to meet close to a royal palace, crawling with police, seems reckless for someone on the run.

A new text arrives on my phone.

I can see you. Follow the path and turn right by the biggest tree.

I do as I'm told, and I get another text telling me to head for the shrub ahead. I am losing patience and text back: *What is this, a treasure hunt?*

But now he's here, in front of me. Facial hair blurs the lines of his jaw, and his eyes are in shadow from the hood of his filthy jacket. If I had glimpsed him as I passed by, I wouldn't have recognised him.

'You stink.'

'I forgot to pack aftershave. Plus BO keeps people at a distance.'

His voice sounds different, but I can't quite work out how. He walks away from the path, towards the furthest edge of the park. It's an effort to keep up but eventually he stops and lowers himself onto the grass, half-facing the open space. His eyes track across the landscape, like a passenger in the window seat of a fast-moving train.

'Am I meant to call you Davy now?'

He sighs. 'Whatever.' It's not only the beard that's new. There's a weariness that makes him seem a decade older.

'Have you been sleeping rough?'

'It's just like being at Scouts camp.'

'You didn't ask me to come here so you could tell me lame jokes, Dex. Davy. Whoever you are.'

He nods. 'I know. Listen, Immi, whatever happens, whatever people say, please believe me. I didn't hurt Lucas . . .' He hesitates.

'There's a but, isn't there?'

'I did find him dead.'

'*What?*'

'I'd seen him earlier that night, drunk and angry. I had decided to leave already and I couldn't sleep so I went up to see if he was OK and . . . Well, he wasn't OK.'

'So, why not call an ambulance, right? Or wake one of us?'

He scans the horizon again. 'I knew he was gone. He was *cold*. And his face? There was nothing left of the person he was, nothing anyone could do.'

'What, you're a fucking doctor, suddenly?'

'No, but I have seen someone . . . overdose before.'

'When? You take photographs, Dex. *Dave*. So unless this was some junkie underworld photoshoot, I don't believe you!'

'I'm not lying. It wasn't work. But it was my fault.'

People cycle past, jog along, throw balls. Anger builds up in me. 'I can't listen to this. You left Lucas. You abandoned me. And now you're saying you've killed someone? Who the hell are you, Dex?'

'I am David Sharp. My family call me Davy. I'm not a kid from the ghetto. I'm from a village between Bristol and Bath.

I rely on my parents' money, because I'm not a good enough photographer to support myself that way.'

I'm struggling to make sense of it. 'OK but why pretend to be someone else?'

'Because of what Davy did. What *I* did. I took on a new name when I came to the Factory because it was meant to be a safe place while I figured out what to do.'

A safe place. 'Who were you hiding from?'

That glazed look magnifies his brown eyes again. 'All sorts of people were after me, that wasn't a lie. I got involved with different stuff. Drugs. I owed money.'

I shake my head. 'You're still lying, Dex, Dave. And you know how I know that? Because the drugs stuff is not enough.'

'Enough for what?'

'Enough for Hanna to blackmail you with.' I close my eyes. 'Why do you think they picked *us* specifically to move in? I'm a boring teacher, you're an underemployed photographer with a fake name.'

He shrugs. 'I never understood why they chose us either.'

'I think it was because they knew they could control us.'

'They? Immi, this has been a very stressful time for you but you're making even less sense than me—'

I hold up my hand to shut him up. 'Listen. Hanna has something on me. You don't need to know what, but it's . . . damaging. And she's using it to keep me at the Factory till this blows over.'

He frowns. 'Why would she care? It's not as if she owns the place.'

I shake my head. 'I don't get it either, but think about it. Zoum is gay, but daren't tell his parents. I'm pretty sure Ashleigh isn't quite what she seems. Lucas was a cokehead. Bernice might have lied about her age and obviously had issues that went a lot deeper . . .'

He thinks about it. 'So what if they did pick people in trouble? They always said the Factory was about helping to create a supportive community.'

I let his words settle around us. 'We both know how that experiment worked out. It's breaking us all.'

He pulls blades of grass out of the earth, shreds them with his fingers. I remember his hands on my body, mine on his. It feels like decades ago. 'Everyone has baggage, Immi. If what you said about Lucas and Bernice is true, that makes it even more likely they took their own lives.'

I scoff. 'It comes to something when that's the best-case scenario.'

The whoops and shouts of the park taunt me, a reminder of how normal people live.

'Do *you* think I killed them?' he asks quietly.

'Did you?'

He shakes his head.

'I want to believe you. But if I do, it means I could still be living with a murderer.'

'Do you genuinely feel at risk there?'

I close my eyes. 'I don't know. The Factory has either made me completely paranoid, or I am in danger.'

'Is there anything I can do, Immi?'

I desperately want to trust him, because I can't trust anyone else. But I'm clutching at straws. 'You're not really in a position to help, are you?'

He scatters the remaining fragments of grass, the tips of his fingers stained bright green. 'Look, I can't go back to the Factory.

But someone needs to sort this out, and you shouldn't have to do it on your own.'

The smell of chlorophyll is potent as coffee. Despite the holes in his story, I am so tired of bearing the weight of this all alone.

And I suddenly think of a way he might be able to help me understand what's really going on.

56

Tuesday 19 June

Dex

The house is twenty-two minutes from the last Tube station on the line. The further I walk, the shabbier the area gets: street after street of ugly houses pebble-dashed with sharp nuggets of stone. Overhead, airplanes take off and land, so close they could give me a buzz cut.

Number 293. There's a kid's bike chained to the rail, and a dog barks loudly in the garden of the neighbour's house. A security camera blinks at me above the front door.

It's probably a big mistake coming here, but I'm not doing it for me. I ring the bell quickly, before I lose my nerve.

A fragile old man answers the door, wearing a cotton shirt three sizes too big.

'If you are a journalist, we have nothing to say.'

His voice is stronger than I expected, and I realise he's younger too, late forties max.

'No. I'm a . . . friend of Zoum. Tell him it's . . . Dex.'

Yesterday, giving Immi my real name felt like surfacing after too long underwater. Now I'm retreating back into the lies.

The line of this man's lips straightens into something like contempt. He walks back into the house and I hear the name *Azoum* along with words in a language I don't recognise.

Zoum appears. When he sees it's me, he shakes his head.

'Just when I thought things could not get any worse . . .'

I open my mouth to apologise, but he holds up his hand. 'My dad had just about got his head around me being a possible serial killer. Now I am best friends with mysterious black men who sleep rough. Terrific.'

I don't know if I'm meant to laugh so I just say, 'It's important, yeah?' in my terrible mockney voice. 'Are you allowed to leave the house?'

'Oh, you want a *play date*. Sure. They don't have me tagged yet.' He pulls on trainers from the bench behind him: there are dozens of pairs of shoes in a row, from flowery girls' sandals to giant loafers. He calls something back into the house in another language.

As we walk, he takes a packet of cigarettes out of his jeans pocket.

'Since when were you a smoker, Zoum?' I ask.

'Since I got bailed to be at home. Gives me an excuse to get out twenty times a day.' There's one cigarette left in the packet. He lights it. 'Why are you here, Dex?'

'Because Immi might be in danger. We need to find out who is behind the death and we've both ruled you out.' This is a lie, but it's what Immi and I agreed I would say. 'She thought you might be able to find stuff online about the Factory, to help clear both our names.'

He gives me a sideways glance. 'Shame she's not here too,' Zoum says. 'What a cosy reunion that would have been.'

'She asked me to come instead of her, because she's worried you'd be angry. She got you arrested.'

Ahead of us there's a small play park, with a group of young teens hanging out near the swings.

Zoum walks through the gates and sits down on a bench. I join him. 'Thing is, Dexter, I told them myself that I'd hacked the security system.'

'*What?*'

'I would never wish to hinder the investigation so I volunteered everything: why I was angry with the committee for their behaviour, the things I did to mess with their heads.'

'But . . .'

'Of course, I hoped they would be able to tell the difference between a prankster and a murderer. It turns out I gave them credit for being more analytical than they really are.'

'They still think you did it?'

Zoum sighs. He's finished his cigarette and his fingers are twitching, as though he needs something else to occupy them. 'They let me go, but only because they want time to find more evidence. I bet I could get back in their good books by calling them up and telling them *you* are here.'

The idea of the police coming right now chills me. 'Why haven't you done that?'

'Curiosity. Who do you think might have done it, Dex, if it is neither me nor you?'

'It's a pretty short list. Immi is very suspicious of Hanna but I suppose it could be Camille, or even Ashleigh.' I shake my head. 'Neither of them seems that likely, though.'

One of the older kids is sloping towards us. They're all in school uniform, and it's the middle of the day so I guess they're bunking off.

'Whaddya want?' the kid asks.

'I'll buy a couple of tabs off you,' Zoum says. The kid looks insulted, but reaches into his blazer pocket to get out a packet. I see the flash of a knife but Zoum doesn't seem to notice, handing over a few coins.

'I like to encourage young enterprise,' Zoum says as the kid swaggers back to his mates. 'Hanna, yes, it could be her. Apart from me, she is the only one with access to every room. But I am afraid you, Dex, are not in the clear either as far as I am concerned.'

'Why not?'

'Because you ran. But also . . . I do not know who you are, but you're definitely not a streetwise photographer called Dex.'

I try not to react, but this is what I was dreading when Immi asked me to come and talk to him. I have to send him off course. 'OK, but there's one other person Immi mentioned and that's Jamie.'

Zoum smiles. 'Trying to distract me, Dex? OK. Let us proceed with the idea of Jamie as a suspect for the moment. He certainly has the motivation to destroy the people who almost destroyed him.'

He reaches into his jacket pocket and for a moment I wonder if he's got a weapon. Instead, he takes out an old phone, scrolls through his gallery and magnifies one image before handing it to me. 'You may also want to tell Immi about this. It is from the open day the weekend that Bernice jumped. Or was pushed.'

It's a picture of a young man outside the entrance door to the Factory. He's moved his head to the side, as though he knows exactly where the cameras are. But still I can make out his jaw-line, slack with puppy fat. 'I'm guessing this is Jamie.'

'Yup.' Zoum nods. 'I don't remember seeing him at any of Ashleigh's wild fermentation workshops on the open day so what *was* he doing there?'

'Does it show him leaving the Factory?'

'Yes. Twenty-six minutes later. So he couldn't have physically *pushed* Bernice off the roof. But what if he said something that made her scared or desperate enough to see jumping as the only way out?'

'Was he in the building on the day Lucas died?'

'I'm not meant to tell you this, but if you *are* the killer, you'd know it already. The more recent CCTV images of people coming and going have been wiped off the server. It's a big coincidence, isn't it? Hanna can do that. Or someone with a lot of money to pay for it to be done.'

'Or you?'

Zoum holds my gaze, his light eyes fixed on mine.

A shriek breaks the spell – we'll never know which of us would have outstared the other. The kids at the other end are opening cans of beer, spilling them over each other.

'Why did *you* really come, Dex? To see if you are off the hook?'

'No. Immi asked me to. She needs help, because Hanna is trying to blackmail her into staying.'

'What on earth could they have on a sweet primary school teacher?'

'She wouldn't tell me. But it's enough to keep her there when she feels unsafe.'

Zoum stands up, grinding the second cigarette under his trainer. 'Even if I wanted to help her and you, the police took away my laptops and mobile. This piece of shit is my mother's old phone, and I only got this photo because I had already uploaded it to the cloud after digging around when Bernice died.'

Part of me feels relieved: if he can't investigate the Factory, he also can't go online to investigate me. But that doesn't help Immi.

I reach into my pocket and pull out £30. 'Zoum, I don't trust you, you don't trust me. But we both care about Immi. There must be an internet café you could use to look into Jamie and Hanna.'

He looks at the money. 'You think I will be able to resist looking into you too?'

'I'd hope you'd focus on them, not me. But it's in both our interests to find out what has really gone on in the Factory.'

Though uncovering that won't change what's going to happen to me.

Zoum takes the money. 'All right, I will try. Your sisters must be missing you.'

I stare at him. Has all this been a bluff? Does he already know who I am and what I've done?

'What makes you think I have sisters?'

'Lucky guess. A man as full of himself as you almost always has devoted sisters who make him feel like a god.'

57

Tuesday 19 June

Immi

I never thought I'd wear this dress again.

The silky fabric is tighter around the hips – maybe because when I last wore it, I was too broke to eat properly. I tug it down, but that makes my neckline too low.

Cleavage or legs, never both. Except when I am Isabella.

Dex waits outside on the street. The state he's in right now the bouncers wouldn't let him through the door, though this wanky place suits Jamie Henderson down to the ground. Zoum tracked down where he's working now, and Dex followed him from his office.

They make an unlikely team but they're all I've got.

'Looks like it's someone's birthday,' Dex said when he called me. 'They're all getting wasted on champagne, and Jamie's pestering all the girls. Tonight could be the night if you want to get him to talk.'

I don't think Jamie would have seen me in the public gallery at court, but just in case, I plaster on as much make-up as I did in the bad old days. Dewy foundation to perk up my sallow skin, kohl to make my eyes smoky, lipstick in a plummy colour. Red would be too tarty.

The lipstick has a chalky texture because it hasn't been used for so long. I lean over the basins, blot my lips, check my teeth.

I'm as ready as I'll ever be.

A bassy dance track plays as I leave the toilets and go up the steps into the main bar. When Jamie finally glances my way, I walk slowly towards him, before veering off towards the counter. In my everyday wear, I struggle to get served. In this outfit, two male bar staff fall over each other to take my order.

'What can I get you?'

'Tonic, please, lots of ice.' I need to stay sober.

Jamie is not sober. His suit is crumpled and his soft face is slack. I position myself in his eyeline again and it's not long before he clocks me. It's almost a double-take and for a moment I hate myself for taking advantage.

No. According to Dex, he is Zoum's only suspect. Though, of course, I can't be sure Dex is telling me the truth.

I sip my drink, look up, look down, lick my lips. The whole thing seems so clumsy and obvious, yet I know from experience that this works with men older and a lot wiser than Jamie.

When I do it a second time, he actually looks behind him, wondering if there's another man I'm trying to attract. He whispers something to a colleague, who checks me out and gives Jamie an encouraging nudge. At last, he breaks away from the group and joins me at the bar.

'You're not a journalist, are you?'

I shake my head. 'No. Why? Are you famous?'

He half smiles and I smell alcohol. 'Infamous maybe.'

'Sounds intriguing.'

'It's really not. Are you waiting for someone?'

'A friend. But she's stood me up, so I'm just finishing my drink before I head home . . .' I tail off, inviting him to make me a better offer.

He hesitates. Even being drunk may not be enough to overcome his shyness. Is this really a man who could have harassed Camille, manipulated Bernice into suicide and murdered Lucas?

I take another sip of my tonic and give him a lingering look. A raw hunger appears in his eyes. 'Could I buy you one for the road?' he says.

I look at my watch and smile. 'I suppose my arm *could* be twisted.'

One drink turns into six. His are doubles, mine end up in a pot plant when he goes to the gents. I have to judge it right: wait till he's drunk enough not to notice how loaded my questions are, but still just sober enough to be capable of answering them.

Through the window of the bar, Dex observes us together like a jealous ex.

Jamie and I have talked about London – the people, the traffic, the *noise*. When we switched to Scotland, his eyes became moist so I almost thought he might begin to cry, but he snapped out of that when I asked about his family. He doesn't mention how rich they are, perhaps because he fears I'm a gold-digger, but casual asides give the game away: the second home, the boarding school education. There's a whiff of entitlement about him, combined with an undercurrent of *poor me*.

'The City reminds me a lot of school,' he tells me.

'Was there that rule where you do whatever the older boys want?'

Jamie shrugs. 'Fagging? Not at my school. But there was bullying. I was a . . . late developer.' He laughs, embarrassed. 'I've caught up now.'

'I'd agree with that,' I say, holding his gaze. But in truth, he seems more like a spoiled kid than a grown-up. 'Where do you live now?'

He tells me about his flat share in Hammersmith. 'I'm in South London,' I say. 'The shittier bit. But one day I'd love to be by the Thames – London Bridge or Bermondsey. I have a mate who lives there.'

'Ugh. I lived there when I first arrived. I'd never go back. Full of liars and psychopaths.'

'That's a bit harsh!'

'Believe me, it's not. My flatmates thought it was a game to mess with each other's heads. Their lives. It almost ended my career.'

'Seriously?'

He nods, and I leave space for him to keep talking. But at the last moment, he shakes his head. 'You don't want to know.'

When he goes to the toilet again, I text Dex. *He's not taking the bait.*

The reply comes back: *Plan B then. But STAY SAFE.*

I hoped I wouldn't have to resort to what I'm about to do.

When Jamie returns, I complain about the heat and suggest a walk. As we leave the pub, I glance up at the CCTV in the corner and hope it's recording us, in case . . . I don't believe this man-child is a killer but my judgement has been proved wrong many times before.

The night is cooler now the sun's gone down. I shiver and he takes off his jacket and drapes it over my bare shoulders. He's working up to a kiss, but he's so drunk I easily step out of the way.

'I'm a bit tipsy, could we sit down?'

The bench overlooks the pedestrian bridge to Embankment. There are plenty of people around so I feel relatively safe.

He leans towards me, his breath almost flammable with vodka fumes.

I hold up my hand to stop him getting closer. 'I don't want you to be angry with me, Jamie, but there's something I need to tell you.'

'You're a prostitute,' he says, then giggles. 'It's OK. I guessed. I have money. How much do you cost?'

A spike of anger runs through me. But let's face it, I dressed and acted like a tart. I can hardly blame him for thinking I am one.

'I'm not a prostitute, Jamie. I am the person who moved into your room at the Factory. And I'm really scared.'

His eyes dart about, as his drunken brain processes this. 'You – they . . .' He shakes his head as though trying to clear it. 'This is a set-up? You *fucking* bitch.'

'I promise, I'm not setting you up. The police don't know I'm here. Hanna doesn't.'

'What about Cam?' There's a tiny note of what sounds like hope in his voice.

'The only other person who knows about me being here is Zoum.'

Jamie frowns. 'OK. He didn't take sides. Though the cops arrested him, right? As well as me . . .' He stops himself. 'If you're scared, leave. But it's got nothing to do with me now.'

He tries to stand up but I grab his hand. 'They won't let me, Jamie. You said it yourself, they're liars and psychopaths. And you think you're in the clear but you're not.'

'What are you talking about?'

I take a breath, hoping the double bluff might work. 'They've got a picture of you at the Factory on the day Bernice died. They must have doctored it because there's no way you would have gone back, right?'

He sits back down again, a numb expression on his face. 'Shit. *Shit!*'

'Oh God. You did go back, didn't you?'

He closes his eyes. 'It was a spur of the moment thing. I still get the emails I signed up for when I came to London, about classes in the area, places to make friends. There was one about Ashleigh's open day. I'd been trying to get on with my life but . . . I was desperate to see Cam.'

I wasn't expecting that. 'Why?'

'She's not like the others. She's . . . vulnerable. I wanted to apologise. I loved her. I *love* her.'

'Surely going to see her was asking for trouble after the court case?'

'That only happened because Bernice and Lucas made her go through with it. They turned something special into something sordid.' He puts his head in his hands and when he speaks, it's more of a whisper. 'I wanted to try one last time to persuade her to leave.'

'What did she say?'

Jamie exhales. 'I never got the chance to see her. Bernice saw me first. We had . . . words. I hate that woman. *Hated* that woman. Everything that went toxic in that building was down to her and her power games.'

'So you didn't hurt Cam then?'

'No, but they twisted it in her mind, to protect themselves. If I'd been able to have a proper relationship with Cam, that would have broken up their little clique.'

What he's saying sounds outlandish – yet given what I know about the bets, can I be sure it's not true? 'What did you say to Bernice?'

'I told her what I thought of her. I wasn't particularly polite.'

'How did she respond?'

'She wasn't like she was before. Barely argued back when I told her what I thought of her. She seemed . . . lost.' He tails off. I think he *does* fear he pushed Bernice, if not physically, then mentally. 'I walked away. It felt like kicking someone when they're down.'

'Did you try to see Cam?'

'No. Bernice begged me not to. Said Cam was already on the edge after the trial, that it would be no good for me or her.'

'So you just left?'

'Yep. I didn't even know Bernice had died until the news broke about Lucas and the police came to talk to me. They didn't tell me about that CCTV picture, though.'

Maybe they were holding it back. I hope I haven't screwed up their case. 'You can understand why they suspect you.'

He nods. 'I won't lie. There were times when I was so mad I wanted to hurt them all – Cam included. But however loathsome Bernice and Lucas were, I never wanted them to *die*.'

I want to believe him. 'So who do *you* think killed them, Jamie?'

He lets out a bitter laugh. 'Pretty much everyone who ever lived at the Factory would have a reason. I was saying to Ronnie the other day that there's a kind of poetic justice to it all.'

'Ronnie?'

'Veronica? She used to be my boss. She's the one who vouched for me and got me into the Factory in the first place.'

I'd almost forgotten about her. 'How is it poetic justice?'

'Because eventually Bernice and Lucas must have encountered someone even more psychopathic than them. What are the odds?'

'It does seem a big coincidence.'

'Are you done with interrogating me now?' Jamie says, interrupting my thoughts.

'Yes.' I hand his jacket back. 'I wouldn't have misled you if I didn't have to.'

He shrugs and stands up a little unsteadily. 'I should have known you were too sodding good to be true.'

Jamie shrugs his jacket back on as he walks off towards Waterloo. The night air is bitter against my bare shoulders and legs. I don't know what – or who – to believe now.

But I do not believe this is over.

58

Wednesday 20 June

Immi

I wake after a disrupted night's sleep and take a coffee up to the terrace, past my old, locked-up studio, and the ones where Lucas and Bernice lived.

Tomorrow's the longest day, and a yellow midsummer fug hangs over the rooftops. The kids will be hot and fractious. At least they might stop me thinking about death.

What Jamie told me last night hasn't clarified anything. The only part that really rang true was what he said about Bernice's mood. That and the part when he speculated about the odds of so many damaged people living together.

Except he didn't say *damaged people*. He said *psychopaths*.

Work is hard-going. At break, my phone buzzes with a message from a number I don't recognise.

This is Zoum. I need to meet you urgently.

I never expected to hear from him. Dex told me Zoum was still angry with me for getting him arrested. I type my reply: *What about? I could get away straight after school.*

The kids are being shepherded back towards the building as I wait for his response.

About Dex. Oxford Circus, 5pm? Bail conditions mean I cannot come near the Factory and I have 8pm curfew.

At home time, I take the bus into town, wondering what Zoum might have to tell me. Despite everything that's happened, part of me is looking forward to seeing him, making sure he's OK. Apart from Dex, he's the only Dyer I had any time for.

Through the grubby window, the cityscape gradually changes from run-down to wealthy. But posh is overrated. Scratch the surface and there's nothing but decay underneath. Once I get my deposit back from the Factory, I'll look for somewhere closer to school, somewhere more real.

Zoum stands on the opposite corner of the big junction at Oxford Circus, head darting from side to side as the crowds swirl around him. He looks fragile and small. I wave but he doesn't notice me until I cross over and step into his eyeline. It makes him jump.

'It's OK. Just me,' I say.

'I hate crowds. Can we find somewhere quieter?'

We end up in the John Lewis café, where most of the other customers are twice our age and have bags-for-life overflowing with haberdashery and cookware and cured Spanish sausage. By silent agreement, Zoum and I wait till our coffees have arrived before I ask him why he wanted to meet. 'Because if it is about streetwise Dex actually being posh Davy from Bath, I already know.'

Zoum looks surprised. 'He told you?'

'Yup.'

'But did he tell you about *this*?' He opens up his messenger bag and takes out a folder of printouts. 'I had to go to an internet café to find all this, and the printer quality was awful. But you will get the idea.'

He slides the top sheet across the table. It's from a news website: DRUG DEATH PROBE AFTER GIRL, 19, DIES AT HOUSE PARTY

The piece, dated early April this year, is one of those horrible stories about a young woman taking a dodgy MDMA and dying before she could get to hospital. Her name isn't mentioned, but the party happened near Hammersmith, in West London.

'And?'

'Once I worked out Dex's real name – reverse photo searches, electoral register, it really was not that hard – I also found out where he had been living before the Factory. It was in *that* house, where the girl died.'

Instantly, I remember what Dex said two days ago, sitting on the grass in Green Park. *I've seen someone overdose.*

I blink, bring myself back to the present. 'Is this all there was in the papers?' I ask Zoum.

He passes a few more sheets across. 'An appeal for people who were at the party to come forward, because the police needed more witnesses. Plus lots of posts by friends about her funeral a couple of weeks ago.'

The final sheet shows her picture: she's pretty-bordering-on-beautiful, with red hair that reminds me of poor Bernice's and a slightly awkward smile that hides retainers on her teeth. She was studying business.

I shudder. 'You think *this* is why Dex came to the Factory? Because he was on the run for supplying drugs to this girl?'

'We cannot be certain. But the timing suggests he was there at the party, then left and applied to the Factory only a week later.'

I close my eyes. He said in the park that he'd seen someone dead before Lucas. It must have been this girl. Another memory comes to me now. When I was trying to sober him up after Bernice died, he warned me he'd hurt someone. *I'm dangerous, Immi . . .*

The girl's overdose doesn't look deliberate. But if Dex has been present at the unexpected deaths of three people, it cannot be a coincidence. 'You think he's some kind of serial killer?' I say it a little too loudly, and two women look up from their lattes in surprise. It would almost be comic if it weren't so terrible.

Zoum sighs. 'I am aware this sounds far-fetched, but so is this situation. The most frightening thing to me is that there seems to be no connection between the death of that girl, and Bernice or Lucas.'

'So Dex is doing it, what, for fun?'

He shrugs. 'Maybe even Dex himself would not know. The bigger question is what do we do now? I cannot see the police taking any allegations I make seriously.'

'Look. I'm so sorry about talking to the police about you.'

'It's nothing. As I said to Dex, I told the police myself. I do not hold you responsible in any way.'

'You told Dex this? He told me you were still angry that I landed you in it.'

Zoum shakes his head. 'Not at all. But clearly Dexter wanted to ensure you would not speak directly to me, for fear of my response.'

What else has he lied about?

'I just . . . I trusted him, Zoum.'

'Do you think *he* trusts *you*? You could call the police but they do not seem to have made much progress finding him so far. If you could ask him outright, and record his answers somehow, we might find out the truth. But this could be risky.'

'Riskier than living in the Factory?' I say, raising my eyebrows.

'If you are worried, you should leave.'

'I can't afford it. Hanna says she'd keep my deposit and pursue me for another month on top. There's no way I'd be able to get a new place.'

He gives me an odd look. 'It must surely be worth living on beans on toast for a few weeks to stand a better chance of staying alive.'

I look down. 'It's . . . more complicated than you might think.'

'Hanna and her files, am I right?'

I say nothing.

'I have not only been researching Dex. I tried to find information about Hanna and the Factory while I lived there, but got nowhere. Strangely, now I am searching in another location, I've found much more of interest.'

'Such as?'

'Such as the fact that Hanna was previously an influential academic specialising in the psychology of groups at the University of Aarhus?'

'That's . . . weird.'

'Also, the holding company that owns the Factory has a link to Formilex, one of the biggest pharma groups in Scandinavia. Do big pharma and communal living seem natural bedfellows?'

'Unless they're drugging us all without us knowing.'

'Again, I will not be sharing that theory with my new friends at the Metropolitan Police.' He looks at his watch. 'I need to get the Tube now so I will be safely home without breaching my bail. Another night in front of *Love Island* with my dear family.'

'And I'm heading back to hell.'

'Where is *real* home for you, Immi?'

I push down the feeling of sadness the word 'home' triggers. 'Cheshire. But I've come a long way since leaving. I don't want to go back.'

'I will keep digging about Formilex and Hanna. It may help you to force their hand regarding your tenancy. And as for Dex, keep your distance. Let us talk in the morning, things may seem clearer then.'

On the Tube to London Bridge, I cannot think straight. What I've learned about Dex is terrifying. Yet I also feel he *wants* to tell someone the truth. Could I persuade him to tell me what happened?

At least he's no longer living at the Factory. But what Zoum told me about Hanna scares me too. Are we rats in some experimental maze she's built for her own research? If so, what was she trying to prove or disprove about the behaviour of groups?

When I get into the Factory, I re-examine every light fitting, every designer detail, to see if I can spot any cameras or microphones that Hanna might have installed as part of some academic experiment. I pour a glass of water, sniff it and take tiny sips, trying to taste or smell something wrong, any trace of pharmaceuticals.

Nothing.

Logically, no drug company would run a trial this way.

Screw logic. I pour the tap water down the sink and fill a fresh glass from the large bottle I bought on the way home.

Dex tries to call me but I let my mobile ring out, knowing he won't dare leave a voicemail. I haven't decided what to do about him yet.

After supper, Ashleigh uses benign emotional blackmail to get me and Camille to join her for a sunset yoga session on the terrace. Camille's limbs are so thin they look like they'd snap if she stretched any further.

'We are so close to the solstice now,' Ashleigh intones. 'It is a time that the earliest humans understood had a huge effect on all life. Let us feel the power of the sun.'

I watch Ashleigh too, her eyes closed as she speaks. Even if Zoum finds something to help get me out of my tenancy, can I abandon Camille to this woman, with her dodgy tattoo and her emotional vampirism?

'Even as the sun's last rays fade, we know we can rely on it rising again tomorrow. Breathe in the warmth, breathe out your fears.'

Afterwards, as we sit on the artificial grass drinking Ashleigh's chamomile tea, I debate whether to tell them anything I discussed with Zoum. I don't want to feed Camille's fears, yet it doesn't feel safe to keep them in complete ignorance.

'I, um, need to mention something to you both, about what's happened here, and about Dex, too.'

Camille looks up sharply.

'I don't want to worry you but I've found out a few things – well, Zoum has – about Dex's past. A girl died, where he was living before, not long before he came to the Factory. And I know he's lied about other things.'

Ashleigh inhales. 'How did she die?'

'She'd taken drugs. At least, that's what the police said.'

Camille shakes her head. 'Like Lucas?'

'We shouldn't jump to conclusions and I'm sure the police are across all of this,' I say. 'Don't forget, we should be safer inside here than anywhere else, thanks to the new security Hanna has organised.'

Ashleigh puts her arm around me and I smell that lavender scent and imagine that spider's web tattoo on her back and I want to throw her off. But I don't, because I know she wants to help and I don't want to hurt her.

'Shh, Immi,' she whispers. 'As you say, the police will be across it. And Hanna has our best interests at heart.'

It's too much.

I shrug her off. 'You think Hanna does? Seriously? You don't know anything about Hanna. None of us do.'

Ashleigh pouts. 'You've never liked her, have you?'

'It's not about liking her, it's about . . .' The frustration builds and I am struggling not to shout. 'She's not some kindly caretaker. She's a psychologist for a university. I think she's been studying us or something. And this building is owned by some Scandinavian drug company. Think about it logically. They could make a fortune selling the building, or just renting it in the normal way. Why set up a community unless there's an ulterior motive?'

Camille shakes her head. 'What would that be?'

Ashleigh looks sceptical. 'Come on, Immi. Are you saying we're being drugged? Used as guinea pigs?'

I think of Bella the guinea pig, dead on Bernice's bed and I have this terrible urge to laugh. Ashleigh makes a strange noise and I realise I am half-expecting Hanna to appear from nowhere and accuse me of screwing up some vital research.

I force myself to exhale and inhale before I speak again. 'I don't have the answers, OK? Maybe it is all legit but the secrecy is doing my head in. Honestly, I don't know how much more of it I can take.'

'Please don't leave us, Immi.' Camille's voice trembles as she says my name. 'I want everything to be the same.' Her forehead is criss-crossed with lines. I reach out to take her hand, and it feels weightless.

Ashleigh sees what I'm doing and reaches for me and Camille as well, making a circle of three.

She smiles. 'It *will* be the same,' she says. 'We'll come through this together. It might even end up better than before.'

59

Thursday 21 June

Immi

Midsummer's day.

At school, I talk to the kids about the solstice and Stonehenge and the mystery of how those four-tonne boulders were moved into place.

'Was it space aliens?' Patrice asks me.

'Anything's possible, that's why it's unexplained.'

But I'm struggling to focus. It's Dex I am thinking about, as I did all last night. I replayed the nights we spent together, wondering if he was plotting to kill *me* as I slept. I think about the young girl with red hair, too. Is it more than chance that Bernice looked similar, and she's now dead too?

A big part of me cannot accept he could kill anyone. But whatever the truth is, he can't keep running. How can I persuade him to get help?

At break, I get a message from Zoum. *Check your email now.*

It's a single document, and the minute I understand what it means, I have to call Dex. He answers within two rings.

'I know why you ran, Dex.' I can't think of him as Davy. 'I know about the party where you used to live, and what happened. You have to go to the police to bring an end to all this. I'll come with you, if you want.'

He says nothing. In the background, I hear the echoes of footsteps and voices, as though he's in a tunnel or an underpass.

'If you know where I lived then you know what I did. Why would you want to help me?'

'Because it wasn't your fault. I've got something to show you that proves it.'

'You're lying.'

'I promise you, I'm not. I have to be in Bermondsey after school to keep an eye on Camille but I could meet up for a short while?'

'You're nuts if you think I'm ever going back to the Factory.'

'Not there, but the park, Leathermarket Gardens? Dex, I promise, you don't have to hide now.'

I hear a sigh. 'How do I know you won't tell the police where I'm going to be, Immi?'

'I could have done that the night we met Jamie but I didn't. Please. You have to trust me.'

Another sigh. 'OK,' he says. 'I'll be there at half past four. But if I think you're trying to trap me, I won't stick around. And you won't ever hear from me again.'

Ashleigh sends me her usual handover message at three, before she heads off to her volunteer job with refugee kids.

What does she get out of it? Before, I thought she did it because she was good. Now I wonder whether working with the vulnerable gives her an element of control.

Don't want to speak too soon but Camille seems a bit better today. I wonder if knowing we're all together has made her a bit less stressed. Hanna is around if you need any help. Ax

As I get off the bus near London Bridge, I feel the sun on my face and I wonder if this might be the beginning of the end, so long as Dex believes me enough to show up.

I buzz myself into the Factory.

'Camille? It's only me, Imogen.'

She doesn't reply but she sleeps a lot these days. My footsteps echo around the quiet space as I climb the stairs. Apart from me, her and Hanna, the place will be completely empty.

I'm slightly breathless by the time I reach the kitchen, so I pour myself water from the tap – all the paranoia I felt yesterday about drugs in the filter system seems ridiculous today.

'Shall I make us a coffee?' I call up, but Camille can't have heard me. Perhaps she's up on the terrace. It *is* a gorgeous afternoon. Maybe I can talk to her about the future and what she might do when she leaves the Factory. It might be easier to get through to her without Little Miss Sunshine there too.

I take my glass of water up to Retreat. I'm going to change out of my work clothes before meeting Dex. I want him to know from the instant he sees me that everything can be OK.

Though I'll have my knife with me. Just in case.

I have my phone ready to buzz into Warsaw, but as I turn my head to call out to Camille a third time, I see something that stops me.

The door to her studio is wide open.

'Camille? Camille, are you there?'

I walk towards Paris, my skin prickling with apprehension and my ears straining for any sounds of life. Not again. Please.

'*Fuck!*'

The glass drops from my hand and smashes on the floor. Water splashes my bare ankles.

Camille's studio has been ransacked.

Pieces of broken glass crunch under my soles as I step inside. I feel a sharp pain as one slips through the gaps in my sandals and pierces my skin.

I shouldn't go any further. If this is what I think it is, forensics will want the scene intact.

But then I spot something on the bed that makes me gasp.

Edward the rabbit: he doesn't look at all injured, but his body is completely lifeless.

Bernice's scream when she found Bella echoes round my head. If that was *her* final warning, what does this mean for Camille?

It's over an hour since Ashleigh sent her message. I dial her number as I run around the building. Retreat is open-plan and I can see no one is hiding where the animals used to live. The door to Edward's empty cage has been closed.

Hi this is Ashleigh, leave me a message.

I ring off and head up the stairs to Play and the terrace, trying not to make any noise in case there's someone in here who shouldn't be.

Someone like Jamie?

I creep down towards the kitchen area again and dial Zoum's number. After eight rings, when I am certain it's about to go to voicemail, he picks up.

'Is everything all right, Immi?'

'I'm in the Factory,' I whisper, aware how sound bounces off the brick walls and hard floors. 'Something's wrong, Zoum. Camille has gone, and her room has been burgled. And the rabbit's dead. On Camille's bed—'

'OK. Hold on. Hold on. You are still in the building?' His voice is soothing – I'm not alone.

'Yeah. I think whoever did this must have gone.'

'You told Dex about the report?'

'I told him he's in the clear, we're meant to be meeting outside so I can show him what you found . . .'

'And is Hanna there?'

'She'll be in the basement, I'm going there next.'

'All right. Stay on the phone to me. I'm in the internet café and I can probably log into the front door CCTV. But if you have even the slightest sense that you are in danger, then get out of the bloody building, Imogen.'

Something about his tone shocks me and I realise: I have never heard him swear before.

I keep the phone pressed against my ear as I tiptoe down the steps, towards the main entrance. The sound of Zoum's rapid touch-typing at the other end of the line reassures me.

'Are you seeing anything online?'

He tuts. 'No. What time did you come into the building?'

'Just after four.' I wait at the top of the stairs to the basement.

'Hold on . . . just fast-forwarding the CCTV, but you're not showing up. But . . . that cab going past at three minutes to . . . It went through at exactly the same time an hour before . . .'

'I'm going into the basement now, Zoum, but I'm not ringing off. Maybe Hanna's hurt.' My hand closes around the knife in my pocket as I take the final rough uneven steps down. 'Keep talking to me . . .'

'Imogen, I think you ought to leave, you should call . . . or I will . . .'

The signal breaks up as I cross the rough concrete towards Hanna's office. There's a light on inside. My heart beats so loud I can hear nothing else, not even my feet on the floor.

'Hanna, are you there? Camille's not upstairs and I'm worried something's happened to her.'

Just before I get to her office, I hear something: a whimper.

And when I step into the doorway I see her.

Not Hanna but Camille, her face a bloodied mess, her mouth closed by thick silver tape, her body tied to a chair. One of her eyes is so badly swollen it's completely shut. The other shows raw terror.

60

Dex

I might as well be standing in the middle of Trafalgar Square wearing a T-shirt reading *Most Wanted*.

Leathermarket Gardens is full of happy families. I used to belong to one. I guess I still do, but they'd disown me if they knew the kind of person I really am.

I check my watch. Immi is late. She told me she had something she *needed to show me*.

I've been trying to work out what it might be: good news, or a trap? Except, there is never good news, not since Jade died.

How did I get to this point? Everything about my upbringing was perfect – the kind of childhood that only ever lasts the first ten minutes of a disaster movie, before everything falls apart.

All that love, but here I am, stinking and hairy-faced, so that mothers keep hurrying their kids away from me, like I'm the bogeyman. They can't think any less of me than I do myself.

Not for much longer. Regardless of what Immi wants to show me, I've decided to stop running and face what I deserve. I'm going to ask Immi to come with me to the police, because she's the closest I have to a friend.

I send an SMS: *I'm here, next to the community hall. Trying not to look like an escaped convict.*

Will I cope with prison? After the Factory, it might be easy. Except people say that men who have killed young women or kids get the roughest ride.

I check my phone. She's ten minutes late. The longer I wait, the more I want to run.

I text Immi again. Try to call her. It goes to voicemail.

The lack of response unnerves me. I pace, going through the words I plan to say at the front desk of whichever police station we go to.

My name is Davy Sharp. You've been looking for me.

Eighteen minutes late now. Has she given up on me? I want to tell her everything, and I begin to walk towards the Factory. I suppose if the police see me now, it won't matter that much.

As I walk, I call Zoum. I still don't trust him, but I am worried not to have heard from Immi.

'Dex!' When he answers, he sounds panicky. 'Are you with Immi?'

'No, I was calling to ask you the same. I'm meant to be meeting her, so she can let me see something. But she hasn't shown up.'

'Shit! Are you near the Factory? I was on the phone to her when it went dead. But there's limited signal in the basement, so I was not sure whether to call the police. But she should have called me back by now . . .'

Immi is in danger. The phone battery burns in my hand and the sounds of the park fade away. I start to run. 'I'm going there now but I don't think my app will still work so I won't have any way to get in.'

'Stay on the line, Dex. If you cannot get an answer on the intercom, I shall telephone the police.'

I tell myself it will be OK but how can I believe that? I do care about Immi, and she seems to care about me too, which is more than I deserve. 'She said things were going to get sorted out.'

'Yes. I found something, Dex. About the girl who died,' Zoum is saying.

Shit. 'Believe me, if I'd known, I'd never have given her the drugs. Not that it makes it better, I know that, but—'

'It was not the drugs that caused Jade's death, Dex.'

I keep running. 'What?'

'I sent Immi the post-mortem report. They thought it was drugs at first, ran so many different tests but her parents paid for a second PM. That's how they found out she was stung by a bee. That is what killed her. A catastrophic anaphylactic reaction to a bee sting on her upper leg.'

A flashback to that night: kissing the girl I'd just met, my housemates jeering . . .

'Are you . . . Are you sure?'

Going out into the garden, kissing her more. The old me had a swagger, and girls liked that. I didn't even know Jade's surname, not then.

'Yes. The police have dropped all their investigations. She never noticed the sting. No one did.'

Crashing into the bushes, the prickle of thorns against my body and the smoothness of her skin. Giggling like kids as we settled on the hard tiles at the back of the garden, out of sight. But continuing, despite the discomfort . . .

It takes me a few seconds to process what Zoum's news means for me. Jade's death was pointless, tragic, devastating. But it wasn't my fault.

The sounds of the street return in a wave, and everything is suddenly more colourful. There is nothing special about today to the kids on their way home from school, or the people vaping outside their office blocks.

But for me, today is the day I am reborn.

My posture's already changing: my body knows I don't have to hide anymore. It's a hot day and I let the hood of my filthy fleece drop away from my head. I pull at the sleeves and tear it off me, dumping it on the street. It's like shedding skin.

Now I can run faster.

Tanner's Walk is quiet, with the windows of the Factory blazing orange in the afternoon sun. I go cold when I think of Bernice jumping off the terrace, onto the cobbles.

'I need to hang up, to see if I can get access via the app.'

'Call me when you're in, or I am calling the police.'

A darkness passes through me. 'Zoum, maybe you should call them anyway.'

As I half-expected, nothing happens when I hold my phone up to the lock. So I press the buzzer. Lean on it, not letting go, sensing the vibration underneath my fingertip, and knowing the alert that'll be sounding on every one of the floors.

No one is coming.

Now I knock against the wood with my fist.

The guy from the café opposite – heavily built as a bouncer, thick hair unnaturally black – takes a few steps towards me. 'They don't answer the door no more, mate, because of all the journalists.'

'I'm meeting someone.'

He shades his eyes from the sun with his hand. 'I recognise you.'

'Yeah, I used to live here.'

'Better off out of it. They should close it down, I've been saying that for years.'

'I'm sorry, I don't have time for this right now.'

He huffs. 'Yeah, well, *I* didn't have time to mop up blood outside my café twice in bloody ten years.'

'Someone died here before?'

'First one jumped after I'd only been here a few months. Only a young kid, too. I knew him. Face-planted onto the stones. Obvious he was dead.' There's a relish in his voice that makes me nauseous.

I look up and shiver. 'How terrible.' I bash on the timber again with my fist but it barely moves. 'Have you got a hammer or a crowbar?'

The man nods, his eyes darting up as he remembers. 'His name was Sam. Polite lad, barely out of university. He came here, every morning, first customer of the day. These kids in the City jobs, they work longer hours even than me.'

'Please! Do you have anything I could use to smash the lock? I'm worried about someone inside. I've been trying to call her and I know she's in there.'

He looks dubious.

'I've called the police already,' I say, 'but it might be a matter of life and death.'

'Well, I suppose.'

'Please hurry up!'

He heads back to the café and I call out, 'Immi! Camille! Are you in there? The police are coming.'

The café owner trots back over, carrying a hammer, prattling on.

'Weirdest thing of all was he was filthy rich, Sam. His family owned the building. Denmark they were from. Hang on, no. They *lived* in Denmark but they came from Finland. Sam said the Finns were famous for Nokia and Moomins and sexy blondes getting their kit off in saunas. To be fair, though, I might have added the bit about sexy blondes myself.'

And deep in my brain, something slots into place and I aim the hammer at the lock with the hardest blow I can manage . . .

61

Immi

'Jesus, Camille, what happened to you?'

I rush forward. Where do I begin? I think of the first-aid class I did in teacher training: airway, first.

I try to pull the tape away from her mouth, in case she's struggling to breathe. Blood has dried around the edges and it's difficult to remove without hurting her.

'This might sting.'

I pull it away with a sharp snap, like taking off a plaster. She licks her lips, which are puckered from dryness.

'Hanna,' she says.

I spin round, half-expecting her to be behind me. 'Is she still here?'

'No. She . . . got me . . .' Her throat sounds raw. 'I asked her . . . about the Finnish drugs company you mentioned and . . .' Camille winces.

Finnish? I knew Formilex was Scandinavian but not which specific country.

'Let me get you some water first, then I'll get you off that chair.'

The water splashes everywhere as I turn on the tap, because my hands are shaking so much.

I should be untying her first, shouldn't I? The poor woman has been through so much.

Yet something stops me.

I hold the glass of water up to her mouth. Her eye swivels around to meet mine, the colour even bluer than usual next to the dark bruises that are already forming.

After she's taken a few sips and nodded, I put the glass down and lean over her to work out how she's been bound and how to release her with the minimum discomfort—

It's like a flash of lightning against the side of my temple.

Harsh.

Sudden.

Blinding.

Noise in my ears. Dull, repeating pain against the back of my head like the second hand of a clock.

Tick

Tock

Tick

Tock

And my arms wrenched so far behind my shoulders they're almost coming out of their sockets.

My eyes don't open immediately but I try again . . . Why is the vaulted ceiling above me moving?

No, it's *me* that's moving, my body being dragged along the floor like a dead weight, my skull bouncing against the hard stone and nothing I can do to stop it.

I can smell wood and blood and the hot dust of an old heater.

I try to breathe through my mouth but it's only now I realise I can't because it's taped shut. The terror goes so deep I almost black out again.

No. I won't let that happen.

A woman pants behind me. Hanna?

I twist my head.

The hands that grip my wrists are young hands.

Camille's hands.

She inhales and, with a grunt, pulls me up and over a threshold and lets go.

Yet when I try to move my arms, I can't.

Now I understand where I am: in the sauna, on the floor, just behind the panelled wood door. It closes behind me and there's a sucking sound as the insulation around the edges makes a seal. And then a clicking sound as a key turns and the door locks. Inside here it's pretty warm, and there's a slight purring noise, but the sauna heater isn't turned on.

Camille's face shows through the small, smoked-glass window halfway up. I'd always taken that blank expression as a sign of how she'd retreated from real life after trauma. Now it looks much more sinister. Both her eyes are open – the bruises look so real.

I suddenly realise I'm not alone in the sauna.

Hanna lies on the top bench in a foetal position. Her mouth, wrists and ankles are bound with that silver tape. She doesn't seem to know I am here. I jab her ankle: no response.

I look back up at Camille, try to speak her name. But my lips hum uselessly against the tape and nothing comes out.

She shakes her head once, as though she's disappointed in me.

And then she's gone. I strain to hear her footsteps as she crosses the basement. Seconds go by. A minute?

I can't be sure, but I think Hanna and I are now alone.

My head throbs and my mouth itches under the tape. The sauna is warm, even though the coals aren't fired up. A whirring noise comes from somewhere close by.

Nothing is making any sense.

Camille must have hurt Hanna, pretended she'd been assaulted herself. Does that mean she also killed Lucas, pushed Bernice off that terrace? Her two closest friends . . .

Before my thoughts spiral, I force myself to focus on now. On getting out.

I try to get up from the floor but with my wrists and ankles taped so tightly, I fall. The second time I do manage to get into a half-sitting position, my back against the lower bench.

Hanna stirs but she is deeply unconscious. From a head injury? There is one small bruise to the side of her right eye. I throw my bound arms up and knock against her ankles. Her eyes open and widen. She tries to say something but it's lost behind the tape gag.

I blink. Panic rises in my chest again but I force it back. I have survived worse. I must try to think clearly.

The first thing must be to get the gags off us so I can call for help or at least breathe properly.

I look around this tiny space. Remember when I was trapped in here before, as Dex and I were cornered by Camille and Lucas.

At that time I thought it was Lucas who instigated the attempt to seduce us, while Camille had been manipulated into it. But it must have been the other way round . . .

Not now. I'll try to make sense of this later, once we're out of here. I suppose Camille has shut us in here to buy herself time. But somebody *will* find us. We are going to be OK.

I try to convey this to Hanna with my eyes, blinking as you do to calm a stray cat. But that's not what's reflected back in her gaze. She tries to lift her head, but it seems too heavy for her and her eyes glaze over.

I survey the sauna for something spiky I can use to try to peel the tape away from my mouth. It's all smooth, sanded wood. Except for the metal that forms a cage protecting the fire basket. The edges are rusty and jagged and the thought of it cutting through my skin makes me nauseous.

I could wait. Someone will come. Dex or Zoum or Ashleigh . . .

Except, the nausea is getting worse and the aching across my forehead blossoms, different from the throbbing where Camille must have struck me when I went to untie her.

I get closer to the fire basket, and the mechanical noise I heard when I was first hauled inside gets louder. It's coming from underneath, where the old dyeing pit is.

What is that sound? Half humming, half spitting.

I peer through the gap and I realise what it is.

A portable gas heater, a really old one. I think I saw it in the big pile of old appliances stacked up in the basement ready for the recycling people who never came.

But what is it doing down there? And why the hell is it turned on . . . ?

Suddenly I understand. The nausea comes in a wave so powerful I taste bile in my throat and have to use everything I have to swallow it down.

Camille knows we will be found eventually.

But she wants to make sure that we are long dead before help arrives.

62

Immi

We are being gassed. Asphyxiated. My breathing rate increases as panic takes over.

Anything but that. With every inhalation, I'm taking in more of the carbon monoxide that must be coming up through the boards from the heater. The older ones are notorious for going wrong, and should never be used in a small space because of the risk of carbon monoxide poisoning.

That is what's happening to me. With every breath I take, the CO is binding with the molecules in my blood, and Hanna's, blocking oxygen, poisoning us by stealth.

Soon I will be unconscious and soon after that, I will die.

Camille is trying to suffocate me. She knows what happened to me when a man did the same for pleasure as I lay terrified underneath him in some lonely hotel room. Does this give her pleasure too?

The last time, I didn't fight back.

This time, I will fight till my last breath.

I have to get the tape off my mouth.

The most jagged edge of the fire basket cage is at the far side. I try to push my cheek against it. Being bound makes me clumsy. I lean, topple, try again.

I find the right spot. First I'm too tentative, scared of being cut.

Except the alternative is so much worse.

So I push so hard that I feel the skin of my face being punctured, sliced into . . .

Try again.

There.

The sharp metal catches just under the corner of the tape and I move my head, trying to unpeel it. The adhesive is heavy-duty but I sense the release of a millimetre or two of skin, so I do it again. And again.

Sometimes it catches and stings. There's a smell of rust which might be the metal but could just as easily be blood.

Maybe I do it fifty times, my eyes locked on Hanna, willing her not to slip into a deeper unconsciousness. I don't know what I'll do once the gag is off but it's the first step.

I've got a third of the tape loose, so I poke my tongue out, trying to force it through, and I bite at the parts of my lips that are still stuck. I picture an animal gnawing off its own paw to escape a trap. The survival instinct is stronger than anything.

There.

'Hanna,' I call out from my prone position on the floor. The edge of the tape still sticks to one side of my cheek but I am no longer silent. 'Hanna, wake up.'

Her eyes open and she looks down, trying to make sense of what she's seeing. I'm relieved she's not yet so severely poisoned that she's beyond any response.

'I need you to breathe as slowly and shallowly as possible,' I say, aware my own voice already sounds slurred. 'I am going to call out for help so don't panic.'

I take a deep breath out of habit and shout out, 'HELP! WE'RE TRAPPED! WE'RE IN THE BASEMENT!'

My voice sounds loud in here, but that's because the wood that's designed to trap the heat in the sauna also absorbs the sound. No one will be able to hear us outside.

'Think, think,' I whisper to myself, trying to vocalise solutions.

I twist my body back towards the door and, after another dangerous deep breath, I kick my tied legs towards where it opens, trying to break the lock.

All the power vibrates back through my body like a shockwave. The door isn't budging. It opens inwards so perhaps every kick makes it fit even more snugly.

Despite that, I kick again. The noise might attract attention. I thump three times, in rapid succession, aware that the effort means I am taking in more poisoned air.

Wait in case someone calls out. *Nothing.*

Because no one can hear us.

No one is coming.

Dex is expecting me in Leathermarket Gardens, but there's no way he'll risk returning to the Factory. Ashleigh isn't due back till after eight.

That'll be too late.

'What else can I do?'

Focus, Imogen. My old teacher's voice is as clear as though she is sitting next to me, whispering in my ear. Is this delirium – a sign that the poisoning has reached the next level?

Logic and science will always provide the answers, if you think carefully.

What we need most of all is clean air to replace the stuff that is killing us.

The tiny window in the pine-clad door is the only way to get that. I can see from down here that it's safety glass, almost impossible to shatter. But I must try. And soon.

The soreness in my head is diminishing, replaced by the urge to sleep . . .

I need to pull myself up and the only thing I can use is my teeth. I angle myself towards the back of the sauna and the edges of the L-shaped bench. Bite hard into the wood and hope that despite childhood neglect, they're strong enough for this job.

Wood splinters under my jaw. I taste it and the tarriness of the finishing oil. Pain. Pressure . . .

But . . . I am now sitting up. I lift my shoulders so that my elbows hook just above the ledge and use all my strength to lever my body up onto the bench. As I do, I hear a tinkling of metal as something falls out of my pocket.

My knife glints against the bottom pine bench.

A tiny seed of hope begins to grow.

I use my teeth to move the handle so it's wedged into a groove between two planks. I know it'll hurt if I get this wrong but I have to try. I shift my body till my face faces the knife and lower my wrists towards the blade.

The point tears through the tape and I feel a stabbing pain where it pierces my skin. But I rock back and forth till I'm sure it's gone as far as it can, then repeat. And repeat. When I try to move my wrists, there's moisture – blood – but for the first time I can feel a little give.

My pulse is fast and my body is fighting my survival instinct, wanting me to breathe faster. I picture ripples spreading across a smooth blue pond . . .

Another attempt and another and finally the tape tears completely and I stare at my ghost-white fingers and my wrists,

which are peppered with tiny cuts. As the circulation returns
to my hands, the bleeding speeds up. Before I can dwell on the
damage, I tear the gag off Hanna's mouth and slice through the
ties on her wrists too.

'Camille . . .' she manages.

I hold my finger to her lips. 'Stay calm. I need to break the glass.'

She doesn't seem to understand me. Is her brain shutting
down? Or maybe I am not actually making the sounds I think
I am. I do know I am very, very tired . . .

I reach back with my arm and jab at the small pane with the
end of the knife.

It bounces off.

'No. NO!'

I turn it round so it's the thicker handle that faces the glass,
and try again. Once, twice, three times. The impact makes my
hand throb but the glass is untouched.

'Imogen . . .'

I turn to see that Hanna is trying to raise her arm in the air, as
though she's writing something. She moves it in what looks like
a circle and then a second time, it's more like a square. Her hand
drops but with what looks like her final reserve of strength, she
nods at the door.

But I understand and turn back and plunge the narrow blade
into the little groove that surrounds the window like a bevelled
frame. It goes into the space, and I hold my breath as I attempt
to move it downwards.

DON'T BREAK.

I pull at the handle and, after a sickening delay, the knife
comes out so I almost fall backwards.

But when I lean forward again, my eyes close to the frame, I see something that gives me hope.

A tiny hole, letting in the dank basement air.

I plunge the knife in half a dozen times.

Slice through the thinner wood and mastic that holds the window in place.

Push it out so it falls onto the floor, still unbroken.

Gasp at the air – three, four, five of the deepest breaths I've ever taken. *Take in your own oxygen before attempting to help others.*

And I remember coming back to life after the client had finished his torture, this 'breath play' he'd promised would be the most life-changing experience I'd ever had.

This, now, is like the moment when he let go of my throat and despite the pain and terror, I was alive.

I *am* alive.

'We're OK, Hanna,' I say, but when I turn back, her eyes are rolling back in her head, and I drag her limp body up towards the hole where the glass was, positioning her face against the gap.

I slap her, like you'd slap a newborn, to encourage it to take its first breath.

Wait.

Nothing.

'Come on, Hanna. *Breathe!*'

When the tiniest inhalation comes, and with it a cough, it's the most joyful sound I have ever heard.

63

Saturday 21 August

Immi

Zoum and I have tidied up especially, clearing away his numerous laptops and my sewing machine so there's space for our guest to sit down in our tiny living room.

When the intercom goes, Zoum pulls a face. 'I am still not sure this is the best idea you have ever had, Immi.'

'We can always kick him out.' I pick up the entryphone but all I can hear is the usual static at the other end, so I press the access button anyway.

A minute later, there's a soft knock at the door. When I answer it, Brian Davies is not the high-flyer I expected. He's in his sixties, stooped and dressed in shades of beige. As he steps straight into the living room, there's an odd smell. What is it? Ham sandwiches.

He looks around. 'Just moved in, have you?'

'A few weeks ago,' Zoum says, 'but we are embracing the chaos. It makes a change from where we used to live.'

'Take a seat while I make tea,' I say. Brian settles himself into the armchair, taking out a clipboard and various books and leaflets.

'Thanks both for filling in my questionnaire in such depth,' he says. 'This is a fascinating case. Really not your run-of-the-mill cult at all.'

I raise my eyebrows at Zoum over the kitchenette counter. We don't tell many people what happened to us, because when they find out, they ask endless questions, and answering them doesn't do anything to help us feel better. But Brian Davies has a professional interest.

Zoum smiles politely. 'I *am* glad. I hate the idea of being seen as ordinary.'

'Ah well, you're definitely not that,' Brian says, missing the sarcasm. 'There are so many things that make the Factory unique, but the one I've really honed in on is the fact it wasn't meant to be a cult at all.'

After Camille's attempt to kill me and Hanna, nothing made sense, either to me or the police. But once Hanna was well enough to be interviewed, the truth about the Factory began to emerge. It wasn't a cult, or a social experiment, or an unlicensed drugs trial.

It was a 'therapeutic community'.

And the patient was Camille Jarvis – or, as she was known in her own country, Camilla Järvinen, the daughter of the unbelievably wealthy Finnish family behind Formilex. They adopted her when she was three, after she'd been taken away from her heroin-addict mother. They tried everything to make up for her chaotic infancy, but she was constantly disruptive. It got so bad they had to leave Finland for Denmark for a fresh start. The only person who could calm her was her adoptive brother, Sam, but the pressure it put on him was unbearable.

He moved to London – his parents were so rich they bought the building that became the Dye Factory so he could live these – but ended up killing himself, unable to cope with the guilt and loneliness.

Grief triggered a desperation in Camilla, which changed her behaviour from difficult to dangerous. Hanna, an old university friend of the Järvinens, tried to help 'fix' Cam. Her ten-year quest culminated in setting up the Factory.

I put the tea tray on the table. 'It's like a riddle. When is a cult not a cult?'

Brian smiles. 'Certainly, Hanna Winther did use cult techniques to bond the community, albeit for broadly benign reasons.'

'Hardly benign when it led to the deaths of two people!' Zoum says.

Brian nods. 'Fair point. But it seems to me they were *intended* to be benign. Even beneficial. I have a police source who tells me Hanna insisted in interview that it was a fair trade. In other words, the luxuries of life in the Factory were adequate compensation for being unwitting therapists to a psychopath.'

'Psychopath?' I am beginning to wonder if Brian is quite the expert we thought he was. 'I think the term they use now is anti-social personality disorder.'

'Political correctness gone mad! What else do you call some-one who uses their own considerable intelligence to manipulate, exploit and cause pain for the fun of it? You were living with a psychopath. And she was running rings around everyone, including Hanna.'

Camille ran rings around the police, too. By the time Dex and the café owner found me with Hanna in the sauna – breathing but still trapped inside – she was long gone. It took the detectives four days to track her down to a five-star hotel less than two miles from the Factory. She'd run up a bill of several thousand pounds but barely touched the champagne or room service food she'd ordered. Never mind that she could easily have paid for it with her parents' money: she seemed to get a kick from the con.

'I thought you might wish to hear techniques I've identified that were employed by both Hanna and Camilla.' Brian pronounces their names in a mannered Finnish accent that makes me want to stick my fingers in my ears. 'Former cultists often gain relief by understanding how they were manipulated, to reassure themselves it wasn't due to some weakness in their own characters.'

Yet as he reads out the strategies – love bombing, replacement of outside relationships, removal of privacy, sleep deprivation – I still believe we were picked precisely because we *were* vulnerable. *Malleable.*

Hanna made sure of it, especially after her Factory 'project' started to veer off track. The first residents didn't have major secrets, but as time went on, Hanna got choosier, realising she needed to have some kind of hold over the Dyers if everything went wrong. I had my escort work, Dex thought he'd killed a girl by giving her dodgy MDMA and as for Ashleigh . . .

'Hanna might have used some of these techniques, but she did believe in what she was doing,' Zoum says. 'She tried to help Camille out of loyalty to Cam's family.'

I shake my head. It's the only thing I disagree with him on. 'Bullshit. It was about wanting to prove her half-baked psychology theories worked. That was bad enough. But to keep going when it was clear that Camille had started to go off the rails was criminal. That was all about avoiding the trouble she'd get into if anyone found out.'

Camille has been charged with Lucas's murder and her trial will follow in the autumn. But the police say they're struggling with finding the right charge for Hanna. She deceived all of us by creating this toxic community, endangering so many lives, including her own. Even the selection process was rigged, with Hanna telling Bernice how to vote. But I don't believe Bernice ever knew the whole story, only that 'poor' Camille needed help.

Brian observes us, scribbles down a note. Anger wells up inside me at the idea of us being a 'case study'. What happened still affects me, but it's early days. A quick temper and claustrophobia are better than being dead.

'Certainly, it seems the patient had a greater understanding of how to manipulate people than the psychologist who was meant to be in charge. Your questionnaire mentions bets that she started having with the others,' Brian says.

'I think it kept her amused,' Zoum says. 'She was always highly intelligent, and the bets must have been fun. But it wasn't just that. Her adoptive parents were scientists, which is where her experiments came from. She generated smells that were fed into people's studios via the pipes to mess with people's heads: alcohol for Dex, baking for Ashleigh. Plus using insulin on Lucas and even the carbon monoxide in the sauna. I think they were her idea of a joke.'

Brian nods. 'It's still a big leap from sick jokes to murder. Do you have any theories about why that happened?'

'Jamie,' I say, at exactly the same time as Zoum.

'This was the young man who was acquitted of sharing a sex tape?' Brian blushes. From what I found out online, Brian's own daughter became involved in a cult, and he now helps other people using what he learned to get her out.

Zoum nods. 'He looked just like her brother Sam. We don't know any of this from the police, but the press printed a picture and loads of background before she was arrested.'

I nod. 'When Veronica brought him for interview, maybe it seemed like fate bringing her brother back to her. Cam was the one who pushed for Jamie to join, even though Bernice and Hanna had their doubts about him.'

Brian makes another note. 'But that should have made her happier, surely?'

'She was at first, I remember it,' Zoum says. 'They got close at the midsummer party, which we now know was nine years to the day after Sam died. But Jamie was messed up in his own way. I believe now that he did do the things he was accused of – used drugs to knock her out enough to have sex. Maybe the betrayal brought back all the pain of her brother's suicide. That's when she began to lash out again.'

I shake my head. 'It's all possible, but she is incapable of telling the truth. She hasn't even said whether she pushed Bernice off the roof. The notebook Bernice wrote in showed she had some dark thoughts, but I still can't believe she killed herself.'

'It cannot be a coincidence that Sam himself died the same way,' Zoum says.

Brian's eyes are wide. 'It really is most extraordinary. But there is hope for both of you. I've worked with many ex-cultists and it will get easier, though you *will* probably experience flashbacks and disorientation for months, if not years. And perhaps a sense of loss, too.'

I don't feel that loss, but I know Zoum does and I give him a sympathetic smile. When he suggested getting a place together, I wasn't sure at first. But of all the people I met at the Factory, he's the one who I find I have the most in common with.

We scraped together enough for the deposit for this place, which has the best broadband in Zone 3, and is a bus ride from school when I start my deputy headship next month. As it turns out, we complement each other pretty well: his messiness challenges my slight OCD, and I am encouraging him to date and even consider a day when he might come out to his parents. Meanwhile, I haven't told *my* mother my new flatmate is a man, but she does know a little of what happened to me at the Factory, and we're trying our best to be kinder to each other.

I suppose we might see the others at Cam's trial. Dex has gone home to his family near Bath. He asked me to come to visit him but I couldn't face it. We were never meant to be 'together' – it was only ever a rebound thing for me, and a way for him to try to forget what he thought he'd done to that girl.

He's ditched his ambition to be a professional photographer. Instead, he's started volunteering with kids in Bristol on a video project – which is what he'd promised to do when he came to the Factory. I hope it works.

And Ashleigh is travelling again, in search of whatever she's missing. The last time I saw her I asked about the tattoo and she told me both she and her brother had fallen in with 'some bad people' when they were growing up. She'd learned her lesson but unfortunately her brother is still in prison. I didn't push it – I don't have any right to know all her secrets any more than she needs to know mine – but I hope she finds what she needs.

Zoum winks at me and I can tell he's already had enough. 'We manage OK. We survived the Factory. Nothing scares me now.'

We show Brian out and afterwards, we pull the keychain across the door, even though it's only seven o'clock. We pour ourselves a gin each, and we tell Alexa to play Northern Soul, as a tribute to Bernice, and as 'Heaven Must Have Sent You' starts, we turn the volume up to ten. We dance on the sofa, not caring that the thing is more shabby than chic, that the tea tray is rattling because the music's so loud, or that – in our private joke – Zoum and I have four left feet between us.

Because this is safe and this is now and *this* is where I belong.

64

Tuesday 20 November

Camilla

She stands on tiptoes so she can see through the window at the top of her compartment in the prison van. She sees walls topped with razor wire and cameras as the vehicle slows to enter her new home.

A shiver passes through Camilla, not from the chilly afternoon, but from the anticipation.

When the van stops, the transfer staff unlock the compartment and bring her out. The place surprises her: it's a fine redbrick Victorian building, not unlike the Factory. There is no sign of life, yet she senses people watching from the arched windows that overlook the entrance. Guards or prisoners.

No, not prisoners. *Patients.* Because, after all, she is *ill* with an abnormality of the mind.

'Promise it's not as grim as it looks. Not inside.' One of the escort staff takes her elbow to encourage her down from the van, mistaking Camilla's calm contemplation for fear.

Camilla shrugs her off, and makes the little jump down on her own.

As she waits for the handover to be completed, she breathes in the air. It smells of leaves and the autumnal perfume of things beginning to rot. It has been a long, hot summer and she's been looking forward to the cold, to remind her of home.

A strange sound makes her look round. It sounded almost like . . . *quacking*.

Ducks trot along the tarmac and onto a stretch of grass. *Ducks.* This is why she adores England – for its eccentricity.

'Let's get you admitted,' says a doughy woman in a black pullover and trousers that hug her dimpled thighs.

Camilla allows herself to be led, passive for now. First impressions are so important. Even as the woman and her colleague take their time conducting a full body search, Camilla doesn't react. Knowing she could is enough.

Her parents want to get her out of here as soon as possible; transfer her out of the barbaric English system and back home. Lawyers are already in place, the best available. What else do Mama and Papa have left to spend their money on now they no longer have to fund the Factory?

But she thinks this place might be her ideal home. The Factory was interesting at first, and Hanna was fun to play with, but the fundamental problem was that everyone else was basically *good*, or at least, wanted to be.

Here Camilla will be among her own: the dangerous, the disordered, the amoral. This should be more of a challenge.

There is only one thing about how it ended that makes her sad, and that is leaving a part of Sam behind. Living in the place where he died had felt special to her.

Some doctors believed it was his death that triggered her 'troubles'. Others claimed it was always there, waiting to emerge, due to her babyhood with her drug-addicted bitch of a mother. Camilla doesn't care either way.

But she did love her adoptive brother more than anyone else before or since. Sam was her prince. She should have been allowed to go with him, to London. He would never have killed himself if she had. Her parents stood up to Camilla for once, refusing to let a thirteen-year-old leave, failing to realise she was always more mature than they were.

'So it's important to remember that we are a hospital, not a prison,' the woman says wearily, as though reading from a script. 'Of course, you are *held* here, for your own safety and that of people outside, but this is not a punishment. You wouldn't be here if the doctors didn't think you could be helped.'

Camilla says nothing but inside, she's laughing.

'You do understand English?'

'I might have a personality disorder but I am not an imbecile.'

The nurse or guard or whatever she was, scowls back. Camilla's mood improves. This dullard is of no interest anyway.

'You might want to think about who is going to look after you before you get snappy with us.'

Camilla made her own amusement at the Factory. The little bets kept her entertained at first. She invented them to keep herself occupied until an audition went her way and she got a role that was worthy of her. Except it never happened. Funny, she could act the part of a normal person in real life, but it never quite worked on camera or on stage.

And then that night Veronica brought Jamie to the interview *everything* suddenly made sense. He was meant to be at the Factory, meant to be with Camilla. He was so like her brother that it made her feel calmer than she had in years. She knew he would be *hers*: even closer than she'd been to Sam. One shrink was convinced her obsession with Sam was a kind of incest, which made it sound so sordid.

But Jamie was not Sam and what he felt for her was the opposite of love. He hurt her. Camilla was surprised she could still feel anything, and not only because of the Rohypnol. Sex to her had always been a power play, a weapon, never a source of pleasure in itself. Another one of the psychs she saw, theorised that development of 'normal' sexual feelings had been arrested because her brother died just as she was on the cusp of puberty.

The sex wasn't the worst part, though.

When Jamie shared that video, and she saw what he'd done while she was unconscious, she felt a curious range of emotions. Humiliation. Loss of control.

Rage.

'Hurry up,' the doughy nurse says, her heavy soles slapping on the lino. 'This isn't an afternoon stroll.'

Bernice was the one who talked her into going to the police, with her naïve ideas about justice. Therefore, when the court case failed, Bernice was to blame. Replacing the antidepressants with something more potent from Camilla's own medicine box made Bernice utterly suggestible. The paranoid scribblings in her notebook helped pinpoint the perfect moment to add something hallucinogenic to the mix. Why push a person off the edge yourself, when you can get someone to jump themselves?

Fly away, Bernice. It did make her smile beforehand, the poetic justice of persuading an air traffic controller to crash out of life like that. Though she couldn't bear to see the body, because that might have been how poor Sam looked too. They jumped from exactly the same spot.

Lucas, too, died in a way that reflected how he lived. Even if he hadn't started to suspect her involvement, she would probably have put him out of his misery sooner or later. In the time Camilla knew him, he'd gone from a vacuous but virile charmer to an impotent voyeur. Getting his kicks from watching was never going to be enough for him.

She regrets that she failed with Immi. It was necessary, as soon as she found out about the connection between the Factory and Formilex. The timing, ten years after Sam left her and the world, was accidental but glorious. There was also a delicious neatness about planning to kill by the asphyxiation Immi so dreaded. The heater worked in seconds when she experimented on the rabbit. *So* close.

Like Immi, Camilla has a fascination for science, thanks in part to her adoptive parents. It has a delicious precision that human emotions lack.

'The ward is through here,' the nurse says, pausing in front of double doors painted what is presumably meant to be a soothing shade of green. 'Don't be intimidated if the others swoop on you. They'll leave you alone once they've said hello, they're just curious. Ready?'

Camilla smiles. 'Absolutely. After so long in solitary before my sentence, I really am craving human interaction.'

Acknowledgements

I spent my twenties researching this book by living in scary flat shares and divided households. Luckily, the life-threatening aspects of this book are *not* based on personal experience, so thanks to Chris Bielby, the Director of Industry Liaison at SGN, for making it such a gas to talk about gasses! Thanks also to consultant psychiatrist Dr Humphrey Needham-Bennett for his insights into abnormalities of mind and secure hospitals.

Giant gins to Cally, Julie, Rowan, Miranda and Tamsyn for being the writers' emergency service. Thanks to the other professional plotters who've helped me unpick tricky bits: Angela Clarke, Tammy Cohen, Ilana Fox, Araminta Hall, Jane Lythell, Sarah Rayner, Sue Teddern, Phil Viner, Sue Wilkins, and Laura Wilkinson. Thanks to Janie and Mickey for the wine, hummus and sunshine.

Cheers to the VIPs: Karen, Bridgett, Margaret, Tracey, Julie, Jacky, Jackie, Debbie, Joanne, Jill, Chris, Natalie, Amanda, Sue, Julie, Donna, Bridget, Debra, Sarah, Edda, Shereen and Helen.

Thanks to friends and neighbours for support and love during a tough year: Lisa, Liz, Neil, Tina, Keith, Christine, Francis, Geri, Jenny and Mike. Extra big love as always to Rich, my sister Toni and my dad Michael.

Huge thanks to Hellie Ogden and all at Janklow and Nesbit, especially Kate Longman and Kirsty Gordon.

Thanks to Katherine Armstrong and Sophie Orme for being an awesome editing double act. Gillian Holmes did a fab job on the copyedit. The entire Zaffre team are fabulous *and* fun to be around – big thanks to Kate Parkin, Jennie Rothwell, Francesca Russell, Sahina Bibi, Felice McKeown, Ellen Turner and Stephen Dumughn. And to anyone I have accidentally left out: you know what I am like . . .

But the most important person to thank is YOU for reading *The House Share*.

I'd love to stay in touch – how about it?

Please do visit my website at www.kate-harrison.com where you can sign up for my newsletter, which I *promise* is never spammy but just tells you what I've been writing and reading, with some book giveaways too.

Or if you want to say hello right now, pop over to Twitter or Instagram where I am @katewritesbooks – I love an excuse to chat about books!

Kate x